BRIDESMAID

Wedding Party Collection

Don't tell the
BRIDE

Wedding Party Collection

Kelly HUNTER   Tessa RADLEY   Cindy KIRK

April 2017

Marrying the
PRINCE

Wedding Party Collection

Kate HEWITT   Sandra HYATT

May 2017

Always the
BACHELOR

Wedding Party Collection

Michelle CELMER   Amanda BERRY   Barbara HANNAY

June 2017

Once a
BRIDESMAID

Wedding Party Collection

Avril TREMAYNE   Sophie PEMBROKE   Gina WILKINS

July 2017

Here Comes the
GROOM

Wedding Party Collection

Rebecca WINTERS   Emma DARCY   Sophie PEMBROKE

August 2017

Proposing to the
PLANNER

Wedding Party Collection

Susan STEPHENS   Aimee CARSON   Teresa CARPENTER

September 2017

Once a
BRIDESMAID

Wedding Party Collection

| Avril | Sophie | Gina |
| TREMAYNE | PEMBROKE | WILKINS |

MILLS & BOON

Published in Great Britain 2017
By Mills & Boon, an imprint of HarperCollins*Publishers*
1 London Bridge Street, London, SE1 9GF

WEDDING PARTY COLLECTION: ONCE A BRIDESMAID…
© 2017 Harlequin Books S.A.

Here Comes the Bridesmaid © 2014 Belinda de Rome
Falling for the Bridesmaid © 2015 Sophie Pembroke
The Bridesmaid's Gifts © 2007 Gina Wilkins

ISBN: 9780263931082

09-0717

Our policy is to use papers that are natural, renewable and recyclable products and made from wood grown in sustainable forests.
The logging and manufacturing processes conform to the legal environmental regulations of the country of origin.

Printed and bound in Spain
by CPI, Barcelona

HERE COMES
THE BRIDESMAID

AVRIL TREMAYNE

Avril Tremayne read *Jane Eyre* as a teenager and has been hooked on tales of passion and romance ever since. An opportunistic insomniac, she has been a lifelong crazy-mad reader, but she took the scenic route to becoming a writer – via gigs as diverse as shoe salesgirl, hot cross bun packer, teacher, and public relations executive. She has spent a good chunk of her life travelling, and has more favourite destinations than should be strictly allowable.

Avril is happily settled in her hometown of Sydney, Australia, where her husband and daughter try to keep her out of trouble – not always successfully. When she's not writing or reading she can generally be found eating – although she does not cook!

Check out her website: www.avriltremayne.com

Or follow her on Twitter: @AvrilTremayne and Facebook: www.facebook.com/avril.tremayne

CHAPTER ONE

TO: Jonathan Jones
FROM: Sunshine Smart
SUBJECT: Bridesmaid meets Best Man
Darling Jon
I've met Leo and I adore him!

We are on the same page, so fear not—your wedding reception will be everything you ever dreamed of!

Wish we could have the actual marriage in Sydney too, but hooray for enlightened New York!

Hugs and kisses to Caleb.
Sunny xxx

TO: Caleb Quartermaine
FROM: Leo Quartermaine
SUBJECT: WTF??????
Caleb
What are you doing to me?

Sunshine Smart cannot be a real name. And she wants to friend me on Facebook! NOT JOKING!

Despite being dropped in it with the lunatic, I will ensure the dinner doesn't turn into a three-ring circus.

Can't wait to meet Jonathan—but please tell me he's nothing like his bridesmaid.

SUNSHINE SMART WAS looking forward to her second meeting with Leo Quartermaine. *Despite* their introductory meeting two days ago, lasting just ten minutes and ending with him declining her request to be Facebook friends.

She loved Leo's restaurants—well, what she'd read about them. Because she'd never actually eaten at one… which she was about to remedy.

She loved him on TV—tough but fair, judging those reality TV would-be chefs, and *dreamy as* when fronting *Cook It Up With Leo.*

She was predisposed to love anyone whose brother was smart enough to marry her best friend Jonathan Jones.

And she just—well, *loved* him. In that *Isn't he adorable?* way of loving people who were just so solid and serious and a teensy bit repressed.

But his hair—or lack thereof—was a problem. There was no *reason* for Leo to shave his head. It wasn't as if he had a comb-over issue. He could have a full head of hair if he wanted! Lush, thick, wheat-blond. She'd seen the 'before shaved head' photos on the internet. And the start of the regrowth at their first meeting. She'd read a comment in an article about it being easier in the kitchen without hair—but she wasn't asking for a ponytail!

Anyway, that could be fixed. There was time for him to grow it. She would just drop a word in his ear.

Sunshine checked her make-up. Her new red lipstick looked fabulous. Her eyes…well, what could you do? The grey eyeshadow was heavily layered; mascara so thick each lash look like a tarantula leg—make-up intended to distract people from her ocular weirdness. About which there was nothing she could do—unlike Leo Quartermaine's hair!

She got out of her car—a bright yellow 1970s rejc and walked purposefully towards Q Brasserie.

* * *

Leo Quartermaine heard Sunshine approach before he saw her.

He associated that tap-tapping rhythm on the polished concrete floor with her, despite only having met her once before.

He was betting she was wearing another pair of ankle-breaking high heels.

To be fair, she *was* a shoe designer. But shoe designers made flats, didn't they? Like those ballet-slipper things. Not that he could picture Sunshine Smart in ballet slippers. Or trainers—crikey!

'Leo!' she called out, as though he were a misplaced winning lottery ticket, suddenly found. He was starting to think 'ecstatic' was her default setting.

'Sunshine,' he said, managing not to roll his eyes. *Sunshine!* How had her parents put that on the birth certificate without gagging?

'So!'

He'd already clocked the fact that she often started her utterances with 'So!' As though an amazing revelation would be out of her mouth on the next breath.

'News!' she said, tap-tapping towards the window table where he was sitting.

And, yep, six inches of spike on her feet. In electric blue patent leather. God help his eyes.

She stripped off her trench coat as she made her way across the floor, causing her long necklace to swing. He'd noticed the necklace last time. Pretty. Three types of gold—a rose gold chain, with a yellow gold sun and white gold moon dangling from it.

Miraculously, her dress was an understated colour—pale grey-blue. But it fitted her like a second skin and had one of those things—pellums? Peplums? Whatever!—that dragged a man's eyes to a woman's waist and hips. She had a hell of a figure, he had to admit. Curvaceous, like the hourglass pin-up girls of the 1950s.

Leo got up to pull out a chair for her on the opposite side of the table. She took the opportunity to kiss him on the cheek, party-girl air-kiss style—except it wasn't like any air-kiss he'd ever had—and he'd had plenty. It was a smacking, relishing kiss. *Not* the kind of kiss to slap on a person you barely knew.

Oblivious to his momentary shock, Sunshine tossed her trench coat carelessly onto a nearby chair, sat, and beamed up at him. 'Did you hear? They've set the date. October twentieth. So we've got two months. A spring wedding. Yay!'

Yay? Who the hell said 'yay'? Leo returned to his seat. 'Not much time, but doable.'

'Oh, it's *oodles* of time,' Sunshine assured him airily. 'So! I've made a list of everything we need to do, and now we can decide who does what, give each task a deadline, and go from there.'

'List?' Leo repeated the word, apprehensive. He liked lists. He worked well with lists. The haphazard approach to life of his wastrel and usually wast*ed* parents had made him a plan-crazy list junkie. But this was a simple dinner he could organise with his eyes closed while he whisked a chocolate soufflé.

For once in his life he *didn't* need a list.

'Yes.' She reached down beside her to where she'd dumped the silver leather bag she'd been swinging when she walked over and pulled out a dazzling chartreuse folder. She removed some paper, peeled off two pages and held them out to him. 'Your copy. I'm actually not really into lists,' she confessed—*surprise, surprise*. 'So it may need some work.'

He looked at the first page. At the big, bold heading: *The Marriage Celebration of Jonathan and Caleb, October 20th.*

Seeing the words was like a punch to the solar plexus. It was real. Happening. Imminent. His baby brother was getting married.

What were the odds? Two Aussie guys who'd never met in their own country moved separately to New York, met at a random party, and—bang!—happy-ever-after.

It didn't matter that Leo didn't know Jonathan, because Jonathan made Caleb happy. It didn't matter that the ceremony was taking place on the other side of the world, because the place was just logistics. It didn't matter that their marriage was only going to be legally recognised in a handful of countries, because *they* knew what it meant wherever they were.

Leo wondered if he would have had more luck meeting the love of his life if *he* were gay. Because it sure wasn't happening for him on his side of the sexuality fence. The succession of glossy glamour-pusses who seemed to be the only women that came his way were certainly lovely to look at—but they didn't *eat*, and they didn't occupy his thoughts for longer than it took to produce a mutual orgasm.

He wanted what Caleb had. The one. Someone to get into his head, under his skin, to intrigue and dazzle and delight him. Someone who burrowed into his core instead of bouncing off his shell. Someone to belong to. And to belong to him.

He thought back to his last failure—beautiful, talented singing sensation Natalie Clarke. She'd told him on their second date that she loved him. But nobody fell in love in two dates! Nope—what she'd loved was the concept of Leo the celebrity chef. She'd wanted them to be part of 'the scene'. And who said 'the scene' with a straight face? He couldn't think of anything worse than 'the scene'…except maybe her predilection for snorting cocaine, because apparently *everyone* on 'the scene' did it.

In any case, she was a relentless salad-with-dressing-on-the-side type. And she liked playing her own cheesy love songs in the bedroom *way* too much.

With a repressed shudder he brought his mind back to the present and ran his eyes down the list.

Budget
Wedding Party
Master of Ceremonies
Venue
Menu
Alcohol
Guest List
Invitations
Flowers
Lighting
Music
Cake
Clothing
Shoes
Hair and Make-up

What the hell…? Why did *that* need a subheading?

Gift Registry
Photographer
Videographer
Wedding Favours
Order of Proceedings
Toasts and Speeches
Printing
Seating Plan

Each item was bullet-pointed with a little box that could be ticked, and accompanied by questions, comments and suggestions.

Good thing she wasn't into lists!

Sunshine must have noticed the stunned look on Leo's face, because she asked, 'Have I screwed it up?'

'This is…' he started, but words actually failed him.

'Exciting?' Sunshine suggested, looking as if she were about to celebrate Christmas, her birthday *and* the wedding all at once.

'Comprehensive,' Leo corrected. He ran a hand across his scalp. Her eyes followed his hand. She was frowning suddenly. He wondered what was going through her mind.

She opened her mouth. Closed it. Opened it. Closed it. Sighed.

Then, 'So!' she said. 'The venue is the first thing. Because it's bound to be tricky, securing somewhere wonderful with only two months' notice.'

'It may have escaped your notice, but I am a restaurateur,' Leo said. 'I *have* venues. I *am* venues. *And* menus. And *booze*.'

Sunshine seemed startled. 'Oh. I just assumed we'd be too late to get a large group booked into one of your places. That's why I've suggested somewhere like the hotel on—'

'My brother is *not* celebrating his marriage in a hotel.'

'Okay. Well, there's that lovely place that used to be a stately home in—'

'Or in an old house.'

'Then perhaps the new convention space—which is not as tragic as it sounds. In fact it has a—'

He slammed his hand on the table. 'No!' He stopped, reined in the spurt of annoyance. 'No.' *Better. Calmer.* 'We have a perfectly…' *Reaching, reaching...* 'Perfectly perfect…' *hmm, thesaurus required* '…private room in this restaurant.'

The only sign that Sunshine had noted his ill-tempered hand-banging incoherence was a tiny twitch at one side of her mouth. He feared—he really feared—she was trying not to laugh.

'Which seats…?' she asked, her head on one side like a bird, with every indication of deep interest.

'Seats?'

'How many people does the private room seat?'

'Twenty-five.'

Sunshine crossed her arms—seemingly unaware of how she was framing her rather spectacular breasts—and looked at him, apologetic. 'See? Me and lists! I got the order wrong. "Guest List" should have come before "Venue". So! Let's take a step back. I have Jon's invitation list. Do you have Caleb's?'

'It's coming today some time.'

'Because there are seventy-five people on our side.'

He stared. 'You are not serious.'

'I assure you, I am. And that's with a savage cull.' She shuddered theatrically as she uncrossed her arms. *'Savage.'*

'Caleb wants an intimate dinner.'

'That's not my understanding, but I'll tell you what—you check with Caleb overnight, and we can reconvene tomorrow.'

His eyes narrowed. 'I hate it when people try to soothe me.'

Sunshine bit her lip. 'Oh, dear, and I was *trying* to sound like I was keeping an open mind. But…okay. I'll tell you straight out, if you prefer: there is no way this is going to be a dinner for twenty-five people. And there's no use getting in a snit about it—it's just the way it is.'

'I'm not in a snit.'

'If you say so.'

'I do. Say so.'

'All right.'

'I'm *not.*'

'All *right.*'

Another mouth-twitch. She was *definitely* trying not to laugh.

And Leo had had enough. 'I have to go,' he said, despite not being needed in the kitchen for fifteen minutes.

'Yes, I can see everything's getting under way here. I love the buzz of restaurants. Jon and I used to try a new restaurant every other week. I miss him. He's so…so important to me.' Her voice wobbled the merest fraction as she added the last bit.

Uh-oh, tears. Leo didn't do tears. He felt himself shrink back. Wanted to run.

But her face morphed into something tortured, right before his eyes, and he froze. It was as if a layer had been ripped off her in one half-second. Her eyes were strained and yet also vacant, as if she were seeing…emptiness. Her lips trembled. Her skin looked ashen. Every trace of happiness was obliterated. The contrast with her normal exuberance was dramatic—almost painful to see.

All this because her best friend had moved overseas and she missed him?

Huh?

Leo wanted to touch her. Pat her hand or…something. Say…something. He who never touched, never comforted, because he didn't know how. His hands fisted uselessly.

Then Sunshine blinked. Shook her head—tiny, tiny movement. And in another half-second everything clicked back to normal and Leo breathed a silent sigh of relief.

'Um…' he said. Yep, he was super-articulate today.

But she was smiling blindingly, as though that moment had never happened, so he did the sensible thing and shut up.

'We haven't got far down the list,' she said. 'What about if I shortcircuit a few things? You know, invitations, et cetera.'

'What do you mean, "shortcircuit"? And "et cetera"?'

he asked, still a little shaken. Everything about her was throwing him off kilter.

'I'll get some options together for us to look over tomorrow. Nothing scary!'

She was completely back to normal. Full-strength perky. Better than the tragic facemask she'd freaked him out with—but only marginally. Leo didn't like perky. And if he were being made to board Sunshine Smart's good ship *Lollipop* for this wedding *he* would be the one at the tiller.

'I thought we'd be emailing the invitations,' he said.

She gave him what could only be termed a pitying smile. 'Did you?'

That was all. She wasn't even going to bother arguing. *Um...no.* That was not how it was going to work. 'It's the twenty-first century,' he said. 'And time is short. I've seen some brilliant cutting-edge online invitations.'

'Well, why don't you bring one of those examples to our meeting tomorrow on your tablet/device/notebook/ whatever you've got, and I'll bring some hard copy snail mail samples appropriate for a chic but traditional wedding celebration.'

'You're doing the soothe thing again.'

'Oh, dear, am I? I'll have to work on that,' she said.

It was obvious to Leo that she had no intention of doing anything of the sort. But he wasn't going to waste his breath pointing that out. He was tired enough from just *looking* at her.

'We'll talk tomorrow—*after* I've checked with Caleb,' he said shortly, and stood abruptly.

'Just one more thing, Leo, before you rush off.'

He looked down at her and she cleared her throat.

'What?' Leo asked, trying not to feel a sense of impending doom.

'Just…something that's going to have to start now, like right this second, if it's going to be ready in two months.'

'And are you going to share with me exactly what this all-important thing is?'

'Promise you won't get mad?'

'No.'

'It's important.'

'Waiting.'

'I wouldn't ask if it wasn't absolutely vital. It's just...' She stopped, ran her hand through her long hair, widened her eyes at him as though she were trying to impart something telepathically. Ran her hand through her hair again.

And he—

God! The eyes. Why hadn't he noticed her eyes before?

She huffed out a breath and pursed her lips. Exasperated because he hadn't read her chaotic mind, probably.

But all he could think about were her eyes.

'Hair,' she explained. 'It only grows one-point-two-five centimetres a month. One-point-three if you're lucky.'

'So?'

'You have to start growing your hair.'

He had no answer. Might well have been gaping like a hooked fish.

'Sorry—but if I didn't raise it now you might have shaved your head tonight and it would be a shame to lose those few millimetres.'

'I don't want to grow my hair,' Leo said. Ultra-reasonable. The way you talked to a person who was certifiably insane.

'But you will look so much better in the photos. And you have lovely hair.'

'And you know this...how?'

'I looked you up online and saw the photos from the launch of this place, when you had hair. Now, I'm not saying you're not very good-looking even *with* the shaved head. Tall, but not in a carnival freaky way. Lean—which is amazing, for a chef, if you ask me. Wonderful sharp cheekbones, brilliant smile— All right, I'm guessing the smile bit, since I haven't actually seen it, but I'm a good guesser. And really lovely eyes—amber is such an unusual colour, you know? Tigerish. But if you look quite delectable now, you will be absolutely, irresistibly *gorgeous* with hair.'

Leo stood there, gobsmacked. 'I've got to get to work,' he said when he could trust himself to speak.

'But you'll think about the hair, won't you?' she asked anxiously. 'And while you're thinking, maybe keep the razor off your scalp…just in case you *do* decide to look absolutely, irresistibly *gorgeous* at your brother's wedding.'

He looked at her. Noted her eyes again. Really stunning eyes. *She* would look absolutely, irresistibly gorgeous herself if she—

Aha.

Leo could have crowed, he was so pleased with himself. 'Let's make a deal—you go into the bathroom and wash off that eye-goop right now, and I will not shave my head…unless I see that crap all over your eyes again. The minute I see it, I'm reaching for the razor.'

And, yes! He'd stumped her. She was the gaping fish now.

He watched as she processed what he'd said. She lifted her bag off the floor and rummaged inside, pulled out a compact. Flipped it open, looked in the mirror. Widened her eyes, then squinted. Turned her head to peer sideways, then switched sides and did it again. 'You know that I have strange eyes, right?' she asked.

'Beautiful eyes.'

'Evil eyes.'

'Yeah, maybe lay off the sci-fi.'

'Oh, it's a real condition. It's called heterochromia iridum, and there are various theories about how you get it. Genetics, melanin levels, trauma, chimerism—which is kind of creepy because it means another foetus has merged with you in the womb, which in my case would mean there were initially three of us, because— Well, anyway, I don't like the idea of absorbing a sibling in the womb—hello, Dr Frankenstein!' Pause for breath. 'All that aside, I'm pretty sure they used to burn people like me at the stake as witches back in the day.'

'Nobody is going to burn you at the stake in modern-day Australia for having one blue and one green eye.'

'I've tried contact lenses, but there is nothing that makes you panic quite like a contact lens that's slipped up under your eyelid and you think it's going to be there for eternity unless you race off to the emergency room and have someone stick some implement in there against your poor squishy eyeball. Talk about bloodshot!' She pursed her lips. 'But I guess I could try them again—maybe some amber ones.' She looked into his eyes, considering. 'Because your eyes really are lovely, and I think I'd look kind of interesting with amber eyes.'

'You do that and I'm shaving my head.'

Sunshine took another look in the mirror, then snapped the compact shut. 'All right. Deal. I may need a little make-up on the actual day of the reception, just so I don't look Plain Janerama, but no camouflage paint in the meantime. I'm keeping the lipstick, though—I can't go completely naked. So! Where's the bathroom?'

Plain Janerama? Leo, speechless, pointed.

Sunshine got to her feet. 'No need to wait,' she told him.

'Oh, I'm waiting.'

She squared her shoulders. 'This is going to be *weird*,' she said, and tap-tapped away.

Leo checked that everything was in order in the kitchen, then returned to the table. He went through the checklist again. Swore under his breath. He suspected Sunshine Smart usually got her way in all things. Which meant she was in for a surprise, because just on principle he wasn't going to let that happen. He hadn't got where he was today by doing what people told him. His survival instinct told him always to go his *own* way, to *get* his own way.

He started jotting down menu ideas—appropriate for a dinner for twenty-five people—but hadn't got far when he heard the tap-tap of Sunshine's returning high heels.

She plonked herself into the chair opposite and did an over-the-top eyelash-bat at him.

Leo stared at her. He couldn't help it. Without the exaggerated eye make-up she looked fresh and clean and sweet as suckable candy. Her dark chocolate hair against the ultra-white skin of her face seemed more dramatic. With the edge of her heavy fringe now damp and misplaced, he could see how fine and dark her eyebrows were, and that they arched intriguingly towards the outer edge. Her eyelashes were thick and black enough to form a fine line around her eyes. And her eyes were simply spectacular. Heavy-lidded, slightly tilted, the colour difference so dramatic without the dark shadow and over-clumped lashes that he couldn't seem to stop looking at them.

'Well?' she asked, batting away.

'Better,' Leo said, with impressive understatement. He got to his feet. 'I'll see you tomorrow, then—an hour earlier, if you can make it. But you'll have to come to Mainefare—it's in the Pig and Poke pub. Do you know it?'

'Yes, I know it—and, yes, that's fine. But before you go can I ask just one more favour?'

Leo eyed her suspiciously.

'I'm staying for dinner,' she explained. 'Don't worry—I have a booking. It's just that my date—Gary, his name is—is a massive foodie, and he'd really love to meet you. Perhaps you could just pop out and say hello…?'

'Oh, sure,' Leo agreed easily. He'd been expecting something worse—maybe that he have a shot of Botox!—

and, anyway, speaking to his customers was part of his routine.

'And do you think I could have this exact table? It has a lovely view over the park. If it's reserved I'll understand, but—'

He caught his impatient sigh before it could erupt. 'You can have the table, Sunshine.'

'And could I have a Campari and soda while I wait for Gary?'

'Fine,' Leo said, irritated that it made him curious about her—because he would have pegged her for a Cosmopolitan girl. And who the hell *cared* what she liked to drink? 'I'll get one sent over.'

'And—'

'Good God, what else?'

'Just that it's Gary's birthday…so if there's a special dessert or something…?'

'Yes. I. Will. Send. Out. A. Special. Dessert. Now, are you all right for socks and undies, or do you need me to get you some of those too?'

'Actually, I never wear socks.' Sunshine smiled serenely. 'And I'm not wearing undies tonight—not under *this* dress!'

Leo could feel his eyes bug out of his head. 'Thanks for that mental picture, Sunshine. Anything else you'd care to share?'

'Well…'

'Yeah, hold that thought,' he said, and made a bolt for the kitchen. Where he leant against the wall and burst out laughing.

His sous chef looked at him as if he'd grown a gigantic unicorn horn.

Clearly it had been a long time since he'd laughed.

Yum.

That was the word that had been popping into Sunshine's head with monotonous regularity from the moment Leo had sent out a bowl of polenta chips with a gorgonzola dipping sauce to snack on while she drank her Campari.

Q Brasserie had an open kitchen, so she could not only smell but also see the magic being wrought on an array of seafood and meat—and, okay, vegetables too, although they were a lot less interesting if you asked her.

She rubbernecked as a steady stream of mouthwatering dishes was whisked past her en route to other diners, agonised over the menu choices and wished she could eat everything.

Sunshine basically Hoovered up her entrée of six plump, perfectly sautéed scallops, served with a Japanese-style dressing of cucumber, rice vinegar, mirin, and ginger. And it took great willpower *not* to beg a taste of Gary's mushrooms with truffle custard. She wouldn't normally covet a vegetarian dish but, come on, truffle custard? *Yum!*

The main meals were sublime. She ate every bite of her Angus beef brisket, served with smoked bone marrow and potato confit, and, giving in to her inner piglet on the date-taste issue, was in the process of polishing off one of Gary's divine king prawns—chargrilled with coriander and lime, *yum, yum, yum*—when up bowled Leo.

He'd changed from his jeans, T-shirt and way cool brown leather lace-ups into a spotlessly clean, double-breasted chef's jacket, finely checked pants and classy black slip-ons, and he looked sigh-worthy.

Leo looked at her well-cleaned plate. At Gary's. At the tiny piece of prawn on the end of her fork. His eyebrows shot up.

Sunshine knew she was presenting as a glutton—but so what? She liked food! Sue her! She calmly finished the last bite of prawn and laid her fork on her plate.

She made the introductions, then retreated as Leo engaged Gary in a conversation about food.

Gary looked a little starstruck. Which was kind of sweet. *He* was kind of sweet. Not that their relationship was going anywhere. This was their third date and from her perspective he'd settled into purely platonic material. She hadn't had even one lascivious thought about him.

The conversation moved on from food and Gary was explaining a little about his job. He was an investment banker—which was more interesting than it sounded. Truly!

'Nice talking to you Gary,' Leo said eventually. 'Dessert is on the house. Happy birthday, and enjoy the rest of your evening.

Leo had been aware of Sunshine beaming her approval all through his talk with Gary. It was irritating, like a tiny pebble stuck in your shoe, to have her there—just there... just...*there*. Like a hyped-up Miss Congeniality.

In fact the whole evening had been irritating, because that damned table he'd pinched from one of his regulars was in his line of sight from the kitchen, so he'd been in Peeping Tom mode all night. Watching as she ate. And ate and ate. As she made Gary laugh. And laugh and laugh.

Gary was clearly besotted with her. Poor guy. He was handsome—a nice man—but not in Sunshine's league. Not that Leo knew what Sunshine's league *was*, only that Gary wasn't in it. Which had been underscored by the expression on Sunshine's face when the Persian nougat glacé had arrived at the table. The way her glowing eyes had closed as she took the first bite, then opened as the taste hit her. How her mouth had oozed over the spoon...

And why hadn't he noticed the shape of her mouth before? Too much coloured gunk, he supposed. But once the lipstick had worn off she hadn't bothered reapplying it. Which was odd, wasn't it? He'd never known a girl *not* to race off and reapply her lipstick *ad nauseam* during dinner.

Not that Sunshine's lipstick habits were any of his business.

Except that now he couldn't miss her too-heavy top lip, glistening as she darted her tongue over it. The wide and chewable bottom lip. She had a little gap between her two front teeth that was kooky-meets-adorable. And she moved her mouth over her spoon as if she were having a food-induced orgasm.

He wondered if he was thinking in orgasm terms because she was going commando tonight. *Not* that he was going there. No way! *And please, God, get the thought out of my head!*

Whatever, she'd clearly appreciated the 2002 Cristal her boyfriend had ordered to go with dessert.

Leo preferred the 1996 vintage.

Talk about splitting hairs. What the hell was wrong with him?

He sighed. Stretched. It had been a long night, that was all. He just needed to get to bed. Right after he emailed Caleb. He was going to get the dinner party back under control at their meeting tomorrow. Put Sunshine the Bulldozer back in the shed.

Sunshine. *Groan!* She was like a six-inch electric blue thorn in his side.

So it didn't make sense that he would be humming as he thought about that manifesto-sized checklist of hers.

And damn if it wasn't that cheesy Natalie Clarke number about love biting you in the ass.

The most diabolically awful song of the century.

Clearly, he needed a drink.

God, he hated Barry White.

CHAPTER TWO

TO: Caleb Quartermaine
FROM: Leo Quartermaine
SUBJECT: Seriously?

Caleb, mate

What's the deal? Where's your invitation list? Are we really talking 150 guests? I thought it was an intimate dinner.

Sunshine is descending on me tomorrow to kick off the invitation process, so it would be nice to know who's got what expectations. So I don't end up looking like a completely clueless moron.

LQ

TO: Jonathan Jones
FROM: Sunshine Smart
SUBJECT: Wedding of the century

Hello, darling

Had dinner at Q Brasserie tonight—fabulous. We're meeting again at one of Leo's other places, Mainefare, tomorrow. Can't wait!

I've worked out that Mainefare is a play on words. Mayfair as in London (it's in a British-style pub) but with Maine as in Quartermaine and fare as in food. Leo is so clever!

Invitation samples attached: (1) ultra-modern, cream and charcoal; (2) dreamy romantic in mauve and violet;

(3) Art Deco—blue and teal with yellow, brown, and grey accents.

PLEASE like the Art Deco one, which I know sounds ghastly, but open it and you'll see!

All else is on track. Party of the year, I'm telling you! Sunny xxx

PS—and, no, in answer to your repeat question—I have not done it yet. You're getting as bad as Mum and Dad.

TAP-TAP-TAP. Same sound effect, just on floorboards.

Leo saw her scan the room. Mainefare wasn't as open as Q Brasserie and it was harder to spot people—so he stood, waved.

His eyes went automatically to Sunshine's feet. Coral suede. Maybe four inches high—he figured the missing inches equalled casual for her. Oddly, no polish on her toenails; now that he thought of it, he hadn't seen colour on her toenails at their previous two meetings. Fingernails either.

Hello, Mr Estee Lauder—since when do you start noticing nail polish?

He *didn't*. Of course he didn't. But she just looked like the kind of girl who wouldn't be seen dead with unpainted nails.

Then again, she didn't look like the kind of girl who would eat like Henry VIII either.

Sunshine gave him her usual beaming smile as she reached him. She was wearing a pair of skintight pants in dark green, with a 1960s-style tunic. The tunic was cream, with a psychedelic red and black swirl on the front that should have looked like crap but didn't. She had on the same sun/moon necklace, but no other jewellery. And that was kind of strange too, wasn't it? Where was the bling?

She kissed him on the cheek, same as yesterday, before he could step out of reach, and sat as though exhausted, thumping an oversized tote—rust-coloured canvas—on the floor beside her chair.

'Whew,' she said. 'I've got lots of samples with me, so that bag is heavy.'

Leo couldn't work out how she could wear colours that didn't match—her shoes, her outfits, her bags always seemed to be different shades and tones—and yet everything looked *I'm-not-even-trying* perfect. He'd been out with models and fashion PR types who didn't make it look that easy.

'Did you sort out the guest list with Caleb?' she asked, and had the nerve to twinkle at him.

'Yes,' Leo said unenthusiastically.

'So! A hundred and fifty, right?'

Gritted teeth. 'Yes, a hundred and fifty. But you can still forget every one of the venues you listed as options.' He sounded grumpy, and that made him grumpier—because there was really nothing to be grumpy *about*. It wasn't *his* damned wedding. But it was just...*galling*!

Sunshine observed him, head tilted to one side in her curious bird guise. 'Does that mean you have somewhere fantastic in mind to fit one hundred and fifty people? Somewhere that will be available with only two months' notice?'

'As a matter of fact I do,' Leo said. 'I have a new place opening next month. But it's not in Sydney. It's an hour and a half's drive south. Actually, it's *called* South.'

He was a bit ashamed of himself for sounding so smug about it—what was he? Fifteen years old?—but his smugness went sailing right by Sunshine, who simply clapped her hands, delighted.

Which made him feel like a *complete* churl.

Sunshine Smart was not good for his mental health.

'Oh, I've read about it!' she exclaimed. 'Perched on

the edge of the escarpment, sweeping views of the ocean. Right?'

'Yep.'

Another enthusiastic hand-clap. 'Perfectamundo. When can we go and see it?'

Perfectamundo? Good Lord! 'Not necessary,' he said repressively. 'I've personally handpicked the staff for South, and they know what they're doing. We can just give them instructions and leave them to it. But I can send you photos of the space.'

Sunshine was staring at him as though he'd taken leave of his senses. 'Of course it's necessary. Your staff may be excellent, but Jon is trusting me to make sure everything is perfect. I know exactly what he likes, you see, and I can't let him down.'

Leo sighed inwardly.

'We have to think about how the tables are going to be arranged,' she went on. 'The best place for speeches, where we'll do welcoming cocktails—I mean, is there an outdoor area for that?' Her hands came up, clasped her head at the temples as if she were about to have a meltdown. 'A *thousand* things.'

Leo felt a throb at the base of his skull. 'Let me think about it,' he said, just to staunch the flow of words. He wasn't *really* going to think about taking her to see the damned restaurant.

'Thank you, Leo!' She was back to twinkling, clearly nowhere *near* a meltdown.

Two months! Two *months* of this manipulative, mendacious wretch.

'So!' she said. 'Let's talk invitations. I have three designs to show you—and I won't tell you which is my favourite because I don't want to influence your opinion.'

'You won't.'

'Well, I wonder if, subliminally, knowing what I like

best might sway you.' Little knowing smile. 'Maybe to deliberately pick something that is *not* my favourite! And that would never do.'

He caught his half-laugh before it could surface. Laughing would only encourage her.

'And since we haven't discounted the email, I've got something to show you too,' he put in smoothly, because he'd be damned if his version was going to be dead in the water without a demo at least. 'It's something we did for the Q Brasserie launch.'

Half an hour later Leo was amazed to find that he'd agreed to a printed Art Deco-style invitation in blue and teal, with yellow, brown, and grey accents.

But he'd had a win too! Sunshine was so impressed with his electronic idea she'd insisted they send something like it as a save-the-date notice, linking to some artsy teaser footage of South's surroundings.

'But we'll keep the venue secret,' she added conspiratorially, 'because it will be fun to have everyone guessing, and they'll be so excited to find out it's South when the printed invitations arrive.'

He hoped—he *really* hoped—he hadn't just been soothed.

Sunshine took on the responsibility for getting the invitations printed and addressed, with names handwritten by a calligrapher she'd dated in the past. She would show Leo—who actually didn't give a damn—the final design before it went to print, along with handwriting samples. Leo was in charge of getting the save-the-date done for Sunshine's approval—and she most certainly *did* give a damn.

He was on the verge of disappearing to the kitchen when Sunshine circled back to South and her need to see it.

'It's not going to happen,' Leo said. 'You can't go on site without me. And the only time I have free is…is…daytime Monday.' *Ha!* 'Shop hours for you, right?'

Sunshine pulled out a clunky-looking diary.

He did a double-take. 'You're on Facebook but you use a paper diary?'

'My mother made it for me so I have to—and, anyway, I like it,' she said. 'Hemp and handmade paper. Jon and Caleb have them too. Play your cards right and you'll get one next year. And, yes! I can do Monday. Yay!'

Again with the *yay*. And the twinkle.

And that throb at the base of his skull.

Sunshine put her diary away. 'My hours are super-flexible. I mostly work from home, and usually at night, when I seem to be more creative—not during the day, and never in the shop unless I'm doing a particular display. Because I have a superb manager who would *not* take kindly to my interfering.'

'I like the sound of your manager.'

'Oh, I can introduce— Ah, I see, sarcasm.' She regarded him with a hint of amused exasperation. 'You know, I'm not generally regarded as an interfering person.'

He couldn't keep the snort in.

'Sarcasm and a *snort*! Better not debate that, then! So! Shall I drive us down?'

'I'm going to take my bike.'

Her face went blank. 'Bike?'

'As in motor,' he clarified.

'You have a car as well, though?'

'No, I don't.'

'Because we could get so much done if we drove down the coast together.'

'Except that I don't have a car.'

'But I have a car. You can come with me.'

'Sunshine, I'd better put this out there right now: you are not going to control me. I don't have a car. I have a bike. I am going to ride down the coast, because that is what I want to do. Why don't you just ride down with me?'

Mental slap of his own head! Why the *hell* had he suggested that? Sunshine Smart plastered against his back for an hour and a half? No, thank you!

Although at least she wouldn't be able to talk to him.

Still, she would annoy him just by *being* there. In her skintight pants...full breasts pressed into his back...breathing against the back of his neck...arms around him...hands sliding up under his leather jacket...

What? No. *No!* Why the hell would her hands need to be sliding up there?

'Thanks, but, no,' she said—and it took Leo a moment to realise she was talking about riding on the bike as opposed to sliding her hands under his jacket. *Thanks, but, no.* Sharp and cool—and not open for discussion, apparently.

And it...*stung!* Dammit.

'Why not?' he asked.

'Because I don't like motorbikes.'

Don't like motorbikes! Well, good. Fine. Who cared if Sunshine Smart didn't like motorbikes? Every other woman he dated couldn't *wait* to hop on the back of his Ducati!

Not that he was dating Sunshine Smart. *Argh.* Horrible, horrible thought.

Just let it go. Let it go, Leo.

'Why? Because you can't wear ten-inch heels on one?' That was letting it go, was it?

'I don't wear ten-inch heels anywhere—I'm not a stilt-walker. It's not about shoes. Or clothes. Or even what those helmets do to your hair.' She tossed said hair. 'It's just...' She shrugged one shoulder, looking suddenly uncomfortable. 'Just an antiquated little notion I have about staying alive.'

'Fine,' he snapped. 'You drive, I'll ride, and we'll meet there.'

And then she sort of slumped…without actually slumping. He had an absurd desire to reach over and touch her damned hair, and tell her…what? Tell her *what*?

That he would drive down the coast with her? Hell, no! Not happening. And he was *not* touching her hair. He didn't touch anyone's hair. Ever.

Leo all but leapt to his feet. 'I'd better get into the kitchen.'

'Right now? But—' Sunshine checked her watch. 'Oh. That took longer than I thought.'

She gave her head a tiny shake. Shaking off the non-slumping slump, he guessed, because the perk zoomed back, full-strength.

'I have other samples in my bag—you know, pictures of floral arrangements and cakes. And I was going to talk to you about shoes. I'm arranging some custom-made shoes for you for the big day.'

'Flowers can't be that urgent. I have a superb baker on staff, so don't get carried away on the cake. And I don't need shoes.'

'The shoes are a gift. From me. I'm doing them for Caleb and Jon too. And I promise it will not be an identical shoe gig—nothing like those ancient wedding parties with six groomsmen all wearing pale blue tuxes with dark blue lapel trim!' Dramatic shudder. 'Oh, please say yes, Leo.'

Leo looked down at his feet, at his well-worn brown leather shoes. Scuffed, but as comfortable as wearing a tub of softened butter. And he had other shoes. Good shoes. *Italian* shoes. He didn't need more. He didn't want her goddamned shoes.

But her hypnotically beautiful mismatched eyes were wide and pleading as he looked back up, and he found himself saying instead, 'I'll think about it.'

She smiled. '*Thank* you. There's a ton of stuff still to talk about, but I understand you're on a tight leash tonight, so you get going. And before we meet on Monday I'll do some legwork on the flowers front. And music… No, I won't do any legwork on that, because I know you used to go out with that gorgeous singer Natalie Clarke, and she would be perfect. I hope—' She stopped, bit her lip. 'Oh, dear, enough about the music. I'm sensing a teensy bit of animosity—that little tic next to your mouth gives it away, you know. But we still have clothes to talk about. Yours and mine, since we're the closest thing they'll have to an official wedding party. We don't want to look too matchy-matchy, but there's so much we *can* do to look part of the overall theme.'

Leo stared. He was doing a lot of that. 'You mean there's a *theme*?'

'I'm not talking about those horrifying Elvis or Medieval or Viking themes. Or Halloween—it's been done! I've seen pictures—with pumpkins! I mean just a touch of complementary colour, a certain style…things like that.'

'You're scaring me.'

'I promise you'll love—'

'*Really* scaring me. Later, okay? *Much* later.'

Sunshine wrinkled up her nose—and Leo had now twigged that this meant she was about to put a new argument, so he held up a 'stop' hand.

'I'll see you Monday, Sunshine. And in the meantime try and remember that the marriage will have already happened. This is just a celebratory dinner.'

'But—'

'Monday.'

She made a muted explosive sound, redolent of frustration. 'All right! Monday! But I'm staying here for dinner—not running away like a good little girl.' She tossed her hair again. Flick. Over her shoulder. 'I have a date.'

Leo kind of liked that huffy hair-flick—it made him feel as if *she* were the one off kilter for a change.

'Then I'll send over a Campari for you while you wait.'
Calm. Reasonable. Charming, even.

'Lovely, thank you,' she responded. Calm, reasonable,
charming.

'I won't be able to come out and speak to Gary tonight,
though.'

'That's okay—Gary's not coming.'

Frown. 'But I thought you said…?'

'Oh, I see.' Little laugh. *Annoying* little laugh. 'No, tonight I'm having dinner with Ben.'

'Another investment banker?'

'No. Ben's an embalmer.'

Leo did the stare thing again. 'You're joking, right?'

'No.' Puzzled. Actually, seriously puzzled. 'Why would
that be a joke?'

'An *embalmer*? How did you even get to *meet* an embalmer? Are you making shoes for corpses?'

'Not that I *wouldn't* make shoes for corpses, but no.'
Pause. He saw the tiny swallow. 'It—it was a subject I
needed to—to research. Two years ago. For my…sister.'

'I didn't know you had a sister.' He thought back…
something about her eyes? In the womb… Triplets…?

Twins!

Oh. Embalmer. Sister. Her twin sister was dead. And
he was such a freaking idiot!

Because—oh, God. *no*—the face-morph. It was happening again. Emptiness. Ashy skin. Trembling lips. What
the hell *was* that?

'Sunshine…?'

No response.

'Sunshine!'

Alarmed.

She shook her head and the look was gone. But her eyes
were filling and she was blinking, blinking, blinking, trying to stop the tears falling.

Crap! He reached over to the next table, snagged a napkin, held it out to her with a gruff, 'Here.'

She took the napkin but just stared at it. Another blink.

He watched, holding his breath… Just one tear, one drop, and he would have to…to… No, he couldn't… could he? Hovering, hovering… His heart was starting to pound…

And then she took a long, slow breath and the tears receded.

Leo took his own long, slow breath, feeling as though disaster had just been averted, and slid into the chair beside her.

'Sorry,' Sunshine said. 'My sister died two years ago. The anniversary is coming up so I'm feeling kind of… emotional about it. I should be over it by now, but every now and then…' That tiny head-shake, then she looked at Leo and smiled. 'Anyway, let's get back to—'

'What was her name? Your sister?' Leo asked, because he was not getting back to *anything* quite that easily.

Sunshine paused, but only for a few seconds—and her smile didn't waver at all. 'Are you ready for this, Leo? It's not for the fainthearted.'

Leo didn't know if he was ready, not ready, or why he had to *be* ready.

In fact he didn't know squat.

He didn't know why he hadn't let her change the subject as she'd clearly wanted to do. Why her unwavering smile was bothering him. Why he wanted to take her by the shoulders and shake her until she let those jammed-up tears fall.

He didn't know a damned thing—*least* of all why he should be interested in Sunshine Smart's dead sister.

But he said, 'Worse than Sunshine?'

'Ouch! But, yes—at least Moonbeam thought so.'

'Moonbeam?' He winced. 'Seriously? I mean…*seriously*?'

Little gurgle of laughter. 'Yep.'

'Good God. Moonbeam. And Sunshine.'

She was playing with the hem on the napkin he'd given her, picking at it with her fingernails.

'So what happened?' Leo asked.

She looked down at the napkin. Pick, pick. 'Hippie parents.'

'No, I mean what hap—?'

'Oh, dear, I've snagged the hem,' Sunshine said, and put the napkin on the table. 'Sorry, Leo.'

'I don't care about the napkin, Sunshine.'

'Actually, table napkins have an interesting history. Did you know that they started out as lumps of dough, rolled and kneaded at the table? Which led, in turn, to using sliced bread to wipe your hands.'

What the hell? 'Er—no, I didn't know that.' Thrown. Completely thrown.

Extra-bright smile. 'But you were asking about Moonbeam. Actually, it's because of her that I'm sitting here with you. She and Jonathan dated as teenagers.'

He was staring again—couldn't help it. 'No way!'

'Yes way! But Moon realised pretty quickly that she'd need to swap an X for a Y chromosome if their relationship was going to get to the next level, even though Jon adored her. So—long story short—she encouraged Jon to leap out of the closet, with me hooked in for moral support, and the three of us became super-close—like a *ménage à trois* minus the sex. And *voilà*—here I am, planning Jon's wedding to your brother.' Her brilliant smile slipped. 'One of the reasons I miss Jon so much is because he's a link to my sister.'

Jon dating a girl. *Ménage à trois* minus the sex. Bread as *table napkins*? Leo didn't know what to say.

'Anyway,' she went on, 'I don't have to explain that to you. I know you miss your brother too.'

'It can't compare.'

'Yeah, I guess…I guess you can jump on a plane if you need to see Caleb.'

'That's more likely to happen in reverse.'

'You mean him jumping on a plane? Oh, no, I see—*him* needing to see *you*.' She looked him over. 'I get that. You're the dominant one, you're the one doling out the goods, and you don't *need* to see anyone.'

The perceptiveness startled him.

'So no emotional combustions! It's a good way to be,' she went on. 'In fact my approach to relationships is based on achieving a similar core of aloofness, of control. Of mastery over my emotions.'

He was a little awed. 'Your approach to relationships?'

'Yes. Separating sex from love, for example—you know, like that *ménage à trois* with me, Jon, and Moon. You have to agree that it makes life easier.'

'Easier, maybe. Not better.'

'Of course it's *easiest* to leave the love out altogether. That's what I do now.'

'What? Why?'

She tapped her chest lightly, over her heart. 'No room in here.'

'You're not that type of person.'

'Well, I *do* have to work hard at it,' she conceded.

'What? Why?' God, he was repeating himself!

'Because my natural inclination is to care too much about people. I have to take precautions to guard against that.'

'What? Why?' Nope—he was *not* doing another repeat! 'I mean, what are you scared of?'

'Pain,' she said simply. 'Because it hurts. To care deeply. It hurts.'

Leo wanted to tell her the whole argument was ridiculous, but the words wouldn't come. What did he know? He was living proof that sex was usually loveless, no matter how much you wished otherwise.

At least Sunshine could actually touch a person without having a panic attack, so she was way ahead of him. For sure Gary and Ben wouldn't have let Sunshine have those mini-meltdowns and sat there like blockheads, handing her restaurant napkins. How was he supposed to find what Caleb had when he couldn't put his arms around a tearful woman? Did he even deserve to, stunted as he was?

'But we were talking about embalming,' Sunshine said, and she was twinkling again. 'Which is much more interesting. A very technical and responsible job. And it does make you think, doesn't it?'

Leo, reeling from the various changes in conversation he'd been subjected to for the past few minutes—shoes, pumpkins, napkins, sex, love, embalming, *napkins*—could only repeat stupidly, 'Think...?'

'Well, cremation or burial? It's something we all need to plan for. If you're interested—as you should be, if you ride a motorbike—I'm sure Ben would be happy to—'

'Er, no—that's fine, thanks.' Leo got to his feet with alacrity. 'I'll send over that drink.'

Halfway through the night, Leo poked his head out of the kitchen. Ostensibly to gauge how the place was humming along, but really—he was honest enough to admit it—to check out Sunshine's date.

And Ben the embalmer was handsome enough to give Alexander Skarsgard a run for his money. Like a freaking Viking!

They'd ordered the roast leg of lamb—a sharing dish that came with crispy roast potatoes, crusty bread rolls and assorted side dishes and condiments. Enough food to feed the entire cast of *The Hobbit*, including the trolls.

Twice more Leo peered out at them. Both times Ben

was laughing and Sunshine was about to shove a laden fork in her mouth. Leo was starting to think Sunshine could single-handedly have eating classified as a championship sport.

Since he thought dining with a woman who actually ate would make a nice change, he didn't know why the sight of Sunshine chomping up a storm with Ben was so annoying.

But it was. Very, *very* annoying.

Another laugh floated through the restaurant and into his straining ears.

Right! He ripped off his apron. He was going to find out what the hell was so funny.

He washed his hands, changed into a clean chef's jacket and headed out.

Sunshine looked up, startled. 'Leo! This is a surprise.'

She quickly performed introductions as one of the waiting staff rushed to find a spare chair for Leo, who was examining the almost demolished lamb leg.

Leo raised his eyebrows. 'Didn't like it, huh?' he said, settling into the quickly produced chair.

Sunshine groaned. 'Not funny. I'll have to start dieting tomorrow.'

'That will be a one-day wonder,' Ben said, and winked at Sunshine.

Winked! Who the hell *winked* at people?

Sunshine laughed. 'Or you could kiss me instead, Ben, because—interestingly—kissing burns six and half calories per minute. As long as it's passionate.' She pursed her lips. 'I guess passion supersizes the metabolic effect.'

Ben, in the process of sipping his wine, choked. 'Where do you get all these facts?'

'The internet.'

Ben grinned. 'Better brush up on your arithmetic, Sunny, because if I kiss you for, say, fifteen minutes—and any longer is just *asking* for chapped lips—it's going to net you a hundred calories max. Basically, we'll burn off two thirds of a bread roll.'

'Are you talking yourself out of a kiss?' Sunshine asked.

She was doing the eyelash-bat thing, and Leo decided it made her look like a vacuous twit. He only just stopped himself from telling her so.

Ben smiled at Sunshine. A very *intimate* smile, by Leo's reckoning. 'You know I'm up for it,' he said. 'But we're going to have to make it a marathon and buy a truckload of lip balm if you keep that up.' He nodded at her fingers, which were hovering over the food.

Sunshine snatched up a small piece of crispy potato and popped it into her mouth. 'It's a vegetable,' she said. 'Doesn't count.'

'Oh, that's a *vegetable*!' Ben laughed. 'And you're a *nut*, Sunshine.'

Sunshine smiled serenely. 'If that's the analogy we're going with, you're a piece of meat.'

Ben gave her a *faux* mournful look. 'Oh, I know I'm just a piece of meat to you. We all are.'

A phone trilled.

'Mine,' Ben said, reaching into his shirt pocket. He checked the caller ID. 'Sorry, I have to take this.'

'*All?*' Leo asked as Ben left the table.

Sunshine laughed. 'Just a "poor me" thing with my exes. They get a bit club-like.'

'What? There's like a *legion* of them?'

Another laugh. 'Not quite.'

Leo leant forward, fixed her with a steady gaze. 'Are you sleeping with both of them? Gary *and* Ben?'

She stopped laughing. 'And you're interested because…?'

'Just wondering where everyone fits in relation to that guff about sex and love you were spouting earlier and the whole pieces of meat thing.'

'It's not guff.'

'*Total* guff.'

She considered him for a moment. 'Well—I've never been in love, but I *have* had sex. And I'll bet you've had enough sex to write *Fifty Shades of Leo*—but no wife. No steady girlfriend, even, right? No…love…perhaps?'

He felt his jaw clamp. God, he'd love to show her fifty shades of Leo. She wouldn't be looking at him in that curious bird way at the end. 'That's not the point,' he ground out.

'That's exactly the point. What's wrong, Leo? Not enough room in there?' She leant over and tapped her fingers on his chest, right over his heart. *Into* his heart, it felt like. 'I don't think you should be lecturing me just because I have sex without love the same as you do.'

'You're supposed to want them both.'

She tossed her head. 'Well, I don't. I won't. Ever. And glowering at me isn't going to change that.'

'I'm not glowering. I don't glower.'

'Oh, you *so* do. It's kind of cute.'

'I'm not cute.'

'Sure you are—in that I'm-a-typical-male-hypocrite kind of way.'

'I'm not a hypocrite either.'

'Go and get yourself nicely monogamised and I'll believe you.'

'Monogamised isn't a real word.'

That twitch at the side of her mouth.

Leo felt his temper surge. 'And I *am* monogamous.'

'Yeah—but one-after-the-other monogamy doesn't count if there's a hundred in the pipeline.'

He wanted to haul her out of her chair and… And what? And *nothing*, that was what. Nothing.

'Ben's coming back so I'll leave you to it,' he said. 'I've got some dessert coming out for you.'

She bit her bottom lip. 'Oh, dear—I really will need to start a diet tomorrow.'

Leo got to his feet. 'Just get Ben to kiss you twice.'

Sunshine grabbed his hand to keep him where he was.

His fingers curled around hers before he could stop them—and then his fingers stiffened. He pulled his hand free, flexed his fingers.

Sunshine's eyes flickered from his hand to his face. There was doubt in her eyes. And concern. And a tenderness that enraged him. He didn't need it. Didn't need Sunshine-bloody-Smart messing with his head or his goddamned hand.

'Why are you upset with me, Leo?' she asked softly.

He was unbearably conscious of the scent of her. Jonquils. A woman who'd just stuffed herself silly with meat shouldn't smell like flowers, so why did she?

'I'm not upset with you,' he said flatly. *Liar.* 'I'll email you a map for Monday.'

He strode back to the kitchen, furious with himself because he *was* upset with her.

But that was the 'what' of the equation. What he couldn't work out was the 'why'.

What? Why?

Oh, for God's sake!

CHAPTER THREE

TO: Jonathan Jones
FROM: Sunshine Smart
SUBJECT: Wedding of the century
Quick update, darling...

Invitations are underway—wording attached. We're going with smart/cocktail as the dress code, although obviously I will be wearing a long dress as befits my bridesmaid status.

Off to check the venue in the morning. It shows every indication of being divine.

Next we'll be working on the menu, but having now eaten at two of Leo's establishments I have no doubt it will be magnificent.

I wish I could meet a chef. Well, obviously I HAVE met one now, but I mean one with jumpable bones!
Sunny xxx

PS—Leo rides a motorbike! And, no, I still haven't done it, but soon.

TO: Caleb Quartermaine
FROM: Leo Quartermaine
SUBJECT: Coming along
Sunshine has the invitations under control and I'm attaching the save-the-date we've decided on. If I don't hear

from you in the next day or so I'll go ahead and get this out as per the War and Peace-sized invitation list.

Meeting Sunshine at South in the morning. And if she raises any concerns you'll have to arrange bail for me because I'll kill her.

I'm growing my hair—hope you're happy. And I am apparently having a pair of shoes custom-made for me. Was that your idea? Because I WILL get you back.

LQ

'Wow,' Sunshine said out loud.

South had to have the best position of any restaurant in the whole world.

Well, all right, she hadn't been everywhere in the whole world, and she was sure there must be oodles of well-situated restaurants all over the planet—in fact she would look up 'most scenic restaurants in the world'—but it was spectacular.

The restaurant was perched on the edge of the cliff. But in some mind-blowing engineering feat the entrance to it was positioned actually *over* the cliff and doubled as a small viewing platform. The floor was transparent, so looking down you could see a landscape of trees curving steeply to the beach. Looking directly forward, you could see the deep blue of the ocean; looking to the side and backwards gave you a view into the restaurant. No tables and chairs in there yet, but the space was sharp and clean, with a seemingly endless use of glass to take advantage of the view.

She breathed in the ultra-fresh air. It was windy, and her hair was flying everywhere, but she didn't care. This venue was perfectly...*perfect* for a wedding celebration.

Perfectly perfect. That had been Leo's description of the private room at Q Brasserie. He'd been annoyed with himself over the way he'd described it, which had made her want to hug him, because it was just *not* something to be annoyed about.

Not that he was the cuddly teddy-bear type you could pat and jolly out of the sullens. He was impatient and stand-offish and most of the time just plain monosyllabic cranky. There was no reason at all to feel that he needed to be hugged more often.

And yet…she wanted to put her arms around him right now.

Wanted to be close to him, held by him. Comforting. Comforted.

Dangerous, debilitating thought.

It had to be the proximity of the ocean messing with her head. For which she should have prepared herself before her arrival. Instead here she was, not knowing when or how hard the jolt would hit her—only knowing that it would.

So she would force it—get it done, dealt with, before she saw Leo. She didn't want to slip up in front of him again.

She took a breath in. Out. Looked out and down, focus-ing her thoughts… And even though she was expecting it to hit, the pain tore her heart. The memory of Moonbeam was so vivid she gasped.

Moonbeam had believed she belonged to the ocean—and Sunshine had always felt invaded, overrun, by the truth of that when she was near the coast, even when she was far above the water, like now.

One of her most poignant memories was of their last time at the beach. Darkness, rain, and Moonbeam exulting as she raced naked into the waves. *'This is where I'm me!'* Moon had yelled, and Sunshine, laughing but alarmed as she tried to coax her out of the freezing, dangerous, roiling surf, had called her a crazy Poseidon-worshipping hippie.

Three days later Moonbeam was dead.

Sunshine touched her sun and moon charms. She longed so keenly for her sister just then she couldn't move, could barely breathe. The loneliness, the hunger to be so close to someone that you were like two sides of the same coin, was like a knife wound. But not a sharp wound; it was a *festering* wound that wouldn't close, wouldn't heal.

'Sunshine?'

She took a moment, forcing the depression to the back of her consciousness with a shake of her head as she'd trained herself to do in public. Defences securely in place, she turned, smiling, to face Leo, who was standing at the doors leading into the restaurant.

'Hi, Leo,' she said.

Leo pushed the heavy doors further open, inviting her to enter. She started to lean up to kiss him as she crossed the threshold, but he jerked away before she could connect and she stumbled. He grabbed her elbow. Released it the nanosecond she regained her balance.

Ah, okay! She got it. He didn't want her to kiss him.

In fact…thinking back over their few meetings…she would go so far as to say he didn't want her to touch him in any way, ever.

And she'd just been daydreaming about putting her arms around him. Way to give the man a heart attack!

Was it just her, or did he have a problem touching all women? And if it was a problem with women generally, how did the man manage to have sex with a human?

Maybe he didn't. Maybe he had a blow-up doll.

Maybe it wasn't just women.

Maybe he had a problem touching men *and* women. Maybe he had a problem touching pets. *And* blow-up dolls.

Maybe he had an obsessive-compulsive disorder, hand-washing thing going on.

Hmm. She'd read something that might help in that case—about systematic desensitisation…or was it exposure therapy…?

In Leo's case it would mean touching him often, to get

him to see that nothing diabolical would happen to him just because of a bit of skin contact.

She could do that.

It would be a public service, almost.

A favour to a man who was going to be family—well, kind of family.

What was more, it would be *fun*.

'Oh, dear. I'm sorry, Leo. I took you by surprise, didn't I?' She bit her lip. 'I should have learned by now not to launch myself at people when they aren't ready! I once ended up in an embarrassing half-kiss, half-handshake, nose-bumping, chokehold situation. Has that ever happened to you?'

'No.'

'Well, just to make sure it never does I'll give you an indicator before I kiss you in future—say…puckering up my lips like a trout, so you'll know it's coming.' She stopped and thought about that. 'Actually, I wonder why they call it a trout pout when women overdo the lip-filler? Trout don't seem to have excessively large lips to me.'

He was looking at her lips now.

'Not that my own lips are artificially inflated, if that's what you're wondering,' she assured him, moving further into the restaurant. 'They're just naturally troutish. If trout really *do* have thick lips, that is. I definitely need to have another look at a photo of a trout.'

Leo's gaze had moved on to her hair. In fact he was looking at it with a moroseness that bordered on the psychotic.

What the *hell* was going on in his head?

'Is something wrong with my hair?' she asked, and flicked a hand at it. 'Do I look like I stuck my finger in an electrical socket? Because it's windy out there.' She reached into her bag—an orange leather tote—and pulled out an elastic band. Bundling the tousled mess of it into a bunch at the back of her head, she tucked the ends under and roughly contained it. 'There—fixed,' she said. 'I need a haircut, but I'm not sure how to style it for the wedding so it has to wait. I have a great hairdresser—actually, I used to date him.'

'*Another* one?'

'Another...? Oh, you mean someone else I used to date? Well, yes. Anyway, Iain—that's my hairdresser—says he needs to see the dress first. Some people might say that's a little neurotic, but he's a genius so I'm not arguing. And, of course, if I did argue it would be a pot-kettle-black thing, because I'm just as neurotic. I can't design your shoes, for example, until I know what you're wearing.'

He looked a heartbeat away from one of those glowers he supposedly didn't do. It was his only response.

'That was a hint, by the way, to let me know what you're wearing.'

'Yep, I got that.'

Silence.

'So!' she said. 'What do you think? About my hair? Should I keep the fringe? It won't grow out completely in two months, but it should be long enough to style differently—say, like...' She pushed the fringe to one side, smoothing it across her temple.

'I like the fringe,' Leo said.

Words! Yay! But he was *still* frowning.

And now he was looking at her dress.

Okay, so it was a little tight—hello! After two nights in a row at his restaurants, never mind yesterday's two-minute noodles, sugar donuts, and family block of chocolate, what did he expect? But nothing *that* remarkable. Kind of conservative. Just a nude-coloured woollen sheath. V-neck, knee-length, three-quarter sleeves, no fussy trim.

His eyes kept going, down her legs to her shoes. Five-inch-high nude pumps.

'Problem?' she asked, when his eyes started travelling back up, and she must have sounded exasperated because that stopped him.

At last he looked in her eyes. 'You look good—as usual.'

Oh. 'Thank you,' she said, and actually felt like preening.

'But I don't want you to break your neck wriggling around in that dress and tottering on those heels. The building is finished but there's still some debris around that you could trip over.'

And we're back!

This was going to be a long day. A long, *fun* day. He was just so irresistibly grumpy!

She stepped towards the windows. 'This is just brilliant!' Turned to shoot him a broad smile. 'Are you going to give me a tour, Leo?'

He nodded—and looked so uninviting that Sunshine almost laughed. Well, there was no time like the present to commence his therapy and start touch, touch, touching!

Brace yourself, Leo darling.

'Yes, but be careful,' Leo was saying, oblivious. 'And leave your bag—it looks heavy.'

Sunshine dropped the bag on the spot. 'Tell you what,' she said, walking back to him, 'I'm just going to hold on to you so you don't have to worry about the state of my fragile limbs.' She took his arm before he could back away. His arm felt hard and unyielding, like a piece of marble. Or petrified wood. Petrified! Perfect. She beamed up at him. 'Lead on, Leo.'

His jaw was shut so tightly she thought he might crack a tooth.

Oh, dear...oh, deary me! This was going to be *good*.

This was *bad*, Leo realised.

Actually, he'd realised it the moment he saw her stand-

ing on the viewing platform outside, looking glamorous
and yet earthy. And wistful. And…sad.

So she was sad—so what? She recovered like lightning,
didn't she? Like the other times. There was no reason for
him to want to… Well, no reason for anything.

And her hair was annoying! Out on the platform the
wind had been blowing it every which way and she hadn't
given a thought to the tangle it was creating, and then she'd
shoved the mess of it into a band as though it didn't matter. She *should* care about her damned hair the way every
other woman he'd ever dated cared.

Not that he was dating her.

It was destabilising, that was all, to have his percep-
tions mucked around with.

As was the way she'd cast that expensive-looking orange leather carry-all thing onto the floor—as though it
were no more valuable than a paper shopping bag.

And the fact that she never wore nail polish.

The way she could make her eyes twinkle at will.

And that fresh flower smell of hers.

The jolt when she took his arm and looked up at him
with mischief printed all over her face like a tattoo.

He didn't want to feel gauche when he pulled away
from her touch and nearly caused her to face-plant—and
then embarrassed because she laughed it off and blamed
herself when he *knew* that *she* knew the fault was his. Because Sunshine, he was coming to realise, was no dummy.

And he certainly didn't want to feel disapproving, like
a damned priest, just because she was dating two men
simultaneously and didn't love either of them. Because
she was right about one thing: who was he to lecture her?

Leo flexed his arm under her hand, which felt disturbingly light and warm and…whatever. It was nothing. Meant
nothing. It was just her keeping her balance. The same as
holding on to a railing.

He took a slow, silent breath. 'Let's start with the kitchen,' he said, and led her though swinging doors into a large room of gleaming white tiles and spotless stainless steel surfaces. 'Everything in here is state of the art, from the appliances to the ventilation system.'

Sunshine let go of his arm—relief!—and turned a slow circle. 'It's kind of daunting. Although I think that about every kitchen.'

'You don't like to cook?'

'I just do *not* cook. I can't. I did once boil an egg, although it ended up hard like the inside of a golf ball.' That stopped her for a moment. Distracted her. 'Have you ever peeled off the outer layer of a golf ball?' she asked. 'It's amazing inside—like an endless rubber band wrapped round and round.'

Not exactly a riveting fact, but she did seem to have an interest in the oddest subjects. 'You boiled it too long,' he said. *Yeah, I kind of think she figured that out herself, genius.*

'I ate it, but I haven't boiled an egg since. And, really, why boil an egg when you can pop out to a café and have one perfectly poached with some sourdough toast?'

'And that's the only thing you've cooked? The egg?'

'I've made two-minute noodles—as recently as yesterday.'

'Didn't you help out at home when you were a kid?'

'That was the problem.' She ran a finger along the pristine edge of one of the cooker tops. 'My hippie parents are vegetarian. It was all bean sprouts, brown rice and tofu— which I actively detest—when I was growing up.' She gave one of those exaggerated shudders that she seemed to luxuriate in. 'Tofu casserole! Who wants to cook *that*?'

She opened an oven, peeked inside.

'You're clearly a *lapsed* vegetarian.'

She turned to face him. 'Capital L, lapsed! From the

moment I bit into a piece of sirloin at the age of fifteen—on a Wednesday, at seven-thirty-eight p.m.—I was a goner. I embraced my inner carnivore with a vengeance. Meat and livestock shares skyrocketed! And two days later I tried coconut ice and life was never the same again. Hello, processed sugar! I don't have *a* sweet tooth—I have a shark's mouth full of them!'

'Shark's mouth?'

'Specifically, a white pointer. Did you know they have something like three hundred and fifty teeth? Fifty teeth in the front row and seven rows of teeth behind, ready to step up to the plate if one drops out.'

This was more interesting than the make-up of a golf ball, but not quite as intriguing as the calorific benefit of a passionate kiss.

And he wished he hadn't remembered that kiss thing— because it came with a vision of her kissing the Viking embalmer.

Sharks. Think about sharks. 'The only thing I know about sharks' teeth is that they can kill you,' he said.

'Hmm, yes, although the chance is remote. Like one in two hundred and fifty million or something. You've got more chance of being killed by bees, or lightning, or even fireworks! But that was just an illustrative example. So! I'm a processed-sugar-craving carnivore, to my parents' chagrin.' She stopped. Took a breath. 'Seriously, I must have the metabolism of a hummingbird, because otherwise I'd be in sumo wrestler territory. You know, hummingbirds can eat three times their own weight every day!' She ran a hand down her side and across her belly. 'Not that I can do *that*, of course,' she said sadly.

'No,' Leo agreed. 'You're not exactly skinny.'

A surprised laugh erupted from her. 'Thank you, Leo. Music to every girl's ears!'

'That wasn't an insult. I'm a chef—I like to see people eating.'

'In that case, stick with me and you'll be in a permanent state of ecstasy.'

And there it was—*wham!*—in his head. The image of her licking the glaceé off her spoon. Ecstasy.

He swallowed—hard. 'You could take a cooking class.'

'I think the cooking gene was bored out of me by the time I left the commune.'

'The commune? So not only are your parents hippies but you lived on a *commune*?'

'And it was *not* cool, if that's what you're thinking. Less of the free love, dope-smoking and contemplating our navels, and more of the sharing of space and chores and vehicles. Scream-inducing. If you have any desire for even a modicum of privacy do *not* join a commune.' She did the twinkle thing. 'And, really, *way* too much hemp clothing. Not that I have anything against hemp—I mean, did you know the hemp industry is about ten thousand years old? Well, probably you didn't know and don't care. But you have to admit that's remarkable.' Stop. Breathe. 'However, let's just say that I don't want to wear it every day.'

Oddly enough, Leo could see her wearing hemp. On weekends, down at the edge of the surf, with her hair blowing all over her face and her polish-free toes in the water.

It must have been the mention of the commune, because that was not a good-time girl Sunshine Smart image.

Enough already! 'Let's move on,' Leo said.

'What about plates, cutlery, glasses, serving dishes? You're sure everything will be here in time?'

'Yes, it will all be here. And it is all brand-new, top-quality, custom-designed.'

'Not that I have any intention of telling you how to stock your restaurant...' She bit her lip. 'But can you send me photos?'

Leo sighed heavily. 'Yes, I can send you photos.'

'Excellent. And can I see the bathrooms?'

She took his arm again, and he didn't quite control a flinch. Thankfully Sunshine seemed oblivious, although he was starting to believe she was oblivious to approximately nothing.

Escorting her into the men's and women's restrooms as though they were out for an arm-in-arm stroll along the Champs-Elysées felt surreal, but Leo knew better than to argue. He wouldn't put it past her to start imparting strange-but-true facts about the toilet habits of some ancient African tribe if he did, and his nerves couldn't take it.

At least she looked suitably dazzled by what she found. Ocean-view glass walls on the escarpment side, with the other walls painted in shifting shades of dreamy blue. Floors that were works of art: murals made of tiny mosaic tiles, depicting waves along the coast. And everything else stark white.

'I could live in here—it's so beautiful!' Sunshine marvelled.

'And I will, of course, send you a photo of the toilet paper we're using,' Leo deadpanned as they walked back to the dining area.

Sunshine looked at him, struck, lips pursing. Leo could almost see the cogs turning.

'You know,' she said slowly, 'I read something somewhere about a pop star who has *red* toilet paper provided when she's on tour, so do you think—?'

'No, I do not,' he interrupted. 'Forget the red toilet paper.'

The nose was wrinkling. 'Well obviously not *red*. I was going to suggest a beautiful ocean-blue. Or sea-green.'

'No blue. Or green. You'll have to content yourself with your victory over my growing hair.'

Sunshine laughed, giving up. 'It's coming along very nicely.'

She ran her hand over the stubble on his head and his whole body went rigid.

Leo stepped away from her, forcing that hand to drop and simultaneously dislodging her other hand from his arm. 'And so are your eyes,' he said, just for something to say—and didn't *that* sound bloody fatuous? How could eyes *come along*? They were just there—from birth!

Although…hmm…something about them wasn't right. Her pupils were a little bigger than they should be, given all the light streaming into the room.

Why were they standing so close that he could see her damned pupils anyway? It wasn't a crowded nightclub. They were the only two people in a big, furniture-free space. There was nothing to bump into. No reason for them to occupy the same square foot of floor. He took another step back from her.

She was considering him with a blinking, slightly dazed look that worried him on a level he didn't want to acknowledge.

And there went that tic beside his mouth.

'I saw my parents yesterday,' she said, and her voice sounded kind of…breathy. 'They like the new natural look—as you could imagine. Mum talked about sending you a thank-you card, so brace yourself for some home-made paper and a haiku poem. Apologies in advance for the haiku!' Stop. Little laugh. 'But strangers are doing a double-take when they look at my eyes now, which makes me feel a bit naked.'

'Don't knock naked. I've had some of my best moments naked,' Leo said, and wondered what the hell was happening to his brain. Disordered. That was what it was. You didn't go from talking about hair to eyes to nakedness. At least *he* didn't.

In fact there was altogether too much talk of underwear, orgasms and sex between them as it was, without tossing *naked* around.

He took yet another step back. Tried to think of something to say about homemade paper instead, because he sure knew nothing about haiku poetry. But Sunshine was giving him that dazed, blinking look, and he couldn't seem to form a word.

'Yeah, me too,' she said.

Leo had a sudden vision of Sunshine naked, lying on his bed. The almost translucent white skin, the long chocolate hair. Voluptuous. Luscious. Steamy hot. Smiling at him, sea-eyes sparkling.

He shook his head, trying to get the image out of his head.

And then Sunshine shook *her* head. 'So! Tables!' she said, and took hold of his arm again—and this time it seemed to hit him straight in the groin.

Leo, looking everywhere *except* at Sunshine, had never enthused so happily about inanimate objects in his life. The choice of wood for the chairs; the elegant curved backs; the crisp white tablecloths and napkins; the bar's marble top and designer stools. And still his bloody erection would not go down!

Go down. Sunshine Smart going down. On him.

Bad.

This was bad, bad, bad.

Walking a little stiffly, he showed her the outdoor terrace. Talked about welcome cocktails. Described the way the decking had been stained to match the wooden floor inside. Back in. Suggested positions for the official table. Indicated places for dancing—except that Caleb had told him that dancing was likely to be off the agenda, so why he was pointing that out was a mystery. Just filling the space with words. *Any* words. Waiting for that erection to subside.

And at the end, when she looked at him with those

twinkling blue and green eyes of hers, he still had a hard-on and he could still—*dammit!*—imagine her naked. On his bed. Kneeling in front of him. Walking towards him. Away from him.

Help!

'Can you email me the layout so I can refresh my memory when I need to?' Sunshine asked. 'Oh—and tomorrow I'll have the invitation design to sign off. Are you happy for me to do it, or would you like to see it?'

'I'd like to see it,' he said, and couldn't believe he'd actually said that. Because He. Did. Not. Care.

'I could email it.'

'No. Not email.'

Sunshine pursed her lips. Her 'thinking' look—not that he knew how he knew that.

'I really do have to be in the store tomorrow,' she said. 'Some new stock is coming in and I have a very specific idea for the display. And you're working tomorrow night, right?'

'No—night off,' he said, and was amazed again. He *never* took a night off.

She brightened. 'Great. Where shall we meet?'

'I'll cook.' Okay. He had lost his mind. He was *not* going to cook for Sunshine Smart. He never cooked for girlfriends. And she wasn't even that. Not even *close* to that. Even if he did want to have sex with her.

Damn, damn, damn. Goddamn.

Sunshine's eyes had lit up like a Christmas tree. 'Really?'

Could he back out? Could he? 'Um. Yes.'

'At my place?'

No—not at her place. Not anywhere. 'Um. Yes.' So he had a vocabulary problem today. Brain-dead. He was brain-dead.

'Just one teensy problem. Most of my kitchen appliances have never been used.'

'I love virgin appliances.' *Arrrgggghhh*. Again with the sexual innuendo. He was clearly on the verge of a nervous breakdown.

'In that case you will have an orgasm when you walk in my kitchen.'

Orgasms. Oh. My. *God*.

Sunshine checked her watch. 'And, speaking of orgasms, I'd better go.'

Huh? What the hell*?*

'I'm being taken to that new Laotian restaurant the Peppercorn Tree tonight,' she said, as though that explained anything. 'I checked the menu online. *Very* excited!'

Okay, he got it. *Whew*. It was the thought of *food* making her orgasmic.

And then her words registered. 'Being taken'. As in date.

'Gary or Ben?' He just couldn't seem to stop himself from asking.

'Neither of them. Tonight it's Marco.'

Marco. *Marco*? *Three* men on a string now? Not to mention the calligrapher. And the hairdresser. And there was probably a butcher, a baker, and a candlestick-maker in there somewhere.

'You sure there was no free love on that commune?' he asked, and thanked heaven and hell that he sounded his normal curt self.

'Love's never free, is it?' Sunshine asked cryptically. And then she smiled. 'That's why I'm only interested in sex.'

Before Leo could think of a response she tap-tapped her way out of the restaurant, clearly with no idea he was having a conniption and might need either medical or psychiatric intervention.

CHAPTER FOUR

TO: Sunshine Smart
FROM: Leo Quartermaine
SUBJECT: Photos
Attached are the images we discussed yesterday, plus the restaurant layout with a sketchy floor plan.

I've also included a photo of the toilet paper. White.

I'll be making pasta tonight, and bringing some home-made gelato.

LQ

TO: Jonathan Jones
FROM: Sunshine Smart
SUBJECT: All going swimmingly—and shoes!
Darling!

Checked out the venue yesterday—scrumptious. Caleb has photos.

Your shoe design is attached. As requested, not too over the top! Black patent with a gorgeous charcoal toe-cap. The shoes will work brilliantly with the dark grey suit and red tie.

I'm sending Caleb's design to him directly—he says you don't get to see his outfit before the big day! And you have the contact number for Bazz in Brooklyn to get the shoes made, so make an appointment, and quickly because he's super-busy.

Leo's are next. And, speaking of Leo...drumroll... tonight he's cooking me dinner!

We'll get onto the wedding menu tonight too. I'm thinking we should lean towards seafood, but with a chicken alternative for those who are allergic, and, of course, a vegetarian (dullsville) option.

Sunny xxx

PS: Was Marco Valetta always such a douche? Had dinner with him last night and he spent the whole meal talking about his inheritance—scared his father is going to gobble it up on overseas travel. Seriously, let the man spend his own money any way he wants! Marco thought he was going to get lucky, but after banging on all night about money and then suddenly switching to the subject of lap dances??????? As if!!!! He is SO off my Christmas card list. I'll bet Leo Quartermaine would never be such a loser.

PPS: I saw a statistic recently that said about twenty-five million dollars is spent on lap dances each year in Vegas alone. Amazing!!!!

TO: Leo Quartermaine
FROM: Caleb Quartermaine
SUBJECT: Loving the Sunshine...

...and I don't mean the New York weather, which is icky-sticky right now.

Just warning you, bro, that my custom-designed shoes are eye-poppers. I love them—but I'm the flamboyant type. Better prepare yourself!

Love the invitations, love the save-the-date, love the fact that you sent Sunshine a photo of the restaurant toilet rolls (yep, she told me). Think I love Sunshine too if she can get you to do that. Jon tells me half the male population of Sydney is in love with her—gay and straight—so I'm in good company.

Also glad about your hair—go, Sunshine! And glad about South.

Can't wait to marry Jon. Seriously, I don't care where or how we do it, as long as we do it. The party is just the icing on an already delicious cake.

Your turn now. Hope you're out there hunting instead of spending every spare minute slaving over assorted hot stoves.

And please tell me the bunny-boiler Natalie is under control. If she turns up at the reception I am getting out the power tools and going for her.

CQ

SUNSHINE LIVED IN an apartment in Surry Hills. The perfect place for people who didn't cook, because wherever you looked there were restaurants. Every price range, every style, and practically every ethnicity.

Leo had sent a ton of supplies and equipment ahead of him, because he had a shrewd understanding of what he could expect to find in Sunshine's cupboards—i.e., nothing much—and the thought of overbalancing the bike while lugging a set of knives was a little too Russian roulette for his liking.

He'd been cursing himself all day about offering to cook for her. Cursing some more that he'd offered to do it at her apartment—his own, with a designer kitchen and every appliance known to man, would have been so much easier. But then, of course, he wouldn't get to see what her place was like. And, all right, he admitted it: he was curious about that. He imagined boldly coloured walls, exotic furniture, vibrant rugs, maybe some kick-ass paintings or a centrepiece sculpture.

He buzzed the apartment and she answered quickly.

'Leo!'

He could hear the excitement in her voice. How did she

do that? Could she really, truly, be that enthusiastic about everything?

'Yep.'

'Fourth floor,' she said, and clicked open the door to the lobby.

She was waiting for him, apartment door wide open, when he got out of the lift.

Her hair was piled on top of her head—kind of messy, but very sexy. She was wearing an ankle-length red kaftan in some silky material that managed to both cling and flow. It had a deep V neckline and was gathered at the base of her sternum behind a fist-sized disc of matching beads. Voluminous sleeves were caught tightly at the wrists. She looked like a cross between a demented crystal healer and a Cossack dancer—but somehow bloody amazing.

His eyes, inevitably, dropped to her feet. She was barefoot. *Good God! Stop the presses.*

'I am *so* looking forward to this,' Sunshine confided, and puckered her lips.

Leo steeled himself, and after the tiniest hesitation she went right ahead and laid the kiss on him.

'That pucker was enough warning, right?' she asked with a cheeky smile. And then she rolled right on before he could answer. 'And I was right—trout do *not* have especially thick lips. So! This way,' she threw over her shoulder, and walked to the kitchen.

She gestured to three boxes on the counter. 'Your stuff arrived about ten minutes ago.'

'Good. I'll unpack everything,' he said, but he was more interested in the uninterrupted view into her apartment afforded by the open-plan kitchen.

And it was…disappointing.

White walls. No paintings. A serviceable four-seater dining suite in one section of a combined living/dining room in a nondescript, pale wood—pine, maybe. The couch was basic, taupe-coloured. A low coffee table in front of the couch matched the dining suite. There was a television atop a cabinet that matched the other furniture. Carpet a similar shade to the couch. Absolutely nothing wrong with any of it, but…no. Just *no*!

He nodded towards the living room. 'What's with the porridge-meets-oatmeal thing out there?' he asked, shrugging out of his leather jacket, and tossing it onto one of the stools on the other side of the kitchen counter.

'Oh, I thought you'd like it.'

Leo was speechless for a moment. Seriously? *That* was how she saw him?

When she came to his apartment she would see just how wrong she was!

Not that she *would* be coming to his apartment. But if she *did*…

Nope, he had to address this now or he wouldn't be able to cook. 'You've seen my restaurants—do they look like they've been furnished from a Design for Dummies catalogue?'

'I guess I didn't imagine you did that part personally. But there's nothing intrinsically wrong with a neutral colour palette, you know! And… Well…' She waved a hand at the living area. 'This part wasn't me, or it would be very different.'

'So who was it?'

'Moonbeam—and she just went for quick, basic, affordable. Out here and in her own room.'

'But aren't twins supposed to…you know…have the same taste?'

'*Negativo.*'

'So that's a no, is it?' Leo asked dryly.

'A big no way, José.'

Eye-roll. 'So, no?'

'Okay! No.' Matching eye-roll. And then she smiled softly. 'Unlike me, Moon didn't care about *stuff*.'

'What did she care about?'

'Life, the earth, the universe…et cetera.'

'So it stands to reason she wouldn't expect you to make a shrine out of a few pieces of pine, right? Why don't you change it?'

'I can't.'

'Why not?'

'I just…can't.' She looked at the boring furniture as though it were some Elysian landscape. 'Don't you ever want to freeze a moment? Just…*freeze* it? Hang on to it?'

'No, Sunshine, never,' he said. 'I want to move on. And on and on.'

She turned to him. 'You're lucky to be able to see things that way.'

'Actually, it's the *absence* of luck that made me see things that way. The desire to *change* my luck. To have more—a better life. To get…everything.'

Their eyes caught…held.

And then Sunshine gave that tiny shake of the head. 'Anyway,' she said, 'there's quite enough me in this apartment. I just keep it behind closed doors because it's scary for the uninitiated.'

Was she talking about her bedroom? 'Closed doors?'

She pointed at a closed door at one end of the living area. 'My office.' Pointed at another closed door behind her. 'Bedroom.'

Leo's mouth had gone dry. Over a freaking *room*? No— over just the *thought* of a room! But he couldn't help it. 'Show me,' he said.

She twinkled at him. 'You're not ready for that, Leo. But think a cross between Regency England and the Mad Hatter's tea party in the office, and Scheherazade meets Marie Antoinette in the bedroom…'

He looked at the bedroom door hard enough to disgust himself. What did he think was going to happen? An 'Open Sesame' reveal? Why did he care anyway?

'So! Leo! How do we start this gastronomic enterprise?'

Leo dragged his Superman-worthy gaze away from the bedroom door and refocused on Sunshine—the vivid, unique, laughing eyes; the luxuriant hair; her free-spirited yet glamorous dress; her naked feet.

'You're not wearing any shoes,' he said. *Duh! Of course she knows she isn't wearing shoes! They're her feet, aren't they?*

'I'm generally barefoot when I'm at home. But I do have a lovely pair of black beaded high heels that I wear with this dress if I'm going out.'

He could picture her, tap-tapping her way into South with sparkles on her feet, the red silk billowing. He knew he was staring at her feet, but they were very sexy feet.

And then his eyes travelled up. Up, up, up… To find her watching him, her eyes dazed and wide, lips slightly parted.

She licked her lips.

'Sunshine…' he said.

'Yes?' It was more a breath than a word.

'Um…' What? What was he doing? *What?* 'Feet.' *Doh!* 'I mean shoes!' he said desperately. 'I mean mine.'

She looked down at his feet. 'I like them. Blue nubuk. Rounded, desert boot-style toe. White sole.' Her eyes were travelling up now, as his had done. 'Perfect with…'

Holy freaking hell. He hoped she couldn't see his erection as she got to—

Argh. He saw the swallow, the blink, the blush. She'd seen it.

'Jeans,' she finished faintly.

Disaster. This was a freaking disaster. *Say something,*

say something, say something. 'I meant for…for the…the wedding,' Leo said.

And, really, it was a valid subject. Because he was starting to get curious about what she would design for him. Although it would probably end up being the shoe equivalent of a Design for Dummies pine bookshelf: plain black leather lace-ups.

'Oh!' She took a breath, smoothed the front of her dress. 'Well! I need to see what you're wearing first, remember?' She blinked, smiled a little uncertainly. 'So! Pasta? I even bought an apron!'

Food. Good. Excellent. Something he could talk about without sounding stupid or crotchety or boring or…or crazed with inappropriate lust.

Because he could *not* be in lust with Sunshine Smart. They were polar opposites in every single possible, conceivable way. Like light and dark. Bright and gloomy. Joyful and… *Oh, for God's sake, get over yourself!*

'You've got pots and pans, right?' he asked.

'Yes. And most of them are even unpacked.'

'*Most* of them? How long have you lived here?'

'Two and a half years.'

Leo ran his hand over his head. If he'd had hair he would have yanked it. Two and a half years was long enough to unpack *all* the pots and pans. 'I need a medium saucepan and a large frying pan. And what about bowls? Plates? Cutlery?'

'Oh, plates and stuff I have.'

'You get all that out while I unpack the food.'

She started humming. Off-key.

Leo peeked as she opened cupboards and slid out drawers. Just the bare minimum.

He opened the fridge to stow the wine he'd brought—empty except for butter, milk, soda water, and a wedge of Camembert.

Freezer: a bottle of vodka and half a loaf of bread.

The kitchen had one of those slide-out pantry contraptions, which he opened with trepidation. A jar of peanut butter. A packet of lemon tea. A box of sugary kids' cereal. A tin of baked beans that looked a thousand years old. And—sigh—three packets of two-minute noodles.

'Right,' she said proudly, and pointed to the pot, pan, bowls, and forks she had lined up on the counter. She reminded him of a hyperactive kitten being given a ball of wool to play with after being cooped up with nothing all day.

'How old are you?' he asked suddenly.

'Twenty-five—why?'

'You look younger. You act younger.'

'So I'm fat *and* immature?'

'You're not fat.'

She laughed. 'But I *am* immature? Just because I can't cook pasta? How unfair. I'm not asking you to design a boot, am I?'

'Yeah, yeah. Just go and put on your apron,' he said, and then wondered what he thought he was doing as she hurried towards a tiny alcove off the kitchen. What *she* thought she was doing! She wasn't going to be in the kitchen with him! She didn't cook! She had scoffed at the idea of cooking classes. So she didn't need a goddamned apron.

But when she came back she was beaming, and he couldn't find the will to tell her to go and watch TV while he made dinner.

He took one look at the slogan on the front of her apron— *Classy, Sassy, and a Bit Smart-Assy*—and had to bite the inside of his cheek to stop the smile. He was *not* going to be charmed. Like Gary and Ben—and probably Marco. Iain. And the tinker, the tailor, the soldier, and the spy.

'Come on, it's cute—admit it!' she said, possibly wondering about the strangled look on his face. 'You know, I used to be called Sunshine Smart-Ass in school, so seeing this in the shop today was like an omen. Not a creepy Damien omen. I mean like a sign that I am going to nail this pasta thing.'

'Smart-Ass. Why am I not surprised?' Leo asked through his slightly twisted mouth. Damn, he wanted to laugh.

She'd messed up her hair, getting the apron on. He could see part of her temple, where her fringe had been pushed aside. He realised he was holding his breath. Because... because he wanted to kiss her there.

Half the male population of Sydney is in love with her, he reminded himself. *And you are not—repeat not—going to become a piece of meat in the boyfriend brigade.*

Leo unpacked his knives and chopping boards, liberated extra plates and dishes from the cupboard, unearthed additional gadgets from his magic boxes.

'Come here so you can see properly,' he said as he started arranging ingredients on the counter.

Sunshine moved enthusiastically to stand beside him. The wave of heat emanating from him was very alluring. She edged a little closer. Breathed in the scent of him, which was just...well, just *him*. Just super-clean Leo. Could she manage to get just a bit closer, so that she was just— *nearly*—touching him, without him panicking and hitting her with a cooking implement?

His arm, naked below the short sleeve of his T-shirt, brushed hers—*that* was how close she was, because there was no way he would have done that on purpose—and she felt like swooning. Wished, quite passionately, that she hadn't worn sleeves so she could feel him skin to skin.

And it had absolutely *nothing* to do with exposure therapy either.

It was, plain and simple, about sexual attraction. *Mu-*

tual sexual attraction—at least she hoped the impressive bulge in his jeans that had taken her by surprise earlier was Sunshine-induced and not some erectile dysfunction... like that condition called priapism she'd read about on the internet...

Not that she was going to ask him that, of course, because men could be sensitive.

But with or without erectile dysfunction, she wanted to have sex with Leo Quartermaine!

Was it because he was cooking for her? There was definitely something off-the-chain seductive about a man—a *chef* man—making her dinner.

But...no. It was more than that.

Something that had been sneaking up on her.

Something to do with the way he jumped a foot inside his skin when she kissed him on the cheek. The little tic at the corner of his mouth that came and went, depending on his level of agitation. The slightly fascinated way he looked at her, as though he couldn't believe his eyes. And listened to her as though he couldn't believe his ears. The way he gave in a lot, but not always. And how, even when he let her have her way, the *way* he did it told her he might not always be so inclined, so she was not to take it for granted.

How bizarre was that? She liked that he gave in—and also that maybe he wouldn't!

She even kind of liked the fact that he tried so hard never to smile or laugh—as though that would be too frivolous for the likes of him. It was a challenge, that. Something to change. Because everyone needed to laugh. The average person laughed thirteen times a day. She would bet her brand-new forest-green leaf-cut stilettoes that Leo Quartermaine didn't get to thirteen even in a whole year! Not good enough.

Now that she'd acknowledged the attraction it felt moth-to-a-flame mesmeric, standing beside him. No, not a moth—that was too fluttery. More like the bat that had flown smack into the power line a block from her apartment. She'd seen it this morning, fried into rigidity, felled by a jolt of electricity.

Poor bat. Just going along, thinking it had everything under control, contemplating its regular upside-down hang for the night, then hitting a force that was greater than it and—*frzzzzz*. All over, red rover.

Poor bat—and poor her if she let herself get too close to Leo. Because she had a feeling he could fry her to a crisp if she let him.

Not that she would let him. She *never* got too close. That was the whole point of her 'four goes and goodbye' rule. Protecting her core.

Leo had managed to move a little away from her— which she rectified.

'This is a simple fettuccine with zucchini, feta, and prosciutto,' he said, clueless.

He moved once more, just a smidgeon. And Sunshine readjusted her position so she was just as close as before. *Poor Leo—you really should just give up!*

He managed another little edge away. 'We're going to fry some garlic, grated zucchini, and lemon zest, and then toss that through the pasta with some parsley, mint, and butter. Finally we'll throw in some feta and prosciutto—again tossed through—with a little lemon juice, salt, and pepper.'

He was—gamely, Sunshine thought—ignoring the fact that she was practically breathing down his neck.

He cleared his throat. Twice. 'This—' he was showing her a container '—is fresh pasta from Q Brasserie. I thought about making it here, but that might have been too much for a two-minute noodler to cope with.' He shot her a teeny-tiny smile—more of a glint than a smile, but *wowee*! *Be still my heart, or what?*

Sunshine watched as Leo started grating the zucchini

with easy, practised efficiency. There was a long scar on his left thumb, and what looked like a healed burn mark close to his right wristbone. Assorted other war wounds. These were not wimpy hands.

And, God, she wanted his sure, capable, scarred hands on her. All over her. It was almost suffocating how much she wanted that.

She kept watching, a little entranced, as Leo set the zucchini to one side, then grated the lemon rind. Next he grabbed some herbs and started tearing with his beautiful strong fingers as he talked...

His voice was deep and kind of gravelly. '...into strips,' Leo said.

Hmm... She had no idea what the start of that sentence had been.

He unwrapped a flat parcel—inside were paper-thin slices of prosciutto—and put it in front of her. 'Okay?' he asked.

'Sure,' she said, figuring out that she was supposed to chop it, and grabbed a knife.

'No,' Leo said, and took the knife away.

Lordy, Lordy. He'd actually touched her.

Sunshine felt every one of the hairs on her arm prickle.

She was staring at him. She knew she was.

He was staring back.

And then he stepped back, cleared his throat again. 'Tear—like this,' he said, and demonstrated. Another clear of the throat. 'You do that and I'll...I'll...find the ...cheese.'

She was humming again as she massacred the prosciutto.

And blow him down if it wasn't a woeful attempt at Natalie's signature song—the truly hideous *'Je t'aime-ich liebe-ti amor You Darling'*.

He started crushing garlic with the flat of his knife as though his life depended on it.

She was still tearing. And humming. *Please* tell him she didn't have the same insane cheesy love song obsession as Natalie. Who was *not* going to be performing at his brother's wedding! Once when he'd been mid-thrust, and Natalie had sung a line of that awful song, he'd choked so hard on a laugh he'd given himself a nosebleed; that evening had *not* ended well.

'Done,' Sunshine said, and looked proudly at the ripped meat in front of her.

Leo winced.

'What do you want me to do next?' she asked, with that damned glow that seemed to emanate from her pores.

'Salad,' he said, sounding as if he'd just announced a massacre.

Which it was likely to be—of the vegetable kind.

'We'll keep it simple,' he said. 'Give these lettuce leaves a wash.'

Sunshine took the lettuce leaves and ran them under the tap, her glow dimming.

'What's wrong?' he asked as he took them from her.

'Salad. It's so…vegetarian.'

She looked so disgruntled Leo found himself wanting to laugh again. He swallowed it. 'It's just a side dish. And there's meat in the pasta, remember?'

She wrinkled her nose. *Oh-oh.* Convoluted argument coming.

'I'll do it with a twist,' he offered quickly. 'I'll put some salmon in it, and do a really awesome dressing that doesn't taste remotely healthy. All right?'

Her nose unwrinkled. 'Okay, *if* you go a little heavy on the salmon and a little light on the lettuce.'

He choked. 'Am I designing that boot for you? No? Then

just shut up and see if you can cut these grape tomatoes into quarters. They're small, so be careful.'

She mumbled something derogatory about tomatoes, but made a swipe with the knife.

'Quarter—not slice,' Leo put in.

She nodded, wielded the knife again.

'And not mash, for God's sake,' he begged.

Sunshine made an exasperated sound and tried again.

Leo turned his back—it was either that or wrench the knife from her—and concentrated on the salmon he'd packed as a failsafe, coating it in herbs, then laying it in a pan to fry.

Sunshine was onto the song about love biting you in the ass, throwing in the occasional excruciating lyric—and he wanted so badly to laugh it was almost painful.

Mid-song, however, *she* laughed. 'Oops—that song is just too, too, *too* much, Hideous,' she said.

Damn if he didn't want to snatch her up and kiss her.

Instead he gave her some terse instructions on trimming the crunchy green beans to go into the salad, which she did abominably.

He put water on for the pasta, then turned back to the bench.

'Next, we'll—' He stopped, hurriedly averting his eyes as Sunshine arranged the salad ingredients in a bowl. 'We'll just slide the salmon on top—' shock stop as his eyes collided with the mangled contents '—and now I'll get you to mix the dressing.'

He lined up a lemon, honey, seeded mustard, sugar, black pepper, and extra virgin olive oil.

Sunshine considered the ingredients with the utmost concentration. 'So, I need to juice the lemon, right?'

'Yes. You only need a tablespoon.'

'How much is a tablespoon?'

Repressing the telltale tic, he opened the cutlery drawer and took out a tablespoon. 'This is a tablespoon.'

'Oh. How much of everything else?'

Limit reached. 'Move out of the way. I'll do it. I put a bottle of wine in the fridge. I think—no, I *know*—I need a nice big glass of it, if you can manage to pour that. Then go around to the other side of the counter, sit on that stool and watch. You've already thrown my kitchen rhythm off so things are woefully out of order.'

'It seems very ordered to me.'

'Well, it's not.'

Sunshine shrugged, unconcerned. 'You know, I feel like one of those contestants on your show.'

A thought too ghastly to contemplate!

Sunshine slid past him on her way to the fridge, brushing against his arm. *God!* God, God, *God*! Her brand of casual friendliness, with the kisses and the random touches, was something he was not used to. At all.

He didn't like it.

Except that he kind of did.

Dinner resembled a physical battle: Sunshine leaning in; Leo leaning *way* out.

A less optimistic woman would have been daunted.

But Sunshine was almost always optimistic.

As they ate the pasta and salad they argued over assorted wedding details, from the choice of MC—*'What are you thinking to suggest anyone but yourself, Leo?'*—to the need for speeches—Sunshine: yes; Leo: no!—to whether to use social media for sharing photos and videos of the function—over Leo's dead body, apparently.

By the time the pannacotta gelato was on the table Sunshine was in 'what the hell?' mode. Seven weeks to go—they had to move things along.

'So!' she said. 'Music!'

He went deer-in-the-headlights still. 'Music.'

'Yes. Music. I hear there's no dancing, so we can scrap the DJ option.'

'Correct.'

She pursed her lips. 'So! I've located a heavy metal band. I also know a great piano accordionist—surprisingly soulful. And I've heard about an Irish trio. What about one of those options? Or maybe a big band—but did you know that a big band has fourteen instruments? And where would we put fourteen musicians? I mean, I know the restaurant is spacious, but—'

'I know what you're doing, Sunshine.'

She blinked at him, the picture of innocence—she knew because she'd practised in the mirror. 'What do you mean, Leo?'

'Suggesting horrific acts and thinking that by the time you get around to naming the option you really want I'll be so relieved I'll agree instantly.'

'But that's not true. Well…not *strictly* true. Because I *have* named what I really want. Natalie Clarke.'

'No.'

'Why not?'

'Because.'

'Because why?'

'Caleb doesn't want her there.'

'Is that the only reason? Because I can talk to Caleb.'

'It's the only reason you're going to get.'

Sunshine gave him a bemused look. 'Is this because you used to date her? You know, I'm good friends with *all* my exes.'

'I, however, am not.'

'Why not?'

Leo scooped up a spoonful of gelato. Ate it. 'I just don't do that.'

'Why not?'

'They're just not that…that kind.'

'Kind?'

'Kind of person. People. Not the kind of people I'm friends with.'

She nodded wisely. 'You're choosing wrong.'

He took another mouthful of gelato. Said nothing.

'Because you don't want someone, really,' she said. 'You're like me.' Sunshine tapped her heart. 'No room in here.'

Leo's spoon clattered into his bowl. 'I've got room. Plenty. But I want…' He stopped, looking confused.

'You want…?'

'Someone…special.'

'Special as in…?'

'As in someone to throw myself off the cliff for, leap into the abyss with,' he said, sounding goaded. 'There! Are you happy?'

'My happiness is not the issue here.'

He dragged a hand over his head. Gave a short, surprised laugh. 'I want all or nothing.'

'And Natalie didn't?'

'She wanted…the illusion. She wanted the illusion of it without the depth.'

'Oh.'

'Yes—*oh*.'

'Not that I think there's anything wrong with not wanting the depth.'

'Of *course* there's something wrong with it,' he said with asperity. 'You're wrong about the whole no-room, sex-not-love thing.'

'Each to his or her own,' Sunshine said. 'And I still don't see why Natalie can't perform at the reception. You wouldn't even have to talk to her. I could do the negotiations.'

He snorted.

'Why the snort?'

'Forget it.'

'I am *not* going to forget it.

'Look—' He stopped, shot a hand across his scalp again. 'No, I don't want to go there.'

'Well, I do!'

'Oh, for God's sake!' Leo looked at her, exasperated. 'Natalie is a bunny-boiler, okay? She would not settle for negotiating with you—she'd be aiming for me. Always, *always* me. Got it?'

Sunshine sat back in her seat. Stared. *'No!'*

'Yes!'

'But…why?'

'How the hell do I know why? I only know the what— like eating at one of my restaurants every week. Driving my staff nuts with questions about me. Sending me stuff. So just leave it, Sunshine. I know another singer. Her name's Kate. I'll give you some CDs to listen to.'

'Is she an ex?'

'No. She's just a good singer with no agenda.'

Sunshine sighed inwardly but admitted defeat. 'Fair enough.' She stretched her arms over her head and arched her back. *'Mmm.* Next time maybe you should teach me how to make paella. I love paella.'

'One problem with that plan,' Leo said. 'I am never entering a kitchen with you again.'

'Oh, that's mean.'

'Think of the poor tomatoes.'

'What was wrong with the tomatoes?'

'Other than the fact that they looked like blood-spatter from a crime scene?'

Sunshine bit her lip against a gurgle of laughter. 'What about the prosciutto? I managed to tear that the way you showed me.'

'Flayed flesh.'

'Ouch,' Sunshine said, but she was laughing. 'What about how I scooped the gelato?'

'Please! Like ooze from a wound.'

'It's a good thing I don't have any coffee, or we'd be up to poison.'

'Since I didn't see an espresso machine in that shell of a kitchen, poison sounds about right.'

Rolling her eyes, Sunshine pushed her chair back from the table. 'Well, then, I will make you some tea—something all well-bred hippies *can* do. Unless you have some words to throw at me about scalded skin. The invitation is on the coffee table, waiting for your approval, so why don't you check it out while I clear up? Something *else* I can do.'

She watched from the corner of her eye as Leo moved to the couch, sat, reached for the invitation.

He was smiling—full-on!—as he slid the pad of his thumb so gently across the card, as though it were something precious. Oh, he did look good when he smiled. It was kind of crooked, with the left side lifting up further than the right. A little rusty. And it just got her—*bang!*—right in the chest.

Fried bat, anyone?

Tearing her eyes away, Sunshine finished making the tea.

'So! Is it okay?' she asked, sliding two mugs onto the coffee table and sitting beside Leo.

He turned to her, smiled again. *Heaven!*

'It's great. The calligraphy too.'

'I guess the next step is to discuss the menu.'

Leo picked up his mug. 'I'm going with a seafood bias, given the location.'

'Uncanny! Exactly what I was thinking.'

'Canapés to start. Local oysters, freshly shucked clams

served ceviche-style, poached prawns with aioli, and hand-milked Yarra Valley caviar with *crème fraîche*.'

'*Ohhhhh...*'

'Buffalo mozzarella and semi-dried tomato on crou-tons, honey-roasted vegetable tartlets, and mini lamb and feta kofta'

'*Mmm...*'

'Just champagne, beer, and sparkling water—we don't need to get too fancy with the drinks to start. But any spe-cial requirements we can accommodate on request.'

'Good, because Jon's mother will insist on single malt whisky—and through *every* course. *Nothing* we say ever dissuades her.'

'Well, it's better than a line of coke with every course.'

She gaped at him. 'Line of...?'

'Natalie,' he said shortly. 'Another reason she will not be performing at the wedding. Just to be absolutely clear.'

'That's...' She waved a hand, lost.

'Anyway, moving on. The first course will be calamari, very lightly battered and deep fried, served with a trio of dipping sauces—lime and coriander, smoked jalapeno mayonnaise, and a sweet plum sauce.'

'Oh, Leo, could you teach me how to make that at least?'

'No. The main meal will be lobster, served with a lemon butter sauce and a variety of salads that I wouldn't dare describe to you.'

'Lobster! Oh.' She took a sip of tea. 'You know, Leo, I saw the most intriguing thing about lobsters on the in-ternet.'

'Yes?' He sounded wary.

'They are actually immortal! They stay alive until they get eaten.'

'That can't be true.'

'Which means coming back as a lobster in the next life wouldn't be such a bad thing. Except...' Nose-wrinkle.

'Well, I'm not sure that when they're caught they're always killed humanely. So you might be lucky enough to live for ever—or you might get thrown into a pot of boiling water and be absolutely screaming, without even having the ability to make a sound, because some sadistic cook couldn't be bothered to kill you first.'

Leo gave a sigh brimming with long suffering. 'Okay—barramundi it is,' he said. 'Coated with lemon and caper butter and wrapped in pancetta, served with in-season asparagus.'

'That sounds divine. And so much more humane.'

'I am *not* a lobster sadist,' Leo said, sounding as if he were gritting his teeth.

'Well, of course not.'

There was the tic. 'And they are not immortal.'

'Well, they might be—who would know? And they can, a hundred per cent, live to about one hundred and forty years. Which is *almost* immortal.'

He regarded her through narrowed eyes. 'How is it you've made it to twenty-five without being murdered?'

'You're definitely watching too many crime shows.'

'Dessert,' he said firmly. 'I'm thinking about figs.'

'Figs. Oh.' Sip of tea.

'"Figs oh" *what*? Is this the fruit version of your vegetarian hang-up? Because there *will* be sugar, you know.'

'It's not th— Actually, it *is* partly that. But, more to the point, I think fig pollination is kind of disgusting.'

He had that fascinated look going on.

'Wasps,' she said.

'Wasps?'

'They burrow into the fig and lay their eggs in the fruit, then die in there. *Ergh*. And it's quite brutal, because on the way in the poor wasp can lose her wings and her antennae—it's a tight fit, I guess. Come on—you have to agree that's a bit repulsive. And sad too.'

Leo had closed his eyes. Tic, tic, tic.

A moment passed. Another. He opened his eyes and looked at her. 'So, we'll serve a variation on the glacé I made for you at Q Brasserie—perhaps with a rose syrup base. And, because it's a wedding, some Persian confetti.'

Sunshine beamed at him. 'That's just perfect.'

'And remember I know your modus operandi, Sunshine Smart-Ass.'

'But I don't have one of those!'

Leo simply put up the 'stop' hand. 'For the non-seafood-lovers there will be ricotta tortellini with burnt-sage butter sauce as an alternative first course, and either chargrilled lime and mint chicken or a Moroccan-style chickpea tagine for your fellow commune dwellers for the main course.'

'Oh, even the chickpea thing sounds good. Because chickpeas are sort of like the meat of vegetables, don't you think?'

'No, I don't.'

'What about the cake?'

'Four options: traditional fruit cake, salted caramel—which we can do with either a chocolate or butterscotch base—or coconut.'

'Oh! *Oh!* Could we do one of those cake-tasting things? You know, where you sit around and try before you buy? I would *so* love to do a cake-tasting.'

'For the love of God, can't we just ask the guys what they want?'

'What would be the fun in that?' Sunshine asked, mystified.

Leo ran that hand over his head. 'I'll talk to Anton—he's my *pâtissier.*'

'And I have the most amazing idea for the decoration. Kind of Art Deco—my current favourite thing. Square tiers, decorated with hand-cut architectural detailing, in white and shades of grey, with painted silver accents. Wait a moment—I've got a photo.'

Sunshine leapt off the couch and raced into her office, grabbed the photo and raced back out. 'What do you think?' she asked, thrusting it at him.

But Leo was looking past her into the office.

She'd forgotten to close the door.

'Oh,' she said, seeing through his eyes the green-striped wallpaper, the reproduction antique furniture painted in vivid blues, reds, and yellows, the framed prints of lusciously coloured shoes through the ages hung on the walls.

The urn with Moonbeam's ashes. In his direct line of sight.

Oh, no! Sunshine raced back to close the door.

'So!' she said, her heart beating hard as she came back to sit beside him. 'So! The cake.'

'I'll talk to Anton,' Leo said absently, still looking at the closed door.

Sunshine decided drastic action was needed—just to make sure he didn't ask to actually go in there.

Going with gut feeling—and, all right, secret desire—she hugged him.

He seemed to freeze for a moment, and then his arms came around her. He gathered her in for one moment. She heard, felt him inhale slowly.

Wow! He was actually touching her! Voluntarily! Except that this wasn't exactly touching—it was more. Better! Absorbing! He was absorbing her! Talk about exclamation mark overload!

His arms were so hard. So was his chest. It should have felt like being pulled against a brick wall…and yet there was something yielding about him. His hand came up, touched the back of her head, fingers sliding into her hair.

Good. But Sunshine wanted more. Much more.

She pulled out of his arms, sat back, looked at him. 'I don't know how you're going to take this, Leo,' she said, 'but I want to have sex with you.'

CHAPTER FIVE

LEO STARED. COULDN'T so much as blink.

A minute ticked by.

She was waiting for him to speak, her head tilted—the curious bird look.

Had he heard correctly?

Had Sunshine Smart just told him, taking matter-of-factness to the level of an art form, that she wanted to have *sex* with him? And that she didn't know how he'd *take* that confession?

'What did you just say?' he asked at last, and his voice sounded as though he hadn't used it for a month.

'Just that I want to have sex with you.' Sunshine pursed her lips, considering him. 'Are you shocked? Horrified? Appalled? Because you don't look interested.'

'Gary. Ben. Marco.' He listed them without elaborating.

'Gary, Ben and Marco?' she said, as though she had no idea what he was getting at.

'How many lovers do you need?'

She gave him an *Aha!* kind of look, then said simply, 'Okay, I'll tell you. I'm not sleeping with any of them. I'm not sleeping with anyone. I *hoped* there would be a spark with Gary, but it never developed. Ben? Twice. But that's ancient history, and we won't talk about his addiction to cheesy love songs in the bedroom.'

Momentary distraction. '*Ben* and cheesy love songs? What *is* it with people and cheesy love songs?'

'I know—it's crazy! So, of course, it was never going to go anywhere. Marco—well, that would be a cold day in hell.' She looked at him. 'But there's no need to talk it to death. If you're not interested let's just move on. We have a tough seven weeks ahead, and there's just not enough time for us to go through an awkward phase.'

'How the hell am I supposed to *move on*?' Leo asked, incredulous.

'I said I wanted to have sex with you—not that I wanted to marry you. And only up to four times, which is my limit.' She looked at him thoughtfully. 'You don't suffer from priapism by any chance, do you?'

'From *what*?'

'Guess not. Well, then—are you, perhaps, a virgin who's signed some sort of pledge?'

'No, of course I'm not a *virgin*.'

'Well, I don't know why you say *"of course"* like that. There are more virgins out there than you realise. In fact I read on the internet that—'

'And what do you mean, only up to four times?' he asked, jumping in before she could give him virgin facts. Because he did *not* want virgin facts.

'Any more than four times and things get messy. You know—emotional. If you don't want to develop a relation-ship it's best to set a limit. And I don't. Want to develop a relationship. I mean; I *do* want to set a limit. Hmm, you're giving me that look.'

'What look?'

'That *she's insane* look.'

'That's because you are. Insane.'

'I'm just sensible, Leo. Men do this stuff all the time. Pick up a girl in a seedy bar—not that we're in a seedy bar, of course, but you get the picture—then race her off to the bedroom, then do the I'll-call-you routine when they have no *intention* of calling. So why can't I? Well, not the I'll-call-you thing—I would never say I'd call someone and then not do it. And there really is no *reason* not to call. Regardless of whether you want to have sex with them again. Because you had to like them in *some* way to get into bed with them in the first place, so you should want to see where the friendship goes, shouldn't you? The sex part is kind of incidental—because sex is just...well, *sex.*'

Pause.

Thank God. Because his head was spinning.

'I guess what I'm saying,' she continued, unabashed, 'is that it's better to be up-front about what you want— just sex, just friendship, sex and then friendship. Whatever! But no tragic *I love you* just to wring an orgasm out of someone.'

'What if you *do* fall in love?'

'I won't. I never have. And I never will. I told you before: I won't let myself care that much.'

'So you're saying Jonathan and Caleb should give up the idea of marriage and just have sex?'

Her face softened. 'No, I'm happy for them. And I know the love thing works for lots of people—my parents are a prime example. It just doesn't work for me.'

'How do you know if you've never been there?'

'Haven't we already had this discussion?'

'Not thoroughly enough, Sunshine.'

Another pause. 'All right, then. The fact is I'm too... intense. I feel things too intensely.'

'Not thoroughly *enough*,' he repeated.

She bit her lower lip, worried it between her teeth. And then, haltingly, she said, 'I didn't recover—not properly— from my sister's death.' The tears were there, being blinked furiously away. 'I can't describe it. The agony. The... *agony.*'

'That's a different kind of love,' he said, but gently.

'A different *kind*, yes. But the *depth*… I just think it's safer, for me, to splash in the shallows—not to swim out of my depth.' She laughed, but there was no humour in it. 'Huh. A line of coke and I'd be Natalie.'

'You're nothing like Natalie. And you already have strong, deep ties—to Jon, to your parents…'

'Yes. I love Jon, and I love my parents. But it was too late to do anything about them; they were already here.' Small tap over the heart. 'I'm just limiting further damage.' She tried to smile. 'And, anyway, the in-love kind of love would be the *most* damaging. Because I know how I'd be in love. Kill for him, die for him…'

'The kind I want.'

'The kind you *say* you want, anyway. Into the abyss, off the cliff. But you'll see, when you've fallen into the abyss, that there's anguish there—in the fear of losing the one you love, or even just losing the love. And I can't—won't— go through that. Because next time I just don't know how I—' She stopped. Blew out a breath. 'Let's not go there. Let's just keep the focus on sex.'

Leo could hear muted noises from outside floating up from the street. Traffic. A laugh. A shout. But inside it was quiet. 'So you've restricted your lovers to a four-night term ever since Moonbeam died? And none of them ever wanted to take things further?'

'They knew it was never going to happen. And I've managed to stay good friends with all of them despite that—which is more than you can say. Well, all of them bar one.'

'And what went wrong with him?'

'He just doesn't like women dictating the terms, so we didn't even make it to the first…what would you call it?… assignation? Yes, assignation.' She did the curious bird thing. 'I'm guessing you're in his camp.'

Leo had no idea, at that point, *what* he thought. But he didn't like Sunshine telling him which camp he was in, thank you very much! 'No, I'm not in that camp.'

Sunshine smiled. 'So! Are you saying you *would* consider it, Leo? Sex, I mean?'

'No, I'm not saying that either.'

Another smile. 'Shall we try a little experiment, then?'

Long silence. And then, 'What kind of experiment?'

'I'll kiss you and you can see how that makes you feel.'

He opened his mouth to say no.

But Sunshine didn't let him get that far.

She simply moved so she was straddling him. She undulated, once, against him, and he thought he would explode on the spot. *Holy hell.* Then she settled, cocooning him between her forearms as she gripped the back of the sofa, one hand on each side of his head. Jonquils. Red silk. Heat and buzz and glow. She dipped her head, nipped his lower lip.

'No, that wasn't the kiss—that was me signalling my intention, as I promised to do.' She smiled. 'So! Ready?'

Any thought of denying her went straight out of his head like a shot of suddenly liberated steam. Leo gripped her hips, ground her against him, wanting her to feel his raging erection—although he didn't know why, unless her form of insanity was contagious—and took over, devouring her mouth with a hard, savaging kiss.

Her mouth was amazing. Open, luscious, drawing him in. His tongue, hot and agile, swept the roof of her mouth, the insides of her cheeks, under her super-sexy top lip. The tart sweetness of the lemony tea was delicious when it was licked from inside her. He could feel that slight gap between her front teeth. He moved his hands, cupped her face to keep her there, just *there*, so he could taste more deeply.

He could feel his heart thundering. Became aware that her hands were now fisted in his shirt as she rocked against him, forced her mouth and his wider still. She was whimpering, alternately jamming her tongue into his mouth and then licking his lips. And rocking, rocking, *rocking* against him until he thought he'd go mad with wanting.

Then her hands were moving between them, fingers plucking at the button of his jeans, which opened in a 'thank God' moment, then sliding his zipper down, freeing him.

'Ah…' he gasped, pulling his mouth away so he could breathe, try to think. But it was no use. He had to kiss her again.

She reeled him back in, pulled him closer, angled him so that when she lay back, flattened on the couch, he was on top of her.

Then his hands were there, pulling up the red silk. Up, up, up. So he could touch her skin, which was like satin. No, not satin—warmer than satin. Velvet…like velvet. His fingers slid higher, closer. He didn't want to wait—couldn't wait—*had* to feel her, to be in her the fastest way he could get there.

Without disengaging his mouth from hers, he plunged his fingers into her. Again. She arched into the touch.

She didn't speak, but breathed out words. His name. *'Leo. Yes, yes. Leo…'*

And then it wasn't his fingers but him needing to be there, buried in her as deep as he could go, panting, straining, wanting this, wanting *her*, silently demanding that she come for him. For *him*.

He felt her body tightening, straining, heard his name explode from her lips as the orgasm gripped her. He pushed hard into her, and kissed her drugging mouth again as he followed her into a life-draining release.

They lay there, connected, in a tangle of clothes, spent.

After a long moment Sunshine gave a shaky laugh. 'That was some kiss,' she said.

But Leo didn't feel like laughing. He felt like diving into her again…and also, contrarily, like getting the hell away from her. From her rules. Her determination to fix him in the place where she wanted him. Just where she wanted him. No further.

Awkwardly, he disengaged himself from her body.

Sunshine sat up, pushing at her hair with one unsteady hand and at her dress with the other. She looked like the cat that had got the cream.

Infuriating.

Mechanically, Leo adjusted his clothing. He was appalled to realise he hadn't even *seen* her during that mad sexual scramble. Did that make him some kind of depraved, desperate sex fiend, that he'd treated her body like a receptacle? But then, he hadn't really *needed* to see her to know very well that it was her driving him wild—so wild he hadn't been able to think past the need to be inside her.

'Are you sorry?' Sunshine asked softly.

She was watching him with wary concern.

'No. Yes. I don't know.'

Tiny laugh. 'Multiple *choice*? How…comprehensive.'

He stood abruptly, shoved his hands in his pockets, not trusting where he'd put them otherwise.

'Leo, don't go. We have to talk about this.'

He shook his head.

She got to her feet, took his hand. 'You will get all angsty if you leave now, because it happened so fast and we weren't expecting it to go like that. We can't have angst; we have too much to do. Come on, sit with me—let's make sure we can get back to normal before you go.'

How did you talk yourself back to *normal* after that?

How did a kiss turn into rip-your-heart-out sex in one blinding flash of a moment? And that complete loss of control… It had never happened to him before. No condom. Not even a *thought* of one! He was shaken. Badly.

And—God!—she was still holding his hand, and he was rubbing his thumb over her knuckles, and he hadn't even noticed he was doing it. He didn't *do* that touchy-feely stuff.

He dropped her hand and stepped back. 'You're dangerous, Sunshine,' he said.

She looked startled. 'It's not like I'm a black widow spider or a praying mantis.'

'What the—? All right, I think I get the black widow spider. But what's so dangerous about a praying mantis?'

Her eyes lit. 'Oh, it's really interesting! Praying mantises can only have sex once the female rips off the male's head. Imagine! At least you still have your head.'

Leo felt his lips twitch. But he was *not* going to laugh. It was not a funny situation. It was an *angsty* one. Angsty? God.

'On that note, I'm going,' he said.

'But we have to talk.'

'Not now. Meet me… I don't know… Tomorrow. At the Rump & Chop Grill. Five o'clock. It's only a few blocks from here. I'll send someone for my kitchen gear in the morning.'

'All right, tomorrow,' she agreed, and walked with him to the door, where she stopped him. 'Leo, just so you can think about it before then…I want to have sex with you again. We have up to three more opportunities, and there doesn't seem to be a reason not to use them. We just need to schedule them so we don't get distracted from the wedding preparations.'

He was staring again. Couldn't help it.

'Far be it from me to distract you, Sunshine,' he said.

So!

Yowzer!

As Sunshine wallowed in her bubble bath, lathering

herself with her favourite jonquil-scented soap, she pondered what had happened.

It sure hadn't been a cheesy-love-song experience. More like heavy metal—hard and loud and banging. But maybe with a clash of cymbal thrown in. She smiled, stretched, almost purred.

She knew she would be reliving the sex for an hour or so—that was par for the course. The sexual post-mortem...a normal female ritual. Remembering exactly what had happened, what had been murmured, who'd put what where.

But at four o'clock in the morning she was still trying to piece it together and parcel it off. She wondered if the difficulty was that she didn't have a precise anatomical memory of the experience. She couldn't recall everything that had been said, every touch, every kiss. She just had an... *awareness*. That it had been so gloriously *right*, somehow.

Which was strange. Because technically it shouldn't have been that memorable. They hadn't taken off their clothes; Leo hadn't touched her breasts—which she'd always counted as her best assets—and he hadn't even bothered to look at the goods before plunging in—which was a waste of her painfully acquired Brazilian!

But none of that seemed to matter because the *can't wait* roughness of it had been more seductive than an hour of foreplay. She hadn't needed foreplay. Hadn't wanted finesse. Hadn't thought about condoms. Hadn't thought about anything. She'd been so hot, so ready for him.

She wondered—if that rough-and-ready first time was any indication—just how magnificent the next time would be.

Because there *would* be a next time. She was going to make sure of it.

TO: Jonathan Jones
FROM: Sunshine Smart
SUBJECT: Party news

Isn't the menu great? Leo=food genius.

Just the wedding cake to go. I'd tell you the options, but if you chose one I wouldn't get my cake-tasting, which you know I've always wanted to do.

Leo cooked the most amazing meal last night. He is so different from the men I usually meet. More mature, steadier. Kind of conservative—I like that.

His hair is coming along too.
Sunny xxx

TO: Sunshine Smart
FROM: Jonathan Jones
SUBJECT: Do not sleep with Leo Quartermaine
DO NOT!!!!! That would be all kinds of hideous.
Jon

TO: Jonathan Jones
FROM: Sunshine Smart
SUBJECT: Re: Do not sleep with Leo Quartermaine
Oops! Too late!

But how did you know? And why hideous?
Sunny

TO: Sunshine Smart
FROM: Jonathan Jones
SUBJECT: Re:Re: Do not sleep with Leo Quartermaine
OH, MY FREAKING GOD, SUNNY!!!!!!!!

How do I know? For starters because every second word you're writing is 'Leo'!

He's not the type to enjoy the ride then buddy up at the end. You know his parents were drug addicts, right? You know he basically dragged Caleb through that hell and into a proper life?

He's a tough hombre, not a poncy investment banker,

soulful embalmer or saucy hairdresser. This is not a man for you to play with.

Let's talk tonight—10 p.m. your time. With video. No arguments.

Jon

Sunshine got to the Rump & Chop Grill fifteen minutes early. Although it was part of a pub, it had a separate entrance on a side road—which was locked.

She decided against knocking and inveigling her way inside to wait. That would have been her usual approach. But Leo already had one bunny-boiler on his tail, as well as being in a state about last night, so it was probably best not to look *too* enthusiastic.

Fortunately there was a café across the road, where she could wait and watch for him. Which would give her time to think.

Because Jon's email had thrown her.

The thing with Leo was a simple sexual arrangement. No need for concern on *anyone's* part.

So he'd had drug addict parents? And, no, of course she hadn't known that! How could she have, unless someone had told her? And why did it make a difference anyway? Unless Leo was a drug addict himself—and given his obvious disgust over his ex-girlfriend's coke habit that seemed unlikely.

Did Jon think the fact that Leo and Caleb had navigated a hellish childhood would put her off him? It clearly hadn't put Jon off Caleb, so why the double standard? And Caleb had come through unscathed. He was a terrific guy—very different from his brother, of course—at least from what she'd seen during their internet chats. Funny and charming and *out there*. Not that Leo wasn't also terrific, but he certainly didn't have Caleb's lightness of spirit.

But it was to Leo's credit, wasn't it, if he was the one

who'd dragged them both out of the gutter? She admired him *more*, not less, because of it. Liked him more.

Okay—*that* could be a problem. She didn't actually *want* to admire or like him more, because admiration and liking could lead to other things. And what she wanted was to keep things just as they were.

Hot man, in her bed, up to three more times. Finish.

As she would tell Jon, very firmly, tonight.

So! For now she would stop thinking about Leo's horrible childhood and concentrate on the wedding reception. *Not* that Jon deserved to have her fussing over it after that email, but...well, she loved Jon. And she was going to make the bastard's wedding reception perfect if it killed her.

While she sat in the café, disgruntled, sipping a coffee she didn't even want, she scanned the checklist. Having the function at South was brilliant, but it did add an extra task: finding accommodation for people who wouldn't want to drive back to Sydney. She figured they would need two options—cheap and cheerful, and sumptuous luxury. If she could get it sorted quickly, hotel booking details could be sent out with the invitations. She was sure Leo wouldn't want to traipse through hotels with her, so she would shoot down the coast herself and just keep him in the loop via email.

Right. The next urgent thing on the list was what Leo was wearing.

At least it was urgent from *her* perspective, because his shoe design hinged on it. And so did her outfit.

She was dying to wear her new 1930s-style dress in platinum charmeuse. It looked almost molten. Hugging her curves—all right, a little dieting might be required—in an elegantly simple torso wrap before tumbling in an understated swirl to the ground. It even had a divine little train. And she could wear her adorable gunmetal satin peep-toes with the retro crystal buckles.

But there was no good glamming to the hilt if Leo was going to play it down. And so far, aside from his pristine chef's whites, she hadn't seen an inclination for dressing up. Just jeans, T-shirts, sweaters. Good shoes, but well-worn and casual.

She heard a roar, and a second later a motorbike—it had to be his—pulled up outside the restaurant. One economical swing of his leg and he was off, reefing his helmet from his head.

Her heart jumped into her throat and her stomach whooshed.

Nope.

This was not going to work.

She couldn't think about clothes or shoes or hotels when he was still riding that damned bike. She was going to have talk to him about it. *Again*. And again and again. Until he got rid of it.

She straightened her spine and set her jaw. She was *not* to going to spend the next seven weeks dreading his death on the road! She stashed the wedding folder into her briefcase, threw some money on the table and exited the café.

Leo saw Sunshine the moment she stepped onto the footpath, his eyes snap-locking on to her from across the road. She looked good, as usual, wearing a winter green skirt suit that fitted her as snugly as the skin on a peach, and high-heeled chocolate-brown pumps.

'Leo, I have to talk to you,' she said.

He waited for that smacking kiss to land on his cheek.

But his cheek remained unsullied. She was clearly agitated—too agitated to bother with the kiss.

Well, good, he thought savagely. She *should* be agitated after last night. *He* certainly was.

'Yep, that was the plan,' Leo said, and unlocked the door.

Sunshine was practically humming with impatience as he relocked the door and escorted her to a table in the middle of the restaurant.

'I'll just check the kitchen and I'll be back,' he said, and almost smiled at the way her face pinched. *Yeah, cool your jets, Sunshine Smart-Ass, because you are not in control here.*

Not that that he was necessarily in control himself, but she didn't have to know that he hadn't been able to think straight since last night—let alone make a decision on her offer of three more pulse-ricocheting bouts of sex.

He was a man—ergo, it was an attractive proposition. But sex just for the sake of sex? Well, not to be arrogant, but he had his pick of scores of women if that was all he wanted. All right, the sex last night had been fairly spectacular, although hardly his most selfless performance, but it was still a commodity in abundant supply.

So, did he want more than sex from Sunshine?

Even as the question darted into his head he rejected it with a big *hell no.*

He didn't like perky and he didn't like breezy. Perky and breezy—AKA Sunshine Smart—were synonyms for negligent in his book. Choosing the shallows over the depths, wallowing in the past instead of confronting life head-on, the whole sex-only mantra. That kind of devil-may-care irresponsibility described his deadbeat parents, who'd not only offered up their bodies and any scrap of dignity for a quick score, but had been so hopeless they'd dropped dead of overdoses within days of each other, orphaning two sons.

Okay, the 'poor little orphans' bit was overcooked, because he and Caleb had stopped relying on them years before their deaths—but the principle remained.

So, no—he did *not* want more than sex from Sunshine.

And he didn't need *just* sex from her either.

All he needed from cheery, perky, breezy, ditzy Sunshine Smart was a hassle-free seven weeks of wedding preparations, after which he would set his compass and sail on.

Pretty clear, then.

Decision made.

Sex was off the table.

And the couch. And the bed. And wherever else she'd been planning on frying his gonads.

And he would enjoy telling her. Quickly—because he'd made this decision several times throughout the day, then gone back to re-mulling the options, and enough was enough.

But when he sat down across from Sunshine, all primed to give her the news, she forestalled him by saying urgently, 'Leo, you need to get rid of that motorbike. It's too dangerous.'

He took a moment to switch gears because he hadn't been expecting that. Sex, yes. Clothes, yes. Shoes, fine. But not the motorbike again.

'Yes, well, as it's my body on it, you can safely leave the decision about my transportation to me.'

'There's no "safely" about it.'

He looked at her closely, saw that there was nothing cheery-perky-breezy-ditzy in her face.

'Whoa,' he said. 'Let's take a step back. What's really behind this?'

'I want you to be alive for the wedding—that's all.'

'That's not all, Sunshine. Tell me, or this discussion is over.'

She dashed a hand across her fringe, pushing it aside impatiently. Looked at him, hard and bright and on edge, and then, 'My sister,' exploded from her mouth.

Leo waited. His hands had clenched into fists. Because

he wanted to touch her again. He felt a little trickle of something suspiciously like fear shiver down his spine.

'You may think it's none of my business—and it's not, strictly speaking,' she said. 'But it's not my way to stand aside and *not* say or do something when death is staring someone in the face. How could I live with myself if I didn't interfere and then something happened to you?'

'And you go around giving this lecture to everyone on a motorbike?'

'No, of course not—only to people I...' She faltered there. 'People I...know,' she finished lamely, putting up her chin.

Leo considered her for a long moment. *Not buying it.* 'Your sister. I want the whole story. I assumed...an illness. Wrong, obviously. I should have asked.'

'I didn't want you to ask. I didn't *let* you ask. Because to talk about that...to you, with your bike...it would have been a link. And I couldn't... But now...' Pause...deep breath while she gathered herself together. 'Sorry. I'm not making sense. I'll be clearer. Moonbeam had a motorbike. She crashed and she died. I was on the back and I survived. We were the cliché identical twins—inseparable. And then suddenly, just like...like...' She clicked her fingers. 'I was...'

The words just petered out. He saw her swallow, as if she had a sharp rock in her throat.

'Alone?' he finished for her.

'Yes. Alone.'

He waited a heartbeat. Two. Three.

She kept her eyes on his face, but apparently she wasn't intending to add anything.

'Sunshine,' he said softly, 'death is *not* staring me in the face. I'm not a teenage hothead burning up the road. I'm thirty. And I'm careful.'

'What if someone not so careful knocks you off?'

'Is that what happened? Did someone run your sister down?'

She shook her head, looking as if she would burst from frustration. 'No. She was going too fast. Missed the corner.'

Leo ran a hand over his head. Tried to find something to say. He was scared to open his mouth in case he promised her that, yes, he would give up the one carefree thing he allowed himself. They'd known each other for one week: she couldn't really care—had said she *wouldn't* care. And he would *not* be seduced into sacrificing his bike by the thought that she did.

'Look,' he started, and then stopped, ran a hand over his head again. 'It's not your job, Sunshine, to worry about me.'

'But I *do* worry about you. *Please*, Leo.'

There was a loud crashing sound from the kitchen. 'I have to check that.' Leo got to his feet, but then he paused, looking down at her. 'I shouldn't have started this. Not here, where there are too many distractions. Go home, and we'll pick it up another time.'

'I'm eating here tonight,' Sunshine said. 'And, no, I am *not* turning into a stalker. I have a date. Iain.'

His eyes narrowed. 'The hairdresser? The ex, who's now just a friend?'

'That's right.'

'As long as it *is* ex. Because while you and I are sleeping together—even if it is only four times—there isn't going to be anyone else in the picture. Got it? I'm not into sharing.' He heard the words come out of his mouth but couldn't quite believe they had. *Okay*, so he'd changed his mind and sex was back on, apparently.

'Well, of course!' Sunshine said. 'Actually, the main reason I asked him to come tonight was to check your head.'

'Check my head?' Leo repeated, not getting it.

'To make sure it's going to be long enough—not your head, because obviously that's not growing any more, but your hair.'

'He is *not* checking my head, Sunshine.'

That damned nose-wrinkle. 'But I think—'

'No,' Leo said, and strode into the kitchen.

Where he burst out laughing and stopped half the staff in their tracks.

'What?' he asked.

But nobody was brave enough to answer.

Sunshine did not enjoy dinner.

Not that the food wasn't great—because who couldn't love a Wagyu beef burger with Stilton, and chilli salt fries on the side?

And Iain had brought sketches of the most fabulous hairstyle for the wedding. Finger waves pinned at the base of the neck and secured with a gorgeous hairclip. Her fringe would be swept aside—*please* let it be long enough—and similarly clipped above her ear.

But neither the food nor the sketches was enough to take her mind off that damned motorbike, and the fact that Leo, who was so sensible, didn't seem to understand that it had to go.

So she fumed. And, because she'd always supposed she didn't carry the fuming gene, the unwelcome evidence that she could get as wound up as a garden variety maniac bothered her.

They'd had sex. That didn't mean she had a hold over him, of course, but it made him...well...someone more important than a casual acquaintance.

She became aware that Iain was sing-songing her name softly from across the table and snapped her attention back to where it should have been all night.

'That's better,' he said.

'Sorry, Iain. I haven't been good company tonight.'

'You're always good company, Sunny.'

She smiled at him. 'You're too nice.'

'Nice?' He gave a short, almost bitter laugh. 'Was that the limiter?'

'What? No!' She looked at him, dismayed. 'The problem was—is always—that I just don't want…that.'

'Someone's going to change your mind, Sunny—and all of us who have been forced to accept the limit are going to be mighty annoyed.'

All of us? Good Lord! 'You make it sound like there's a zombie camp of men out there, slavishly doing my bidding! And nobody is going to get annoyed—because I'm *not* changing my mind, ever. *And* I also happen to know you're dating Louise, so— Oh!'

She stopped abruptly. Stared past Iain.

Because Natalie Clarke, accompanied by a pretty guy vaguely familiar as a model—Rob-something—was being seated at the next table.

Natalie was stunning. Gold skin, glorious copper hair, perfect rosebud mouth, pale grey eyes. She was superslender, wearing a tight black leather skirt and a cropped black jacket. Black suede boots that made Sunshine green with envy.

Natalie shrugged out of her jacket to reveal a teensy white top; a black demi-bra was clearly visible underneath.

Iain's eyes went straight to the mother lode!

Sunshine, swallowing a laugh, kicked Iain under the table. *Bolt-ons,* she mouthed at him.

So? He mouthed back, and the laugh erupted after all.

Natalie, venom in her grey eyes, looked sharply, suspiciously, over at Sunshine and Iain.

Oh. That was just *nasty.* Imagine if Natalie ever got wind of what she'd done with Leo last night! Crime scene for sure—blood spatter, flayed flesh, ooze, *and* poison, and possibly a meat cleaver in there as well!

Then Sunshine noticed the tattooed butterflies flitting down Natalie's arms, and laughed again before she could stop herself.

Oops. *Extra* venom. And not much of a sense of humour, obviously.

Sunshine shifted her attention back to Iain and made a valiant effort to ignore Natalie—but it was impossible not to hear the overly loud one-way conversation from Natalie to Rob-the-model. All about Leo!

Blah-blah…so boring that Leo never, ever cooked for people outside his restaurants. *Ha! Prosciutto fettuccine, anyone?* Blah-blah…swank parties with Leo. Blah-blah… celebrities she and Leo had met. Blah-blah…she and Leo, part of the scene. *And who said 'the scene' with a straight face?* Blah-blah, blah-*blah*!

Natalie was pushing food around her plate as she talked; Rob was at least eating, but he was also smirking. *Smirking*—was that the most infuriating facial expression in the world?

The two of them would intermittently disappear to the bathroom, then come back talking too fast and too loud. When they disappeared for the fourth time Iain mimed coke-sniffing and Sunshine grimaced.

Natalie and Rob returned to the table and within moments were back on topic: Leo. And then, clear as a bell, 'I'll take Leo back when I'm ready—because, no matter what, he's good in bed.'

Tittering laugh from Rob.

People at about six different tables were staring at Natalie, entranced.

Sunshine felt her blood pressure shoot up. If she wasn't a pacifist she would want to slap Natalie for doing this to Leo—and in his own restaurant, dammit! Sunshine's heart was racing, her brain fizzing. She felt light-headed. She was going to have to do something to stop this.

'Really, *really* good,' Natalie continued, taking in her audience, 'which is kind of psycho, because he can't even touch you unless he's fu—'

Sunshine let out a loud, long peal of exaggerated laughter, drawing all eyes. She felt like a prize idiot, and Iain was obviously uncomfortable, but it was the only option she could immediately think of to shut Natalie up.

Sunshine was racking her brain for a way to proceed when Rob solved the dilemma by jumping to his feet and clutching at his neck.

Natalie stared ineffectually at her choking date.

Someone called out for a doctor.

The manager was racing to the kitchen.

Two diffident waiters approached the table, probably hoping someone would get there before them.

The diners—apparently not a doctor amongst them—seemed frozen. No movement. Just watching.

Sunshine got to her feet with a sinking heart. On the bright side, this dramatic development had shut Natalie up. On the not so bright side, Sunshine suspected she was about to star in the next scene. She hovered for a few seconds. *Please someone else help...please.* But—nope! Sunshine sighed. So be it.

Focusing her mind, Sunshine strode to the table. 'Out of the way,' she said, pushing past a still gaping Natalie.

Sunshine thumped Rob on the back. *Nothing.* Again. Once more.

Nope. Whatever was lodged in his throat wasn't going to be beaten out of him. Rob wasn't coughing, wasn't making a sound; he was just turning blue. His eyes stared, entreating. His hands tugged at his shirt collar.

Okay, here goes. Quickly, calmly, Sunshine moved behind him, wrapped her arms around him and placed a fist between his ribcage and where she guessed his navel was. Then she covered the fist with her other hand and gave one sharp tug upwards and inwards.

A piece of meat came flying out of Rob's mouth and he staggered, grabbing at his chair, dragging in breaths.

The restaurant broke into spontaneous applause and Sunshine felt her face heat.

Thank God the waiters were now taking control.

She started to return to her table and saw Leo standing just outside the kitchen. He was staring at her as though he'd just witnessed the Second Coming.

Sunshine couldn't remember ever being so embarrassed.

She was almost relieved when Natalie's squeal snagged his attention.

His eyes widened, then narrowed as they returned to Sunshine. Not happy!

Sunshine would have laughed if she hadn't felt so shaken. What on earth did he believe had just happened? That she and Natalie had been having a friendly chat while Rob stood there choking? Maybe that Sunshine was persuading Natalie, mid-Heimlich manoeuvre, to sing at the wedding reception against Leo's express wishes?

At this point Sunshine would prefer to hire *herself* to warble a few off-key songs!

She was almost glad when Natalie, squealing again, rushed towards Leo and threw herself into his arms. Leo, looking frazzled, backed into the kitchen, pulling Natalie with him.

Frazzle away, you idiot, Sunshine said in her head, and quickly returned to Iain.

'You're amazing,' he said, standing to pull out her chair.

'Anyone could have done it,' she said dismissively. 'I'm just glad I didn't break any of his ribs—that's the main danger. And I don't want to sit, Iain. I want to go home. I have another high drama to get through tonight: a video call with Jon.'

'Why high drama?'

Sunshine sighed. 'You're not the only one worried about the zombies.'

'Jon, you're wrong.'

Those were the first words Sunshine had managed to edge into the conversation since her initial 'Hello' three minutes earlier.

Not that 'conversation' described the incendiary soliloquy Jon had been delivering, which covered her unsatisfactory outlook on life, her ill-preparedness to deal with a man of Leo's darkness, a disjointed reminder to ensure she was taking precautions—which caused her a momentary pang of guilt about the unprecedented lack of a condom last night, although she *was* on the pill and that had to count for something—and the general benefits of not actively courting disaster.

'No, Sunshine, I'm not wrong,' Jon said, and seemed ready to relaunch.

Sunshine headed him off by jamming her fingers in her ears. She raised her eyebrows, waiting. And at last he smiled.

She removed her fingers from her ears. 'This is not worth so much anxiety, Jonathan.'

'I'm worried about you, Sunny. About the way you've been living—no, only half living—since...'

She held her breath. Watched as Jonathan hesitated...

'Ever since Moon, Sunny,' he continued, but more gently. 'This four-times-only thing. The blocking yourself off from anything more. It's not *you*!'

'Yes, it is.'

'It's not.' Sigh. 'I know I'm wasting my breath.' Another sigh. 'Well, you will not be able to dictate terms to Leo

Quartermaine. Look, Leo is going to be my brother-in-law, and you're like a sister to me. I need you two to like each other. Calmly, rationally, *like* each other.'

'I'm always friends with the men I've slept with.'

'He is not like the others.'

She rolled her eyes. The zombie camp! 'There aren't that many of them, you know!'

'I know Sunshine—you talk a good game, but you don't fool me. You never have. Sleeping with a guy is the exception, not the rule. But, whether it's two or ten or a hundred guys, Leo is not like them and he will not be your friend at the end. There are other men in Sydney, and a ridiculous number of them seem happy to have you lead them around by their sex organs. Why did you have to pick Leo?'

'It kind of— He kind of— Look, the situation picked itself. That's all.'

'You mean you had no control over it? Neither of you?'

Sunshine thought back to last night. The way 'no-touch' Leo had gathered her in when she'd given him that one hug. How she'd melted just from the feel of his fingers in her hair. The way the kiss had spiralled…

'Apparently not, Jonathan.'

'This is bad, Sunny.'

'I promise not to let it interfere with the wedding.'

'You can't promise that. There are two of you.'

'I'm not going to start asking your permission before sleeping with someone,' she said, exasperated.

Pause. Silence. Jon looked morose.

'Jon?'

More silence.

'Jon—where does that leave us?'

'It leaves us, very unsatisfactorily, at loggerheads,' he said. 'And while we're there I'm going to raise the other subject you hate. Where are Moonbeam's ashes, Sunshine?'

Sunshine stiffened. 'They are in the urn, here in my office, where they've always been. Want to see them?'

'Don't be flippant. Not about this. She'd hate it, Sunny. You know she would. When are you going to do it?'

Sunshine managed a, 'Soon.' But it wasn't easy getting the word out of a suddenly clogged throat.

'You've been saying that for two years.'

'Soon,' she repeated. 'But now I have to go. I have to finish the new handbag designs.'

'I'll keep asking.'

'I will do it. Just…not yet.'

'I love you, Sunny,' Jon said, looking so sad it tore at Sunshine's heart. 'But this isn't fair. Not on Moon. Not on your parents. Not on you. You've got to let yourself get over her death.'

'I…can't. I can't, Jon.'

'You have to.' Another sigh. 'We'll speak soon.'

Sunshine signed off.

Work. She would work for a while.

But half an hour later she was still sitting there, staring at the urn that held Moonbeam's ashes. The urn was centred very precisely on top of the bureau Sunshine had painted in her sister's favourite colour—'cobalt dazzle', Moon had called it.

Sunny tapped at the computer, found her list of Moonbeam's favourite beaches. The options she'd chosen for scattering the ashes.

But not one of the options felt right. Not one!

She put her head on the desk and cried.

When Leo left the restaurant, a little after midnight, he intended to ride home, throw down a large brandy, think about life, and go to sleep.

What a night. Sunshine. Natalie. And the Heimlich manoeuvre.

The bloody Heimlich manoeuvre.

Just when he needed so badly to think of Sunshine as frippery and irresponsible she had to go and save someone's life—and then look surprised when people applauded her for it. The difference between Sunshine's calm, embarrassed heroism and Natalie's ineffectual hysterics had been an eye-opener of epic proportions.

And it had come after the Moonbeam story, which had already had his heart lurching around in his chest like a drunk.

So he needed home. Brandy. Thinking time. Bed.

He wasn't sure, then, why he left his motorbike where it was and walked to Sunshine's apartment block.

She would be asleep, he told himself as he reached the glass doors of the entrance. But his finger was on the apartment's intercom anyway.

'Hello?'

Her voice was not sleepy. And he remembered, then, that she worked mostly at night.

'It's Leo.'

Pause. Then buzz, click, open.

She was waiting at her door. Barefoot. In a kimono. Seriously, did this woman not own a pair of jeans or some track pants? Who slummed around alone in their own home after midnight looking like an advertisement for *Vogue* magazine in a purple kimono complete with a bloody *obi*?

Her hair was loose, her face pale, her eyes strained.

He was going to thank her for saving Rob's life.

He was going to ask her why she knew how to do the Heimlich manoeuvre.

He was going to tell her that he'd found out exactly what had happened and that he was an idiot for thinking, when he'd seen her near Natalie, that—

She cleared her throat. 'I didn't talk to Natalie except to tell her to move out of the way.'

'I don't care about Natalie,' he said—and realised that he really, *really* didn't.

'Then why are you here?'

'I'm claiming assignation number two,' he said, and kissed her.

CHAPTER SIX

SUNSHINE DREW HIM backwards into the apartment. Kiss unbroken.

Leo slammed the door with his heel. Kiss unbroken.

Sex—just sex, Sunshine said to herself.

Leo pulled back as though she'd voiced the thought, looking at her with eyes smouldering like a hungry lion's.

Sunshine grabbed his hand and dragged him to the bedroom. Kissed him again as she flipped the light switch and the fairy's lair lights she'd had embedded in the ceiling winked to life.

He angled her so he could kiss her harder, *harder*. He started to shake—she could feel it—and he broke the kiss, his breathing ragged. He rested his cheek on the top of her head as he held her in his arms, his freight train heartbeat beneath her ear.

She heard him laugh softly and pulled back, watching as he took in the room.

It was pink. Every shade of pink from pale petal, to vibrant sari, to raspberry. The walls were the colour of cherry blossoms, stencilled in white in a riot of floral shapes and curlicues—like an extended henna tattoo. There was a chaise-longue, footstools, a window seat curtained off with diaphanous drapes. At one end of the room was a half-wall that divided the bedroom from the dressing room, with its orderly arrangement of garments, shoes, and bags, which in turn led through to her bathroom.

A scene was painted on the dividing wall: a woman donning a flowing deep rose robe. Sunshine had made it a 3D work of art, building an actual Louis XIV gilded dressing table and mirror into the scene.

There was *a lot* to look at.

Leo moved towards the bed, which was king-sized, shrouded by fuchsia hangings and piled high with cushions in macaroon pastels. He touched the gauzy curtains.

'Seriously, Sunshine?' he asked, a smile in his voice.

Sunshine arched an eyebrow. 'If you want to get laid tonight, I suggest you keep a civil tongue in your head.'

'That's not where my tongue wants to be.'

Those words made her toes curl.

'Come here, let me undress you, and we'll find some place to put it,' Leo said softly.

Sunshine walked over to him, her heart jumping.

His hands reached for the *obi*.

'Wait,' she said. 'I need to warn you—I'm…scarred.'

He waited, hands at her waist.

'The accident. I have a…a scar. Two, actually. Not… small.' She hunched a shoulder, suddenly self-conscious. 'I don't want you to be shocked.'

His response was to slowly, slowly unwrap the *obi* from around her waist, then the under-sash. The kimono fell open and Leo sucked in an audible breath.

'My God,' he said, in a voice just above a raspy whisper.

'I know—they're awful.'

Leo's fingers reached, traced along the incision marks. He shook his head. 'The *My God* wasn't about the scars, Sunshine.'

Sunshine was having trouble catching a thought, her breath. 'Then…what?'

'*My God*, you are so beautiful. And *my God*, I am itching to put my hands all over you.'

'Then do it,' she whispered. 'I have no intention of stopping you.'

His fingers tensed against her flesh. And then, with both hands, he reached for her shoulders, sliding his hands under the kimono, pushing it back until the heavy fabric dropped with a quiet whoosh to the floor. He stood gazing at her.

Sunshine kept absolutely still, watching him as his nostrils flared, his hands fisted at his sides. It was both torture and delight to stand motionless as lust shimmered between them. Leo was still fully clothed, and that somehow made her feel more wanton, sexier. Her nipples were hardened points; she could feel them throbbing. Could feel a swelling between her legs as his gaze moved over her. Down, up, down. The suspense was almost unbearable. And yet she wanted the delay. Wanted to draw things out. Slow everything down so that she could wallow in this overwhelming need caused by nothing more than his eyes on her.

Then both his hands moved. With the tips of his trembling fingers he touched the centre of her forehead. Slowly his fingers moved to the bridge of her nose, across her eyebrows, down her cheeks to her mouth, her jaw, neck, collarbones. When he got to her breasts he paused at her nipples to circle and pinch. Her knees almost buckled. But inexorably his hands moved again, fingers sliding across the long, straight scar that ran over her ribs, down to her hips, across her belly, then to the juncture of her thighs.

He stopped there. Looked intently at her bare mound, licked his lips. 'Very, very pretty,' he said.

Both hands slid between her legs, fingers playing there while her breathing quickened.

'I think we've found a place for my tongue,' he said,

suddenly finding that one excruciatingly sensitive nub, focusing there.

'Are you going to take off your clothes?' Sunshine asked breathily as his fingers continued to tease her.

'Yes. But first...'

His fingers shifted, exploring her, dipping and sliding and slipping, but always returning to that one tiny place. Sunshine gasped again. Her legs were trembling as he continued to work her, pinching, stroking, rolling, lunging into her.

'Ah, Leo— God!' Sunshine cried out, and came suddenly, with a long groan.

Her head dropped back as his fingers continued to caress her, soothing now, and then one hand cupped her possessively, stilled.

Easing away from her, he started removing his clothes with short, efficient movements. The leather jacket was shrugged off and dropped to the floor. Sweater and then T-shirt were ripped over his head. Boots were yanked off. Jeans shoved down, kicked aside.

Good Lord. He was...divine. Not a steroid-pumped muscle in his whole body. Just perfectly defined, hard, lean lines of strength. Broad shoulders. Beautifully crafted biceps. Smooth, hairless, sculpted torso with that wonderful V leading to his groin. Narrow hips. Long legs. And the jut of him, big and hard, rising from that gorgeous dark blond nest, was mouth-watering. She wanted her mouth there. And her hands. And the inside of her.

'Come here,' he said. 'I want to feel you all over me.'

Sunshine thought she might swoon, just hearing the words—except that she was desperate to take him up on that offer. She *wanted* to be all over him.

She walked into his open arms and they closed around her. The top of her head didn't even reach his chin, and the feeling of being cocooned, surrounded by him, was glorious.

'You feel good there.'

'I feel *very* good,' she said throatily, and he laughed. 'And so do you,' she added as his erection nudged her belly. 'We can get that part of you a little closer, I think.'

'No rush tonight,' he said. 'If we only have three assignations left I'm going to make them count. So…now I'd like to see you spread out on that Taj Mahal bed.'

He edged her backwards, reaching out to push the hangings aside, following her down onto the bed, kissing her as he lay on top of her.

For one fraught moment he slid between her thighs, held still, teasing both of them with the promise of the length of him as it pulsed there against her wet opening. He buried his face against her neck and sucked in a breath, another, one more.

'God, it's hard to wait,' he groaned against her hair.

'Then don't,' Sunshine said, shifting to try and get him to slip inside.

He withdrew. 'I want to play with you for a while first. And this time we won't forget the condom.'

With great concentration he arranged Sunshine on the bed against the cushions, raising her arms above her head so that her breasts were tightened and jutting, the chain she always wore caught between them.

He kissed her eyelids closed and then put his mouth at the corner of hers, his tongue flicking out to taste. She gasped, and his tongue slid smoothly inside her mouth, swirled once, then retreated to lick at the corner again. He kissed down her chin, her throat, then…nothing.

She opened her eyes to find him sitting back on his heels, looking at her. 'What's wrong?' she asked.

'Nothing,' he said. 'I just like looking at you. I don't think I've ever seen skin as pale as yours. And these…' His hands reached out, hovered over her breasts. 'I'm almost scared to touch in case I come in three seconds.'

'I want you to come.'

'No—don't move your arms,' Leo ordered, and his hands settled on her breasts, squeezed gently, massaged. 'God. God, God, God...' he said, and it really did sound like a prayer.

He lowered his head and closed his lips over one nipple, sucked it sharply so that she moaned.

He stopped instantly. 'Sorry—but you're driving me crazy. Did I hurt you?'

'No,' she said, her legs moving restlessly. 'I just want you so much. *So much,*' she wailed as his mouth sucked hard again.

He commenced a steady rhythm, tugging, tonguing, pulling back to lick.

When he shifted to the other breast she couldn't help herself—her arms came down to circle him, to pull him closer, closer.

'Come inside me,' she whispered. 'Please, Leo.'

He shook his head and started moving lower. He stopped again as his mouth touched the scar. He pulled back to see it, then touched it gently with his fingers, running them over the length of it, then across the dissecting scar that ran perpendicular to it, across her ribs towards her back.

Sunshine held her breath, waiting for...what? She didn't know. Didn't want to believe that it mattered, what he thought of her imperfections. All that mattered—all that *could* matter—was the promise of the orgasm flickering low in her belly.

And yet she didn't release her breath until he moved again, kissing his way to her mound. He stopped again. Shuddered out a breath against her. Then he was kissing her there, over and over again.

'Beautiful. Delicious,' he murmured in between licking kisses, his tongue dipping just low enough to make her squirm. 'Open wider for me.'

She shifted her legs, hips rising off the bed, soundlessly urging him to shift, to slide that clever mouth right between her spread legs. When, finally, he did, using the very tip of his tongue to separate the lips of her sex, breathing deeply as he slid the flat of his tongue along the seam, she screamed his name and climaxed almost violently.

He kept his mouth there, his tongue on that fizzing knot of nerves, until the waves receded.

And then, with a groan, he slid back up her body and thrust inside her. 'Ah, thank you, God,' he groaned, and any semblance of control snapped.

He pounded into her, teeth gritted, gripping her hips as though his life depended on leveraging himself off them so he could go harder, deeper.

Sunshine could feel his orgasm building and tightened her inner muscles, holding, wanting... 'Come, come,' she said, and then the explosion ripped through him.

Long moments later he rolled onto his back, bringing Sunshine with him so that she was lying on top, her thighs falling either side of him. 'Forgot the condom again,' he said.

Sunshine frowned. 'I've never forgotten before.'

'Do we need to talk about it?'

'Only if you have a disease.'

'Then we don't need to talk.' He secured her more tightly against his chest. One hand was in her hair, smoothing through the strands.

Silence. Minutes dragged on.

Then, 'The Heimlich thing... Why?' he asked.

She shrugged, self-conscious. 'I saw a story on the internet about a woman who choked to death. If someone had known what to do she wouldn't have died. So I...I learned.

Just in case. Typical that the first time I had to use it was on Natalie's boyfriend!'

'He's not her boyfriend. He's her bitch.'

'Ouch.'

'I wish I could say that was me being malicious, but it's just the truth.'

'I certainly don't understand what you saw in her.'

'Me neither. I guess we get what we deserve.'

She looked up at him, perplexed. 'Why would you think you deserved her? Deserved...*that*?'

Leo shook his head, shrugged, clearly uncomfortable. 'Just history. Perpetuating the crappiness of my life. Because she wasn't my first mistake—just the most persistent.'

Mistake. Something about the word made Sunshine shiver. Mistake...

'You're cold,' Leo said. 'And I have a brilliant idea— let's actually get *in* the bed.'

Sunshine latched onto being cold as a viable excuse for the sudden chill prickling along her skin. She slid under the covers, busied herself positioning cushions so that she was propped up against the bedhead, half turned to him.

She toyed with her chain, rubbing the sun and moon charms between her fingers.

'Sun and moon,' Leo said, watching her. 'For Sunshine and Moonbeam?'

'Yes. The business is called Sun & Moon too. Not sure what we were going to do when we changed our names.'

'You were going to change your names? Don't tell me: Sue and Jenny?'

'Do I look like a Sue?'

'Actually, you look like a Sunshine.'

'Harsh! Well, Moonbeam was definitely *not* a Jenny! She was going to be Amaya—it means Night Rain. She figured it was a close enough association with the night, if not with the moon specifically.'

'Nice. And yours?'

'Allyn. Do I look like an Allyn?'

'I told you—you look like a Sunshine.'

'Oh, dear. Daunting. Well, Moon said Allyn meant Bright and Shining One. Close enough to sunshine, in her opinion. And she said it suited me.' She frowned, thinking. 'I've thought a lot over the past two years about making the change. Wondered if doing the thing we planned to do together on my own would help me accept…move on. My parents aren't so sure.'

'Tell me about them,' Leo said.

'My parents? Oh, they're very zen! Quite mad. And completely wonderful. Always there. Supportive, but never smothering. They let Moon and me leave the commune when we were fifteen, so we could see a different way and make informed decisions about how we wanted to live. They made sure we had a safe place to stay, a good school to go to, money for whatever we needed, while we worked it out. And they seemed to understand even before we did that Moon was the true hippie and I was… well, something in between a hippie and an urbanite. Moon would have raced straight back to the commune if not for me being anchored in the city.' She smiled, remembering. 'We started our business with money our father inherited but didn't need. It was given to us simply, with love, on our eighteenth birthday.'

'Lucky.'

'Yes. But it's not all sparkles and roses, you know. There's the haiku to deal with!'

'Ah, the haiku. What is it?'

'You'll find out—that poem is coming.'

'Can't wait.'

'You have no idea!'

'But…they were okay with you girls changing your names?'

'They weren't insulted, if that's what you mean. They were fine with it if we wanted to do it.' She bit her lip. 'But Dad had a sidebar conversation with me because he thought Moonbeam was browbeating me.'

'And was she?'

'Not browbeating—nothing that brutish. She was… *persuading*!' Sunshine said, and smiled, remembering. 'But I was happy enough to be persuaded if she wanted it that badly. And I owed her, for staying.'

Sunshine closed her eyes, picturing her sister.

'Tell me more about Moonbeam,' Leo said.

Opening her eyes on a sigh, Sunshine adjusted her position in the bed. 'Well, you know what she looked like—me! But slimmer. And with the most beautiful green eyes— both of them. Other than looks, though, we were completely different. I was the carnivore; she was vegetarian. I was…well, as you see me. Friendly, touchy-feely, chirpy.'

'And…?'

Sunshine fiddled with her necklace. 'Moon was… intriguing. I was *Mary Poppins*; she was *Crouching Tiger, Hidden Dragon*. When the kids made fun of my devil eyes I would laugh it off, but she would go all superhero.' She laughed suddenly. '*Is* there a hippie superhero? What a wonderful idea. I'm going to do a web search on that.'

'So she was your protector?'

'Oh, yes. And my cheer squad. And my…everything. She was smart, and had an amazing flair for numbers, so although the business was my idea she was the CEO. And she didn't even want to be in the city!'

Sunshine adjusted the quilt. Fussed with a cushion.

'She said that left me to concentrate on the creative stuff because she was not into fashion like I was. She would wear a suit for business if I chose it for her; otherwise she

would drag on whatever clothes and shoes came to hand.
I, on the other hand, was obsessed with colour and shape
and style.' She shrugged, a little sheepish. 'And I really
love shoes!'

'Funny, I hadn't noticed that.'

She hit him with the cushion. 'Don't make me take
you behind that wall and show you my shoe collection. I
haven't known a man yet who could cope with the sight.'

'Are you *really* going there? Talking about the men
you've had in here? I'll go there if you want, Sunshine,
but I don't think you'll like it.'

She opened her eyes at him. 'Oh, that sounds very alpha
male.'

He didn't smile. 'You'll see alpha, beta, gamma, *and*
zeta male if you go near another man, Sunshine.'

'Oh, alpha, beta, *and* zeta?'

'Alpha-beta-*gamma*-zeta. And don't roll your eyes.'

'Sorry.'

'I said don't roll your eyes.'

'All *right*!' Sunshine said, laughing.

'So, I think,' Leo said quietly, after a long moment,
'we're up to the bike, aren't we?'

Sunshine nodded, sat a little straighter. 'The bike,' she
said. She pulled a different cushion onto her lap and started
playing with the fringe. 'She bought it because she liked
the wind in her face and the freedom of riding. It was too
big for her, but she wouldn't be told.'

She stopped there.

'And...?' he prompted.

Sunshine reached for the charms. 'We were at a party.
Her boyfriend *du jour*—Jeff—mixed us up and tried
to kiss me. Moonbeam went into melodrama mode and
stormed off, dragging me with her.'

'Was she angry with you?'

'God, no! She knew I would never poach. And truthfully...? She wasn't even angry with Jeff. She was just restless. Bored with being in the city. And tired of Jeff. So what he did gave her an excuse to dump him. She thought...she thought he'd done it accidentally-on-purpose because he actually preferred me. We were dressed so differently, you see, it couldn't have been a mix-up.'

'Did that happen often? A boyfriend switching sides?'

'No. Never before.'

'And so...?'

'And so we clambered onto the bike.' She shivered. 'She was wild that night, riding too fast. She took a turn badly, and...well. Moonbeam died instantly. Her neck snapped at the base of the helmet.' She swallowed. 'I got carted off to hospital, where I went through twenty-eight pints of blood.' She moved restlessly. 'Internal bleeding. They had to take my spleen—which apparently you don't really need, so go figure! And they took half my liver, which was haemorrhaging. Actually, did you know that the liver regenerates? Which means the chunk of my liver they cut out has probably grown back. Amazing!'

'I'm sorry, Sunshine,' Leo said.

She rearranged herself in the bed again—flustery, unnecessary activity. 'Which brings us to the important part of this discussion. Getting rid of your motorbike.'

Leo said nothing.

'Leo? You understand, don't you?'

He nodded slowly. 'I understand why you hate motorbikes—because you blame yourself for the accident. You feel guilty because you couldn't talk your sister out of that bike. Because she stayed in the city only for you, where she was an unhappy fish out of water. Because of what her boyfriend did. The way all those things led to both of you being on the bike at that precise moment at that speed. Because she died and you didn't. And you're here and she's not.'

Sunshine brushed away a tear. 'That's about the sum of it. I just miss her so much. And I'd do anything to have her back.' She looked at him. 'But you can't bring someone back from the dead. So *please* get rid of it, Leo. Please?'

'You don't understand what that bike means to me.' He grimaced. 'My parents…they were druggies, and they didn't give a damn. Your parents made sure you had support. I was my own support—and Caleb's. Your parents made sure you had money, but when I was still a child I had to steal it, beg it, or make it—and I did all three! There was never food on the table unless I put it there. So I haunted restaurants around the city, pleading for leftovers. Eventually one of the chefs took pity on me and I got a job in a kitchen, and…' Shrug. 'Here I am.'

Sunshine touched his hand.

He looked at where her hand was, on his, with an odd expression on his face. And then he drew his hand away.

'I'm not telling you all that to get sympathy, just to explain,' he said. 'And it could have been a lot worse. We weren't sexually abused. Or beaten—well, not Caleb. And me not often, or more than I could take. Mainly we were just not important. Like a giant mistake that you can't fix so you try to forget it. I grew up fast and hard—I had to. The upshot is that I don't do frivolity. I'm not sociable unless there's something in it for me. I don't stop to smell the roses and hug the trees. I just push on, without indulging myself. Except for my bike.'

'I see,' Sunshine said. And she did. It was so very simple. Leo had his bike the way she had Moon's ashes. Something that connected you to what you'd lost—what you couldn't have: in her case her sister; in his a carefree youth.

She swallowed around a sudden lump. 'We're not going to find common ground on this, are we? Because you deserve one piece of youthful folly and I can't bear what that piece happens to be.'

She got out of bed, grabbed her kimono off the floor, quickly pulled it on, and turned to face him. 'This means, of course, that we'll have to call it quits at two.'

'At two…what? O'clock?'

'Two *times*—as in not *four*. As in assignations.'

'Why?'

Why? She had a sudden memory of that electri-fried bat. 'Because the thought of you on that bike already upsets me too much. That's going to get harder, not easier, to cope with if we keep doing…*this*.'

'This?'

'Sex,' she said impatiently. 'It's my fault for starting it, and I'll cop to that. I threw myself at you when you didn't want to go there. The blame is squarely here, with me.'

'If we're talking blame, I threw myself at you tonight.'

Sunshine dragged the edges of the kimono closed and started looking around for her sash. 'Well, let's *un*throw ourselves.'

'Come back to bed, Sunshine, and we'll talk about it.'

'Bed is the wrong place to talk.'

'Four assignations was what we agreed on,' Leo said.

'*Up to!* They're the salient words. *Up to* four. I've never got to four before. I've never got past two! And you can see why. It gets too emotional.'

Leo shoved the quilt aside, got out of bed. 'I'll do you a deal on the motorbike,' he offered, and started tugging on his clothes.

'What kind of deal?'

Wary. *Very* wary.

'I'll get rid of the bike the day after our fourth assignation. Or when you change your name to Allyn. Whichever comes first.'

She licked her lips nervously. 'That's an odd deal.'

'Is it? I'm offering to give up a piece of a past I never really had—the bike. In return, you give up something you can't accept is past its use-by date—your sister's two-year hold over you.'

'She doesn't have a hold over me.'

'If she didn't have a hold over you the four times thing wouldn't exist. So—my bike for going where no man has gone before and risking the magic number four.'

'No.'

'Then take the alternative option and change your name. You said it might be a way of moving on, so do it. Move on, Sunshine, one way or the other.'

'I...I don't know,' she said, agonised.

'Take some time and think about it,' he said. 'But not too long. Because—in case you haven't quite figured me out yet—I don't wait for what I want. I just go out and get it. Even if I have to steal it.'

'You don't really want me.'

'I'm like an immortal lobster—who really knows? Let's get to number four and see.'

'Well, you can't *steal me*.'

'Don't bet on it, sweetheart. I've spent my life getting my own way. And I can take things from you that you never knew you had.'

She located her *obi* and whipped it up off the floor. 'That's not even worth a response.'

Leo just smiled and started pulling on his boots.

She tried, twice, to tie the sash, but her fingers were clumsy.

And Leo's hands were suddenly there—capable, efficient, tying it easily.

'Thank you,' she said stiffly when he had finished, and flicked her hair over her shoulders. 'I'll see you out.'

She walked Leo to the apartment door. 'So!' she said. 'I'll email you about...about the clothes for the wedding and a few other things. And then... Well...'

'And then...well...?' Leo repeated, looking a little too

wolfish and a lot too jaunty for a man who was waiting for an answer about sex that could, should—no, *would*!—go against him. And then he leant down and kissed her quickly on the mouth.

She jumped back as though he'd scalded her.

'It's just a *stolen* kiss, Sunshine,' he murmured. 'Think of the calories.'

Sunshine stared into the darkness long after returning to bed.

Leo would give up his motorbike.

Into her head popped an image of Moonbeam—laughing as they left the party that night. Giving a wild shout as she started the bike. Zooming off with Sunshine on the back, gripping her tightly.

And then darkness. And that feeling. Waking up in hospital and knowing, without needing to be told, that Moonbeam was gone. She never wanted to experience that desolating ache again.

Leo didn't understand what it would do to her if something happened to him. And that said it all, didn't it? She'd only known him for one week, and already she was terrified that something would happen to him.

What a conundrum. She could get him to give up his bike if she slept with him twice more. But if she slept with him twice more she would be getting dangerously close to him. And she couldn't risk that.

Or...

She could get him to give up his bike if she changed her name. And she just wasn't sure what that would mean. Maybe it would help her accept Moon's death. But maybe it would be a betrayal—taking a twins' decision and making it a solo decision. Moving on when Moon couldn't.

And did anything matter more than keeping Leo safe?

Sunshine threw off the covers—what a restless night

this was turning out to be!—and yanked on her kimono, leaving it fluttering as she raced from the room and into her office.

There, on the high-gloss blue bureau, was her sister. Her sister, who had wanted her ashes to be scattered at a beach under a full moon.

Instead here she was. Beautifully housed in a stunning antique cloisonné urn featuring all the colours of the rainbow.

But an urn—no matter how beautiful—wasn't the ocean.

And the ocean was where Moonbeam belonged.

Leo stared into the darkness, thinking about the simple pleasure of touch.

It didn't take a psychologist to work out what his issue was—the fact that his parents had never touched him the way other parents touched their children. Because there had been more important things to do than give their son the affection he craved. Like shoot up. Suck in the crack. Snort up the meth.

It had been different for Caleb, because Leo had made it so. Leo had looked after Caleb, put his needs first, fought his battles, protected him. And so Caleb wasn't reserved, wary, driven, and damaged—like Leo. Caleb attracted affection and gentleness and love. Leo attracted people like Natalie, for whom his remoteness was a challenge and his celebrity something to use.

'You're choosing wrong,' Sunshine had said—but what if he was choosing *right* and he was getting exactly what he deserved?

It wasn't as if he could choose Sunshine Smart as an alternative. She didn't *want* to be chosen by anyone.

So why he was offering to give up his motorbike for her was a mystery.

So what if he never had sex with her again?

So what if she went on grieving for her sister for the rest of the life?

Leo punched his pillow. Forced his eyes closed.

And there she was, warning him about her scars. So beautiful. And damaged, like him. But wanting to *stay* damaged—*unlike* him.

His eyes popped open and he punched the pillow again.

God, but she irked him.

Her perkiness irked him. Partly because he wanted to think that it made her shallow…and yet she'd learned the Heimlich manoeuvre and wasn't afraid to use it.

The way she chucked crazy facts into her arguments—about the sexual habits of praying mantises, the questionable immortality of lobsters, regenerating livers, and so on and on and on—irked him. Because most of the time that stuff was fascinating. And even if it wasn't, it was fascinating to watch those unique eyes glow with the wonder of it.

Her boring living room irked him, because it shouldn't be like that. Not that her décor was any of his business. And the fact that he could be bothered to think of her apartment irking him irked him too.

Her pink bedroom irked him. All right, it didn't—because it was kind of amazing. But it *should* irk him, and the fact that it *didn't* irk him irked him.

Her propensity to kiss and touch and pet him irked him. And it had irked him even more when she hadn't kissed him hello at the restaurant.

Her four-times maximum irked him. And the fact that he'd refused to accept that they were stopping at two irked him.

Two times. *Two.* Not three, not four—two! Her terms. Everything on her terms, right from the moment she'd ambushed him on the couch.

Well, he'd picked her as a wily little dictator from Day One. But she was *not* going to dictate to Leo Quartermaine. He would have her as many damned times as he *wanted* to have her.

He punched his pillow again. Hard.

CHAPTER SEVEN

TO: Leo Quartermaine
FROM: Sunshine Smart
SUBJECT: Wedding update
Hi Leo

I'm attaching a photo of my dress. If you can send me one of your suit and tie—I'm assuming a tie?—I'll know if this is okay or if I have to go back to the drawing board. And I can get your shoe design finished too.

So, the shoes. You'll need three fittings—twenty mins each time—and you can schedule these to suit yourself as I won't be needed. I'm attaching Seb's business card—Seb is the shoemaker—and once you've approved my design all you need to do is call him.

And, trust me, once you've had custom-made shoes you'll never go back. Which might not be good, now I think of it, because they're hellishly expensive (not these particular shoes, of course, because it's a special deal for me, as well as being a present).

The other attachment is of some floral arrangements for the restaurant. I think the all-white ones, so as not to distract from the view. What do you think?

I'm going to scoot down the coast on Sunday to check out some hotel options for guests who want to stay overnight. I know you're super-busy so I can handle this and email all the info to you.

And then we need to confirm the music—Kate is amazing—when you have a minute.

Hope all is well.
Sunshine

OH, NO, SUNSHINE Smart-Ass, you are not going down the coast without me.

That was the first thought to leap to Leo's mind after he read the email.

The second was that she had a bloody nerve adding the 'Hope all is well', because she had to know all was *not* well. Not by a country *mile* was all 'well'. 'All' wouldn't be 'well' until he had her exactly where he wanted her.

A sudden image of her naked, in his arms, had him erect and almost groaning. Even though that was not what he'd meant. What he'd meant was on her knees and—

Argh. Another image.

Figuratively speaking on her knees, not physically.

But—nope, the image wouldn't budge.

He took a steadying breath and forced himself to open Sunshine's attachment, hoping it wouldn't be her *in* the damned dress—which, of course, it was. Looking very hot. And, of course, she had her foot stuck out so he could see her amazingly sexy shoes.

And, since he knew he had to see her in the flesh in that dress, he would up the ante on his suit so that he matched the formality—*and* send her the damned photo so he could get his shoe design.

And he would tell her that he would most definitely meet her at South on Sunday, when they would discuss flowers and confirm music and go and see the hotels *together.*

Ha!

Hope all is well.

Bloody, *bloody* nerve.

* * *

Sunshine, who had laboured long and hard over the wording of her email to Leo to give it just the right sense of moving-on friendliness, opened Leo's reply with some trepidation.

She wasn't sure what to expect—but the three terse lines certainly hadn't been laboured over.

Meet you at South at two p.m. Sunday. Will confirm everything then. Suit pic attached.

So! She guessed she'd better start working on getting rid of the horrible fluttery feeling in her stomach before Sunday. *Surely* she could be her normal carefree self in four days!

Cautiously she opened the attachment he'd sent.

And—oh—flutter, flutter, flutter. And he wasn't even *in* the photo!

The suit, photographed on a dummy so she got the full effect, was in a beautiful mid-grey. Three pieces, including a waistcoat, which she adored. The pants were narrow and cuffed. The two-button jacket was ultra-contemporary, but also sexily conservative. A white shirt, a tie in a fine black, silver and white check, and a purple and silver pocket square shoved insouciantly into the left breast pocket.

That suit, his physique, his dourly handsome face, his hair... He would have all the female guests drooling over him.

Maybe she shouldn't have made him grow his hair... *And where did* that *unworthy thought come from? If three centimetres of hair snares him a new bed partner—good!*

Well, every woman might be drooling, but only one woman could design his shoes. All right, that sounded incredibly lame. But so what?

She was going to do the design right now. And give it

to him on Sunday. And he was going to love—not like, but *love*—his shoes, dammit!

The motorbike was in pole position when Sunshine pulled up outside South. He couldn't have made it more visible if he'd had it on a dais under a spotlight.

She knew right then that he would be yanking her chain all day. *Stealing* her sanity!

Her stomach, which had finally started to settle into a relatively stable buzz, started rioting again. She sat in her car, taking some deep breaths and giving herself a stern talking-to: he was not a teenage hothead and he would *not* kill himself; she didn't care if he *did* kill himself; *she'd* kill him if he didn't get rid of the bike. And so on.

Not the most intelligent conversation she'd ever had with herself. And completely ineffectual, because her stomach was still going crazy.

If *only* she'd had the nous to call it quits with Leo after the first time she might still be a properly functioning adult.

Well, spilt milk and all that. She would just have to find a way back to normality before it affected the wedding preparations. Because the wedding was what was important. Not her, not Leo—the wedding!

She straightened her shoulders, flung open the door, and scrambled out of the car. She would have liked to have *disembarked* from the car, in case Leo was watching, but she was wearing her most complicated shoes and a too-tight dress! Compensating, she practically glided to the boot and, with what she considered great panache, swung her portfolio out. She left the briefcase behind, though—it was hard to look cucumber-cool when you were carrying a briefcase *and* a portfolio. Not that it usually bothered her, but... Well, *but*!

She took another deep breath as she entered the restaurant and saw Leo.

His hair was at Number Three buzz-cut stage. His jeans were black. He was wearing a fitted black superfine wool sweater. Sex on a stick. Even the black biker boots didn't have the power to dampen the desire that hit her like a punch.

He walked towards her—a purposeful kind of prowl that made her tongue want to loll. *Not* that there would be any tongue-lolling going on today.

She went to give him a reflex kiss on the cheek, but pulled back as it hit her that this was now fraught with difficulty.

His slow smile told her he'd registered her state of confusion. And then, to her shock, he leant down and kissed *her*. Sweet, slow, warm brush of lips against her cheek.

'Oh,' she said inanely.

He simply raised his eyebrows. And she knew what he was doing. He was playing the *Dare You* game! *Dare you to question that.* Well, she would *not* be dared.

He gestured to the dining area. 'As you can see, the tables and chairs are in,' he said. 'We're basically ready. I'm doing a trial dinner in two weeks, then we'll have a month to tweak. It will be a full moon on the trial night, so the view should be amazing. I'm inviting mostly locals, and some food and lifestyle media, but because it's a rehearsal for the wedding you'll have to come—obviously.'

Dare you! Dare you not to come.

Oh, how she wanted to say she couldn't make it. But that would be a mammoth case of cutting off her nose to spite her face, which he knew very well.

So, 'Of course,' she said.

He nodded at the portfolio in her hand. 'What's that?'

'Your shoe design.'

'Let's have a look,' Leo said.

Ordinarily, Sunshine would have gone a little theatrical, starting with a narrative and then positioning the designs on an easel. But today she merely pulled out the sheets and thrust them at Leo.

She watched, trying not to care, as he flicked through them.

She saw the shock come over his face and wished she could snatch the drawings out of his hands and rip them up.

Leo took them further into the restaurant and laid the pages on a window table, where light streamed brightly through.

He darted a looked up at her. 'Not what I was expecting,' he said.

'What *were* you expecting?'

Small pause. Quick smile. 'What's the shoe equivalent of a pine bookshelf?'

Huh? 'I guess…black leather lace-ups…?'

'Bingo.'

'Not that there's anything wrong with black leather lace-ups.'

'And yet…?'

Sunshine shrugged. 'And…yet.'

Okay. Leo admitted it. He wanted the damned shoes.

The design was sharp, lean, streamlined. No decorative stitching. Toes that were subtly rounded but also somehow pointed. No laces—monkstraps, fastened with sleek silver side buckles.

Plain and yet edgy.

And the colour was astounding. They looked black, but there was a suggestion…a sheen…of purple.

He cleared his throat. 'Thanks.'

'Do you…do you think you'll wear them?'

'Can you really get that colour? And those buckles?'

'I have the black-violet leather reserved. And I've already ordered the buckles—they're real silver.'

Black-violet. Perfect. 'Then, yes, I'll wear them, Sunshine.'

She smiled, her eyes glowing with joy, and he felt his heart start that heavy thump he'd hoped wouldn't happen. Not today—not when he wanted to be securely in the driver's seat for a change, keeping Sunshine a little off balance.

Of course his first sight of her, hauling herself out of that ancient, minuscule bright yellow car—Holy Mother of God, could a car *be* more perfect for her?—had almost derailed that plan on the spot, because *he* was the one who'd felt suddenly off balance.

It was the dress, he told himself. It was a monumental distraction, that dress. Petal-pink, too damned tight, too damned short.

And the black heels—too bloody high, with little black pearls studded in the leather and those crisscrossed ribbons around her ankles. How could a man *not* think about sucking her toes when he saw those shoes?

Thank God he'd got that first surge of heat under control enough to kiss her cheek instead of shoving his tongue halfway down her throat. Because that had been touch and go!

Now, however, the heart-thump suggested derailment was imminent again.

Well, he would just have to share the derailment around.

'So, then, let's go check out hotels,' he said.

'Are you—? Are you going to come with me? In the car?'

He thought about saying no—he'd realised that seeing him on the bike was going to be her breaking point and he wanted to get to that point fast. But in that tiny car of hers they would be very close to each other. So close she'd be able to feel him even without touching. He could use that. He was *sure* he could use that.

'Yes,' he said. 'The car.'

But when he squeezed himself into the passenger seat, and the scent of jonquils hit him like Thor's hammer, he thought perhaps he had made a tactical error. He just freaking *loved* that smell.

'Seat belt,' she said, and waited like a good little Girl Scout until he'd buckled up before starting the car.

He could see a faint blush on her cheeks. She'd get a shock if he touched her there. One finger along the rosy heat.

So he did, finding it shockingly easy to do.

But touchy-feely Sunshine swivelled as though he'd slapped her.

She stared at him.

He stared back.

And then he smiled. 'You know, Sunshine—your pupils are dilated. Got any internet facts to share about dilated pupils?'

Yes, Sunshine knew all about dilated pupils.

But she wasn't answering that.

Not with visions of straddling him right there in his seat popping into her head. He was so close that every time she changed gears her hand brushed his thigh. She had a sneaking suspicion he was deliberately putting his leg in the way. Another yank of her chain? She'd said hands-off, so he—the great un-toucher—had decided it was hands-*on*, just to needle her into a decision. And she'd thought he'd needed exposure therapy for his touching phobia!

It was just as well the first hotel was close to the restaurant. It was such a relief to be out of the car and in the open air.

Until Leo put his hand in the small of her back to guide

her across the car park to the hotel entrance—*enough with the touching, already!*—and she wanted to slap him.

She was a *pacifist*—she should *not* want to slap!

Sunshine stepped away from Leo the moment they were inside the hotel.

'I loved what I saw on the internet about this place,' she said, with an enthusiasm that actually managed to sound insincere even though she truly meant it.

That was what Leo was doing to her. Making her over-babble.

She looked around, taking in the use of dark wood, the pale stone floor. 'I think I'm going to book my own room here. Are you planning on staying overnight? I think you should. You know, you don't want to…to ride…after the party.'

Babbling. Shut up, shut up!

'I won't be riding home if I don't have a bike,' he pointed out calmly. Yanking her goddamned chain! 'But in any case I have a house here, and hopefully there'll be furniture by then.'

'A house? By then?'

Ugh. She'd turned into a parrot. A babbling parrot.

'The house was only built last year, and it's largely a furniture-free zone.'

'Are you going to live down here permanently?'

'Not permanently. I have too much on my plate in Sydney.'

Sunshine knew all about having too much on your plate. It kept you nicely occupied so you only had to think, not feel.

Think. Not feel.

That sounded good.

Think, not feel.

If she just remembered that everything would be all right.

And if she thought—ha—*thought!*—about Leo's full plate, it was clear that although he might talk about this mythical abyss-jumping woman of his dreams he was no different from her. He couldn't *fit* that kind of commitment into his life. Otherwise he would have it by now. He had enough women to choose from, for God's sake! She'd looked him up on the internet again yesterday, and seen the paparazzi photos. And, all right, that particular bit of searching had been a weak moment that she would not be repeating!

So! He didn't have it because he didn't want it.

And neither did she.

So she could stop the silly panicking.

Think, not feel.

'You could stay with me,' Leo said as one of the hotel staff approached them. 'The night of the reception.'

Okay, she couldn't stop panicking just yet, because her stomach was rioting again. 'I don't think that would be a good idea.'

'Don't have to think,' Leo said, and touched her cheek. 'You can just feel.'

How the *hell* did he lock on to her thoughts like that? 'You are freaking me out, Leo.'

'Am I?' He sounded delighted. 'All you have to do is agree to two more times and I'll stop!'

Sunshine turned gratefully to the hotel manager.

Introductions. Small talk. All good.

And then the manager asked, 'Shall we start the tour with the honeymoon suite?'

Sunshine choked on a laugh.

Which made Leo choke on a laugh.

So much unresolved between them—seething lust, and different takes on life, and twisted psyches—and here they were, being whisked off to the honeymoon suite like a couple of newlyweds.

'Wonderful,' Leo said, biting the inside of his cheek as Sunshine choked again.

She carefully kept her eyes off him when they reached the suite, looking around with a desperate kind of eagerness.

The suite had a touch of Bali about it, with a low bed of dark carved wood and a beautiful wood floor leading out to a private bamboo garden and plunge pool.

'Oh, so perfect! I might book it for myself,' Sunshine gushed.

Oh, no, you won't. 'Or for the actual honeymooners, perhaps?'

'Oops. Got carried away! Bamboo does that to me.'

'*Bamboo* does that?'

'Yes. Did you know it produces up to thirty-five per cent more oxygen than hardwood trees and absorbs four times as much carbon?'

'No, Sunshine, I did not. But I can see how that would make you want to honeymoon with it. There's something so sexy about carbon absorption.'

She giggled, then choked again as she tried to stop it. 'Well, I'm sure there are other wonderful rooms here that will suit me very well,' she said.

'I'm sure there are, but you'll like my place better,' Leo said, and almost laughed to see the flicker of panic race across her face.

Her face was flushed, her eyes wide, her lips parted so he could see that little gap between her teeth.

And, God, he wanted her. Wanted to run his hands up her legs and under her dress. To put his mouth on her, make her beg. Wanted to hear her sigh his name, feel her shudder. Wanted—

Ouch. To do something with his painful erection.

Okay—they were going to have to rush through this hotel tour.

Then rush through the next hotel.

Because it was three o'clock.

And by four o'clock he intended to have her at his house, preferably naked.

'So! Leo!' Sunshine said, pulling up at South at a quarter to four. 'Accommodation is sorted. I'll cover the card with the list of charities for donations in lieu of gifts and get that included with the invitation. Roger to no MC—just you welcoming the guests. No official speeches, just a repeat of their wedding vows. Clothes are done. Shoes underway. Kate is on board to sing. I think we can cover everything else via email.'

Leo hadn't made a move to get out of the car. He just sat there.

'Cake,' he said.

'The—the guys can just pick that, can't they? Like you originally suggested.'

'Sunshine, I brought down four miniature decorated cakes because you wanted a tasting, and if you think I'm taking them, untouched, back to Anton—who is monumentally temperamental and had to be talked into making them in the first place—you can think again.' *Forgive me, mild-mannered Anton...*

'Oh, then I guess... Or maybe I could cut a piece of each and—'

'And then there's the seating plan. I've got the night off.' *Go, Pinocchio.* 'I don't know when I'll get another, so we may as well get that sorted.'

'But I—I...I have a date.'

'Date?'

'Er...Tony. The calligrapher.'

'The calligrapher is an ex. Break the date.'

'How do you know he's an—? Oh, I told you, didn't I?'

'Yep. And in any case we haven't resolved the two versus four issue—you're mine until we do.'

Sunshine dragged in a breath. Held it.

'Breathe, Sunshine. It's just cake.' *Like hell.* 'And I also have a sample Anton made as a potential wedding favour to show you.'

She was looking torn. 'But we could do *that* via email.'

'And I have everything I need to make meat-lovers' pizza.'

Her mouth fell open. 'Oh, well, in that case.' She started getting out of the car.

'What are you doing?' Leo asked.

'Going into the restaurant.'

'No, we're going to my house.'

'I thought there wasn't any furniture.'

'It's not quite *that* basic. There's a completely fitted-out kitchen. With food. And a makeshift dining suite, although the table is on wheels. Some balcony furniture. Bathroom stuff. A mattress.'

Dare you! Dare you to come!

Her nose was wrinkling up; he could practically see the arguments bouncing around in her head.

'Think of the cake, Sunshine.'

'All right,' she said, with the air of a Christian martyr marching towards the lions' den.

'Good,' Leo said, and started getting out of the car.

'What are you doing?'

'I'll take the bike. You follow me. I'll grab my jacket and keys while you call Tony.'

'Tony?' she asked, blankly. And then, 'Oh, yes. Tony. I…'

'Forgot Tony? Poor Tony.'

For the first time ever Leo rode like a bat out of hell.

He didn't feel good about it, because he knew Sunshine

would be in a state—but he also knew it was the most effective way to smash through the wall she was trying to erect between them. The best way to *not* end up like Tony and all the others who had never got to the magical fourth assignation.

Well, Leo Quartermaine was not a piece of meat. He was getting to number four, and if it took the damned motorbike to get there so be it.

He was going so fast he had to pass the house and double back twice so Sunshine could keep sight of him. She was still lagging behind when he zoomed off the road and into the carport, but he was sure she'd been watching him closely and would find her way.

He wondered what she'd think of his place. The nondescript carport gave no hint that it was the gateway to a modern architectural masterpiece. Once they left the carport, however, and headed down a steep set of steps, it would be like entering a different world. The house was basically a long, horizontal strip of wood and glass cut into the side of a low cliff. A second set of steps led from the house to a beach so secluded it was like Leo's private patch of ocean.

The Fiat finally puttered in and Leo braced himself for her reaction, looking closely at her partly averted face as she got out of the car.

Very blank, very pale.

Without speaking to him she went to the boot, took out a cherry-red briefcase, fixed the strap over her shoulder. And then she turned towards him, and he saw that the weird face-morph thing had happened, that she was trembling.

And Leo knew he could never do that to her again.

She followed him to the top of the stairs, where he stopped. 'Are you all right?'

She merely looked at him, but he was relieved to see things settling back into place.

'Take off your shoes,' Leo said. 'It will be safer.'

'Don't talk to me about *safe*.'

'Then give me your briefcase.'

'No. Let's just see how you like thinking about my breaking body tumbling down those stairs, with my anklebones smashed in these heels and my briefcase cracking my skull open.'

'All right. I'm sorry I rode like that.'

She was speechless for a moment, and then she drew back her arm and punched him in the shoulder. At least it looked like a punch; it felt more like a slap with a cushion. 'You told me you weren't a teenage hothead,' she said shakily.

'I'm not. I'm sorry.'

'Shut up, Leo. I'm too angry with you to hear an apology. And there had better be six kinds of meat on that pizza after putting me through that! And *buffalo* mozzarella!'

Buffalo mozzarella—what a zinger.

He only barely managed not to laugh. 'Just give me the damned briefcase,' he said, biting the inside of his cheek.

She punched him again. Same shoulder. She clearly wasn't a candidate for cage fighting if that was the best she could do. 'You are *not* carrying my briefcase, Mr Alpha-Beta-Zeta,' Sunshine said.

'Don't forget the Gamma.'

She tossed her hair over her shoulder and waved him imperiously on: start the descent.

Leo took the first step, and the next, and the next, navigating slowly, staying just a half-step ahead. If Sunshine stumbled, if she even gasped, he would turn and catch her and toss her over his shoulder and carry her even if she kicked and screamed all the way.

But Sunshine—the epitome of high-heeled confidence—didn't put a foot wrong, and they arrived at the entrance to the house without incident. He opened the door and gestured her in ahead of him.

The use of glass was similar to what he'd done at South, except that where South had windows the house had full-length glass doors, opening onto a long veranda. The view was just as stunning. But because the house was so much lower, and perched within a cove, it had a more intimate connection with the beach.

Sunshine was walking slowly, uncertainly, to the glass doors.

'Go out,' Leo urged, stripping off his jacket and tossing it onto one of the few chairs.

She put down her briefcase and slid one of the doors open. Stepped onto the wooden deck, walked over to the edge.

He followed her out, wondering what was going through her head as she looked out.

'My sister would have loved this,' she said.

Moonbeam. *Quelle surprise.* 'And you?'

She half turned, looked into his eyes. He could see the tears swimming.

Because of Moonbeam? Or him and his bone-headed motorbike stunt?

Whatever! Leo simply reeled her in, held her close.

So mind-bogglingly easy to touch her now he'd set his course. So easy...

Her head was on his shoulder, and then she turned her face to kiss the shoulder she had punched earlier.

'I'm sorry for punching you,' she said. 'I've never punched anyone before.'

'I don't know how to break it to you, but those punches didn't hurt.'

'Then I hope it hurts washing my Beige Amour lipstick out of your woollen top. And I won't be sorry if it *doesn't* come out.'

'You can draw a map on the back in Beige Amour, okay? I deserve it.'

He could feel her breath, her spiky lashes against his neck.

'You made me so mad,' she said.

'I know. I'm sorry.'

'And you're supposed to have haphephobia. We shouldn't be standing like this.'

'I'm supposed to have *what*?'

'Fear of touch.'

He swallowed the laugh. This was *not* the time to make fun of her. 'But, Sunshine, we *are* standing like this. Maybe that means I'm making progress on my phobia. So...how's *your* phobia tracking?'

He heard her breath hitch, felt it catch in her chest. She pulled out of his arms and turned back to the view for a long moment. He thought she wasn't going to answer, but then she turned back.

'If you mean my reluctance to get emotionally close to people, that's not a phobia—it's an active choice.'

'The wrong choice.'

'The right choice for me.' And then she gave a shuddery kind of sound that was like a cross between a sigh and a laugh. 'Okay, you've yanked my chain. I've punched you. Let's move on before I start boring myself. We have things to do, so onwards and upwards: let them eat cake! Did you know that Marie Antoinette never actually said that?'

Sunshine took herself off to explore the house while Leo prepared the cakes.

The house was designed to give most rooms a view. There was a generous living/dining area, a cosy library, which had shelves but no books, and two private wings—the main bedroom/bathroom wing, with an atrium that reminded her of the honeymoon suite at the hotel, except that it was plant-free, and the other with three bedrooms, each with an en suite bathroom.

Leo had thrown a roll of paper towels at her when she'd poked her head in the kitchen, so she wasn't sure what that looked like, but she was in love with the rest of the house.

It just needed interior designing. Because the only decorative item in it so far was a massive ornate mirror on the wall in the living room. Some kind of feng shui thing—reflecting the water view for peace and prosperity? She would have to look that up.

Leo was looking inscrutable as he wheeled the dining table over to her, which made her suspicious—because what was there about cakes, plates, cutlery, napkins, and glasses to warrant inscrutability?

Well, she was not going to be inscrutabilised—and she didn't *care* if that wasn't a real word! She was simply going to eat the cake, and later the pizza, like a rational woman who did not care about anything but the state of her stomach, and then drive home.

She examined the four perfectly decorated cakes. Oh, dear, she was on the cusp of a ten-kilo weight-gain.

Then she noted that Leo was pouring champagne.

'Careful—I'm fat *and* I'm driving,' she said.

'You're not fat. And driving...? We'll see.'

'Just cut the cake, Leo,' she said, not about to get into an argument so soon after she'd punched him. He couldn't *force* the champagne down her throat anyway.

Leo cut and served slices of the first cake. 'Traditional fruit cake, fondant icing.'

Sunshine took a bite. It was moist, rich, and utterly delicious. 'This one, for sure!' she said, and scooped up another forkful.

'Pace yourself. Don't vote too soon,' Leo said.

She didn't bother responding—her mouth was too full.

'You *can* have another piece, you know,' Leo offered as she scraped up a last smear of icing.

'I have to lose weight or I won't fit into my dress,' Sunshine said repressively—and then she realised the absurdity of that, given the state of her plate, and burst out laughing.

'Hey, eat as much as you want! I was just trying to protect the plate—it looked like you were trying to dig a trench in it.'

'Leo!'

He held up *I surrender* hands.

'Oh, just cut the next one,' she said, gurgling.

'Salted caramel Mark One. Pastry base covered with a film of sticky salted caramel, topped with chocolate cake layers interspersed with caramel and cream filling.'

Sunshine took a bite. Closed her eyes as flavour flooded her. She took another forkful from her plate. Sipped champagne. 'It is *so* rich and delicious.'

Leo waited while she took one more bite. Another. One more. A sip. One more. 'Finished?' he asked at last, deadpan.

Mournfully, she examined her empty plate. 'I told you I had an unhealthy interest in desserts.'

'"A shark's mouth full of sweet teeth" was how you put it.'

'It may be worse than that. It could be more like a hadrosaur's teeth. They have nine hundred and sixty—*and* they're self-sharpening!'

'What the hell is a hadrosaur?'

'A type of dinosaur.' She sighed, dispirited. 'So! I am a dinosaur—and not even a meat-eating one!'

Leo laughed so suddenly it came out as a snort.

Which made Sunshine laugh. 'Let's get onto salted caramel Mark Two before I lapse into a state of abject depression.'

'You? Abject depression while eating *cake*? That would be something to see!'

'And you will see it, I promise you, if you don't look after my hadrosauric teeth and cut me a piece of cake.'

He cut a slice and handed it over. 'Your wish, my command! Similar to Mark One, but with butterscotch cake layers.'

Sunshine ate, interspersing mouthfuls with an occasional moan of ecstasy. 'Do you have a favourite?' she asked, forking up the last mouthful. 'Because I have to tell you this is harder than I thought and I don't think I'm going to be able to choose.'

'As it turns out, I do have a favourite—but I'm not telling,' he said. 'Subliminally, knowing what I like best might sway you—maybe to deliberately pick something that is *not* my favourite—and that would never do.'

'Oh! I see what you did there! Bouncing my own words about the invitation design back at me.'

'For my next trick I will spout random facts about the mating habits of the tsetse fly.'

Sunshine laughed. 'I'm going to look that up, and next time I see you—'

'I beg you—no!' He slapped another piece of cake on her plate. 'Coconut vanilla bean cake, layered with coconut meringue butter cream.'

Sunshine stared at it, not sure if she could actually fit in another bite. But it looked so good. She picked up her fork. Ate. Sipped more champagne, then looked at her glass. 'Hey—you refilled that.'

'It was empty,' Leo explained.

Sunshine huffed, but her concentration was already moving back to her plate. One more forkful. Another. Again. Empty plate. She licked her lips, looking at the rest of the cake longingly.

'See? You didn't need to know my favourite,' Leo said. 'You decided on your own. The coconut.'

'Yes. Coconut. It would almost be *worth* getting married just to have that cake. Do you think I could have another tiny piece?'

'You can eat the whole damned cake as far as I'm concerned.'

'Dieting from tomorrow, then,' she said, holding out her plate.

Leo cut another slice. 'Don't diet, Sunshine. I like the feel of you just as you are.'

The words, the tone of his voice, made the hairs on the back of her neck stand up. 'That's…that's…immaterial. But, anyway, wh-what's your favourite?'

He smiled. A narrow-eyed smile. She didn't trust that smile.

'The fruit cake,' he said. 'But I have an idea for how we can both get our way. Compromise is my new speciality.'

Was that supposed to be meaningful? 'Both get our way with what?' she asked cautiously.

'With the cake,' Leo said, all innocence, and put the extra slice on Sunshine's plate.

He looked at her for a long moment and Sunshine saw that little tic jump to life near his mouth. She was so nervous she almost couldn't sit still. She stuck her fork into her cake, raised it to her mouth.

'And with our assignations,' Leo said smoothly.

Sunshine jerked, and the piece of cake hit her just at the corner of her bottom lip and fell.

'Two, four…there's a three in the middle,' he said, in that same dangerously soft voice.

And then, before she could string a lucid thought together, he leant in and licked the corner of her mouth.

'Just thought I'd…steal…that little drop of cream,' Leo said softly.

Dare you.

Tic-tic-tic, beside his mouth.

'I'll tell you what,' he said silkily. 'I'm going into the kitchen to organise the first compromise I was talking about. You sit here, finish your cake, look at the view, and think about the second. Think about why it is that a woman like you, who believes sex is just sex—you did say that, right?—is so freaked out by the idea that a man actually does want to have just sex with her.'

With a last piercing look at her, and a short laugh, he left the room.

And, oh, how hard it was to have her words come back to bite her. Because she had said that. Sex was just…sex.

Except that it seemed in this particular case it wasn't.

Because she was thinking about Leo too much, and caring too much, and worrying too much. The motorbike. The damned motorbike. Maybe without the motorbike they would be entwined right now on assignation three and she would be blithely uninterested in anything except his moving body parts.

So do the deal, Sunshine, and he'll get rid of the bike.

Sex twice more. Or change her name.

She touched the corner of her mouth, where he'd licked the cream, and her skin seemed to tingle.

Restless, she got to her feet, walked out onto the veranda.

'*Look at the view,*' he'd said.

But even that wasn't simple.

He had no idea what the view did to her. And here the beach was so disturbingly close…

She hadn't been on a beach in two years.

Leo was right: Moonbeam did have a hold over her. A hold she seemed unable to break. A hold she was too… scared…to break. Well, she would go down to the beach now and yank her *own* chain and see what happened. And

then she would tell Leo. She would tell him—she would...
God, she didn't know what she would say. Or do.

But one drama at a time.

Deep breath.

Beach.

Heart hammering, she bent to remove her shoes. Took
the first step before she could think again, kept going until
the sand was beneath her feet.

It felt strange. And good. Comforting, almost, to have
her feet sink into the sand. The scratch of salt on her face,
the roar and rush of surf sounding in her ears.

Sunshine felt her sister in the wild, careless, regal,
lovely essence of the place. Pulling at her, drawing her
closer and closer, until she was at the water's edge and the
waves were slapping at her ankles.

She let out the breath she hadn't realised she was holding on a long sigh.

This tiny private beach was it.

What she'd been looking for. Waiting to find.

Leo's beach was her sister's final resting place.

She felt tears start, and swiped a shaking hand over
her eyes.

And then she felt Leo behind her.

CHAPTER EIGHT

'I'M NOT VAIN enough to think you're crying over me, Sunshine—so why don't you tell me what the big deal is about the beach?' Leo asked.

Heartbeat. Two. Three. 'Moonbeam.'

'I thought we'd get around to Moonbeam. Everything always circles back to her.'

She turned sharply towards him. 'What's wrong with that?'

'Just the fact that she's *dead*.'

She covered her ears, gave an anguished cry, and the next thing she knew she was in his arms.

'I'm sorry. *Sorry*,' he said, and kissed her temple. 'But, Sunshine, your sister doesn't sound like the kind of person who would have wanted you to freeze, to mark time just because she wasn't there.'

'She—she wasn't. But I can't help it, Leo.'

Long moment. And then Leo said, 'So let me help you. Tell me—talk. About Moonbeam and the beach.'

She waited, shivering in his steady hold, until the urge to weep had passed, and then she pulled out of his arms and stood beside him, looking out at the horizon.

'Sunshine?'

'She told me that when she died she wanted her ashes scattered at the beach—to mix with the ocean.' She turned to look up at him. 'Why would she say that when she was so young? Do you think she knew what was going to happen?'

'I don't know, Sunshine.'

'I didn't do what she wanted. I couldn't. Can't.'

'So…where is she?'

'In an urn in my office. You were looking straight at her—that night you cooked me dinner. I was scared you'd guessed. But it was just my guilty conscience getting the better of me. Because why would you ever guess?'

'There's no need to feel guilty, Sunshine.'

'I've got my sister in an urn in my office—the exact opposite of what she wanted. What does that say about me?'

'That you're grieving.' He smoothed a windblown lock of her hair. 'You'll find a way to do what she asked. But even if you never do it won't matter to Moonbeam. It's not really Moonbeam in that urn. She's in your heart and your head. Not in the urn, Sunshine.'

She turned back to the ocean, gazing out. 'A full moon. A quiet beach. She said it would be up to me to do it on my own—no friends, no family. Just me and her.' The tears were shimmering and she desperately blinked them back. 'I think she knew how hard it would be for me. I think she knew I would take a long time. I think she didn't want to pressure me into doing anything before I was ready. I want to do it, Leo. I *do*. But…'

'Well, we have a beach,' Leo said slowly. 'And a full moon coming up. You'll be here…'

He let the words hang.

She was still. So still. And then she turned to him again. 'You wouldn't mind?' Haltingly. 'You'd let me do that?'

'Yes, I would let you. And, no, I wouldn't mind.'

'I'll…I'll think about it. I'm not sure… Not yet…'

'That's fine. The beach will always be here, and there are plenty of full moons to choose from.'

She shivered.

'You're cold,' he said. 'Come back to the house.'

She could feel him behind her as she walked across the sand and up the steps. Like a tingle inside her nerve-endings. She could feel him watching as she brushed the sand from her feet, slipped on her shoes, retied the ankle laces.

And then, 'What next?' she asked, breathless. Wanting, wanting… *What?*

But Leo merely gestured for her to go into the house.

He'd cleared the table and positioned in the middle of it a small white cardboard box with Art Deco patterning. 'Open it,' he said.

Sunshine lifted the lid to find a one-portion replica of one of the wedding cake choices. Except that on top was a decorative three-dimensional love knot formed from two men's ties.

'Compromise number one,' Leo said. 'Fruit cake—for the wedding favours. It lasts longer than the other cakes, so can be made in advance. The ties will be identical to what Caleb and Jonathan are wearing on the day.'

'Anton is a genius.' She turned to him, felt her heart stutter at the hungry look on his face. 'So! We nail the seating plan now and we're done, right?'

Leo stepped closer to her. 'That makes you happy, Sunshine, doesn't it?'

'Of—of course.'

'The fact that we've done all the planning? Or that you don't have to see me again?'

'But I *do* have to see you,' she said faintly. 'At the trial dinner.'

'You're scared of me.'

'That's…insane.'

'Prove it.'

'There's nothing to prove. And how could I prove it anyway?'

'Kiss me.'

She goggled at him. 'Excuse me?'

'You used to. Every time you saw me. Before we had sex, at least. I thought things didn't change for you just because you had sex with someone.'

'They…they don't.'

'Then kiss me hello. Or you can make it goodbye, if you want. But do it. The way you used to. Just a kiss on the cheek.'

She shook her head.

He smiled. 'Ah. So *you're* the one who won't touch now, Sunshine.'

'I—I do. I mean, I can. But it's not… I just…'

He reached out, grabbed her elbow, and she jumped back.

'See?' he said. 'What's the problem? You've stayed friends with all your exes. Why not me?'

'You're not an ex.' Her eyes widened as she realised what she'd said. 'I mean, you *are*.' Stop. Breathe. Swallow. Hair toss. 'Of course we're friends.'

'So kiss me.'

She gave an exaggerated, exasperated sigh. 'All right,' she said. She leant forward and kissed his cheek. 'There! Satisfied?'

'No. Do it again. Slower. And touch me this time. Your hand, somewhere on me.'

'Ridiculous,' she muttered.

'Just do it.'

She touched his wrist, the burn mark. 'What happened there?'

'Hot pan, don't change the subject—and that's not touching.'

'Okay—where do you want me to touch you?' she asked, rolling her eyes with great theatricality.

His eyebrows shot up. He blinked. Slowly. Again.

Seriously? He was thinking about *there*?

But, 'Improvise…' was what he said.

With the air of a person suffering a fool, and *not* gladly, she ran her fingers up his forearm. 'There.'

'Now do that and kiss me at the same time.'

'This is stupid.'

'Do it.'

Huffing out an agitated breath, Sunshine leant up and gave him a fleeting kiss on the cheek while her hand gripped his forearm.

'There! Satisfied?' she said again. Hmm. That had come out a little too breathy.

'Not good enough—you're not usually that tentative. Try again.'

She stood there, chewing her lip for a moment, and then, as though going into battle, she grabbed him by both arms and kissed him lingeringly on the cheek.

She felt the sizzle, the almost convulsive need to press into him. Jerked back. Stared. 'So!' she said, a little unsteadily.

'It's not going to work, Sunshine,' he said.

'I did it. It worked.'

'You know what I mean.'

'If you're talking about sex, I—I told you. Two times. Over. Done with. Moving on.'

He stepped closer. 'I didn't agree to two. You're not moving on—not in any sense. And I still want you.'

He looked into her eyes. She could feel the lust pulsing out of him. She could smell it. Almost taste the musky promise of it.

'You want me too,' he said. 'I can *see* it. Your eyes… You know, the size of a person's pupils is the result of a balancing act between the autonomic nervous system, which controls the fight-or-flight response, and the parasympathetic system, known for its rest and digest functions—I read that online. Another fact to add to your collection.'

He stepped closer still.

'But I prefer a simpler explanation—sexual interest in what you're looking at makes your pupils dilate. And yours, Sunshine, are looking mighty dilated.'

He pulled her into his arms, kissed her hard.

'Compromise number two, Sunshine. And assignation number three. You're not leaving here until it's done.'

CHAPTER NINE

WITHOUT WAITING FOR a response he reached for the zipper at the back of her dress and slid it down. He peeled the dress over her shoulders, down to her hips.

The dress fell to the floor and she stood there in her underwear. He'd never seen her underwear before, but wasn't surprised to find it was the sexiest in the world. Petal-pink, the same colour as her dress—and he had a sudden insight that Sunshine's underwear would always match her clothes. He'd never been a lingerie man. Until today, when he was confronted by Sunshine's wispy, lacy bra, with its tiny ribbon bows, and the matching French knickers that reminded him of a frothy strawberry dessert.

His heart was hammering wildly in his chest. He touched the bra, the knickers. 'These are staying on,' he said, and turned her to face the mirror, where they could both watch as his hands covered her breasts, caressed her through the lace, slid down her body.

When his fingers dived beneath the elastic of those gorgeous knickers he could see her eyes close, her mouth gasp open. That gap between her teeth looked so damned *hot*!

Then she threw her head back against his shoulder, opened herself to him, and he couldn't think about anything except his desperate need to have her.

'Touch me—touch me, please,' she whimpered, and his

hand slid down, between her legs, where the heat and the wetness of her almost made him come on the spot.

She orgasmed quietly—a single, sighing groan easing through her parted lips; she went so boneless she would have melted to the floor if he hadn't been holding her.

But Leo wasn't done. He kissed her ear. 'Watch,' he said, and she opened her eyes, watching in the mirror again.

He lifted her right leg slightly up and outwards, so she could see the movement of his fingers as they slid beneath the silk of her knickers.

'I love these,' he said, tugging the crotch aside a little, then dragging the waist down so she was just a little exposed, open to him.

Behind her, he smoothly, quietly, undid his jeans. Her eyes were heavy-lidded, glittering, fixed on his as he sheathed himself inside her. It was almost gentle, the way he moved—and it was a test of his control, because he was wild for her. But this time, this coupling, was all about acceptance. And so he moved slowly, stayed still inside her for long moments…and when he did move it was by infinitesimal degrees, never withdrawing from her, always there. Hands running across her skin, along the scars. Until that groaning release of hers again, when he gripped her hips and followed her, groaning her name, holding her, as the waves washed over them, unhurried, sweet, delicious.

At last she stepped away from him, bent to retrieve her dress, slid it on. She turned her back for him to zip her into it.

The he turned her to face him. Put his hands on her shoulders. 'Sunshine?' His voice had that gravelly post-coital timbre to it.

No smile. Just a haunted look unlike any he'd ever seen on her face.

'I—I'm going to go now.'

'The champagne. It's too soon to drive. You should wait.'

'I didn't want all that champagne.'

'We'll do the seating plan. Over pizza, remember?'

'The *seating* plan?' She sounded incredulous.

'I— Yes. No. Whatever you want.'

'Leo, I can't do this. I don't want to.'

'The seating plan?'

'No, not the damned seating plan. The sex. The chat. The post-coital friend routine.'

'You said you were always friends afterwards.'

'It's different. I…I care about you. And it's not kind or—or…fair to do this to me.'

'Do what?'

'Try and put me in a position where I will end up caring *more*—because that's what will happen. I don't know why you'd bother, unless it's some twisted game. Or a challenge just because I set the rules.'

'I don't play by the rules, Sunshine.'

'And I don't want to be a challenge.' She pushed tiredly at her fringe. Then squared her shoulders. 'So! I'll tell you what. You win. You come and claim your fourth time. Let's just do it. The sooner the better. And then the deal is done. Because I am not going past that.'

She could see the triumph flare in his eyes.

'Deal,' he said. 'But before we get to that I'm going to make you pizza. Then we're going to dot every *i* and cross every *t* of this wedding and get it the hell out of our relationship. And then I'm going to take you to bed and make love to you, and draw a line under assignation number three.'

She could feel her breathing quicken, her pulse start skittering, the throbbing rush between her legs.

And then Leo, smiling, added, 'But first I'm going to

read you the haiku poem your mother sent me—which I have to say I kind of liked.'

No.

No, no, no, *no*!

But it didn't seem to matter how many times she said no in her head.

Because it was there, hurting her chest, stretching her heart.

Shimmering brightly, beautifully. Overwhelming and terrifying.

She was in love with Leo Quartermaine.

It was hardly surprising that she'd fallen in love with him, Sunshine thought on her drive back to Sydney the next morning.

The best sex of her life—possibly of *anyone's* life…in the *whole history of mankind*. Meat-lovers' pizza. Tiramisu. The offer to scatter her sister's ashes a stone's throw from his house. But, really, the absolutely unfair kicker—an appreciation of her mother's haiku poetry: evidence that he was probably seriously nuts.

The eyes are sublime
Glowing without the blackness
Liberated now

What had her mother been *thinking*?

And who the hell could actually *like* that?

And how could you *not* fall in love with a guy who did?

The signs were there already that this gobsmacking love was going to be an absolute misery. She'd asked Leo to text her so that she'd know he'd got home safely—and instead of telling her not to be a lunatic Leo had smiled and said, 'Sure.'

He'd smiled! *Smiled*!

What was going to come next—checking him for cuts and scalds after a shift in the kitchen?

Er...*no*! Thank you very much.

Well, it was a new thing. Maybe it wouldn't last. Maybe they would have their fourth assignation and then, once they'd gone their separate ways, it would fade.

Except...she was already feeling a little distraught at the idea of going their separate ways.

So, no. No time to waste.

She had to take action immediately.

Their relationship had to be reversed. They had to return to the way they'd been before she'd hugged him on the couch and started this killer snowball rolling down the mountain.

They had to be friends. Just friends. Without the depth. The way they should have been all along.

Which meant no fourth assignation.

And if she didn't want to renege on their deal that meant...

Sigh.

One name-change, coming up.

To: Leo Quartermaine
From: Sunshine Smart
Subject: Loose ends
Hi Leo
Here is a copy of my name-change application. So no need for assignation number four.

The process apparently takes about four weeks. Please let me know when you've sold the bike. You will find cars are so much more convenient. Well, maybe not for parking. But think of getting around when it's raining.

I know we're all sorted for the wedding, which is great because I am up to the gills in handbags for the next week or so, but let's catch up before the trial dinner.

(Allyn) Sunshine Smart

PS: I'm assuming it's okay for me to invite a date to the trial dinner, because I owe Tony.

Leo read the note three times before it sank in.

Allyn.

She'd chosen the name-change option over more sex with him.

Well, what moron had offered her that *out?*

And then one fact pierced him like a nice, long, sharp lance between the eyes: he didn't want her to change her name for *any* reason. She was *Sunshine.* Sunshine *suited* her. Okay, he was perhaps a little unhinged, because Sunshine wasn't an appropriate name for any human being— only for dish-washing liquid—but it bloody well did suit *her*, dammit.

The second fact smacked him behind the head like one of those quintain things that swung on a pole when you hit it with your lance: maybe the sex wasn't as good for her as it was for him.

After one appalled moment he discounted that. He recognised melt-your-socks sex when he saw it, tasted it, touched it, did it.

So did she, obviously. And it scared the crap out of her.

But to go straight from his bed to the Registry of Births, Deaths and Marriages…?

Well, sorry, but that was just an insult!

He thought back to last night.

He'd read her the haiku and she had looked like some kind of wax mannequin…but then, she'd made it obvious she wasn't a haiku fan.

She'd rallied to argue with him over the remaining wedding preparations. Par for the course.

She'd eaten the pizza as though it were going to be her last earthly meal—no surprises there.

Dinnertime conversation had been as peculiar as usual,

with Sunshine imparting strange but true facts. Leonardo Da Vinci had invented scissors—*who knew?*—there was a maze in England shaped like a Dalek—*how cool was that?*—forest fires moved faster uphill than downhill, and the crack in a breaking glass moved faster than three thousand miles per hour.

Then they'd had more amazing sex, using tiramisu in ways that would make it his favourite dessert for eternity.

And this morning she'd kissed him goodbye. On the mouth. As though she did it every day. And he'd *liked* that.

She'd asked him to text her when he got home. And he'd *done* it—*happily.*

So…*what*? Now he was supposed to accept that it was all over?

And what was the deal with *let's catch up before the trial dinner*?

Was she freaking *kidding* him? He was not *catching up* with her. Unless it was to bang her brains out in assignation number four.

Did she think he didn't know when he was being friend-zoned?

He *wasn't* going to be friend-zoned by Sunshine Smart.

He was not Gary or Ben or Iain or Tony—relegated to coffee catch-ups, Facebook status updates, and being taken to dinner to check people's hair-length.

He was *not* her freaking friend.

His brain felt as if it were foaming with rage.

He would email her telling her he would *not* be catching up with her before the trial dinner. And when he saw her at the trial dinner he would drag her aside and force her to tell him that she—

His brain stuttered to a halt there.

Tell him that she…that she…

That she…

Into his head popped a picture of her kissing him good-bye that morning.

Asking him to text her when he got home.

That she...

That *he*...

Oh, my God.

All or nothing. Off the cliff. Into the abyss.

She was the one.

She would fight tooth and nail not to be, but that was what she was.

The one.

And Leo had no idea what to do about it.

It's hemp, Jim, but not as we know it.

Leo had done a double-take the moment he'd seen Sunshine.

Hemp was not sexy.

Everyone knew that.

So why did the sight of Sunshine Smart wearing it make him want to drool?

A simple loose ankle-length column of dark bronze—and, God, he'd love to see her underwear in *that* colour—with two tiny straps fastened at the shoulders in untie-me-please bows. She'd left off the lipstick as well as the eye-goop and looked fresh as a sea breeze. Her hair was loose. Towering heels in gold. Gold drop earrings, straight as arrows, pointing to those mind-game bows. She also had a thick gold cuff clasped around one arm, just above the elbow. But she never wore jewellery...

Well, obviously she does *sometimes, imbecile.*

Yep. A hundred and fifty guests to feed, and he was pondering Sunshine's jewellery-wearing habits. *Great.*

He strode over to her. 'Sunshine.'

'Allyn,' she corrected.

'Not yet, though, right? And—' he turned to the guy

who had popped up beside her like a cork in a pool '—you must be Tony. Let me show you to your table.'

Leo led them to their seats, introduced them to the others at their table.

And then… Well, her fringe was getting long. She'd brushed it aside—training it for the wedding, he figured—but one piece had sprung back over her forehead. He smoothed it back to where it was supposed to be.

Her gorgeous eyes widened. He heard her quick intake of breath, saw the daze in her eyes. It felt like a 'moment'—one of those bubble-like moments where everything was right with the world.

He sensed Tony watching him. Everyone else at the table too.

Good, he thought savagely. *I'm marking my territory, people, and she belongs to me.*

It had been two weeks since Sunshine had seen Leo—two weeks in which the only contact he'd made had come in the form of three niggardly emails: one rebuffing her suggestion that they catch up before tonight—which had hit her like a blow—the second a message about wines for the wedding, with the most *casual* mention that he'd sold his bike and bought a 'nice safe Volvo'—how dared he be casual about that?—and the third with details of tonight's trial dinner. She suspected it was the same email he'd sent to all guests, except that to hers he'd added, *Don't forget to bring your sister.*

With so little encouragement to pine for him, and fewer reasons to worry about him now that he was *sans* motorbike, Sunshine figured she should have managed to get her wayward emotions under control. But the bike sale hadn't seemed to lessen her anxiety over him. She thought, and thought, and thought about him. *All the goddamned time.* Exactly what she'd been trying to avoid.

And then that one touch of his, brushing her fringe aside, and her emotions had surged so suddenly she'd almost thrown herself at him.

Now just the sight of him walking to the middle of the restaurant and clapping his hands to get everyone's attention, looking so delicious in that crisp white jacket, started her stomach jumping like popping candy.

He made a welcome speech—explained what would happen, ran through the menu, asked people to make sure they passed on all feedback, good and bad—and all through it Sunshine stared at him as though he were a nice big bowl of tiramisu...

When he left for the kitchen the whole night suddenly felt flat—and it didn't reshape itself except when he made his occasional forays from the kitchen to take a momentarily empty seat and chat to guests.

But never at Sunshine's table. And she didn't know whether to be happy about that or not. On the one hand she wouldn't have had to strain every minuscule cilia in her ears, trying to hear what he was saying. But on the other he'd surely notice that she had become, in just two weeks, the equivalent of a fried bat.

And then he was at the table next to hers, and Sunshine caught his eyes on her for the first time since he'd shown her to her table.

The hairs on the back of her neck stood up. She couldn't breathe. Couldn't think. Couldn't even seem to swallow. He was nodding at something the woman next to him was saying but he was looking at Sunshine.

After ignoring her for two whole weeks he was daring to look at her as if he would drag her off to a corner, rip off her clothes and—

His head jerked to the side, towards the entrance, and Sunshine's eyes jerked reflexively. There was a disturbance going down, being played out in a series of split-seconds.

An escalating pitch of voice. A scuffling sound. A shift of bodies. And—

Natalie Clarke. *Uh-oh.*

Within seconds Leo was up and walking swiftly over to Natalie, taking her arm, murmuring to the restaurant manager who'd been trying to handle the situation, and escorting Natalie out onto the viewing platform.

Sunshine felt a little as she had that night at the Rump & Chop Grill. Light-headed with fury on Leo's behalf... desperate to protect him. She didn't even wait for her head to tell her heart it was none of her business. With a fixed smile and an incoherent murmur about a 'wedding issue', Sunshine took off after Leo.

CHAPTER TEN

SUNSHINE REACHED THE viewing platform just in time to see Natalie land a swinging slap against Leo's cheek.

The burst of rage that flared in her head made her shake. 'What the *hell's* going on?' she demanded, grabbing Natalie's hand as it drew back for a second go.

'Go back inside, Sunshine,' Leo said, and tried to shove her behind him.

'You!' Natalie said contemptuously. 'Choke-girl! *You're* the Sunshine person?' She looked Sunshine up and down. 'They say at Q Brasserie that he's besotted with you. But he doesn't know *how* to love someone. He's not capable. He can't even *touch* you.'

Sunshine didn't bother answering. She simply manoeuvred herself beside Leo—which required a sharp nudge with her elbow, since he seemed determined to keep her out of harm's way—and then took his hand in hers, brought it to her lips, kissed it, rubbed it against her cheek.

'Really?' she asked Natalie, with a raise of her eyebrows.

Surrendering, Leo drew Sunshine protectively against his side. 'Natalie,' he said, 'tonight is a private function. And there are journalists inside who are probably wondering what the hell's going on out here. Can we *not* play this out in a blaze of publicity? Go back to Sydney—or there's a hotel nearby if you don't feel up to driving back tonight.'

'Why don't I go and wait at your house, Leo?' Natalie purred the question, shrugging out of her coat. She shimmied a little, sinuous as a snake.

Sunshine, beset by another burst of rage, stiffened, and Leo squeezed her hand slightly. Telling her to let it go.

And she should. She knew she should...

But Natalie licked her lips and raised one eyebrow, and the rage consumed her.

Sunshine laughed—a brittle laugh that sounded nothing like her. 'I'd forgotten about the tattoos,' she said. 'Butterflies. They're the gang rapists of the insect world, you know.'

She heard Leo choke on a laugh and she squeezed *his* hand. Hard.

Natalie fluttered one arm out to look at her tattoos. 'Don't be ridiculous.'

'They are so desperate to mate they perch on a female pupa—that's the metamorphosis stage, you know, where they go from larva to—'

'This is disgusting.'

'I *know*!' Wide-eyed. 'Especially because they perch there in a pack and wait for the female to emerge. And she's still limp, and her wings haven't even opened, and the first male just kind of grabs her and...well, you get the picture. And then the others take their turn.'

'That's...' Words seemed to fail Natalie.

Sunshine was contemplating Natalie's arms sadly. 'Next time get an eagle; at least they mate for life.'

Natalie stood there, quivering with impotent rage, staring from Sunshine to Leo.

One fraught moment. Another. Three people on one small viewing platform. Nobody moving.

And then, with a last look of loathing at Sunshine, Natalie turned on her heel and stalked off the platform.

Sunshine dropped Leo's hand and stepped back. '*Now* I'll go back in,' she said.

'Why did you even come out?'

'I just…I just thought you might need some support.'

'It looked a little like a leap into the abyss to me.'

No. *No!* 'I just don't like violence. And she slapped you. It made me…mad.' She looked at his face, which was still reddened where Natalie's hand had connected.

Half-laugh as he ran his fingers over his cheek. 'Yeah, you'll have to lift some weights if you want to match her.'

Sunshine, conscience-stricken, felt the colour drain from her face. 'Oh, my God, you're right. I'm just like her.'

Leo took her hands in his, pulled her towards him. 'You're nothing like her.'

'But I punched you!'

'And then you kissed it better, remember?'

'I— Yes, I remember.'

She shivered.

'Are you cold?

Nod. 'I brought a coat, but it's in my car.'

'Then come here,' he said softly, and drew her in, folding his arms around her. 'And Moonbeam? Is she in the car too?'

She nodded again.

'So it's happening?' he asked gently.

Another nod. 'Yes, if you're sure you don't mind.' And then, just a whisper, 'Tomorrow is the anniversary of… of…'

'Ah, Sunshine.' He stroked his hand over her hair and they stayed like that for a long moment. 'We'll disappear as soon as dessert is cleared, okay?'

'Tony…'

'Yeah—I don't give a rat's ass about Tony, and neither do you.'

'I don't think rats' asses are an apt comparison.'

'A horse's ass, then.'

She giggled, and then buried her face against his chest to stifle it. Because it wasn't funny.

'Whatever he is, he can fend for himself,' Leo said. 'Because I know he didn't drive down with you. Aside from anything else, I know you wouldn't have him in the car with Moonbeam.'

'How do you know that?'

'Because I just do.' Slight pause. 'So that stuff about butterflies—was it true?'

'Well, it's true of *certain* species,' Sunshine said, drawing slowly out of his arms. 'I'm not sure about *all* species.'

He opened the door to the restaurant, laughing. 'Poor Natalie. Probably *not* arms full of rapists.'

'Do you think I should tell her?' Sunshine asked, feeling suddenly guilty.

'If I could find pupil dilation on the internet I'm sure Natalie can find rapist butterflies,' Leo said. 'I like the thing about the eagles, though. Mating for life.'

It was time.

Sunshine was standing on his veranda at the top of the stairs, barefoot, with the urn in her arms. She was wearing a long knitted garment over her hemp dress. It flowed down to her ankles. No fastenings. A little bit witchy, a little bit hippie—perfect for a ceremonial ash-tossing.

'Right,' she said, and stood there looking irresolute.

Leo simply waited.

'Right,' she said again, with a tiny nod this time. And then she shot a look at Leo over her shoulder. 'I have to do this myself.'

'I know. I'll come down to the beach, just in case you need me, but I'll stay at the base of the steps.'

'I won't need you.'

'In case.' Implacable.

She looked paler than usual. Tense. And oddly hopeful.

And then she straightened her shoulders and started down the steps.

Leo waited two minutes, then followed. By the time he reached the sand her toes were in the wash.

He knew he would never forget the image of Sunshine, alone, surrounded by moon, surf, sand, night, as she lifted the urn to her face, kissed it.

And then she took off the lid and threw it behind her, discarded.

As if on cue an offshore breeze stirred, and Sunshine threw her head back, hugging the urn to her chest for one brief moment. Then, in one sudden, decisive movement, she threw the ashes up and out towards the water. She repeated the move once more. Then she bent, filled the urn with the seawater rushing in, waited while the water receded, then raced in again…tipped the urn so its contents hit the sand just as the new wave broke. And the last of Moonbeam's ashes were carried out to the ocean.

The minutes ticked by.

The breeze died away.

The rhythmic whooshing of surf on sand continued.

Life goes on.

And then Sunshine tossed that beautiful urn aside as though it were nothing but a broken shard of shell and walked back up the beach towards him, silent, tears streaming.

He opened his arms and she walked right into them. He said nothing. Just held her as her tears gradually eased, then stopped.

Staying in the circle of his arms, she looked up. 'Thank you,' she said. 'You know, she would have loved you.'

And you? he wanted to ask. But instead he said, 'Come to bed, Sunshine.'

She looked at his face in the moonlight. Touched his cheek. Nodded. 'One last time.'

She woke wearing one of Leo's shirts, alone on the mattress.

The makeshift curtains were drawn, except for a crack through which a piercing sliver of light beamed.

She got out of bed to tug the curtains back—and there it was: Moonbeam's beach. Wild and beautiful and... peaceful. Perfect.

Leo wandered in, wearing unbuttoned jeans and a navy blue T-shirt.

And the feeling of peace evaporated as her stomach started its usual Leo-induced cha-cha.

Time for reality.

'I'm about to make you an omelette,' he said, smiling. 'It will only be a few minutes, if you want to come out on the veranda when you're ready. And don't worry—there will be chorizo in there.'

A dart of panic stabbed her. 'No. I don't want it.'

'Don't like chorizo?'

'It's not about the ingredients.'

The smile vanished. 'Then what is it about?'

'The fact that you never cook for people.'

'And yet I do it for you.'

Her breath hitched. 'But I—I don't want you to cook for me.'

'Why not?'

'Because it's not what you do. You shouldn't change for me. Because...'

'Because...?'

'Because I can't change for you.'

'I haven't asked you to.'

'Oh.' That took the wind out of her sails. 'That's...good. I was scared because...'

'Because?'

'Well, Natalie said last night the people at Q Brasserie…they think you're besotted with me. That wouldn't be good.'

'I'm not besotted,' he said. 'Does that reassure you?'

'Yes. No. I don't know.'

'Multiple *choice*, Sunshine? How…comprehensive.'

'No. I mean—yes, it reassures me,' she said. 'I just… want us to be on the same page.'

'What specific page are you talking about?'

'Page number four,' she said. 'Four assignations. All settled. And I'm glad we did it. I was feeling guilty because you gave up your bike, and I never got around to filing the papers to change my name—because it didn't feel right, somehow. And I still…owed you.'

'Is that what last night was about? Honouring the deal?'

Last night came rushing back at her—the gentleness and joy of it. The way he'd hovered over her, lavishing her with his touch. Hands so sure and wonderful. The layered feelings of his mouth sliding over her, sometimes gentle, sometimes demanding. Worshipping her body with his— that's what it had felt like. Whenever she'd made a sound he'd been there, kissing her, soothing her. And even when she'd made no sound he'd been just there—something of his, on her.

But now, the morning after, with the terror of love choking her, she wanted to throw herself at his feet and beg him never to go, never to die.

But he couldn't promise that.

'Yes,' she whispered. 'I owed you and now we're done.'

She snatched her dress off the floor and started walking away.

'Where are you going?' Leo asked

'To the bathroom. To change.'

Leo folded his arms over his chest. 'Not only have my

eyes been all over your body, but so have my hands and my mouth. And now you're running to the bathroom?'

She paused, undecided. And then, with a defiant shrug, she ripped off the shirt she was wearing, dragged her dress over her head.

Leo bent, scooped something off the floor. 'Forgetting these?' he asked.

She snatched the tiny bronze-coloured panties from him and struggled into them while trying to stay covered.

'There,' she said. 'Happy?'

He watched her, brooding, hooded. 'No.'

'Leo, what do you want from me?'

'I want to know where you think we go from here—one month out from the wedding.'

'Well, we're going to be family. Sort of...'

'I'm not your brother.'

'I meant more like...like surrogate family. Like friends.'

'I'm not your friend.'

'But we *could* be friends.'

'I told you way back when that I don't do that.'

'I know you don't, usually—but I'm not like your other exes.'

'And I'm not like yours. I won't be Facebook "friending" you, making it to a movie, popping out for a coffee, or catching up over a casual dinner where we give each other a kiss on the cheek goodnight.'

'But why not?'

'Because I want you.'

She stared helplessly at him as her heart thudded in her aching chest. 'You already said you *didn't* want me.'

'I didn't say that.'

'You said you weren't besotted.'

'That's different. I want you, all right...the same way you want me. And it's got nothing to do with friendship.'

She swallowed. God. God, God, *God*. 'I—I don't want to…to want you like that.'

He moved like lightning, grabbing her arms and hauling her up on her toes. 'But you do. Your pupils are telling me you do, Sunshine,' he said, and smiled. 'Nice and big—for me.' He nudged his pelvis against her. 'Like that—nice and big. For you.'

She swallowed convulsively. 'You know I can't let myself love you.' The words sounded torn from her throat.

'Who mentioned love? Not me—*you* did, Sunshine. You.' He kissed her, a hard, drugging, wrenching scorch of mouth and tongue that made her melt and steam and long for him.

She almost cried out a protest when he stopped.

'Call this thing between us anything you want—except friendship,' he said. 'Because I will *never* be your friend.'

He let her go suddenly, and she stumbled backwards.

'I'm giving you fair warning, Sunshine: I *will* have you again. Five, six, seven times. Or ten, twenty. Anything except four. I will have you again, and there will be nothing friendly about it.'

Frustrated and furious, Leo went down to the beach after Sunshine had left.

No—she hadn't 'left'; she had run away, as if all the demons of hell were after her.

He needed a swim to snap his tortured brain back to a modicum of intelligence. And he hoped the water was frigid. He hoped—

Oh.

Oh, God.

There, a metre from the water, skewed in the sand, was the urn Sunshine had tossed aside last night.

And it was more effective than a swim in frigid water ever could have been.

Because it brought back every heartbreaking moment of that scene on the beach as the woman he loved had finally found the courage to say goodbye to her sister. The way she had given herself to him so sweetly afterwards, with gentleness and acceptance and yearning, and a heated desire that had seemed insatiable.

The contrast to this morning was not pretty.

He ran his hands over his head. Today was the anniversary of Moonbeam's death. And what had he done? Pushed and pushed her, without even giving her a chance to think. All but demanding that she strip for him, forcing her to kiss him, telling her he would take whatever he wanted, when he wanted.

It had been his survival instinct—alive and kicking—telling him to go his own way, *get* his own way, no matter what *she* wanted.

But seeing the urn was a concrete reminder that his way was not hers.

She had taken two years to farewell the sister she adored. She wasn't ready to love anyone else. Was too scared of the pain of it and too guilt-stricken to reach for what her sister could never have.

And he didn't have the right to force the love from her.

Not the right, and not the power.

She didn't want him to have all of her, the way he craved.

And if she couldn't give him her all, he was going to have to find a way to settle for nothing.

CHAPTER ELEVEN

'I WILL HAVE you again, and there will be nothing friendly about it.'

Those words had been going around and around in Sunshine's head incessantly for four long weeks, until she'd started to wonder if she'd be too scared to go to the wedding.

She hadn't even been able to pluck up the courage to go to the airport to meet Jon's flight, because she was so certain Leo would be there—ready either to pounce on her or ignore her, and she didn't know which would be worse.

Now she'd finally got to see Jonathan, he didn't waste time on small talk. She barely had time to slap a Campari into his hand as he took a seat on her couch before he fixed his eagle eye on her across the coffee table and asked, 'What's going on with Leo, Sunshine?'

'What do you mean?

'Only that you went from mentioning his name in your emails to the point where I wanted to vomit to complete radio silence a month ago. And he did the same to Caleb.'

'Oh.'

'Yes, *oh*. I did warn you it wouldn't be hands across the water singing "Kumbaya" at the end.'

'Strictly speaking, that's hands around the campfire.'

'I will build a campfire and throw you on it if you give

me internet facts in the middle of this discussion. What happened?'

'It was the four-times rule.'

Jon rolled his eyes. 'Yes?'

'I wanted to stop at two, because I was…liking him too much, I guess. And he didn't want to stop.'

'But you stopped anyway?'

'Well…no. I couldn't seem to resist.'

'And the problem is… ?'

'That I just… I can't stop. Wanting him, I mean.'

'So *have* him.'

'You know I can't do that.'

'What I know, Sunny, is that you tell yourself a lot of crap! How do you know it's too painful to love a man when you've never done it? And don't hide behind the four-times rule. It's easy for you to pretend you've always stopped at one or two or even none because you're scared of caring too much. But the truth is you stop because you don't care *enough*! Which brings me back to Leo and the fact that you obviously finally *do* care enough. *What* is the problem?'

'I'm scared.'

'Sunny—love *is* scary. Not just for you, for everyone.'

'He doesn't love me. He only *wants* me.'

'So make him love you.'

'You can't make someone love you.'

'The Sunshine Smart *I* know can—if she wants to.'

'Well, she *doesn't* want to.'

'Just think about it.'

'No.'

'Then I'm telling your mother you asked for a book of original haiku poems for Christmas.'

She sputtered out a laugh. 'You're a rat, Jonathan.'

'Pour me another Campari and get me the computer. I'm going to look up Sydney's hottest models and try to choose Leo's next girlfriend. And when he nails her I am going to hire a skywriter to scrawl "I TOLD YOU SO" over Bondi Beach.'

And then Jonathan left his seat, came over to her, lifted her onto his lap. 'Sunny, darling one, give yourself a break and grab him.'

'How can I when…when Moonbeam…?'

'Moonbeam! *Sunny.* God, Sunny! Is *that* what this is about? She can't have love so you won't? She never wanted you to throw yourself onto her funeral pyre. That is so *not* her. And reverse the situation—would you have wanted *her* to give up living?'

'No. Of course not! And I know she would have loved him…and that makes it easier. If only…'

'If only?'

'If only he would never die,' she said, and buried her face against his chest.

'Oh, Sunny.' Jon kissed the top of her head. 'Would it really hurt any less just because you're not together? Wouldn't that be worse?'

'It's so hard. *Too* hard.'

'Yeah, life's hard. So why make it harder?'

Sipping a gin and tonic, Caleb leant back in his chair and examined his brother, head on one side.

It reminded Leo of Sunshine's curious bird look. And he couldn't bear it. He surged to his feet and paced the room, trying to shed some of the nervous energy that had infiltrated his body as the countdown to the wedding—to when he would see Sunshine again—began.

'Now that it's just us, suppose you tell me what's going on with Sunshine?' Caleb suggested.

'Nothing.'

'What happened? Did she fall in love with you and you had to hurt her feelings?'

Silence as Leo slid into his seat, picked up his drink and took a long swallow.

'Well?' Caleb prompted. And then his gaze sharpened. 'Oh, boy.'

'"Oh, boy"—*what*?'

'It was the other way around. You fell in love with *her*, and she had to hurt *your* feelings.'

'Not exactly.'

'Blood from a stone, or what?'

Leo put down his drink, ran his hands through his three centimetres of hair. 'We had an agreement—sex only. Four times.'

Caleb nodded, understanding. 'The four-times rule.'

Leo shot a startled look at Caleb. 'You *know* about that?'

'Yep. And you obviously agreed to it. Idiot. So then what?'

'And then she wanted…less.'

'She wanted less. Why? You were no good in the sack? Because that's not what I've heard.'

'Because she didn't want to care about me. Not just me—about anyone.'

'That is the dumbest thing ever.'

'It's a long story that I'm not going to go into except to say that she's not looking for romantic attachments. She only wants to be friends. But I pushed it. I pushed and pushed until I got all four times. But it didn't work. '

Caleb choked on his drink. 'She didn't *friend*-zone you!'

'She tried. I refused.' Deep sigh. 'And I ended up with nothing.'

Caleb was staring at him, flabbergasted. 'You are one dumb bastard.'

'Thank you,' Leo said dryly, and jumped to his feet again, pacing.

'So what are you going to do?' Caleb asked.

'Get through the wedding. Try to accept it's over.'

'That's not the Leo Quartermaine I know.'

'She was up-front from day one and I should have accepted it. The thing with her sister—it was devastating for her. I should have understood and left her alone, but I...' Stop. Start again. 'Instead I pushed her and pushed her.' Stop. Start again. 'And what right do I have to push her into feeling something she's not ready for?'

'We're never ready—none of us—for love.'

'She didn't fall in love with me. She wouldn't let herself.'

'So change her mind.'

Leo came to a stop in front of Caleb. 'She won't do it. She says that she would be anguished in love—live for him, die for him. That's the only way for her to love.' He stared at his brother. 'And I don't think I...'

'You don't think you...?'

'Deserve it. Deserve *her*. All I could say to her the last time I saw her was that I would *not* be her friend, that I would have her again—and again, and again—and that she couldn't stop me.' He was shaking now. 'That's the kind of thing someone like Natalie would want to hear, not Sunshine. The Natalie Clarkes are for me, not the Sunshine Smarts.'

A hopeless, helpless shrug.

'And she ran for the door faster than you could blink. And then I went down to the beach and I saw the urn and it hit me—what she'd been through the night before, when all I'd wanted was to help her find peace. But that morning...the anniversary...I was pushing her because I wanted more.' He scrubbed his hands over his face. 'No wonder she ran away from me.'

Three paces away. Three back.

'As soon as I saw the urn, Caleb, I knew that she would never belong to someone who's clawed and scraped his way out of hell, who's learned to grab and take and steal. Well,

I won't steal from *her*. I mean, who am I to steal from her what she doesn't want to freely give? Why would I think I'm special enough to—?' Stop. Start again. 'Who am I to even *want* it?'

Caleb stood slowly. 'Who are *you*, Leo? Just the bravest, best, most wonderful—' He broke off, grabbed Leo in a fierce hug.

For long moments they clung together. And then Caleb drew back, tears in his eyes.

'Now, I don't pretend to know the significance of the urn. But I know this: you deserve *everything*. And I'm going to give you an argument that will appeal to the noble, valiant, chivalrous, gallant core of you that our pathetic parents did *not* manage to destroy, no matter what you think.'

He gripped Leo by the shirtfront, looking fiercely into his eyes.

'You know why you deserve her? Because you will look after her better than any other man on the planet. Because you will live for *her*, die for *her*. How will you forgive yourself if some substandard joker breaks down her defences—someone who *won't* live and die for her? Who won't throw himself into that freaking abyss you carp on and on about? Think about that, Leo. Think about *that*.'

Leo stared at his brother.

And then he smiled.

CHAPTER TWELVE

THE WEDDING DAY was perfection.

It was warm, the sun was shining, and the restaurant sparkled.

A romantic day. A glorious day.

A day for *not* throwing yourself at the drop-dead gorgeous man that you were head over ears in love with. Even if every hair on your body tingled the moment you saw him stepping onto the terrace in shoes *you'd* designed, as if he owned the world and knew exactly what to do with it.

Even if you wanted to run your fingers through his newly grown hair and slide your hands over the lapels of his sharp and sexy suit, to lean in and take the clean, soapy smell of him into your brain via your nasal cavity.

Sunshine had thought getting her first Leo sighting out of the way would take the pressure off her, but it seemed to have had the opposite effect. Every one of her senses had sprung to life and seemed to crave something that could be found only in his immediate orbit.

Despite her wildly thumping heart and her clammy hands she tried to look serene as she made her way around the terrace, greeting, smiling, chatting. Her parents were looking as deliriously happy as usual. They'd brought Leo a batch of carob and walnut cookies. And a homemade diary for next year. And a haiku poem, framed, as a thank-you for inviting them to the beach that morning to see Moonbeam's final resting place.

They'd told her that he'd loved everything, that he was wonderful. She'd thought for an insane moment they intended to adopt him!

Sunshine was wondering whether to apologise to him about the framed haiku—at least it would be a valid reason to approach him—when, amazingly, she saw him go over to her parents. The three of them looked like a secret club as they whispered together, and then Leo was enfolded in her mother's arms and hugged almost convulsively. And then her father hugged him. The three of them were laughing, looking so *right* together. And then Leo kissed her mother on the cheek, shook her father's hand in a two-handed grip, and moved away.

Oh, my God. How the hell was she supposed to fall out of love with a man who was like *that* with her parents?

He really, *really* must like haiku!

There was just one thing left on Leo's wedding to-do list: make Sunshine fall in love with him before the cake-cutting.

Caleb was sure he could do it. Jonathan had threatened him with violence if he didn't at least try. And even her parents had given him a few pointers.

But he knew she was going to be a tough nut to crack.

Watching her do the rounds in that glistening, shimmering, silver dress, practically floating in those amazing shoes, he had felt his heart both soar and ache.

She'd painted her nails silver, and was wearing glittery earrings and a matching ring in addition to the swinging sun and moon chain. Her hair was perfect—even the fringe was behaving itself. She was wearing a slick of eyeliner;

she'd told him she would way back, when they'd struck their deal, so it was allowed. And deep rose lipstick.

Gorgeous, gorgeous, *gorgeous*.

Five times he'd tried to approach her. Five times he'd lost his nerve.

The upshot was that by the time everyone was seated they hadn't spoken a word to each other. Not one word.

But he nevertheless felt as connected to her as a piano wire to its tuning pin—he was sure if they just got the tension right the music would soar. How poetic was that?

He was aware of every mouthful she ate during dinner, and every mouthful she didn't. He heard every laugh. Caught every quickly averted look from those miraculous eyes whenever he glanced in her direction.

And then Jon and Caleb were moving to the small podium. Standing there, holding hands. Leo started to panic.

Time was almost up.

Jonathan cleared his throat, tapped his glass, and Sunshine held her breath as all eyes turned to the newlyweds.

'It's *that* time of the evening,' Jonathan said. 'All of you here tonight are close to one of us—and hence to both of us. You've shared our journey. You know our story. We are so happy to be home, to be here, to be with you. So happy that we don't intend to bore you to death with speeches! All we want to do is share with you the vows we spoke to each other last week in New York.

'They're short vows—but the words are very important to us. So…here goes: *Caleb, you are the one. When I look in your eyes I see my yearning...and the truth. When you smile at me I know I can tell you anything and find everything. When we touch I feel it in every breath, every nerve, every heartbeat. When we kiss it is magic and delight. And home as well. When you laugh, when you cry, when you rage, and even when you sneer—because you sure can sneer—I am with you. You are everything to me and always will be. Caleb, my one, this is my vow to you.'*

Caleb blinked hard.

'Oh,' he said. 'That's the second time—and it gets me just as much as it did the first time. My turn: *My Jonathan. I have known love before. Friends, colleagues. Most importantly brother—and off-script, because Jon won't mind, Leo, by God, you know how important you are to me— but never before this love. This love is wrenching. Lovely. Scared. Careful. Proud. This love calms me. Excites me. Reassures me. Delights me. This love is everything. This love—my love—I will not and cannot be without. This love I give back to you—you will never be without it. Jonathan, this is my vow to you.'*

Sunshine, her breath caught somewhere in her chest, felt an acrid sting at the back of her nose. Tears. She was going to cry.

Because *she* wanted that kind of love. *Wanted* it. *So* much.

Leo had told her a month ago that he would not be her friend, that she would come to him. But she had been too scared. And now it was too late. Because Leo hadn't even spoken to her—had barely looked at her today. And she was *still* too scared.

She walked quickly towards the entrance, smiling, eyes full of tears. Four steps away. Three. Two. One—

Her arm was grabbed. She was spun around. And Leo was there. Unsmiling.

'What is it, Sunshine?' he asked. 'Did it hit you? Finally? That it's what you want?'

'I can't, Leo.'

'Enough! I've had *enough*, Sunshine. You damned well *can*. I'm lonely without you. I need you.'

Her heart ached, throbbed. But she shook her head.

He ignored the head-shake, took her hand, dragged her to the ladies' restroom.

'A restroom?' she asked. 'We're going to have this discussion in a restroom?'

'Oh, it's not just a restroom,' he said. 'It's a restroom with custom-made blue and green toilet paper.'

She stared at him. 'With…?' She whirled. Raced into one of the cubicles. Laughed.

He'd followed her in and she turned. 'Why?' she asked.

'Because I love you,' he said.

'What kind of juxtaposition is that? Toilet paper and love?' She could hear the breathiness in her voice. *Oh, God—oh, my God. Is this happening?*

'The toilet paper is a big deal, Sunshine. A *very* big deal. Because I said I'd never do it—and yet I did. People can do that, you know. Say they'll never do something and then do it. Like fall in love when they say they have no room in their hearts.'

'You s-said…you t-told me…you were not—*not*—besotted with me.'

'I'm *not* besotted with you. Besotted is for amateurs. I'm madly, crazily, violently in love with you. It's not the same thing. We're talking a massive abyss, no parachute.'

She swallowed. 'Leo, I—I…'

'Think about it,' he urged, stepping closer. 'You suck at making lists—I excel. Complementary.'

Impossible laughter. Choked off. 'Romantic,' she said.

'You do your best work at night, and so do I. So we're synchronised.'

'*Very* romantic.'

'You know stupid stuff and I want to hear it.'

She slapped a hand over her mouth, swallowing the giggle.

'You eat,' he said, starting to smile. 'I cook.'

'Hmm…'

'Getting closer, am I? Because I will cook for you morning, noon, and night—sending people all over Sydney into a state of shock! I will name a cut of meat after you. I will teach you to cook paella. I will invent a five-course degustation dessert menu just so I can watch you devour sugar.'

Half-laugh, half-tears. 'Oh, Leo.'

'I will play *"Je t'aime-ich liebe-ti amor You Darling"* in the bedroom.'

'You will not!' she said.

'That was a trick one. But you can *decorate* the bedroom. The bamboo is ordered, just in case you want a Balinese honeymoon suite, but you can do it any way you want. Perhaps go easy on the pink, though. And— Look, don't you *get* it? Do I really have to keep going?'

She was almost breathless. Staring. Hoping. Wanting this—him. 'What do I have to do in return?'

He grabbed her hand, flattened it against his heart. 'You get the easy bit. All you have to do is love me.'

She looked into his eyes. Knew that there still wasn't any room in her heart—because he'd taken up every bit of it.

'That's too easy. Because I already do love you.' Her eyes widened. 'Oh, my God, I said it. I love you. I've jumped. No parachute.'

He closed his eyes, took a deep breath. Opened them. So serious. 'I have a very particular kind of love in mind. I have to belong. To you. I have to *belong* to you, Sunshine.'

'I know,' she said. 'You want me to throw myself off the cliff. Sink into that damned abyss. Pour my soul into you and drown in you so that you are everything. Live for you, die for you. Too easy, I'm telling you!'

He let her hands go to pull her into his arms, kissed her mouth. 'And I want you to look at our beach and know that your sister is at peace, and that I am always with you to bear whatever grief you have.'

She was crying now, and he was wiping her tears with his thumbs.

'And children,' he said. 'I want a daughter named Amaya Moonbeam.'

More tears. 'Oh, Leo.'

'And a second daughter who can take on Allyn. And a son named whatever the hell you want. Only perhaps not Oaktree or Thunderbolt or Mountain.'

How could you laugh and cry at the same time? 'I can manage that.'

He kissed her again. 'And shoes. I want custom-made shoes. I'm not wearing any other kind from now on.'

'Well, that goes without saying.'

'And maybe a weekly haiku.'

'Um—no! We are *not* encouraging my mother in that.'

'Okay. But your parents get their own wing in the beach house, so they can be close to their daughters any time they want and teach me how to be the kind of parent who brings up wonderful kids.'

Crying hard. 'Leo!'

'And I still want you to change your name. But only your surname—to make you mine, Sunshine Quartermaine. With a ten-tier coconut vanilla bean wedding cake to seal the deal.'

Sunshine sighed and leant into him. Kissed him so hard his heart leapt. 'The medulla oblongata,' she said, rubbing her hand over his heart.

He felt the laugh building. 'The what?'

'The part of the brain that controls the heartbeat,' she said.

'God, I love you,' he said. 'So! Let's go and give the old medulla oblongata a real workout. Because what I really, really want right now, Sunshine, is assignation number five. And tomorrow morning we'll go for number six. And I— God, someone's coming in. What the *hell* are we doing in a restroom? Let's blow this joint.'

* * * * *

FALLING FOR
THE BRIDESMAID

SOPHIE PEMBROKE

For George and Karen,
for making this book possible through
coffee, childcare and cheerleading!
Thank you both, so much.

Sophie Pembroke has been reading and writing romance ever since she read her first Mills & Boon at university, so getting to write them for a living is a dream come true!

Sophie lives in a little Hertfordshire market town in the UK with her scientist husband and her incredibly imaginative five-year-old daughter. She writes stories about friends, family and falling in love, usually while drinking too much tea and eating homemade cakes. She also keeps a blog at www.SophiePembroke.com.

CHAPTER ONE

THE SWEET SMELL of rose petals filled the evening air, giving the falling dusk a sultry warmth. Music sang out from the band on the patio, romantic with just an undertone of sexy. Fairy lights twinkled in the branches of the trees and inside the marquees, and around them leaves rustled in the still warm breeze.

The whole set-up was so perfectly loved-up Violet thought she might be physically ill if she had to suffer through it a moment longer.

Glaring down at her lavender bridesmaid's dress, she slunk to the edge of the celebrations where she could watch the live band play in peace. She needed to make more of an effort to enjoy the evening, and maybe the music would help. Her parents' vow renewal ceremony had been beautiful, and the party that followed a huge success. Later, she had no doubt, her dad and the boys from The Screaming Lemons would take to the stage and wow the remaining guests all over again, even though they'd finished their official set an hour ago. Knowing Dad, it would probably be a lower key, acoustic set the second time around.

Keeping Dad off the stage was always more trouble than getting him on there, and he always wanted one more encore. But for now the support act seemed to be doing well enough. The courtyard in front of the stage was filled with people dancing, or just holding each other, or kissing. Falling in love.

Violet scowled and looked away.

Of course, the situation wasn't helped by her family. There, leaning against her new husband—Lord Sebastian Beresford, Earl of Holgate, if you please—was her youngest sister, Daisy. No, the Lady Holgate now. Hard to believe that Daisy-Waisy was an honest-to-God countess, but somehow not quite as impossible to process as the slight swell of her baby bump under her carefully chosen emerald-green bridesmaid's dress.

Just a few more months and Violet would officially be the maiden aunt of the family. Hell, she was already doing the church flowers most weekends, and taking tea with her mother's 'ladies who lunch' crowd. Maybe she should just skip straight ahead to adopting a three-legged cat and taking up crochet.

Actually, she'd quite like to learn to crochet, but that wasn't the point.

Seb rested his hand against his wife's stomach, and Daisy's soft smile grew into a fully fledged grin as she tilted her face for a kiss. Violet turned away, suddenly embarrassed to be staring.

But unfortunately her gaze just landed on Rose and Will, looking equally wrapped up in each other. Her twin sister and her best friend. Violet had to admit she really hadn't seen that one coming either. An attraction, perhaps, or maybe even a fling. Not that Will would give up his runaway groom status for good and marry into her family. But there Rose stood in her own wedding dress, after sneaking away for their own secret marriage ceremony once their parents' vow renewal service was over.

Maybe she just had no sort of love radar at all. Or maybe it was broken. That would explain a hell of a lot, really.

Will glanced up at just the wrong moment and, this time, Violet couldn't look away quick enough. Even staring pointedly at the band, she couldn't miss the whispered conversation between Rose and *her* new husband. Probably trying to decide whose responsibility Violet's hurt feelings were now.

Violet sighed. It wasn't that she wasn't happy for her sisters—she really, truly was. And she knew that their happiness shouldn't make her own sorry situation feel so much worse. But it did.

Swallowing, she looked down at her feet, and the high heels pinching her toes. It would pass, she knew. Any day now she'd be able to look at all the happy and loved-up people around her and just smile, without the bitter tinge that threatened to colour her whole world.

That day just wasn't yet, that was all.

'She thinks you're cross with her, you know. Or me, possibly,' Will said, standing beside her with his hands in his pockets. Such a familiar sight at these events. Usually Will's presence was a comfort, a reliable soul to help her through the amused looks, the only half-whispered comments, and the occasional drunken suggestion from guys she barely knew but who clearly thought they knew all about her—and her sexual proclivities.

Today, though, he was just a reminder that things wouldn't ever be the same again.

'Cross with Rose?' Violet asked, mustering up a smile. 'Why on earth would I be cross with her? For stealing you away from me? Good riddance, I say.'

The startled look on Will's face told her she'd misjudged something very badly.

'Uh, no. She thinks you're mad because you got landed with picking up that reporter guy from the airport tonight, so you're missing out on the good champagne. That or the whole Benefit Concert thing.'

Ah, that. Yeah, that would make more sense. Especially since she hadn't been completely silent about her unhappiness that the reporter was coming at all.

'I hadn't really…you think she stole me away from you?'

Violet gave him a withering stare. 'Yes, Will. I've been lusting after you, pining away for you through every one of your ridiculous engagements and runaway groom stunts. And now you've finally married my sister, I don't think I will ever recover.'

Her deadpan delivery apparently sold it because Will laughed with obvious relief. 'Good. That's…okay, then. And you're not mad about the reporter either?'

'I'm mad about the champagne. Otherwise, I'll cope.'

'You're sure? I know you're a little…'

Violet tried to guess the word he was avoiding saying. Nervous? Worried? Paranoid?

Probably paranoid.

'Apprehensive about him coming,' Will finished.

Violet sighed. Apprehensive wasn't the half of it. But her dad had made up his mind that he wanted to tell his story, have that official biography on the shelves, and he'd picked this guy to do it. Rose had looked at her with worried eyes when he'd announced it, but even she admitted it made sense to do it now, ahead of the new tour and album. The reporter guy would have exclusive access, in-depth interviews and enough connections to get a real buzz going in the media.

'Rose says he's nice,' Will tried. 'They met in New York before she came home.'

'I'm sure he's a doll,' Violet replied. It didn't matter who he was. He was press, and only interested in them as a story, as something he could sell.

Violet had learned that lesson the hard way.

Will frowned. 'Maybe if you talk to your dad…'

Shaking her head, Violet gave him a gentle smile. 'It's fine. I promise.' Dad had made up his mind and that was it. As always. Nothing Will, Daisy, Rose or Violet could do to change it. And so there was no point dwelling on it. She'd just stay out of his way as much as possible and hope for the best.

What else could she do?

'And about the Benefit Concert—' he started, but Violet cut him off.

'Go on, Will.' She pushed against his arm. 'Go whisk Rose away on your honeymoon. I'll take care of things here, I promise. Since you've apparently already texted the reporter guy my phone number, he's my responsibility now, and I think I can manage one airport pick-up. You two go relax for a bit. Get used to being married for once, instead of just temporarily engaged.'

'Okay. See you soon, kid.' With a quick hug and a peck on the cheek, he headed back towards Rose, and Violet was alone again.

As usual.

She hadn't exactly *lied* to Will, she decided. She had never thought of Will as husband material—or even one-night stand material. He was worth far more to her as a friend, and she'd never felt that spark, that flash of something more that hinted that they could be anything else.

It was just kind of weird that he obviously felt that flash with *Rose* of all people. Her so-identical-it-was-actually-spooky twin sister.

Although, really, she should be used to people seeing something in Rose that they never saw in her. After all, hadn't their parents made Rose stay home instead of going back to the States after Daisy's wedding, just so she could organise their vow renewal ceremony and party? Even though Violet had been right there, with time on her hands, happy to help?

Not that she was bitter. She knew why they hadn't asked—because they'd been sure she wouldn't want to do it. Wouldn't want to have to deal with so many people, so many knowing eyes.

And they were probably right.

Will hadn't thought about that as he'd told her where to find Rose's black planner, though, and asked her to make sure everything kept ticking over for the annual Huntingdon Hall Benefit Concert while they were away on their honeymoon. Maybe he'd just been too caught up in the flush of true love to think about it. Or maybe he expected her to hand it over to some agency person, hired to cover Rose's job.

Maybe she should. After all, she knew absolutely nothing about how to organise a concert for thousands of people. Will had insisted that Rose had already done all the hard work, that there'd be practically nothing left for Violet to do.

Because obviously otherwise they'd have found someone more competent to put in charge.

Violet shook her head. She was being ridiculous. She hadn't wanted to organise the vow renewal anyway. Or the Benefit Concert, come to that. She had other obligations. But now that Rose had told their dad she'd be stepping down from her job managing the PR and events for The Screaming Lemons once she got back from her honeymoon...well, someone would have to do it. And Violet couldn't ignore the very small part of her brain that thought that person could be her.

No. She had no experience, and no desire to deal with people who laughed at her behind her back all day long.

She'd just stick to things she knew she was good at. Like arranging flowers, thank you very much.

The flower displays she'd designed for the vow renewal were, she decided, by far her best displays yet. Lots of exotic blooms in deep jewel colours. Striking and memorable, just like her parents. Her flowers rocked, everyone said so.

There you had it. Twenty-seven years on the planet, and that was all she could say about herself.

Violet Huntingdon-Cross—kick-ass flower arranger, wannabe crocheter. Potential cat lady in waiting.

No, that wasn't all. That was just all that other people saw—and she was happy to keep it that way. She made a difference in the lives of young people and teenagers every day, even if no one ever knew it was her. After all, if word got around that Violet Huntingdon-Cross was manning the phones at the troubled teen helpline, their calls would skyrocket with people wanting to ask her about her own past, or just talk to a minor celebrity—and the kids she really wanted to help wouldn't be able to get through at all. So she helped where she could. Even if she wished she could do more.

Her parents did the same, helping out charities anonymously when they could. The only difference was, they also did enough charity work—as well as music and the occasional modelling gig respectively—in public that everyone assumed they already knew everything there was to know about Rick and Sherry Cross.

But with Violet…well, Violet could only imagine what they were *still* saying about her. Probably the nicest was that she'd become a recluse.

Still, that was a hell of a lot better than what they'd been saying about her eight years ago.

Pulling her phone from her tiny clutch bag, she checked the time and then double-checked the email Will had sent her from Rose's account with the reporter guy's flight details. Thomas Buckley…that was his name. She must make an effort not to just call him reporter guy all the time. Although it never hurt to have a reminder that the press were press and always on the record, whatever they said. Not something she ever wanted to forget again.

Time to go. She'd get changed out of her bridesmaid's dress, grab the ridiculous name card Rose had left for her and be at Heathrow in plenty of time to grab a coffee before his flight landed. And, best of all, she wouldn't be stuck in romance central another minute.

Moving towards the side door to Huntingdon Hall, Violet paused as she caught sight of her parents, dancing in the light of the just risen moon. So wrapped up in each other that the couple of hundred people watching, who'd come all this way to celebrate with them, might not even be there at all. Sherry Huntingdon and Rick Cross were famously crazy about each other, but it wasn't until Violet caught them in moments like this that she really believed the media hype.

And that, she finally admitted to herself, was the real reason all this love stuff was getting to her. Deep down, she'd always believed that she'd just fall into a perfect relationship like her parents had, like both her sisters had now found too.

Instead, she'd got something else entirely. Like anti-love. The sort of relationship that tore up your insides and made you someone else. After that, if she was honest, Violet wasn't sure she'd ever have the courage to try again.

Her phone rang in her hand and Violet answered it automatically, glad for the distraction. 'Hello?'

'I was under the impression that you, whoever you are, were supposed to be meeting me at the airport about twenty minutes ago.' The American drawl made Violet's eyes widen. The reporter guy. Except Rose's email had him landing in an hour and a half. Dammit!

'I'm so sorry, Mr...' Oh, God, what was his name?

'Buckley.' He bit the surname out. 'And I could care less about apologies. Just get here, will you? I'll be in the bar.'

And, with that, the line went dead.

Picking up her skirt, Violet dashed for the garage and prayed no one had blocked her car in. She'd have to borrow one of her dad's if they had. No time to change now, or even pick up that specially made name card of Rose's. If she ever wanted to be relied on for more than flowers, she needed to not screw this up. And since the bad impression she—and by extension her family—had made on the reporter guy was already done, she needed to find a way to fix it. Starting with getting to Heathrow as fast as humanly possible, *before* he started drafting his story. She knew journalists. The truth seldom got in the way of a good story, and once they thought they knew all about a person it was almost impossible to convince them otherwise.

And Violet had already earned the Huntingdon-Cross family enough bad press to last a lifetime.

CHAPTER TWO

TOM PUSHED HIS way to the counter, dragging his suitcase behind him like a weapon. A coffee shop. What the hell kind of use to him was that, especially at this time of night? He needed a drink—a proper one. But that was arrivals for you—never as good as the departures lounge. After so many years travelling the world, you'd think he'd remember that. Except he was usually being collected straight off a plane these days, and got whisked through arrivals to some hotel or another without even clocking his surroundings.

He'd just have to hope that whoever the ditsy woman Rose had assigned to pick him up was would check her phone and see his text telling her to meet him here instead.

Staring at the menu above the counter with bleary eyes, Tom tried to figure out his best option. He'd already consumed so much caffeine in the last two weeks that his muscles appeared to be permanently twitching. Add that to the distinct lack of sleep, and he wasn't sure another shot of the black stuff was quite what he needed. Of course, what he *needed* was a big bed with cool sheets, a blackout blind and about twenty-four hours' solid rest.

None of which was a remote possibility until his ride pitched up.

Ordering a decaf something-or-other, Tom tossed his

jacket and laptop into the nearest bucket chair and hovered impatiently between it and the counter while he waited for his drink. If he'd flown first class, or even business, he could have had as many free drinks as he liked on the plane. But old habits died hard and, since this job was entirely on spec and therefore on his own dime, he'd been paying for his own flight. Something inside him still baulked at shelling out that much cash just for a better seat, even though money wasn't really an object any more. Certainly not the way it had been growing up.

His music journalism career had taken off enough in the past few years that he could rely on his contacts for a good life and a better income. He'd come a long way from his first big, explosive story, almost ten years ago.

So yeah, he could have afforded the upgrade, easily, and without tapping those savings. And if he'd remembered about the free booze aspect of things, he probably would have done. As it was…

Snatching his coffee from the girl behind the counter, he settled at his table and prepared to hang around a while. God only knew how long it would take his ride to get there from wherever she was, but he might as well get some work done while he waited. Even if he felt as if his eyes might jump right out of his head if he didn't close them soon.

At least the work was worth travelling all the way from New York for. A story like this, a break this big…it could make him, permanently. He'd be the go-to person for anything to do with The Screaming Lemons, and that was serious currency in the industry. It would give him access, and opportunities with the newer bands coming through. He'd have the pick of jobs.

He'd already made a pretty good name for himself with the bigger music magazines, websites and even the colour supplements. But this trip, these interviews, this was something more—it was a book in the making. That was what Rick Cross had promised him. And Tom was going to make sure the old man made good on his word.

He was annoyed to have missed all the upheaval in the Huntingdon-Cross family over the past two months, but it couldn't be helped. He'd already been committed to another project at home in the States and, anyway, who could have predicted that one of Rick and Sherry's famously blonde and beautiful daughters would get married and knocked up all within the space of eight weeks? And who knew what was going on with Rose now? She'd been in the press recently herself, he remembered, pictured with the famous Runaway Groom—who he'd *thought* was famously her sister *Violet's* best friend. Maybe something had happened there—and he'd missed it, again. All *he'd* had was a text message when he turned his phone back on after the flight, with a contact number and the information that, due to unforeseen but brilliant circumstances, someone else would be collecting him.

Or not, as the case might be.

Tom sighed. He'd just have to make sure he got good interviews with them all when he could. And, wherever Rose might be, at least one daughter was still living at home—probably the most famous one, if you counted notorious Internet celebrity, which Tom did.

Opening his laptop, he pulled up his notes on the family. He was staying at the family home, Huntingdon Hall, so he needed to be prepared from the get-go. He'd spent weeks compiling old interviews, articles and photos of the whole family, and felt he had it pretty much down. And after speaking with Rose in New York and on the phone while planning the trip, he'd thought he had at least one ally there—until she'd decided to swan off and abandon him with no notice.

Presumably she'd got an offer too good to refuse, no matter how much it inconvenienced anyone else. Celebrity kids—always the centre of their own world, however nice and normal Rose had seemed when they met. He needed to remember that.

He'd only had one conversation with the man he was really there to see, though—Rick Cross himself. Rock star, family man, reformed wide boy. The interviews Tom had on file dated back almost thirty years, back to when The Screaming Lemons were the next big thing on the rock scene. Nowadays, they were the old standards—and they had to try harder to shock or surprise.

With his plans for a tell-all book about the band and his family's history, it looked as if Rick had plans to do both.

Tom had asked him, 'Why now?' It couldn't be money— the band still sold enough greatest hits records and got more than enough airplay that it didn't matter if their latest album tanked. But all Rick would say was that it was time.

Scrolling through his family crib sheet, Tom reminded himself of all the most pertinent facts.

Most people in Britain and the States could pick Rick Cross out of a line-up and tell you his story. Same for his wife, the beautiful and rich mostly ex-model and now English society stalwart, Sherry Huntingdon. With his fame and her family, they made quite the impact.

Then there were the girls. The youngest, Daisy, was the newest Lady Holgate, which seemed pretty much par for the course for celebrity kids, Tom decided. After all, if you already had money and fame, surely a title was the only thing left to go for? Especially in the UK.

The twins were a few years older at twenty-seven. Rose, he knew from personal meetings with her, had been living in New York for the last few years, although she had planned to be in England until the annual benefit concert at least.

And then there was Violet. Tom had enjoyed the hell out of researching her. The thought made him smile even as he rubbed at his gritty eyes.

A commotion at the counter made him look up, and he blinked at the sight of a tall blonde in a ridiculous dress and heels crashing past a table full of customers. Was that Rose? Or a sleep deprivation induced hallucination?

'Sorry!' the blonde yelped, and he decided that she was probably real. Hallucinations didn't usually yelp, in his experience.

Shaking his head to try and wake up, Tom packed up his laptop. It looked as if his ride had made it after all. Any time now he could fall into that nice, peaceful, quiet bed and sleep for a week. Or at least until Rick Cross summoned him for his first interview.

From all the reports he'd read, Tom was pretty sure Rick wasn't an early riser. That lie-in was practically in the bag.

'Rose,' he said, hoisting his bag onto his shoulder and reaching for the handle of his suitcase. 'I thought you were going away? You didn't have to come all the way out here just because the idiot you asked to pick me up forgot. I could have just caught a cab, you know.'

Rose looked up, eyes wide, her hands still gripping her skirt. 'Oh, um, no, it's fine. Thomas. It's fine, Thomas.'

Why did she keep repeating his name? And why was she calling him *Thomas* instead of Tom all of a sudden? They'd spoken plenty of times before, and even had lunch once. It wasn't as if she might have forgotten it all of a sudden.

Unless…

The smirk formed unbidden on his lips. 'I'm sorry, *Violet*. I thought you were your sister for a moment. And it's Tom.'

'That's okay. You're not the only one to get confused.' She pulled a frustrated face, and Thomas couldn't help but laugh. It was just so *familiar*. And not from Rose.

'What?' Violet asked, obviously startled by his outburst. Maybe he should have had caffeinated coffee. Obviously the sleep deprivation was starting to affect him.

'I'm sorry,' he managed, trying to keep his smirk in check. 'But for a moment you looked just like you did in the—' Self-preservation kicked in as her face turned stony and he cut himself off.

'No, really. Do continue.' Her cut glass accent was sharp enough to wound, and any humour Tom had found in the situation ebbed away. 'I believe you were about to finish that sentence with the words "leaked sex tape", right?'

'I'm sorry,' Tom started, realising he'd apologised to this woman more in the first three minutes of meeting her than he'd normally need to in even a month of *dating* someone. But Violet interrupted before he could get to the part about sleep deprivation and inadequate impulse control.

'That's right,' she said, a little louder than Tom thought was strictly necessary. 'I'm the famous Huntingdon-Cross Sex Tape Twin. Not one of the two sisters who found true love and settled down. The one who men only want so they can film us together and put it on the Internet. Get your autographs here.'

The café was almost empty, but a couple of guys sitting at the table nearest the front definitely had their camera phones out. What kind of audacity did it take to stand up in public and admit to being the star of a ridiculously explicit sex tape watched by half the world? The sort only the rich and famous had.

'And apparently, according to the frustrated and annoyed look on my face, it can't even have been good sex. Personally, I don't remember, but Mr Buckley here has obviously watched it often enough to be considered an expert. Do feel free to ask him questions, if you like. I'm not in a hurry. I mean, I'm only missing my parents' marriage renewal ceremony to be here. Carry on.'

Waving an imperious hand towards him, Violet perched on the edge of a stool by the counter and waited. Feeling the heat of embarrassment in his cheeks, Tom grabbed the last of his things from the table and headed for the exit. Violet Huntingdon-Cross might be used to this sort of exposure, but he certainly wasn't.

'No questions? Oh, what a shame. I suppose we'd better be on our way, then.' Violet hopped down and followed him out into the arrivals hall.

'I suppose I deserved that,' he muttered as she held the door of the terminal open for him. He had laughed first. But she'd been over an hour and a half late to collect him. So the sleep deprivation was at least partly her fault, right?

'I suppose you did,' she replied. 'And I'm very sorry for being late to collect you. Rose gave me the wrong flight times.'

Damn. There went that argument.

'This is where you apologise to me for humiliating me in front of a crowd of people,' Violet prompted, and Tom raised his eyebrows.

'Me? Trust me, sweetheart, you did the humiliating all by yourself.' As if a performance of that sort was second nature to her. Which, judging by the sex tape, it might well be. He'd heard that Violet had calmed down in more recent years, but maybe the family had just got better at hiding her exploits from the media.

Her whole face flushed bright red at his words, and she pushed past him as they left the terminal. 'I'm parked in the short stay car park,' she called back over his shoulder.

He was pretty sure he wasn't supposed to hear her muttered words as she strode off towards the car, but he did. 'Hopefully not as short as your stay with us, though.'

Tom allowed himself a smile. Violet Huntingdon-Cross was definitely a worthy interview subject. And if he could get some new or hidden scandals on the eldest family wild child to help sell his book proposal, well, he'd be an idiot not to. Right?

CHAPTER THREE

VIOLET'S HANDS WERE still shaking as she tried to get the key into the ignition. At the back of the car, Tom was struggling to open the boot for his cases, but she had no intention of helping. Not least because the way her body was trembling meant she'd probably be even worse at it than him.

What on earth had possessed her? Eight years of best behaviour, of keeping her head down, of politely ignoring all the comments and jokes—all gone in one moment of frustration and humiliation in an airport coffee shop.

It had been his laugh, she decided, as the key finally slid home. It had made it so abundantly clear that she wasn't a real person to him, just a hilarious anecdote. One she had probably now ensured he would be dining out on for all time.

She was used to being seen as a public figure more than herself. She was always Rick and Sherry's daughter first, and often Rose or Daisy's sister before she was ever a person in her own right. Except when she was the Sex Tape Twin. And, quite honestly, she'd rather be nobody than *that*.

Except that was all she ever seemed to be to anyone outside her own family. And God, was she sick of it.

The car boot slammed shut; Tom must have managed to stow his cases away. Any moment now he'd slide into

SOPHIE PEMBROKE 25

the passenger seat beside her and they'd have to make polite conversation all the way home. That, or sit in frosty
silence. Violet wasn't sure which would be worse.

She sighed. Yes, she was. Silence would be worse. Because only her dad had any idea how long Thomas Buckley
would be staying at their house, and she couldn't simply
send him to Coventry indefinitely. This wasn't boarding
school; it was real life. And somehow that had turned out
to be even more confining and stifling than the strict Cath-
olic school they'd all been sent to.

She was a grown-up now. The mistakes of her youth
were *supposed* to be in the past. She was more than the
stories people told about her. Which meant sucking it up
and making nice with the offensive American music journalist who would be writing some sort of tell-all about her
family and their life any time now. And hoping he'd forget
what a disaster this whole night had been.

It was like her dad had said, back when That Tape had
first hit the internet and suddenly her sex face was splashed
all over magazines and newspapers everywhere. He'd left
the rest of the band in some hotel somewhere, mid-tour,
and come home to check on her. While she'd lain sobbing
on her bed, he'd rubbed her back and told her, 'At least you
know now, honey. Not everyone out there wants what's best
for you. And only you can decide who to trust.'

Well. There was an easy answer to that one, Violet had
found. Don't trust anyone—except family.

Will had been an exception to the rule, and a hard-won
one at that. But it helped that he'd only ever been friend
material. She wouldn't trust even her best friend with her
whole heart. Not like Rose had done.

The passenger door opened and Violet sucked in a
breath before plastering on a smile. 'All okay?'

Tom gave her a slightly wary look, as if uncertain

whether she might just drive off with him half in and half out of the car. She couldn't really blame him; she hadn't been exactly consistent since they'd met.

Time to start mending fences before he started writing articles.

'Fine.' Tom slid into the seat beside her. 'And, uh, you?'

She forced her smile to brighten further. 'Just dandy.'

'Right. And are you always prone to such extreme mood swings?'

Oh, God, he was probably thinking that she was on drugs, or bipolar, or something else that would make a good story. This was *not* going well.

Violet sighed. Time to try honesty. 'Okay, look. We got off to a rotten start here, I know. But Dad wants you staying with us, working with him, and Dad doesn't change his mind once it's made up. So I just have to suck it up and get on with things, right? And since I don't particularly want to spend the next however many weeks avoiding you or trading insults on sight, I figure the easiest thing is to pretend the last half an hour didn't happen. Okay?' Partial honesty, anyway. She didn't need to mention—

'Plus you don't want me to tell the story of this evening in any future articles or books?'

Damn. 'Well, do you blame me?'

Tom was quiet so long that she had to glance over to check that he hadn't fallen asleep. When she looked, he was holding out his hand.

Eyebrows raised, she took it, biting her lip at the slight tingle she felt at his skin against hers. For heaven's sake, it was a handshake! Had it really been so long since someone she wasn't related to by blood or marriage had touched her that her body had forgotten what it felt like?

'I'm Tom Buckley,' he said with a half smile. 'Nice to meet you. Thanks for coming to pick me up.'

'Violet Huntingdon-Cross. Sorry I was an hour and a half late.'

He chuckled. 'Let's just blame Rose for everything, yeah?'

'That's what I've been trying to do for the last twenty-seven years,' Violet said, and sighed. 'Sadly, it never seems to stick.'

At Tom's laugh, she slipped the car into gear and pulled out of the parking space. 'Come on. Let's get you home. I bet you're tired after your long journey.'

'Exhausted,' Tom admitted, and when she looked she could see the dark circles under his eyes, even in the poor lighting of the airport car park. 'That's kind of my excuse, actually. For, well, everything. Sleep deprivation. It's been a hell of a week.'

'I'm sure. Rose said you were working out in Miami?'

He nodded. 'For the last week. Then a flying visit home to New York to repack my bags, then straight here. I feel like I haven't slept in a month. I'm looking forward to some peace and quiet, actually. Your dad told me that Huntingdon Hall is out in the middle of nowhere, right?'

'Ye—es,' Violet said, biting her lip as she remembered the party she'd left just a couple of hours before. It was long gone midnight. Surely everyone would have gone home by the time they arrived, right? Oh, who was she kidding? Rick and Sherry's parties were legendary. They'd be lucky if they didn't find anyone passed out on the tennis court in the morning, this time.

'That sounds ominous,' Tom said. 'Do they have guests? Wait…' Glancing over, she saw him frown, the moment it clicked into place for him. 'Oh, hell. It's their vow renewal today, right? You said you were missing it… That's why you were so annoyed about having to come and fetch me?'

'And why I'm wearing this fetching yet inappropriate

dress,' Violet confirmed. No need for him to know that, actually, she'd been happy to get out of there. 'I'm afraid there's a very real chance the party might still be ongoing.' She glanced at the dashboard clock. 'In fact, I think Dad and the boys will probably be taking the stage for their encore session right about now.'

Tom groaned and let his head fall back against the headrest. 'So, no sleep tonight is what you're telling me.'

'Basically. Sorry! Maybe you can get some sleep in the car?' She should feel worse about this. The guy was obviously exhausted to the point of losing all social niceties. She should feel bad that her parents and their friends were going to keep him up for *another* night.

She really, really didn't, though.

It seemed to Tom that no sooner had he closed his eyes than a car door was slamming, then another opening, and cool night air flooded over his face. Followed swiftly by his ears being assaulted by one of The Screaming Lemons' classic hits being played as an acoustic number.

Normally, he'd be up at the front of the stage, soaking in the moment, tucking the memories away for future articles, trying to find the right words to describe the perfection of that three and a half minutes.

Tonight—or rather this morning—he just wanted it all to go away. Including Violet Huntingdon-Cross.

'Wake up, Sleeping Beauty,' she said, in a voice far too jolly for someone who had recently glared at him with such loathing. 'You're missing the party.'

He cracked open one eyelid and waited for the yellow blur of her hair, the pale fuzz of her face and the purple blotch that was her dress to come into focus. Then he blinked; she was closer than he'd thought, and suddenly the only things in focus at all were her bright blue eyes, peering down at him.

'Oh, good,' she said, straightening up. 'I thought for a moment I was going to have to leave you here for the night. That or get someone to come carry you to bed. That sort of thing never makes a terribly good first impression, you know.'

Unlike, for instance, pointing out a woman's sex tape history within five minutes of meeting her. God, when he woke up properly he was going to have to work at getting Violet back onside. As the only daughter living at home, he had a feeling she could make life difficult for him if she wanted.

And he rather suspected she might more than want to. It might actually be her burning life ambition at this point.

'I'm awake,' he half lied, forcing himself to straighten up. Another couple of moments and he might even make it out of the car.

Violet grabbed his hand and, even through his sleep fog, he couldn't help but be aware of the feel of her smooth, cool skin, or the way something indefinable crept up his arm at her touch. Something that seemed to crackle with possibilities.

Something that woke him up completely.

Blinking again, he twisted round to get his feet firmly on the ground and stood up, belatedly aware that he was still gripping onto Violet's hand, probably rather tighter than she'd like.

He dropped it fast, but her blue, blue eyes were still fixed on his and the puzzled crease between her eyebrows told him that whatever he'd felt, she'd felt it too.

At least he had the excuse of sleep deprivation. What justification was she using?

Violet shook her head and stepped back, nicely out of

his personal space. 'I know you're exhausted. But given that sleep is likely to be impossible for the next couple of hours at least, and since you *are* here to observe and interview and write about the band… Why don't you come and meet Dad?'

Dad. Even after an hour in the company of one of the most famous celebrity kids in the world, it still felt strange to hear her refer to the infamous Rick Cross as 'Dad'. How different a world must Violet live in to the real one he inhabited, to so casually be able to think of Huntingdon Hall as home, and one of the most recognisable couples ever as Mum and Dad?

Different, certainly, to the kid from New York who never even knew who his father was, only that he wouldn't have done him any good in life if he'd stuck around anyway. The kid whose mother had so disapproved of the method he'd used to get out of the gutter, she hadn't spoken to him for three years before her death.

Yeah, there were worlds between him and Violet. And however long he stayed at Huntingdon Hall, he had to remember that.

'Isn't he still playing?' Tom said, hoping it wasn't painfully obvious he was stalling. Rick had seemed sharp on the phone, the sort to see through people's masks. He wanted to be on top form when he sat down with Rick for the first time.

Violet tilted her head to the left, listening to the music, he presumed. 'This is usually his last number. He'll be off stage soon and still on that performance high. It's a good time to meet him if you want him to like you.'

'And do *you* want him to like me?' Tom asked. It seemed strange that she would, given everything.

A look of annoyance flashed across Violet's face, as if

she weren't used to being asked this many questions about her motives and feelings. Maybe she wasn't. 'Yes.'

Tom couldn't resist. 'Why?'

'Does it matter?' Violet tossed her hair back over her shoulder as the last chord rang out from the stage. 'We're going to miss him.'

'You haven't answered my question.' Tom folded his arms, leant back against the car and waited.

With an impatient huff, Violet grabbed his hand and started dragging him towards the stage. Tom didn't budge until she started talking.

'Because Dad makes up his mind about people and things in an instant, and that's it. You're here; you're going to be writing about him and us. If he likes you, he'll show you his best side, the stuff *I* want you to be writing about. If he takes a dislike to you…'

'Things could get messy?' Tom guessed.

Violet sighed as they reached the edge of the stage area. Even though the party was obviously filled with friends and family, the cheering as the band came off stage was still as loud as Tom had heard in any stadium.

'Let's just say this whole experience will be a lot less fun. For all of us.'

Suddenly, the familiar craggy face of Rick Cross appeared at the top of the stage steps, mouth open and laughing at something his band mate was saying behind him.

'Showtime,' Tom whispered, and Violet flashed him a quick grin—the first honest smile he'd seen from her.

Tom took a breath. Time to meet the parents.

CHAPTER FOUR

VIOLET HID A grin at the slightly shell-shocked look on Tom's face as Dad and the boys traipsed down the temporary stairs at the side of the stage set, all laughing, chatting and still clearly caught up in their own world—a world that consisted of music, noise and melodies.

She knew the kind of impact they could have, just off stage. When she was younger, just old enough to be allowed to stay up to watch the occasional gig from the wings, she and Rose had found it hard to understand this part—when Dad wasn't Dad, just for a moment. He was all Rick Cross, rock star, right now. And that was a sight to behold.

The adrenaline would wear off soon enough, Violet knew. He'd come down, hug his wife, ask for a drink, and before too long he'd be heading to bed to sleep it off. Well, maybe after a little more time with his closest friends—drinking and talking and probably singing.

Right now, in this moment, he was exactly who Tom Buckley had come here to interview. She hadn't lied when she said that this was the best time for Tom to make a good impression with her father. But it was also the best time to remind Tom that this wasn't just *anybody* he'd come here to write about.

The press could publish all the stories they liked about

her and her sisters—and heaven knew they would. But they couldn't touch her parents. Rick and Sherry were rock royalty, beyond reproach. There were no affairs, no addictions, no mistakes made—nothing to latch on to and use to make their lives hell. It might have been different back in the day, but not any more.

Now they were national treasures, and Violet was unbearably proud of them for it.

'Mr Cross.' Stepping forward, Tom stuck out his hand, smiling warmly. Violet had to give him credit—if he hadn't been slumped over in her passenger seat for the last forty-five minutes, she'd never have known he was utterly exhausted. He looked professional, ready to do a great job.

She just hoped that Dad's idea of a good job and Tom's meshed.

'Mr Buckley, I presume!' Rick's famous smile spread across his face. 'Great to have you here.' He shook Tom's hand with what looked like painful enthusiasm. 'Boys, this is the guy I've invited over to write our musical life story.'

'And your family's,' Tom put in. Violet rolled her eyes. As if any of them would forget that he was here to expose all their private lives as well as their public personas.

'Oh, he's here for the dirt, Rick.' Jez—Uncle Jez to the girls—the band's lead guitarist and Rick's best man, elbowed his friend in the ribs. 'Time to hide those skeletons in better closets!'

Rick laughed, his head tipped back in pure amusement and joy. Violet bit the inside of her cheek and just prayed there wasn't anything hidden there that she didn't know about. She couldn't imagine how there could be, given how closely she'd been involved in her parents' lives and work since she'd moved back home eight years ago.

But you could never be too careful when it came to the

press. And if Dad had any secrets, Uncle Jez would be the one to know them.

'Trust me, I'm just here to write the best, most honest story I can for your legion of fans. They're only interested in the truth.' Unlike Tom, presumably.

'And that's just what you'll get.' Rick clapped a hand on Tom's back, and Violet knew the reporter had passed some test that no one but her father would ever understand. 'The complete unvarnished truth, ready to be written down for posterity.'

Relief warred with apprehension inside her, and Violet clenched her fists so tightly her nails bit into the palms of her hands. On the one hand, the fact that her dad liked Tom would make the interviews go more smoothly, reducing the chances of a story about a recalcitrant, difficult star. On the other, it opened up the opportunity that Rick would get *too* close to Tom. As much as he talked about the unvarnished truth, surely her father realised there were some parts of their family lives, and history, that none of them wanted shared with the world. For the umpteenth time in some cases.

Well, there was nothing for it now but to see how things went. And try and keep tabs on both Tom and Rick, so she could try and head off any prospective trouble *before* it turned up in the papers this time.

'Darlings, you were brilliant as always.' Sherry floated up to them, kissing each of the band members on the cheek before planting a rather more thorough kiss on her husband. Tom, Violet noticed, was politely staring at the floor. Everyone else was too used to it to even bother.

'Mum, this is Tom Buckley,' Violet said once the public display of affection was over. Might as well get all the introductions over in one go. 'He's the writer Dad—'

'The writer who's going to tell our little story! Of

course.' Sherry held out a hand, although whether she intended it to be kissed or shaken Violet wasn't sure.

Tom went for the handshake. Not fully charmed yet, then. Mum might have her work cut out with this one. Obviously he wasn't taken in by her disingenuous description of his subject matter. Nobody in the world would describe the history of The Screaming Lemons and the Huntingdon-Cross family a 'little story'. Least of all anyone who had lived it.

'It's a pleasure to meet you, Mrs Huntingdon-Cross,' Tom said, releasing her hand.

'Oh, call me Sherry, please.' Mum flashed that legendary wide smile, the one that had been seen in magazines and on billboards for decades now. 'Anyone who stays here at Huntingdon Hall rather automatically becomes part of the family, I'm afraid. You might as well get used to it!'

Tom Buckley, part of the family? Not on Violet's watch.

But that was the problem with her parents. It wasn't that they were overly trusting or naïve, particularly. They knew the dangers of fame as well as anyone, and took care to live their lives circumspectly. But once they'd taken someone in and claimed them as a friend…it took a lot to shake their faith in them. And that could be dangerous.

'Where's Daisy?' Violet asked. She needed backup here and, with Rose and Will already gone on their honeymoon, Daisy-Waisy was going to have to be it.

'Oh, she and Seb have already turned in, I think,' Sherry said with a dismissive wave of her hand. 'Daisy was exhausted, poor thing—pregnancy is extraordinarily tiring, you know,' she added as an aside to Tom, who nodded, despite the puzzled crease between his eyebrows. 'And I think Seb wants to get off back to Hawkesley first thing.'

Curses. With Tom about to collapse from sleep deprivation, the chances weren't good that he'd be up in time to meet Daisy before she left. Which meant Violet was on her own trying to keep this whole project from blowing up in their faces. Lovely.

'And Rose has already left?' Tom asked politely. 'I met her in New York last month, and I know she'd planned to be here right through until the concert…' He left the sentence open. Not actually a question, so not really prying, but enough that politeness insisted that someone fill the gap. Tricky.

'Oh, yes,' Sherry said, beaming. 'She and Will left on their honeymoon a couple of hours ago.'

Tom's eyebrows inched up towards his hairline, and Violet winced. 'Honeymoon?' he asked. 'I didn't realise that she was planning a wedding.'

Or that she was even dating anyone, just like the rest of them. In fact, Violet was willing to bet that what Tom really meant was: *Two daughters married in a suspiciously short space of time, and one of them pregnant…there has to be a story here.* Especially if he'd seen the photos of Will and Rose in the papers.

Time to put a stop to that.

'Oh, yes,' she said, smiling cheerily. 'Will has practically been a part of the family for years now. We're delighted that they've made it official.' All true—Will *was* part of the family—certainly more than Tom Buckley ever would be. And why did he need to know that up until the last month or so, Will had only been there as Violet's best friend? And if he never realised that Will and Rose hadn't met until Daisy's wedding…well, that would be great. She just hoped that Tom Buckley didn't keep up with the UK celebrity gossip too closely.

Rick slung an arm around Tom's shoulders as the rest of the band wandered off in search of a drink or a bed. He had to reach up quite a bit to do it, Violet realised.

'That's the only downside of having daughters, you know,' Rick said, grinning at Violet. 'Having to give them away to unworthy men.'

'Oh, hush,' Sherry said. 'You know you adore Will. And Seb is going to be a wonderful son-in-law.'

'True. I have lucked out.' Rick turned his wicked grin onto Violet, and she felt her stomach clench at what he might come out with next. The inability to keep his inappropriate comments to himself was definitely a downside to the post-performance adrenaline. 'Makes me worry who Violet might decide to bring home. I can't possibly get that lucky three times in a row.'

Heat flooded Violet's cheeks. She'd spent more time blushing in front of Tom Buckley than actually talking to him at this point, she was sure.

'*Not* something you need to be worrying about, Dad.' Or be talking about in front of reporters.

Rick's face turned a little sad. 'No, I suppose not.'

'Anyway, Rose will be back soon enough, and you'll be able to catch up with her then,' Violet said with forced jollity. Tom gave her a look that left her in no doubt he knew exactly what she was doing—steering the conversation away from anything interesting. Violet made a mental note to warn Rose that it might look better if her whirlwind romance with Will hadn't been quite so…whirlwind-like. Rose would understand. Once she got home, everything would be so much easier.

'Actually, darling,' Sherry said, her smile just a little too wide, 'I spoke to Will as they were leaving. I understand they're going to be away for four weeks.'

Four weeks. Suddenly, with Tom Buckley standing there, it seemed longer than ever. Just when she really needed her twin at home with her. What had Will been thinking? Not about his best friend, stuck at home with the man who wanted to ferret out all her secrets. No, he'd been thinking about getting her twin sister naked for longer.

Damn men and their inability to think about more than one thing at once.

'That's right,' she said, forcing a smile. 'Although I couldn't get him to say where they were going.'

'Me neither,' Rick said. 'Will said he couldn't risk it. You know your mum would have texted Rose on the way to the airport and ruined the surprise.'

'Anyway. They won't be back until two days before the Benefit Concert, but Will said he'd left Rose's notes with you.' Mum had her 'tiptoeing' voice on. As if she was taking the long way round getting to the point.

'Yeah, it's all in Rose's study, apparently. Her black planner and all the files and contracts and stuff.'

'And…Will mentioned that you'd agreed to, well, keep an eye on things while they were away.' Ah, that was what Mum was working up to. Of course. Concern that Violet had agreed to something that, when it came down to it, she wouldn't be able to, or want to do.

Well, maybe it was time for her to prove her parents— and Tom Buckley—wrong. If Rose could organise a benefit concert, so could she.

'That's right.' And she'd do it too. But she really didn't want to get into this with Tom standing right there. Then again, there wasn't a chance of her getting any sleep tonight if they didn't agree a plan for the concert. The last thing they needed was the annual benefit being an utter disaster zone because Rose wasn't there, the one year they had a reporter on site recording all the behind the scenes activity for posterity.

Damn it! How could Will and Rose do this? Clearly, love had driven them crazy. It was the only explanation.

'You're looking worried, honey.' Her dad wrapped an

arm around her waist and hauled her close for a hug. 'But there's nothing to fret about. Rose has been running this thing like clockwork for years. The set-up's all done; everything's been booked for months.'

Violet turned her head to raise her eyebrows at her father. If everything was already sorted, then why was Rose always running around like a mad thing in the last few weeks before the concert every other year?

'Maybe your dad is being a little optimistic,' Sherry said. 'But really, darling, everything is in hand. All that's left is the fiddly last-minute stuff. And I'm sure we can find someone to handle that, if you don't want to. Rose and Will would understand. I'll call up an agency or something.'

Agency staff. Another stranger in their home all the time, taking responsibility for the biggest concert in The Screaming Lemons' calendar. Someone who had absolutely no reason to care if things went perfectly or just well enough to get paid.

Violet risked a glance at Tom. She could almost read the story writing itself behind his tired eyes. Thoughtless wild child celebrity daughter disappears on eve of major charity event after whirlwind romance, leaving benefit concert in chaos. Sex Tape Twin decides she'd rather pick flowers than take on the job.

Almost as bad a start as her scene in the coffee shop.

'No. I can do it. We don't need to call the agency. I'll take care of the concert. I've seen Rose do it, and I'm sure she's left really good notes. I can do it. I'd like to.'

A complete lie. The last thing she wanted to do, when she should be keeping an eye on Tom, was take on a high profile project that would put her in the public eye and require speaking to all the people she'd been happily avoiding for eight years. But sometimes proving a point—especially to someone like Tom Buckley—required sacrifice.

'Are you sure, darling?' Her mother's perfect face crinkled up into a frown. 'It doesn't really seem like...well, like your sort of thing.'

Of course it didn't. As much as she might have moaned about her parents calling Rose in to organise their wedding, she knew exactly why they'd done it. To spare Violet the misery of having to brave the public and the publicity again. It was bad enough doing so as a guest at endless charity functions, or just appearing at the benefit concert. Anywhere there were cameras, her nerves started to tremble. And this...this would mean liaising with pop stars, working with celebrities.

There were going to be a *lot* of cameras. Her fingers felt shaky just thinking about it.

'I'm sure,' she said as firmly as she could. 'The Benefit Concert is important. I want to make sure everything goes just as well as it would if Rose was here.'

Maybe she could just pretend to be Rose. Maybe no one would notice that she was actually the *other* twin. You know the one.

'Well, honey, if you're sure.' Rick's forehead had matching creases. Then he broke into a smile and clapped Tom on the back. 'Hey, maybe Tom here can give you a hand!'

CHAPTER FIVE

TOM COULDN'T BE sure if it was the sleep deprivation or if he really was missing something in the conversation going on around him. It felt as if there were actually two discussions taking place—one with words and one entirely conducted through concerned eyebrow gestures.

Still, he was pretty sure he didn't stand a chance of understanding the eyebrow conversation until he got some actual sleep. In fact, he was just plotting the best way to get shown to his room when Rick volunteered him.

'Me?' Tom wished that had come out slightly less squeakily. 'Help with the Benefit Concert?'

Sherry clapped her hands together. 'What a brilliant idea! I knew I married you for a reason.' She planted another kiss on her husband.

Violet, Tom noticed, hadn't responded at all. In fact, she looked as though she'd been sent into a state of severe shock and might need therapy to even deal with the idea.

God, he just had the best way with women, didn't he?

'Unless...Violet, darling, are you sure you really want to do this?' Sherry's eyebrows were doing the very concerned thing again, mirrored by Rick's. Yeah, Tom was definitely missing something here.

But Violet shook off the shock, smiled widely and said, 'Of course I do! And I'd appreciate any help that Tom is

able to give me, in between the work he's *actually* here
to do.' She even managed a sincere smile for him as she
spoke, which Tom thought might be a first.

'Well, that's settled then.' Rick clapped his hands together, but his eyebrows suggested that nothing was settled
at all. Tom suspected there'd be some private family conver-
sations going on once he'd finally found a bed to fall into.

Well, so be it. Despite Sherry's enthusiastic welcome,
he wasn't actually family. He didn't need to know all their
tiny moments and their every word. He just wanted the
stories. And, he'd admit it, the secrets. *They* were what
would set his book apart from everything else ever written about Rick Cross and co.

And he was pretty sure he'd get them. Starting tomorrow.

'Guys, if I'm going to be ready to start interviews, write
a book *and* organise the best concert in the history of benefit concerts, I'd better get some sleep.' Tom gave them all
his friendliest all-in-this-together smile.

'Oh, of course!' Sherry immediately went into hostess
mode, something Tom imagined she had honed and per-
fected over years of events, guests and parties. 'Violet,
why don't you show Tom to his room, darling?'

Violet's smile was starting to look a little fixed, but
no one except Tom seemed to notice. 'Of course. I might
turn in myself.' She kissed her parents on their cheeks.
'It was a brilliant day. Here's to many more happy years
of marriage.'

Tom followed Violet away from the stage, across the
gardens. The party had obviously started to wind down
after the Lemons had left the stage. The fairy lights in the
trees shone down on abandoned glasses and plates and
grass-stained marquee floors. A few stragglers still loi-
tered by the temporary bar, where the last remaining bar-

maid yawned expansively, but most people had already headed home to bed.

Tom applauded their sensible natures. Of course, it was gone 4:00 a.m., so maybe they weren't that sensible.

Glancing over his shoulder, Tom saw Rick and Sherry making their way across to where the rest of the band sat with their partners or friends under the moonlight. Jez was strumming an acoustic guitar and laughter and conversation floated among the notes in the night air.

'I don't know how they're still going,' Violet said, following his gaze. 'I'm knackered. But they're always the last ones standing at a party. I think it's a point of pride these days. And they always finish the night together, just the gang of them who've been there from the start.'

He should be over there, soaking up the moment. Taking in the atmosphere that would make his book authentic. Except...it was a private moment and he was new on the scene. He couldn't force his way into that close-knit group. He had to earn his place, and that would take time and trust.

Violet was giving him an odd considering look. 'You still want to go to bed?' A slight flush of colour hit her cheeks in the pale lights, and he knew somehow that she was waiting for him to make a joke about whether that was an offer to join him. So he didn't.

'Alone, I mean. Not with me,' Violet babbled, as if he had. She must get that a lot, although he'd expected her to just brush it off or turn it back on the joker to embarrass *them*. After her display in the airport café, he knew she had the confidence and the fire.

Except...here, now, this seemed like a different Violet. One who'd known humiliation and pain. One he hadn't expected to meet when he'd sat in Miami and New York reading up about the wild child Sex Tape Twin without shame.

She'd never even put out a statement, he remembered. No apology for being a bad role model, for letting down her fans or those young girls who looked up to her. No regret for the shame and embarrassment she'd brought on her family.

Why was that? Suddenly, he desperately wanted to know. But those questions too required patience and trust to be earned. Maybe in a few weeks. After all, they were going to be working on the concert together. He had all the time he needed to learn everything there was to know about Violet Huntingdon-Cross, and her family.

'Honestly, Violet, I think I'd pass out on you tonight even if it was an offer.' He gave her a friendly smile to show it was a joke, that he didn't mean any offence. But, as her gaze met his, even his exhausted body had a moment where it wished that wasn't the case. That maybe, just maybe, this beautiful, confusing woman might actually make that offer to him.

Which was clearly ridiculous. They had nothing in common. She'd never understand him or his life, and he'd long since grown out of sleeping with any beautiful woman who offered. He liked his sexual encounters to mean something these days. Maybe not true love and forever, but a meaningful connection at least.

He couldn't really imagine any connection between him and the self-absorbed daughter of a celebrity. Still, he felt a little relief as the colour in her cheeks faded and she gave a quick nod.

'Come on then. Your bedroom's this way.' Violet started off towards the main staircase.

Tom bit his tongue to stop himself asking where hers was as he followed.

Violet woke up exhausted. Maybe it was all the excitement and chaos of the day and weeks before, but even once the big vow renewal was over and Rose was safely off on honeymoon she couldn't relax enough to sleep—despite the fact it had been gone four by the time she'd made it to bed. Eventually, after an hour of fitful tossing and turning, she'd given up and turned on her bedside light to read for a while.

She'd woken up four hours later, with the light still on and her face smooshed against her book. Not the perfect start to the day.

Scrubbing a hand across her face to try and persuade her eyes to stay open, she glanced at the clock. Nine thirty a.m. Chances were, the rest of the household would be sleeping in until well after lunch, but there was a nervous energy running through Violet's veins that she knew from experience wouldn't let her go back to sleep.

A shower, her most comfortable jeans and a T-shirt in her favourite shade of lavender-blue made her feel a little more human. She scraped her hair back into a clip to dry naturally, slathered on what claimed to be a rejuvenating moisturiser and headed downstairs in search of coffee.

'Coffee will make all things better,' she murmured as she switched on the espresso machine. The lie was a soothing one, at least. How could one poor drink be expected to deal with all the worries that had piled on in the last twenty-four hours?

'Think it can even help your poor old dad?' Rick leant against the door frame from the hall, his weathered face looking a little grey under his summer tan. 'I think I'm getting too old for the partying lark, honey.'

'Never.' Violet grabbed another espresso cup from the shelf. 'You'll still be rocking with a walking stick when the rest of us have grown old and boring.'

Except she didn't even need to age to grow old and boring; she was already there, wasn't she? Her entire existence already fitted within the grounds of Huntingdon Hall. Or it had. Maybe the Benefit Concert would be her chance to spread her wings.

'Only if I have my girls there to help hold me up,' Rick said, settling himself into one of the chairs at the kitchen table. 'Wouldn't be any fun without you all.'

'Mum sleeping in?' Violet handed her dad his coffee, then sat down to blow across the surface of her own cup.

'She says she needs her beauty sleep.' Rick laughed. 'Course, we all know she's plenty beautiful without it.'

'I didn't expect anyone else to be up for hours,' Violet said.

'I've got a shift down at the centre this morning,' Rick said. 'No one else could cover, so…' He shrugged.

Violet gave him a sympathetic smile. While everyone knew that Rick and Sherry supported all sorts of charities publicly, very few people were aware of all the private time they put in. Her dad did a lot of work for Alzheimer's charities, as well as helping out at a local drug rehabilitation centre, while her mum put in time on a children's helpline, amongst other things. Would they share that side of themselves with Tom? Violet had no idea.

'I'll be back to give Tom his first interview this afternoon, though,' Rick said, suggesting that he might. Violet was glad; more people should know about all the good they did. 'And what are you up to today?'

Violet sipped her coffee. 'I was planning on raiding Rose's files to get an idea of what I've let myself in for with this Benefit Concert.'

Rick's face turned serious. 'Now, honey, you know you don't have to take that on. It's not too late to change your mind.'

'Don't think I can do it, huh?' Violet said, eyebrows raised.

'Violet, I truly believe you could do anything in the world you dreamt of, if you decided to. It just comes down to if you really *want* to.'

Violet bit her lip. Dad thought she could do it. He had faith in her. And maybe, just maybe, he knew something she didn't. At the very least, she wanted the *chance* to prove him right.

'I want to do it,' she said, ignoring the way her whole body felt as if it might start trembling any second. This was her chance—her golden opportunity to do that *something more* she'd been wishing for. 'It's important to me, and I think it's time.' Time to stop hiding behind the walls of Huntingdon Hall at last. Time to start living in the real world again, even if it was still filled with monsters.

The smile that split Rick's craggy face was reward enough for her decision. 'I think you might be right, honey,' he said, and pressed a kiss to her hand across the table. 'I think it's time the whole world got used to seeing the *real* Violet Huntingdon-Cross for once.'

Violet smiled back through her nerves. *Wouldn't that be something?*

CHAPTER SIX

HUNTINGDON HALL WAS ridiculously large, Tom decided, after getting lost on the way to the kitchen for the third time. Tastefully redecorated, with none of the attempts to recreate the Regency or whatever that he'd half expected from the almost aristocracy. But then, this family were unusual in almost every other way, why not this one too?

There were so many contradictions for him to uncover, but that was half the fun.

Contradiction one. Sherry had inherited this hall from her blue blood family—but had obviously renovated it entirely using her husband's money—or her own, Tom supposed. She had enjoyed a very lucrative modelling career, after all. Anyway, the point was, while the outside of Huntingdon Hall still looked like something from a period novel, the inside was entirely modern.

As Tom made his way down a corridor that looked almost exactly like the one he'd just explored, Violet's directions from the night before seemed even more ridiculous. *Just follow the walls,* she'd said. *Eventually all of them lead back to the main staircase.* Follow the walls? What kind of advice was that? Especially since it appeared he'd been following the walls in the wrong direction for the last five minutes. Why wasn't there a helpful servant around here somewhere?

Of course that led him to contradiction two. In a house this size, with a family this rich, he'd have expected dozens of flunkies running around doing things for them. But he'd seen nobody. Oh, he was sure there was a housekeeper somewhere, and he highly doubted that Sherry did her own cleaning, but apart from that? Everything seemed to be kept in the family. Rose took care of the band's PR and everything else that needed organising, it seemed.

At least until she ran away on her honeymoon and Violet stepped in, rather than hire someone else.

Violet was, without a doubt, most definitely contradiction number three.

Tom turned another corner, dutifully following the wall and, finally, stumbled across the staircase. At last, his path towards coffee and maybe even breakfast was clear.

He hopped down the stairs in double time, smiling as he heard voices coming from what he hoped would prove to be the kitchen. Part of him was surprised not to be the first up—it had been a ridiculously late night, but even with his exhaustion level he'd found it impossible to sleep past ten. Too many years of risking missing the tour bus or a flight somewhere had left him a very light sleeper.

'Good morning.' Both Rick and Violet looked up at his words, and Tom got the unerring feeling that he'd interrupted something.

'Ah! Our guest awakes.' Rick moved towards the coffee pot. 'Strong and black? Or do you drink what can only be described as "warm milk with a coffee scent" like my daughter?'

'Strong and black, please,' Tom replied. Actually, he normally preferred it somewhere in between, but he wasn't taking the chance of failing the Rick Cross coffee test. Or any other tests he threw his way before Rick actually opened up to him and gave him the material he needed.

Rick nodded as he poured. 'Good choice. Now, about today.' He handed Tom a tiny steaming espresso cup with an apologetic smile that made Tom's heart sink. There were going to be no interviews today, he just knew it.

This was always the risk in coming here. Staying at Huntingdon Hall gave Tom unprecedented access, yes. But it also gave the subject the illusion of limitless time—and plenty of excuses to dodge sitting down and talking to him.

Tom did not have limitless time, and he needed this story.

'I was hoping we could make a start on some questions about what the Lemons are doing now,' Tom said, hoping the allure of potential publicity for the new album would draw him in. 'I've got a couple of possible slots in magazines and supplements coming up, and it would be good to let people know what's next for the band.'

'Rose would kick me if she heard me turning down the publicity, but I'm afraid I have some commitments today that I need to take care of before I can sit down with you.' Rick reached for his own coffee mug—which, Tom noticed, had milk in it, damn him. 'Sorry, Tom. I'll be back this afternoon, though. And I'll get Sherry to book some time with you too, as well as the boys from the band. I want us to get the bulk of the first few interviews down over the next week or two, so we've all got more time to focus on the Benefit Concert when it comes around. That sound okay to you?'

'That's…great, actually.' So much for the old man trying to avoid the interviews. Maybe Rick Cross was as serious about this book as Tom hoped after all. 'And I can probably find something to entertain me around here this morning.'

He hadn't meant to look at Violet, but somehow his gaze just sort of slid over in her direction. Her blonde hair looked darker—was it wet?—and strands were curling around her face. In jeans and a bright blue T-shirt, without make-up, she looked a lot younger than she had the night before. And, from the redness around her eyes, more vulnerable.

What had she been discussing with her father before he walked in? Suddenly, Tom wished he'd stopped outside to eavesdrop.

'You can help Violet go through all Rose's files!' Rick sounded immensely pleased with himself at the idea. 'Get up to speed on all the plans for the Benefit Concert. I just know my Violet is going to knock this one out of the park.'

He reached across and squeezed his daughter's shoulder, and she gave him a rather weak smile in return.

'Still, everyone needs a little help sometimes, right, honey?' Rick went on.

'Yeah, I guess.' With a deep breath, Violet straightened her shoulders visibly and looked him in the eye. 'So, Mr Buckley, how about it? You up for a challenge?'

'Absolutely.' Tom drained his espresso and smiled, unsure if the challenge was the concert or understanding the woman sitting in front of him.

'Okay. So…Will said that Rose left everything she had to do with the Benefit Concert in here.' Violet approached the door to the seldom used study on the first floor with more than a little trepidation. She hadn't been in this room since it was their homework room, years ago. Since she'd handed in her dissertation, she hadn't so much as opened the door.

It was Rose's room, not hers. As close as the twins were, Violet had to admit that they'd lived very separate lives over the last few years. With Rose in New York, that distance had only grown.

Oh, they still talked about pretty much everything. Violet still knew her sister's mind and heart, and she knew that if she needed anything Rose would be there in a heartbeat. But their lives were different. Rose jetted around the world, building her career working for The Screaming Lemons' PR, but also cultivating her passion making jewellery. The wedding rings she'd crafted for Seb and Daisy, and the bracelet she'd designed and made for their mother, were amongst the most beautiful things Violet had ever seen. Rose had real talent, and Violet knew that Will would encourage that—especially now Rose had made the decision to give up the PR side of things and follow her dreams.

Maybe it was time for Violet to do that too, she thought as she pushed open the door. Starting with the Benefit Concert.

'Huh.' Behind her, Tom stared over her shoulder. 'Did Will say where, exactly?'

It was a valid question. Violet's heart sank as she took in the piles of paperwork, the overflowing files and the stack of wedding magazines on the desk. Poor Rose had been swamped for the last month or more, with preparations for the band's latest tour, album promotion and not to mention planning their parents' vow renewal service and party. No wonder she hadn't had time to tidy up.

Well, that just made step one in the 'get-back-out-there-and-show-the-world-what-Violet-Huntingdon-Cross-is-really-made-of' plan all the more obvious.

'We need to start with a clean sweep,' she said, picking up Rose's battered, precious black planner from the middle of the piles covering the desk. 'We'll sort through everything in here, clear up and find all the relevant stuff, then set up my office in here. Will sent me the link to the Dropbox folder Rose was using for all the electronic stuff, and she's given me access to the email account she uses for the Benefit Concert each year. So I should have everything I need to get started…'

'Once you can find the desk,' Tom finished for her.

'Yeah.' She turned to look at him. 'Sorry. This probably isn't what you were hoping to do this morning.'

Tom shrugged. 'Not entirely. But this afternoon should make up for it. And it doesn't have to be a total waste. I can ask you some basic interview questions while we're working.' He pulled out his smartphone and scrolled through to an app with a microphone logo. 'You don't mind being taped, right?'

Violet's body froze, her back so stiff she thought it might snap. At least he was asking, she supposed. She hadn't been given that courtesy last time.

'I think maybe today we should just focus on getting this office sorted.' She knew her voice was stilted, but she couldn't seem to do anything about it. 'If I'm going to be on the record, I want to be sure I'm giving your questions my full attention.' That way, it would be harder for him to sneak in trick questions, or twist her words around later. She'd spent some time, after everything, researching the best way to deal with the media. Of course, when every question was about a sex tape, there was only so much you could do. But she knew more now than she had at nineteen and that knowledge gave her a little confidence, at least.

She could deal with Tom Buckley. As long as she kept her wits sharp.

'Okay. Fair enough.' Tom slipped the phone back into his pocket and Violet's shoulders dropped back to their usual level. If he had any idea why his request had her so rattled—and surely he must—Tom didn't show it. He was a professional, she supposed. 'So, where do we start?'

Violet surveyed the room. 'The desk? I mean, that's probably going to have her most recent stuff on it. And once we've cleared that, at least we have somewhere to work.'

'Sounds like a plan.' Shifting a pile of papers and a red polka dot cardigan from the leather chair on the visitor's side of the desk, Tom grabbed the first stack of files from the edge of the desk and took a seat.

Selecting her own pile, Violet settled into the desk chair and started to read.

'So, is your sister always this messy when she works?' Tom asked, and Violet's hackles instantly rose.

'She's been incredibly busy recently,' Violet said. 'I'm sure that, if she were here, she'd know exactly where everything was, though. She's very efficient.'

'I'm sure she is.' Tom dropped his first file onto the floor. 'That's my "wedding vow renewal" pile, by the way. I guess that must have taken up a lot of her time. You all helped, though?'

'Where we could,' Violet replied. Of course, with Daisy suffering from first trimester woes, and herself relegated to flower arranging, it had mostly been Rose. As usual. 'Mum was pretty burnt out from organising Daisy and Seb's wedding, so she left a lot of it to Rose. I took care of the flowers, though.'

Tom's gaze flicked up to meet hers, faint disbelief marring his expression. 'You arrange flowers?'

'I do.' Violet looked back down at the file in her hands. This, at least, had to be a safe topic. No one expected the Sex Tape Twin to spend her weekends fiddling with oasis and floristry wire in the church hall, right? 'I took over the local church flower committee a few years ago now.'

That, of course, had been a local scandal in its own way—she was too young, too inexperienced, or just had too much of a reputation. But, whatever anyone said, that scandal hadn't made the national press, at least.

'Huh. I always imagined church flower ladies were...'
Tom trailed off and Violet raised her eyebrows at him as
she waited for him to finish the sentence. 'Married?' he
said finally, as if asking her to tell him what to say to get
out of the conversation.

Violet huffed a laugh and reached for the next file.
'Married. That's the best you could do?'

'Well, okay, fine. I thought they were older, more boring, greyer and considerably less beautiful than you.'

Despite the warmth filling her cheeks, Violet resisted
the urge to say, *You think I'm beautiful?*

He'd just think she was fishing for compliments, anyway.

'As it happens, I'll have you know that floristry is more
popular than ever.' She had no idea if that were actually
true, but it sounded good. 'Young women across the country are taking courses in flower arranging.' Probably.

'Did you?' Tom asked. 'Take a course, I mean?'

'Not...exactly.' Damn. There went the legitimacy of
her words.

'So how on earth did you get to be head of the church
flower committee? I've watched enough rural British murder mysteries to know that kind of job is usually enough
to kill over.'

'We live in Buckinghamshire, not Midsomer,' Violet
pointed out. 'We haven't had a murder in the village in
almost seventy years.'

'Still, I bet there was a queue of blue-haired ladies waiting to take over. Weren't they a tad annoyed when you
swanned in and stole it from right under their noses?'

Well, yes, of course they had been. But Tom made it
sound as if she'd just rocked up and demanded she be given
the job because of who her parents were, just like some

people she'd known back in the day had demanded access to exclusive nightclubs. And usually been let in, too.

'I'd been trained up by the last head of the committee for five years,' Violet said, trying not to notice the lump that still formed in her throat when she thought about Kathleen. 'When she got sick, she insisted that I take over. She dictated arrangements to me over the phone, made me bring her photos to show her I was doing it right. When she died…I was voted in the day after the funeral.' Kathleen had actually tried to leave her the position in her will, but of course it hadn't been hers to give. So there had to be a ballot of the whole committee—which she'd won by just one vote.

Still, Violet hoped she'd won over the doubters over the last few years. God knew, she'd achieved very little else. Until now. It might be a bit of a jump from flower arranging to concert arranging but, come hell or high water, she'd prove herself here just like she had on the committee.

'But you obviously wanted it.' Tom tilted his head to one side as he studied her. It made Violet want to flinch, so she worked really hard at keeping her muscles still instead. He *wanted* her to flinch, she was sure of it. And she wasn't giving Tom Buckley *anything* he wanted.

'It meant a lot to Kathleen that I take it on,' she said evenly. 'And I get a lot of pleasure from working with flowers.'

He nodded absently, as if taking everything she said as accepted truth. But then he fixed her with his clear green eyes and said, 'So, tell me. How did the daughter of rock royalty go from starring in her very own porno to arranging the Easter flowers?'

CHAPTER SEVEN

VIOLET WENT VERY still for a moment, the fingers clutching her file almost white from tension. Tom sat back and waited. He knew this part. In any usual interview, this was the bit where the subject tried to recall all the advice from the PR guru on how to spin their misdeeds in the best possible light.

And Miss Violet Huntingdon-Cross had clearly had some ambitious PR advice, probably from her twin sister, actually. Keep your head down, take on some charity work, or work in the community. Rehabilitate your character until everyone forgets the part about how they saw you naked on the internet, mid pretty boring sex.

Was this why Rick had pushed for him to help her out with the Benefit Concert? Tom had no doubt that Rick's first concern was publicity for the band, but maybe the relaunch of his eldest daughter as an upstanding member of society was a nice side benefit. Hell, maybe that was why he was doing all this now. With two daughters married, he could happily portray them as settled down and mature—and Violet could ride in on their coat-tails.

Except Tom had seen her lose it in the middle of an airport café. He'd glimpsed the real passionate, wild Violet—and he really wasn't buying the Sunday school teacher act.

'I thought we agreed that this wasn't the time for an interview,' Violet said, her voice stiff and prim.

Tom shrugged. 'It's not. I'm not recording anything. Just asking an idle question.'

'Sure.' Violet's mouth twisted up into a bitter smile. 'I bet we're off the record and everything, right? No, thanks. I know how that works.'

'If I say something is off the record, I mean it.' Tom sat up straighter, bristling a little at the implication. 'Your dad brought me here because he knows my reputation as a fair, honest, accurate reporter. I'm not trying to trick you into anything here, Violet.'

He'd worked too hard at building up that reputation—after the story that made his name—to risk it now, over one blonde wild child. If his mother were still alive, even she'd have to admit that he'd turned it around. He was respectable now, dammit.

Violet met his gaze, her blue eyes wide and vulnerable. She'd probably practised that look in the mirror, too. 'Okay, then,' she said finally, giving him a small nod.

But she didn't answer his question. Instead, she turned back to the file in her hand, giving it her full attention as a little crease started to form between her eyebrows. Tom wanted to ask her what she was reading—until he realised there was a much more pressing question to be answered.

'What did you mean, when you said you "know how that works"?'

Violet shrugged, not looking up. 'You know. Off the record is only valid until someone says something worth breaking the rules for.'

'That's not true.' The defence of his profession was automatic—even as he admitted to himself that for some reporters it was entirely true. The sort of reporter who would hack voicemails or intercept emails didn't care very much about a verbal agreement about 'the record'. Hell, it was barely more than a social convention anyway, a nicety to make interview subjects feel more comfortable.

But he'd stuck by that convention for his entire career, bar one story. And he didn't intend to ever break it again.

'Really?' Violet raised her pale brows at him in disbelief. 'You really believe that all reporters honour the privacy of things said off the record?' She shook her head without waiting for an answer. 'The only way to be safe is to assume that you're on the record at all times. Whatever anyone says.' The way she said it, the conviction she gave the words…this wasn't just some advice from a media expert. This was the mantra Violet lived her life by—or at least it was now.

'When talking to reporters?' Tom asked, wanting her to admit to what he suspected. 'Or when talking to anybody?'

Her gaze slipped away from his. 'Depends on who you're talking to. And whether you trust them not to sell your story to the papers.'

'And who do you trust that much?' Tom had an inkling it would be a very short list.

'Who do you?' Violet threw his own question back at him, and he blinked in surprise.

'Trust me, no one is interested in any story about me.' Just the idea of it made him laugh. He was a reporter, always behind the scenes, shedding light on other people's lives. No one ever needed to examine his—and he really didn't want them to.

'Just suppose they were. Hypothetically.' Violet leant forward and, even with the desk between them, her piercing stare made her feel uncomfortably close. 'Imagine that something happened in your life—you won the lottery, or wrote the next Harry Potter, or married a celebrity, whatever. Suddenly everyone in the world wants to know your secrets. Who would you still tell the truth to?'

No one. The thought felt empty and hollow even as it echoed through his brain. There was no one he trusted with that much of him. No one he'd tell about his hopes and dreams—and no one he'd trust with his failures or regrets.

Oh, he had friends, plenty of them. Enough in every country that he always had someone he could meet for dinner, or go out for drinks with. And he'd had girlfriends, too—also plenty. The fact he didn't have one right now made absolutely no difference to the trusted person question. He hadn't told any of the previous ones any more than he thought they needed to know. His mother had probably been the last person he'd trusted that way, and she was a long time gone. Not to mention the fact that even telling *her* the truth hadn't ended so well.

He wasn't the story. He never was. That was kind of the point of being a reporter.

'Never happen,' he said as breezily as he could. 'My utter unremarkableness is one of the main reasons I've managed to build up a successful career as a music journalist. So, go on, your turn. Who do you trust that much? Rose, I imagine. And Daisy and your parents. Who else?'

'I think that's plenty, don't you?' Violet sat back and picked up her file again. 'After all, it's obviously still four more people than you have,' she added, not looking up.

Tom didn't have an answer to that one, either.

It was going to take them forever to wade through all of Rose's files. Violet bit back a sigh—Tom would only have a sigh-related question waiting for her. Maybe ask her if she was frustrated by her sister's departure or, worse, in love with her new brother-in-law. She had a feeling it was only a matter of time before someone noticed that Rose had married the man who'd been squiring her twin around for the last few years and jumped to the obvious—but erroneous—conclusion that there was a really juicy story there. She'd place money on it being Tom, and before the week was out.

Sneaking a glance at him across the desk, Violet considered the way he'd evaded his own question about who to trust in this world. On the one hand, she'd been surprised to find someone whose list was shorter than her own. But then, given his profession, perhaps that wasn't so surprising. He had to know that everyone had their price, when the story—or tape—was good enough.

Still, she'd have expected him to have *someone*. A trusty sidekick best friend, perhaps. Or a loyal, long-suffering girlfriend. Not everyone was lucky enough to have a built-in best friend from the day they were born, like she and Rose had been, but she'd have thought he'd have found at least one person to trust over the last few decades.

Strangest of all was the feeling she'd got, watching him dodge the question. The odd sensation that in that moment they'd both looked past a mask neither of them usually lifted, and seen something they never intended the other to see. Had he really seen her fear, her mistrust in a way that even her family couldn't quite grasp? Or had she imagined that strangely searching look?

And what about him? Had she truly recognised another person who understood that the truth was a private thing, that who a person was deep down didn't always need to be shared? At the least she knew he didn't trust people any more than she did.

Was he lonely? Or did he like being alone? Did it make it easier for him to do his job, not worrying about friends or family who might be disappointed in him, or disapprove of the stories he chose to tell?

Or had he had someone once and betrayed them for a story, like Nick had done to her?

Shaking her head, Violet looked back down at the file in her hand. She was projecting now. Whatever Tom's history was, and whomever he chose not to share it with, she was pretty sure it had nothing in common with hers.

Violet added the file in her hand to the 'album promo' pile and was just reaching for the next one when her phone buzzed in her back pocket. Standing to fish it out, she checked the name on the screen.

'It's Rose,' she said, her finger hovering over 'answer'. 'I'll go take it in the other room.'

'See if you can find out where she's hidden all the bands' contracts while you're at it,' Tom said. 'And the notes on the riders. They'd be really useful around now.'

Violet nodded and escaped into the sitting room next door to talk to her sister. She really didn't want an unreliable audience when she was talking to one of her four people.

'Hey, where are you?' Violet shut the door carefully behind her, just in case Tom got it into his head to eavesdrop. 'Is it glorious and sunny and beautiful?'

'All of the above,' Rose said with a laugh. 'I have to admit, Will has outdone himself. But you'll have to wait and see the photos when we get back. I want to see who guesses where we've been first.'

'Meanie.' Violet pouted but, since her sister couldn't see her, the effect was rather wasted. 'Are you happy, though?'

'Very,' Rose promised, her tone suddenly serious. 'Really, Vi…I'm so much happier than I thought I could be. Ever.'

Violet's heart ached at the truth in her sister's words. 'I'm so, so happy for you,' she said as sincerely as she could. But even as she spoke, she rubbed the space between her breasts, just over her heart, and wished that she could find such happiness.

'What about you?' Rose asked. 'How are things there?'

That, Violet knew, was her cue to tell her sister light-hearted stories about everything that had happened in the less than twenty-four hours since she'd left. Only problem was, she was struggling to think of any.

'Um, fine. Nothing much to report, really. Mum and Dad stayed up super-late with the guys, and Dad headed off for his shift at the centre today looking half dead, even after a couple of coffees. Mum still hadn't surfaced last time I checked.'

'So, the usual,' Rose summarised.

'Pretty much, yeah.'

'How about Tom? Did you find him okay at the airport?'

'Yeah, eventually.' Violet bit the inside of her cheek. She really, really wanted to point out that Rose had given her the wrong flight times. But if she did she'd have to explain what happened next. She was just trying to think of a way to fudge the subject when Rose spoke again.

'Hel—lo. What happened? Tell me immediately.'

'I don't know what you're talking about,' Violet lied.

'Yes, you do. That was your "I'm mad at you but don't know how to tell you" voice. Twin here, remember?'

'Okay, fine. You gave me the wrong flight times! He ended up calling and demanding to know where I was, so I rushed all the way over to Heathrow in my bridesmaid's dress and heels then humiliated myself in front of everyone in the coffee shop.' Violet finally took a breath and relaxed once the words were out. Not telling Rose stuff took far more energy than just telling her everything.

'Will just forwarded you his email with the flights on,' Rose said mildly. 'If they were wrong, it was his own stupid fault. Now, humiliated yourself how, exactly?'

Maybe it would have been worth holding back that part, though.

'His fault? Fantastic. So it was all over nothing in the end, anyway.' Violet sighed. 'I was so determined to make a good impression—to make him like us so he'd write nice things about us. But after his call and the traffic, I was kind of flustered. And it had been a really, really long day.' A long, loved-up, excruciating sort of day for the one single girl in a family of people madly in love with their spouses.

'Oh, God, what did you do?' Rose asked with the sort of dismayed expectation that came from having been witness to every single one of Violet's screw-ups for the past twenty-seven years.

'He thought I was you!' Violet said. Rose knew how much she hated that. And after the day she'd had...well, some sort of blow-up was inevitable.

'Tell me you didn't berate that poor man in public for not being able to tell apart identical twins he's barely met.'

'Of course not! In fact, I played along for a moment or two, but he figured it out pretty quickly.' Violet swallowed at the memory. She hated this bit, but Rose was going to hate it even more. 'He said he recognised my facial expression. From the video.' No need to say which one.

Silence on the other end. But only while Rose caught her breath, Violet imagined.

'I will fly home right now and beat him up if you want.' Rose swore, quite impressively. Violet recognised a few words they hadn't learnt at boarding school. 'I can't believe I thought he seemed like a good guy! I thought we could trust him with this interview, with Dad. But now... I'll call Dad. Get him to send him back to whichever rock he crawled out from under.'

Warmth filled Violet's chest at her sister's unqualified

support. But part of her couldn't help but feel a little responsible too.

'In fairness, he was severely sleep deprived and over-caffeinated at the time,' she said. 'And he didn't really say it in an offensive manner. Well, as far as you can remind someone of the biggest mistake of their life without meaning to offend them.'

'It wasn't your fault,' Rose said automatically, just as she had every time it had been mentioned for the last eight years. 'You trusted him. And you had no idea he was filming you—let alone that he'd put it out on the internet. Do not blame yourself for the actions of Nefarious Nick.'

'*Anyway,* I don't think Tom meant to cause offence. And I might have overreacted a little bit.'

'Overreacted?' Violet was pretty sure she could *hear* Rose wincing. 'What did you do?'

'Announced to the whole coffee shop that yes, I was the Huntingdon-Cross Sex Tape Twin and if they had any questions they should ask Tom, since he'd clearly watched it plenty of times.'

Rose let out a burst of laughter. '*Really?* Oh, that's brilliant. And the first time I've ever heard you joke about the whole thing.'

'I wasn't joking,' Violet muttered.

'So, did he make it to Huntingdon Hall alive? How are things going? I mean, after that kind of a start I'm assuming he's probably part of the family already.' Apparently, Rose's romantic happiness hadn't dulled her ability for sarcasm.

'Actually, we agreed to start over. He's helping me with the Benefit Concert.'

'You took it on?' Rose asked. 'I kind of hoped you might when Will said you'd agreed to take care of things. But I wasn't sure if you'd…well, feel comfortable doing it. You know, you can always get someone in from the agency we use if you're not happy.'

'It's fine. I said I'd do it and I will.' And hearing how everyone else expected her to pull out every five minutes was only making her more determined that it would be a raging success. 'Although we're having some fun trying to sort through all your papers.'

'Yeah, sorry about the mess. But there's a system, I promise.'

'Care to explain it to me?' Violet asked, settling back on the sofa to take detailed notes as Rose explained the meanings of different file colours, and how the left side of the desk was only ever used for pending stuff. She just hoped she and Tom hadn't already messed up whatever weird system Rose had developed...

CHAPTER EIGHT

TOM STARED AT the blank laptop screen in front of him, then rubbed his eyes. He'd been at Huntingdon Hall for almost a week, sat down for detailed, open interviews with both Rick and Sherry, plus most of the band members. He had hours of audiotape, plus a whole notebook full of scrawled notes. He'd even managed to put together a preliminary article for one of his favourite editors, talking about the exciting opportunity he had, staying at Huntingdon Hall. When it went to print in one of the supplements this weekend, it should build excitement for the Benefit Concert, help with the album promo and even start some buzz for the eventual band biography. It had been a productive, worthwhile week.

So why the hell was he still thinking about Violet Huntingdon-Cross, drowning in paperwork in her sister's study?

She was the only one he wasn't certain he could get to open up, that was all. He had appointments to talk with Daisy, and even her new husband, in a couple of weeks when they came for the benefit, and he felt sure he could collar Rose and the new Mr when they got back from their honeymoon. But Violet…she was right there in the house with him, and yet he couldn't get close. Even when they were in the same room, she made it very clear there was an exclusion zone around her—one he would never enter.

Maybe he'd got too close with their conversation about trust—even if he had come out the worst for it. But that only meant he needed to push a little further.

Tom closed his laptop. He could take a break from writing if it meant getting Violet to open up. After all, her parents were off doing the first of many promos for the Benefit Concert—radio today—her sisters were both busy being married and happy...it was just the two of them there now. They might as well get used to each other's company.

Another thing he had managed over the last week was learning his way around Huntingdon Hall. At least he no longer got lost looking for the kitchen.

Tom knocked on the study door, waiting for Violet to call for him to come in, but she didn't answer.

After a moment, Tom pushed the door open, just enough to peer through the crack.

'Yes, I understand that, Mr Collins. But—' Violet sat at the desk, phone clamped to her ear. Strands of hair were escaping from the clip she'd used to keep it back, and she rubbed her forehead with her free hand. 'And, as I've already told you—' A sigh, as she was presumably cut off again.

Slipping through the open door, Tom took the seat opposite the desk and she glanced up at the movement.

'Who is it?' he whispered.

'Olivia's manager,' she mouthed back. Damn it. Olivia was the hot new American act Rose had booked for the benefit. Tom had interviewed her once or twice before, and each time the star's list of demands had grown. Word in the industry was that no one could wait until her star burned out and she had to start begging *them* for the press. But while the kids were still downloading her music...

Reaching over, Tom stabbed the speakerphone button with his finger, and Mr Collins's diatribe became audible.

'All I'm saying is that I think I need to talk with some-one with a little more authority over there. Olivia isn't just some local act, taking part for the exposure. She's the big-gest thing in pop music right now, and I don't think that some girl who's only famous for who her parents are and for getting naked on the internet can really appreciate—'

'Mr Collins—' Tom struggled to keep his tone profes-sional as inside him indignation and anger burned brighter '—this is Tom Buckley. We've spoken before, when I've been commissioned to write pieces about Olivia.'

'Tom. Right.' A little unease threaded through Mr Col-lins's words now he knew he was talking to the press. Tom didn't imagine for a moment that he had *much* power in the world, but the ability to make famous people look un-grateful, stupid or plain mean was always worth some-thing. 'You're covering this concert?'

'I'm helping Miss Huntingdon-Cross organise it this year.' Maybe his words were a little sharp, but Mr Collins deserved a hell of a lot worse. 'All for charity, you know. I've got Olivia's rider right here.' He held out a hand and Violet passed it over. Tom scanned through the pop star's list of demands for her performance and backstage re-quirements, eyebrows raised. 'She does realise that all the profits from the day go to very worthwhile charities, yes?'

'Well, of course she does,' Mr Collins blustered. 'She's always keen to help those less fortunate than herself.'

'In which case, I'd imagine that she wouldn't want the sixty-seven requests she's made to result in us not being able to meet our giving targets for the year, right? I mean, I'm sure that nobody would ever say that Olivia places more importance on having the appropriately named Diva vodka available backstage than she does on starving chil-dren getting a hot meal, but…well, you have to admit, it doesn't look all that good.'

There was a pause on the other end of the line. Tom waited it out. The next move had to be the manager's.

'I'm sure Olivia would be satisfied with a more…easily available vodka,' Mr Collins said eventually.

Tom drew a gleeful line through the words reading 'Three bottles of Diva vodka' on the piece of paper in front of him. 'I'm sure she would too. In fact, why don't you go back to her and see which other items she might be willing to forgo? For the sake of the children.' And her publicity, of course. Tom was under no illusions about that.

'I'll see what I can do.' Mr Collins hung up.

Beaming, Tom handed the rider back to Violet. 'And that is how you deal with ungrateful, self-important, egotistical teenage stars.'

'By threatening to expose them in the press as terrible people?' Violet, for some reason, didn't look quite as pleased with his victory as Tom thought she should.

'By making them aware of the truth of their situation,' he replied. 'They're public figures, and their attitudes and behaviour are noted. Don't you think the world should know that she wanted a bottle of three-thousand-dollar vodka more than she wanted to help the charity she was supposed to be appearing for?'

'No. Yes.' Frustration crossed Violet's face. 'Look, the point is, I didn't need you to save me. I could have dealt with it myself.'

'I'm sure you could.' Something told him this might be the time to tread gently. 'But sometimes these guys react better to the press than to…' Hell, now he was stuck. How to describe her in a way that wouldn't make her fly off the handle?

'Some girl who's only famous for who her parents are and for getting naked on the internet?' Bitterness filled Violet's voice as she quoted Mr Collins.

'Okay, I definitely wasn't going to say *that*.'

'But it's what you were thinking, right?' Violet gave him a sad smile. 'I know how people see me.'

The disappointment on her face made her look more fragile than he'd imagined she could, especially after their explosive first meeting in the airport. This wasn't a woman who revelled in her notoriety, who defended her mistakes and delighted in the press coverage. This wasn't the woman he'd watched—very briefly, before embarrassment got the better of him—in that sex tape.

'Does that happen a lot?' he asked, suddenly furious at the idea that it wasn't just one stupid man belittling Violet, but a whole host of them.

'Mr Collins?' She shrugged. 'Sometimes. I don't… Mostly, I'm not around people like that, so it's fine. If we're at a charity event or something, usually people won't say it to my face. But I hear the snickers and see the smiles, you know? I guess it's the only thing I'm famous for, so it's all anyone wants to talk about.'

'But it's not all that you are.' It surprised him how strongly he believed that—and how ashamed he felt that, when he'd arrived, he'd probably thought the same. What had changed?

'Was this why you didn't want to be in charge of the Benefit Concert?' he asked.

'I do want to do it,' she snapped. 'But…it's why my parents were worried about me doing it, yeah.' Her hands were busy playing with some stress toy she'd found in Rose's drawer when they were sorting the study—a globe that she could stretch and squeeze. After less than a week, it already looked considerably more worn than when they'd discovered it. 'They know I don't enjoy dealing with people so much these days. That was always left to Rose, really.'

These days. Since the sex tape? Tom frowned. Since

then, she'd stopped trusting anyone outside her immediate family, and avoided other people as much as possible.

Huh. Perhaps the stories he'd read when researching Violet Huntingdon-Cross weren't all there was to know. And he was a reporter—he always wanted to get to the truth, the real story.

Standing up, Tom reached across the desk and rescued the poor battered globe from between her fingers. 'Come on.' He took her hand and pulled her to her feet.

'What? Where are we going?' That puzzled frown line between her eyebrows was actually kind of cute, Tom decided.

'Lunch,' he told her. 'Completely off the record. I promise.'

It quickly emerged that Tom had no idea where they could actually go for lunch. 'Hey, you live here,' he said. 'Where's good?'

Rolling her eyes, Violet grabbed her handbag and car keys. 'Come on.'

As she started the engine, and tried to ignore Tom fiddling with the radio, she weighed up her options. There was the Peacock in the village, but that was just across the road from the church and the vicar's favourite afternoon haunt. She could almost guarantee that having lunch there with Tom would mean that the whole flower committee would be talking about her again by Sunday. There was the Three Tuns in the next village over, but Mum and her ladies sometimes took lunch there mid-week, and Violet couldn't remember if it was one of those days. Even if Mum wasn't there, the ladies might be.

So that left the Fox and Hounds, three villages over and with hand-cut chips to die for. Violet felt she could live with that.

'Is there any reason we're crossing county lines to grab a sandwich?' Tom asked as they drove past the turning for the village.

'Hand-cut chips,' Violet replied. It was only a partial lie, at least.

'Fair enough.' Tom settled back into his seat, the radio playing something obscure and jazzy, and folded his hands behind his head.

'So, these questions you want to ask...' It made Violet a little nervous, how relaxed he was. As if he already knew the answers to the things he was going to ask.

'When we get to the pub.' Were his eyes closed? Violet snapped her gaze away from the road ahead just long enough to check. Yep, he was half asleep in her car. Again.

'Okay, but you know I don't believe in off the record, right? I distinctly remember having that conversation.' That too revealing, too intimate conversation. Since then, she'd taken care to keep their interactions to a minimum. When he'd stopped by to see if he could help with the Benefit Concert a few days ago, she'd handed him a call sheet and left him to it. And when he'd been helping her sort the study, it had been easy to just boss him around.

Until today. Violet was under no illusions who was in charge today, even if she was the one holding the steering wheel. And she really didn't like it.

Beside her, Tom sighed, brought his hands down to rest in his lap and opened his eyes. 'Okay, look. This is how this is going to work. We are going to have lunch. Over lunch, we will make friendly conversation. We will probably talk about our families, our friends, our lives. Because that's what people do when they go out for lunch.'

'Not always,' Violet interjected. 'When we have flower committee lunches we mostly talk about other people. In fact, most lunches I've ever been to have been filled with people talking about other people.' Seemed people were always more comfortable gossiping about people they barely knew than about themselves. In fact, they especially seemed to like talking about her, she'd found.

'Fair point,' Tom conceded. 'Okay, then, imagine we're at some sort of internet dating meet-up thing.'

Violet couldn't help but laugh. 'No way.'

'Why not?'

'Because no logical computer programme in the world would ever put us together!' The journalist and the woman who got screwed over—quite literally and in front of millions—by one. Not a natural match.

'You don't know that!' Tom twisted in his seat to grin at her. 'We're both relatively young, relatively attractive…'

Violet tossed her hair over her shoulder, the way her mum did when she was dealing with idiots who didn't know they were idiots. 'Relatively?'

'In your case, relative to the pop stars and supermodels of this world. In mine…relative to everyone else.' Tom shrugged, as if to admit he knew the argument was kind of weak.

Violet raised her eyebrows as she pulled into the car park of the Fox and Hounds.

'Regardless of our relative attractiveness levels, I can assure you that our personality profiles would be very, very different.' Violet switched off the engine.

'Oh, I think we could have stuff in common.'

'How would you know? You don't know the first thing about me, apart from what you've read on the internet.' And watched, of course, although she didn't feel the need to remind him of that.

'Exactly.' Tom flashed her a grin and opened the door. 'And you don't know anything about me.'

'Except that you're a reporter.'

'That's my job, not who I am.' He got out of the car.

'So who are you then?' Violet called after him.

'Come to lunch and find out.' Tom leant down, rested him arms on the door frame and peered in at her. 'I'll do you a deal. For every question you answer of mine, I'll answer one of yours. Off the record.'

'I told you, I don't believe in that.'

'You might by the end of lunch. Now come on. I'm starving.'

CHAPTER NINE

VIOLET HAD BEEN RIGHT—the hand-cut chips were definitely worth the trip. The conversation, not so much. So far, over a pint of bitter for him and an orange juice for her, they'd discussed the menu, the merits of starters over puddings and the general preference for both, whether a table by the window might be nicer than one by the bar, and if the couple arguing in the car park were ever coming in.

But now, as the waitress retreated after leaving them their meals, he had his chance.

'So, do you want to go first, or shall I?' Tom popped another chip in his mouth while Violet considered her answer. Then, since it seemed to be taking her a while, he ate another. 'That wasn't meant to be such a brainteaser, you know.'

'It's a big decision!' Violet said. 'Like that bit in *The Princess Bride* with the iocane powder. You know… *Are you the sort of person who'd put poison in your glass or my glass?* That bit.' She looked down and selected her own chip, biting it in half.

'How, exactly, is lunch with me like deciding whether to drink poison or not?'

'Not lunch. The question thing,' Violet said. 'I mean, if you ask first, then I'll know the sort of level of questions we're asking, which makes it easier for me to come

up with mine. But if I go first, then I can see how good
your answers are before deciding how good *my* answers
should be. See?'

'Sure.' Or, you know, not at all. 'So, you like movies?'
Tom asked, oddly charmed by her uncertainty.

Violet's gaze flew up to meet his. 'Is that your first
question? Because I hadn't decided…'

'Okay. Not an official question. Just an idle wondering.'
Anything that got her talking was good with him.

'Then, yes. I like movies.' She took a breath. 'So, my
turn.'

'You've decided, then?'

Violet nodded. 'I think so.'

'So was that me going first, or did that one not count
and this next question is you going first?' He grinned at
the frustration that crossed her face.

'Does it matter?'

'Not really, I suppose.' Tom settled back in his chair.
'Go on, then. Ask away.'

'Why did you agree to come and stay at Huntingdon
Hall, and work on this book for Dad?'

Was that an easy one, to lull him into a false sense of
security? Or did she just have no idea what to ask? Either
way, he wasn't going to be so gentle.

'Because it's the chance of a lifetime,' he said with a
shrug. Faint disappointment coloured Violet's face, and
he realised suddenly that maybe this wasn't an easy question. Maybe she was asking more than he'd first thought.
He paused, and considered the real answer. 'The Screaming Lemons were my mum's favourite band; they were
the soundtrack to my childhood. So even if this wasn't a
great opportunity to really make my name—and hopefully some money—I'd still have wanted to take the job.
Your dad, his friends, your family—you're part of mod-

ern history. You matter to the collective memory of music lovers everywhere. I don't want that to be lost when we're all dead and gone.'

'The music would live on,' Violet said, her head tipped slightly to one side as she studied him. 'Isn't that enough?'

'In lots of ways, yes. But the Lemons were more than just the music. They're people too—people who mean a lot to their fans, like my mother. And I don't want the truth of who they are to be lost to the stories and anecdotes of people who barely knew them.' Had he even realised why this mattered to him until she'd asked? He didn't think so. Until this moment, he'd thought he was just there to do a job—a fun, fulfilling and hopefully lucrative job, but a job nonetheless. Now it felt more like a vocation.

'So is your mum pleased you're doing it?' Violet asked.

'That's a separate question,' Tom pointed out with a frown. Why had he even mentioned his mother? She was the last thing he wanted to talk about, and he had put the idea in her head. He was normally sharper than this. 'My turn first.'

Violet took a deep breath, as if steeling herself for something deeply unpleasant. 'Go on, then.'

What to ask? Or, rather, what to ask first? He had a lengthy list in his head of things he wanted to know, but where to start? If he went in with something too heavy, she might shy away. But if he started out gentle and they ran out of time, or she called a halt earlier than he'd like, he might never get to the important questions. Tricky.

In the end, he went for something in the middle.

'How do you feel about your twin sister marrying your best friend?'

Violet rolled her eyes and picked up her sandwich with both hands. 'I wondered how long it would take you to get to that.' She took a bite of her sandwich—a stalling tactic,

Tom decided. Something to make her look busy while she considered her answer.

'You promised me the truth,' he reminded her.

Violet swallowed her mouthful. 'I know, I know. Okay, it's a little bit weird, but I'm honestly really happy for them. I thought I was going to have to spend the rest of my life pretending to like Will's fiancées, then celebrating when he inevitably ran off and left them at the altar. This time, I was praying for him to go through with it. They're a good match.'

'So why is it weird?' Tom asked, hoping she wouldn't notice him slipping in the extra question.

Violet tilted her head to the side, considering. 'I guess just because it was never like that with us. Rose is practically my double, but there's a chemistry and a connection between them that just never existed between me and Will. And now it's my turn again.'

She smiled, her gaze catching his, and Tom found himself mesmerised by those bright blue eyes once more. He knew what she meant about the chemistry. He'd met Rose, had a very pleasant lunch and conversation with her. But he'd never found himself wanting to uncover all her secrets, or wanting to reach across and tuck a rogue strand of hair behind her ear. If Rose had told him that no dating agency in the world would set them up, he'd have laughed with her—not stubbornly set out to prove her wrong.

Which was ridiculous. Violet was right—they had nothing in common, no shared history or world. So why was he trying so hard to find a connection between them? Even he wasn't oblivious enough to pretend it was just for a story.

'Go on, then,' he said, breaking away from the look first. 'Ask.'

'I already have. Is your mum pleased you're doing this story?' Violet asked, and Tom's gaze flew away from hers.

'Sorry, only...you mentioned her before—that she was a big fan of Dad's. I just wondered if you were close, I guess.'

'She's dead,' Tom said, wincing at how blunt it came out. 'I mean, she died, about seven years ago now. So, uh, she doesn't know I'm here, but if she did...yeah, I think she'd be pleased. I think she'd have wanted to come too!'

'I'm sorry.' Violet's eyes were wide and sad. 'The way you talked about her, I just assumed... It must have been awful.'

Tom shrugged. 'It was. Still is, in lots of ways. I miss her, of course. And I think about her a lot. But...' Did he want to tell her this? One confidence in the hope of winning a lot more from her in return. 'When she died...we weren't on the best of terms. That's what I regret most. Not having the time to make things right with her before she died.'

He'd expected the sympathy in Violet's eyes, but not the sadness. 'I really am sorry, Tom. But I think she must have known how much you loved her—I can tell just from five minutes speaking with you, and she knew you your whole life.'

'I hope so.' Tom reached for his pint as a distraction. 'My turn. So...' This was it. This was his chance to ask the question he really wanted to know the answer to, while she was still feeling sorry for him. So why didn't he want to ask it, all of a sudden?

He pushed himself to, though. 'The sex tape. Why did you never issue a statement about it? An apology or an explanation?'

'Because it was nobody's damn business,' Violet snapped. 'If they want to watch it, fine, I can't stop them. But I don't have to acknowledge it.'

'Yeah, but a leaked sex tape... There's always talk that the subject might have put it out themselves. For the publicity or whatever. You didn't even deny that.' And *every-body* denied that. That was what made the whole Sex Tape Twin scandal so strange.

Violet looked him straight in the eye, her mouth hard and her jaw tight. 'Since I didn't even know I was being filmed at the time, it seems unlikely that I'd have been able to leak it to the media, doesn't it?'

'You didn't…you honestly didn't know you were being filmed?' Because that made it a whole different story. That…well, that explained a lot about why Violet was so touchy on the subject of trust.

'Of course I didn't! Do you really think I'd let someone film me doing…that?' She shook her head. 'Of course you do. Because you don't know me at all, just like I said. All you know about me is what you've read on the internet, the same as everyone else. Despite the fact you've spent the last week in my home—and apparently learnt nothing at all.'

'I didn't… I just assumed…' His arguments sounded stupid now. Of course Violet wouldn't—this was the woman who trusted no one outside her family. Why would she trust someone to film her being that vulnerable? Except, of course, something had to have happened to make her that wary. And it would make sense for this to be it. 'You looked straight into the camera, Violet. You had to know it was there.'

She blinked at him, shock in those blue eyes. 'I…I did? God, how many times did you watch it, Tom?'

'Not even once all the way through,' he promised. 'But there are stills…'

'Oh, I know. Someone sent a whole pack of them to my parents, along with a note that read "Your daughter is a whore" in bright red lipstick.'

'That's…wow. That's awful.'

'Yeah.' Reaching over, Violet stole his pint and took a sip. Then she sighed. 'Okay, look. I will tell you the story of the sex tape saga. But then that's it for today, yeah? And if you use *any* of it in this damn book of yours—'

'I should. You should want me to,' Tom interrupted. 'The world thinks that you filmed that tape on purpose. Half of them probably think you leaked it yourself. That's all the world knows of you. Don't you want them to know the truth?'

'I just want them all to forget,' Violet whispered, and something in Tom's chest clenched tight at the misery in her voice.

'Tell me what happened,' he said, reaching across the table to take her hand.

Violet looked up, her eyes wide and sad, and said, 'Okay.'

Oh, God, she didn't want to talk about this. Didn't want to admit all over again how stupid she'd been. Stupid, naïve and blind. Or, as Rose put it, nineteen.

'So, after I left boarding school, I took a gap year. I did some work experience at a newspaper because I thought I wanted to study journalism.'

'*You* wanted to become a reporter? You?'

Violet rolled her eyes at the mocking disbelief on Tom's face.

'Yes. I was eighteen then, and a totally different person. And this will go a lot quicker if you don't question everything.' If he interrupted her too much, Violet wasn't sure she could get through to the end of the story at all.

'Sorry. Carry on.' Tom took a big bite of his burger to show he wasn't going to talk any more.

'Okay, so I was working on this paper where no one cared who my parents were—or if they did, it was mostly only to complain about it. I wasn't getting paid, and mostly I fetched coffee, made photocopies and—eventually, once they realised I wasn't an idiot—checked copy and wrote filler pieces from press releases that got emailed in.'

'Sounds familiar,' Tom said through a mouthful of lunch.

'While I was there, I met a guy.'

'Less familiar.'

Violet tried to smile, to acknowledge his attempt to lighten the mood. But just thinking back to those days made her chest hurt. She'd been so young, so carefree. She'd really believed she could do anything she wanted, could be anyone if she just worked at it hard enough.

Finding out she was wrong had almost broken her.

'He was called Nick. He was one of the paper's senior reporters and he kind of took me under his wing. At first I thought it might be because of who my parents were—even then, I was used to people trying to get close to me just so they could get closer to *them*. But Nick didn't seem interested in them. Only me.' He'd made her feel so special—as if her family were the least interesting thing about her. No one had ever managed that before.

Of course, it was all a lie, which might have made it easier.

'What happened?' Tom's expression was already grim, knowing how the story ended. Violet didn't blame him. It wasn't pretty.

'We dated for a bit. He took me places I'd never even thought of going before. I thought...' So, so naïve. 'I thought it was something real. That he loved me as much as I believed I loved him.'

'But he didn't?' There was no pity in Tom's eyes, which she appreciated. The pity was almost worse than the laughter.

'He filmed us in bed together without my knowledge, then put it out on the internet. I believe he also sold some of the photos to the highest bidder first.'

'Bastard.' Violet had never heard quite so much vehemence put into two syllables before.

'The worst thing was…it took me a while to realise what he'd done. I thought it was a fake, or that someone had filmed us without our knowledge…' She swallowed, not wanting to relive the next part. But she'd promised him the truth. 'I went to see him, talking about lawyers and what we could do to get it taken down…and he laughed at me. As did the woman who was in his bed at the time.'

Tom winced at that. 'Jesus. That's…what a piece of work. No wonder you've been hiding out at Huntingdon Hall for the last eight years.'

Violet shrugged. 'It's safe there. I don't have to deal with the press, or the public, or what everyone thinks they know about me, most of the time.'

'So…that's when you stopped trusting people?'

'Do you blame me?' Violet asked.

Tom shook his head. 'No. But one thing I don't understand. Why didn't you let people know the truth? Put out a statement, or sue the scumbag?'

Rose had wanted her to, Violet remembered. Had wanted her to fight back, to fight as dirty as Nick had. She'd wanted to use every connection their parents had to ruin Nick's life the way he'd wrecked hers.

But Violet had said no.

'I didn't want to be that person,' she said, wondering if Tom would understand. Rose had, eventually, but it had taken years. 'I didn't want to drag things out in the papers and on the news. I didn't want to make things all about me. I just wanted it to go away. For people to forget.'

'Except they never did,' Tom said.

Violet stared down at her plate. 'No. They didn't. And it's too late now to change anyone's ideas about me.'

'Maybe not.' Tom leant back in his chair, studying her so intently that it made Violet's skin itch.

'What do you mean?'

Tom shrugged. 'I just wondered if maybe your dad's determination to have me write this book, now, might have something to do with telling the truth about your story, too. Letting the world know what really happened at last.'

Violet shook her head. It wasn't enough. 'Why would they believe it? It's too late now, anyway. It's much harder to change entrenched beliefs than just telling the truth.'

Tom's smile was slow and full of promise. 'Then you clearly haven't read much of my writing. Just wait and see what I can do.'

CHAPTER TEN

'So, WHERE DO you want to start today?' Rick Cross lounged back in his chair in the little sitting room off his studio, looking utterly relaxed. A complete contrast to how his daughter had looked when Tom had asked *her* a few innocent questions over lunch at the start of the week.

Focus, Tom. He had *the* Rick Cross here ready to interview, and he did not have time to be distracted by thoughts of Violet.

'Well, we've covered the basic history of the band—although there are lots of areas I want to dig deeper into later, when we have more time. But since I know you need to head out again in an hour…maybe we should use the time to talk about where The Screaming Lemons are today, and where they're headed next?'

'And the family. Don't forget that,' Rick said. 'I want the story of my family to be told, as much as the band. And it's exciting times around here at the moment.'

'Of course.' Including, presumably, Violet's story. How did she feel about that? he wondered. On the one hand, it would mean everyone knowing the truth—and hadn't he promised her he'd change the minds of the Great British—and American—public with his words? But even if the new press attention was more positive than it had ever been before, it would still put her front and centre again. And leave people talking about her sex life more than ever.

From what he'd learned of Violet, that wasn't going to go down well.

'But let's start with the band,' Tom said. He wanted to talk to Violet some more himself before he started discussing her with her father.

Rick gave him a knowing look. 'Okay. What do you want to know?'

Tom already had every detail of the upcoming tour and album launch, what singles they were planning to release when, who'd written most of which song, and who'd done the cover art—and nothing that he couldn't have got from an informative press release.

He needed to go deeper.

'What issues did you run into writing and recording this album that you maybe haven't had to worry about before?' he asked.

Rick smirked. 'You mean broken hips and playing the guitar with a walking frame now we're all so old?'

'Not necessarily.' Tom gave him an apologetic smile. 'But your last album was five years ago now, and life has to have changed for you all. Two of your daughters have got married, your first grandchild is on the way... Jez got divorced a couple of years ago, right?' Rick nodded. 'And the world—the music scene particularly—has changed too. How did that affect things?'

Leaning back in his chair, Rick brought one ankle up to rest on his opposite knee, obviously belying the need for hip replacements. He was only sixty, if that, Tom thought. There was a lot more music to come from the Lemons yet.

'I think...the music scene changes by the minute. You can't write songs to that. I let the marketing people worry about it, and we just get on with writing the best tunes we can. As for the family stuff… Every year we become more settled, happier in the place we're in. We're fortunate. We're all healthy, living the lives we want to live.' An uncomfortable look crossed his face and Tom knew he couldn't *not* ask any more.

'Except Violet,' he said softly.

'Except my Violet,' Rick confirmed.

Tom put down his notepad on the low table between them, dropping his pen on top of it. His phone was still recording, of course, but he knew he wouldn't use whatever Rick said next. Not officially, anyway.

'Is that one of the reasons you asked me here?'

Rick raised an eyebrow. 'You think you can make Violet happy? Get her to follow her dreams at last?'

'Not that.' Tom shook his head, hoping he wasn't actually blushing in front of a rock legend. As if he'd be so presumptuous as to think he could fix Violet's life. 'I meant…the world never got to hear the true story. Their image of Violet, their beliefs about her—that's a large part of what keeps her hiding away here. It did cross my mind that you might want this book to change that. To let people see the real Violet.'

Rick studied him for a long moment before answering, and Tom fought his impulse to look away. He had a feeling that this moment in time, this answer, would set the tone for every interview that followed. That Rick was judging him and his abilities right now, making a decision about how much to tell him—for this question and every one that came after.

And Tom really, really wanted to be found worthy.

'I think, in the end, that Violet will be the one to show the world what she's really made of. She'll be the one to stand up and say, *You were wrong about me.*' Rick flashed a quick smile. 'But anything you can do to help that along would be appreciated.'

Violet glared at the piece of paper in front of her as the phone in her hand clicked over to voicemail again.

'You've reached Jake Collins, music agent. You know what to do at the beep.'

She hung up. If Olivia's manager hadn't responded to any of the other messages she'd left him in the days since their last phone call, not to mention the emails, then why would this message be any different?

Maybe she should threaten him, like Tom had. Except she was very afraid that Mr Collins would just laugh at her and go right back to ignoring her. Not ideal.

Placing her phone back on the desk, she read through Olivia's contract to appear in the concert again. That, at least, was signed. But since she'd somehow got a clause included that meant it was only valid with the accompanying agreed and signed rider, it wasn't worth the paper it was printed on. The rider was not only unsigned, but nowhere near agreed.

Violet had emailed over a revised version after their last conversation, deleting the request for ridiculously over-priced vodka amongst other things, and leaving in the more reasonable stuff. Since then, she'd heard nothing from Olivia's camp.

A knock on the door roused her from her thoughts and she looked up to see Tom loitering in the doorway. She scowled at him by reflex.

'What did I do to put such a look on your face today?' he asked good-naturedly, dropping to sit in what Violet had somehow come to think of as his chair. 'Since you haven't actually seen me since breakfast, when I think I was mostly inoffensive.'

'Jake Collins isn't answering my calls. Or my emails.'

'Olivia's manager?' Tom shook his head. 'He likes his games, that one.'

'I'd rather figured that out for myself, actually,' Violet snapped. 'And this particular game is down to you, I think.'

'You think he's ignoring you because of what I said to him the other day?' Tom shrugged. 'He still deserved it.'

Which was true, but not particularly helpful. 'I think he's stringing me along, making me fret until the very last moment when he'll show up with both the signed rider and my big name act for the concert.'

'Then why are you worrying?' Tom asked. 'Just ignore his little mind games and get on with everything else.'

He made it sound so easy. 'Because there's always the possibility that he's playing a different game. Olivia's contract is pretty much meaningless without the signed rider and if they pull out at the last minute, once all the concert publicity is done and the programmes printed...'

Tom winced at the implication. 'So what are you going to do?'

And wasn't that the three thousand dollar bottle of vodka question? What did she do? Keep phoning and emailing like a desperate person? The ballsy thing to do would be to cancel Olivia altogether, unless the rider was signed by the end of the day—Violet was sure that was what Rose would do. But Violet didn't have Rose's connections to help her find a suitably starry replacement at the last moment.

Which only left door number three.

'I'm going to go and find Jake Collins and his teenage pop idol and get a signature on this bloody rider, that's what I'm going to do.' Violet wished she felt as confident as she sounded. Turning her laptop so Tom could see, she elaborated. 'Olivia's in the middle of a UK arena tour at the moment. Today's Friday, so she's in…' she ran a finger down the list of tour dates on the screen '…Brighton. So that's where I'm going.'

Tom blinked at her, then a slow smile spread across his face. 'Road trip. Cool. When do we leave?'

'We?' That wasn't the plan at all. 'No we. Just me. I need to do this myself.'

'Hey, I'm not planning on interfering,' Tom said, holding his hands up in a surrender pose. 'I just want to see you take Jake Collins down yourself this time. Off the record, of course.'

'Of course,' Violet echoed with disbelief. As much as, oddly, she found she wouldn't mind Tom's company on the trip, she wasn't sure this was an episode she wanted finding its way into his book.

'Besides, I know the PR staff at the venue. I can probably get us press credentials to get us into the gig in the first place.'

Okay, now that would be useful. She hadn't even thought beyond getting to Brighton to how she'd actually get past security to see the star and her manager.

Decision made, Violet closed the lid of her laptop. 'Better grab your stuff then. If I want to get there before the gig, I need to leave in…' she checked her watch '…twenty minutes.'

Tom grinned and jumped to his feet. 'I'll be ready in fifteen.'

Which was all very well for him. Violet wasn't sure she'd ever be ready for a road trip with Tom Buckley.

CHAPTER ELEVEN

TOM WAS ALREADY leaning against the car when Violet emerged from Huntingdon Hall eighteen minutes later, overnight bag in hand. He hadn't wanted to risk her disappearing without him.

Inviting himself along on her little road trip had been a spur of the moment decision, but he'd decided while packing that it was a good one. From a purely professional standpoint, watching Violet take on Jake Collins could be pure gold for the book—not to mention the fact that a couple of hours trapped in a car together would give him plenty of time to interview her on the way to Brighton. For once, she wouldn't be able to escape his questions.

He was less comfortable with his other reasons for wanting to accompany her. Because he had to admit the truth—to himself, if not to Violet—that when he'd made the decision to join her he hadn't been thinking professionally at all. He'd been thinking about the look on her face when Jake Collins had spoken to her as if she were nothing. He'd been thinking about her plucking up the courage to face him and demand a signature.

He'd been thinking that he didn't want her to have to do it alone. And he wasn't sure he wanted to know why it mattered so much to him that he would be there to protect her.

Shaking his head to clear his rebellious thoughts, Tom grinned at Violet as she drew close. 'Ready?'

'As I'll ever be.' She gave him a less certain smile. 'You know, you really don't have to come. I'll be fine.'

Tom shrugged. 'I know. But I've been in the country for over a week now, and still haven't seen anything but the airport and Huntingdon Hall. I'm ready for a road trip.'

Violet opened the trunk and they both stashed their bags. 'You've been to Britain before, though, right?' she asked as she slid into the driver's seat.

'Loads of times,' Tom admitted. 'But I've never seen any of it with you.'

She opened her mouth as if about to answer, then closed it again, frowning at the steering wheel. 'We should get going, then.'

Tom settled back into the passenger seat as Violet started the engine, turned on the radio and pulled out onto the long driveway. At least he wasn't the only one a little unsettled by their connection.

They travelled mostly in silence, content to listen to the radio, until they reached the motorway—and stationary traffic. Tom's only attempts at conversation—gentle precursors to the questions he actually wanted to ask—had been rebuffed by a sharp, 'I'm trying to concentrate on the road right now,' from Violet. Not that he believed her. He knew a stalling tactic when he heard one.

But as the motionless cars spread out ahead of them as they crested the slip road, he straightened up in his seat and prepared to try again.

'Looks like we might have to catch Olivia after her performance,' he said, as casually as he could.

Violet swore in response, and he hid a grin. Where had a nice girl like her learnt words like that?

'That was off the record, by the way,' she added.

'Of course,' Tom said, as seriously as he could manage.

'Dammit.' Violet thumped a hand against the steering wheel. 'Can you check the traffic reports? See how bad this is likely to be?'

Tom nodded and reached for his phone but, before he could find it, a shrill ringing filled the car.

'That's mine.' Violet nodded towards where her phone sat in a little space below the dashboard. Cars up ahead jerked forward, just enough for her to try and edge the car onto the main motorway. 'Is it Mr Collins?'

Tom fished out the phone and looked. 'It's your mother.'

'Of course.' Violet sighed. 'I'll call her back when we get there.'

'Or I could just…' Tom swiped the screen to answer, and gave Violet an innocent smile in response to her glare. 'Hello, Sherry. Violet's just driving at the moment. Can I help?'

'Tom, great—yes, please. Can you tell her that I just had Frances Littlewood on the phone, asking who Violet is bringing as her plus one for Henry's wedding next weekend? She says one of Henry's ushers is single if she's stuck…'

Sherry sounded harried, which was very unlike her. But then, Henry Littlewood's wedding was the theatre dynasty event of the summer. In fact, he had a feeling that Rick and Sherry were godparents to Henry himself. The Littlewoods had the same sort of money, prestige and power in the acting world as Rick and Sherry had in the music one. It was bound to be quite the event. Quite the *public* event. Just the sort of thing Violet usually avoided, as far as Tom could tell.

He covered the phone with his hand. 'She wants to know who you're taking to Henry Littlewood's wedding next weekend. Otherwise, Frances Littlewood is setting you up with an usher.'

Violet swore again and Tom grinned, glad Sherry couldn't hear.

'Not looking forward to it?' he asked, already pretty sure of the answer.

'Henry's a family friend, and his mother made his fiancée make me one of her bridesmaids too, which she probably hates me for.' Violet sighed. 'I want to go for him, and Mum and Dad will be there, probably Daisy and Seb too… It's just…'

'You don't want to face all the people. And the cameras.'

'Yeah.'

Tom considered. There was a chance Violet might never forgive him for what he was about to do. On the other hand, if he could convince her of the truth—that it was the act of a friend, that he honestly had no ulterior motive for this… maybe it could bring them closer.

Maybe, one day, Violet would learn to trust him.

He lifted the phone to his ear again.

'Sherry, if it's okay with you and Rick, I'm going to accompany Violet. As her date, not a reporter on this occasion!'

'Well,' Sherry said, sounding taken aback, 'that sounds lovely. I'm sure we'll all have a delightful day.'

'Me too.' Although, judging by the shocked glare on Violet's face, only if he lived that long. 'See you later, Sherry.'

Silence reined in the motionless car for a long, long moment.

Then Violet said, 'You are never answering my phone again.'

What was he thinking? Well, actually, Violet was pretty sure she knew exactly what he was thinking—what a perfect way to further his career by sneaking into a society wedding under the guise of being her date. It wasn't as if she hadn't got used to being used for her name and family over the years, but this one really did take the biscuit.

'I meant what I said,' Tom told her, his expression deceptively earnest. 'I'm not going to the wedding as a journalist.'

'No, you said you were going as my date. Aren't you supposed to *ask* a girl before declaring something a date?' Because if he'd asked she could have said no. And she almost certainly would have. Probably.

'Well, it was kind of a spur of the moment decision. Much like this road trip.' He shot her a sideways glance she pretended not to see. 'Is it such a bad idea?'

'Yes!'

'Why?'

'Because…oh, so many reasons. Because you're not my boyfriend; you're the guy who's here to research and write about me and my family. Because you're always, always a reporter, no matter how much you pretend you're taking a day off. Journalists don't do off-duty.'

'Okay, answer me this one question honestly.' Violet stared out of the windscreen at the road as he talked. Because she needed to concentrate on driving, not because she was ignoring him. Really. Even if the car wasn't moving. 'Will the wedding be more or less fun with me there to keep you company?'

Damn him. Violet bit the inside of her cheek to keep from answering. Even with Daisy and her parents there, it would be better with Tom. Because Daisy and Seb would be all loved-up again, and so would Mum and Dad probably, and everyone would start telling stories about their own weddings or engagements or romantic moments… and, for once, she wouldn't have to sit there as sorry single Violet whose heart had been betrayed and broken by the only man she'd ever loved.

'Violet? More or less fun?' Tom pressed.

'More.' The word came out begrudgingly.

'Great! Then it's all settled.' Tom beamed at her and Violet almost missed her chance to move forward two metres.

Settled wasn't the word she'd use at all. In fact, things felt more unsettled than ever to Violet.

'So, how many times will you have been a bridesmaid this year, after this one?' Tom asked.

Violet tried to pretend her cheeks weren't getting warm. 'Three, including Mum and Dad's renewal. And you know what they say…'

'No idea, actually,' Tom said cheerfully.

'Three times the bridesmaid, never the bride,' Violet quoted. 'Of course, this is actually the sixteenth time I've been a bridesmaid, so I think we're long past worrying about that.' Not that that would stop everyone there thinking it, or whispering it behind her back, she was sure.

Tom let out a low whistle. 'Sixteen. That's, wow. A lot.'

'Yeah. Most of them were as kids—you know, family friends or people who just wanted cute, famous twin girls to walk down the aisle with them or to make sure Rick and Sherry were photographed at their wedding. You know how it goes.'

'Yeah, I guess.'

'I've only done it five or six times since I left university. Mostly for friends.' Why was she still talking about this? He couldn't possibly care.

'Still, it's a good job you look so great in bridesmaid dresses,' Tom said with a grin.

No pretending she wasn't blushing this time. But thinking about bridesmaid dresses just made her remember the one she was wearing when she'd met him, and what had followed next.

Still not her finest moment.

'Did you check that traffic report?' she asked, eager for a change of subject.

Tom pulled out his own phone and jabbed at the screen for a while. 'Okay, it looks like this carries on for the next couple of junctions. Then we should be clear.'

Violet sighed. 'So, after the gig it is. There's no way we'll make it before at this rate.' They'd been cutting it close as it was. And by the time the gig was over she was going to be exhausted, even if things went well.

'Want me to see if I can find us rooms at a hotel somewhere near the arena?' Tom asked, as if he'd read her mind. It was kind of disconcerting.

She bit her lip. Did she? It would mean a whole night away with Tom Buckley, plus the drive home tomorrow. He was bound to use that to his advantage, even if she was slightly reassured by his use of the plural 'rooms'. But was that more dangerous than driving home exhausted? No. Of course it wasn't.

She sighed. 'Yeah, I guess so.'

They inched forward another few metres as Tom frowned at his phone screen. Eventually he gave a little cheer of triumph, and tucked his phone away again.

'Got something?'

'Nothing near the arena,' Tom said, 'but I got us two rooms right on the front, in some hotel with an old-fashioned name. I'm not sure I've ever seen the ocean in Britain.'

'It's the sea here,' Violet corrected him. 'And the British seaside is an institution, I suppose. You should see it.'

A broad smile split Tom's face. 'Great! Only thing I

can't figure out is why one of the rooms was half the price of the other.'

Violet could guess. Not all of those old seaside hotels were in the best of repair these days. 'Well, tell you what, you can take that room and find out. Okay?'

Tom's smile didn't even fade an iota. 'Whatever you say, boss.'

Violet turned her attention back to the traffic ahead of her. She had a feeling it was going to be a very long night.

CHAPTER TWELVE

THE CONCERT HAD to be well underway by the time Violet
swung her little car into the car park nearest to the arena.
Tom had exercised discretion as the better part of valour
and avoided asking too many questions for the latter part
of the journey, as Violet's expression grew stony and set
as the traffic worsened.

He almost pitied Jake Collins, the mood she was in.
But only almost.

'You can definitely get us in there, yes?' Violet asked,
switching off the engine and lights. At high summer, the
sun was still going down but it still felt late.

'It's done.' Tom stretched his legs out of the door, feeling his back pop as he arched it. 'There should be passes
waiting for us at the door.' He didn't mention exactly how
much favour currency he'd exchanged for that privilege.

Violet stalked off in what he presumed was the direction of the arena and he hurried to catch her up, pausing
only briefly to admire the look of her determined walk
and her behind in tight blue jeans.

As he'd promised, they were waved through backstage
without any noticeable delays. From the amused look one
of the security guards gave Violet, Tom had a feeling that
she could probably have talked her way in there without

him anyway. She had a very famous face, after all. Not to mention the rest of her.

Violet paused for a moment in the empty corridor backstage as they approached the star dressing room. The sound of Olivia's latest hit echoed around the hallways. Tom stood beside her as she leant against the cool painted wall.

'You ready for this?' he asked, his voice low, relying on his close proximity to ensure he was heard.

'No.' She gave him a wobbly smile. 'But I'm going to do it anyway.'

God, you had to admire that kind of spirit. That kind of grit. The woman he'd thought she was when they met wouldn't have been afraid, and the one he'd come to know in his first days at Huntingdon Hall wouldn't have dared. But this Violet—the woman he was beginning to think of as his Violet, without any justification—she was braver than either of those other women he'd thought he knew.

She was magnificent.

'I'll be right here,' Tom promised. 'But you won't need me.'

Her smile firmed up a little at that, and something in his chest grew warmer. Was it his heart? It had been so long he could hardly tell.

Slowly, Tom leant forward to press a kiss against her forehead, but she tilted her head up to look at him and then…well, it was only natural for him to place that kiss on her lips, right?

'Yeah? Well, you tell them not to call me again until we're talking about top billing, okay? My girl headlines or nothing at all.'

The terse voice cut through what Tom thought was pretty much a perfect moment. Violet jerked back, putting unwelcome inches between them, and Tom bit back a growl of frustration.

'Mr Collins,' Violet said, in what Tom recognised as a dangerously sweet voice. Shaking off the kiss fog that had filled his brain, he tried to focus on what was happening in front of him. How much had the agent seen?

Jake Collins blinked, then jabbed at the screen of his smartphone and slipped it into his pocket. 'Miss Huntingdon-Cross. What a…surprise. And Mr Buckley, correct? Now, what can I do for you two lovebirds?'

Damn. That answered the question of whether Jake had noticed them kissing. Violet's cheeks grew a little pink and Tom cursed his lack of impulse control. Couldn't he have waited to kiss the girl *after* she'd taken care of business?

'I won't take more than a moment of your time, Mr Collins,' Violet continued smoothly, ignoring Jake's amused look and raised eyebrows. Tom stayed a few steps away to the side, close enough to see everything, but not so close that Jake Collins would be able to turn things round and try to deal with him instead. This was Violet's rodeo.

'We're actually in the middle of a pretty big gig here right now, in case you haven't noticed.' Jake's gaze flicked over to Tom. 'I realise you may have had other distractions to deal with.'

Again, Violet ignored the innuendo, so Tom resisted the urge to land a punch on the manager's face. Just.

'Trust me, Mr Collins, I'm here on business,' Violet said crisply. 'Olivia hasn't signed the revised rider yet. You may not be aware but the contract for her to appear at the Benefit Concert is void without the signed rider.' Jake's mouth twitched up at that. Of course he was aware. But Violet kept talking. 'Since I couldn't get hold of you by phone or email, I thought the simplest thing would be to come down here in person with the rider.' She pulled a folder out of her bag and handed it over.

Jake didn't even open it. 'Obviously you realise that

Olivia needs to sign this? And she's a little busy right now.'
As if to punctuate his statement, Olivia hit the high note
of her latest single and the walls around them vibrated
with the sound.

'We can wait.' Violet smiled patiently and Tom brought
his hand to his mouth to hide his own grin.

With a sigh, Jake flipped open the cover of the folder
and glared at the paper inside. 'This isn't what I agreed
with your sister.'

'That is the standard rider that every other act appearing in the concert has signed, plus a couple of the more
reasonable requests from Olivia's original list,' Violet said.
'If it isn't acceptable to you, or to Olivia, I need you to tell
me now. We have just over a week until the concert and if
I need to find a replacement I need to do it immediately.
I'm sure you understand.'

Tom glanced down at Violet's hands, resting at her
sides, and noticed they were trembling, just slightly. Jake
wouldn't have noticed, he was sure. No one who wasn't
looking, or who didn't know Violet, would. She sounded
completely in control of the moment, of the man even.

Only Tom knew she was terrified.

Had she been scared that night at the airport? He hadn't
known to look for the signs, then. Had just assumed that
she was the cocky, self-assured celebrity kid he was expecting.

Now he knew her better. And cared for her all the more
for it.

'You really think you could find an act of the same calibre as Olivia in a week?' Jake shook his head and laughed.

'It's not the calibre I'd be worried about,' Violet shot
back. 'The same level of fame may be a problem, but I
could call a dozen better acts and have them on the stage
in moments.' Tom winced at the sting in her words.

'Of course, the real problem would be the fans,' Jake threw back. 'Because, whatever you think of her talent, Olivia is the one they want to see. I'd like to see you fill that concert without her.'

Violet nodded, her face solemn. 'And I'm sure Olivia would hate to let down her fans. Which is why, if she's not planning to appear, it would be best to know now. So I can put out an official statement apologising to her fans on Olivia's behalf. I'm sure they'll understand when I explain that we were unable to divert enough money from the charity account to satisfy her. Especially when that information comes in a paragraph after a detailed description of all the good causes that money is used to support.' She looked thoughtful for a moment. 'Maybe I'll get Dad to put out the statement. After all, it's his concert, and his charities. We could include a list of all the acts who waived their fee for the concert altogether for comparison. What do you think?'

It was more or less the same threat Jake had made himself, but with more teeth. If Olivia pulled out now, Violet would eviscerate her reputation. Jake didn't want a diva on his books—even if that was what he had. He needed Olivia to appear wholesome and loving and giving, so the kids' mums would let their pre-teens buy her music.

Jake Collins glared at Violet for a long moment before flicking his gaze over to Tom. With a 'What can you do?' smile, Tom shrugged.

'Fine.' Jake snapped the word out as he flicked the folder closed again. 'I'll get her to sign it tonight and courier it to you tomorrow.'

'Perfect.' Violet's smile was sharp, with a hint of teeth. 'And if it's not with me by Monday, I'll issue that press release.' She held out a hand, which Jake took, obviously reluctantly. 'I'm so glad we were able to clear this up. I hope the rest of the tour goes well.'

Jake Collins turned on his heel and stalked away down the corridor without so much as a goodbye. Tom watched him go, aware Violet was doing the same. Then, once he'd disappeared around the corner, Tom let out a long breath.

'You did it,' he said.

'I really, really did.' Violet's eyes were wide, her expression stunned. 'I did it, all by myself.'

Tom grinned. 'So what now?'

The shock faded from Violet's face, replaced by elation. 'Now we celebrate!'

CHAPTER THIRTEEN

THE HOTEL BAR was mostly deserted, but Violet managed to scare up a barman to fetch them some drinks, while Tom carried their bags in from the car and got them checked in. She was glad of the few minutes alone; it gave her a chance to process everything that had happened since they'd arrived in Brighton. And somehow the confrontation with Jake Collins was fading in her memory, compared to the brief, soft, mesmerising kiss she'd shared with Tom beforehand.

But all too soon Tom was back and Violet found herself trying very hard not to stare at his mouth. Why had he kissed her? And was he planning on doing it again?

And if he wasn't, would she?

'Here's to beating that scumbag at his own game.' Tom raised his pint to Violet's glass of wine, and she dutifully chinked them together.

'You don't think I went too far?' Violet asked. After all, it was one thing to stop Jake Collins from trying to ruin her concert, another to behave just as badly to get her own way.

Tom shook his head. 'Trust me, I've seen too far. That was just far enough. Your sister would be proud.'

'Except we're not going to tell her about this, right?' Violet said. 'And it's definitely not going in your book.'

'But it's such a great story!' Tom protested.

'About me,' Violet replied. 'A story about me. And the book is supposed to be about the band, in case you've forgotten.'

'And your family. Your dad has been very specific about that.'

Violet rolled her eyes. 'I have no idea why. Him and Mum, yeah, I get. People want to read about their epic romance. And okay, maybe a tiny section on Daisy marrying into the aristocracy, or looking at all the work Rose has done with the band. But what is there to write about me except a sex scandal I'd much rather no one ever mentioned again?'

'I don't know,' Tom said. 'That's what I've been trying to find out.'

'By asking a thousand questions.'

'That you don't answer.' Tom raised his eyebrows. 'Why is that?'

God, he was unstoppable. 'I answered every question you asked me at lunch the other day. I told you everything you could possibly want to know.'

'About one bad experience with a guy eight years ago, yeah,' Tom said. 'But what about who you are now? What's happened in your life since? Your entire existence can't revolve around one bad sex tape, Violet.'

Except it did, however much it hurt to admit. 'Why does it matter so much to you that you know everything about my life?'

'Because I want to understand you!' Violet glanced around her to make sure no one else had come into the bar and started listening, but Tom obviously didn't care if they had. He was on a roll. 'Violet, you are a mystery to me. And uncovering mysteries is kind of my job.'

'But why do you care?' Violet whispered, knowing she

was really asking *Why did you kiss me?* and wishing she didn't need to know the answer so much. How had he got so cleanly under her skin? She'd only known the man a couple of weeks, but suddenly all she wanted in the world was to hear him say that she mattered to him.

'Because...because you're more than your past. You're...God, Violet, you could be anything you wanted, and you're hiding away at Huntingdon Hall. I want to understand you, to know the truth of you. I want...I want you to trust me.'

Didn't it always come down to that? Violet took a breath. 'I came here today, didn't I?'

'You did,' Tom admitted. 'And why was that? I mean, why did you take on the concert at all if you're not desperate to get back to doing *something* with your life?'

Why had she? It seemed so long ago already that she'd agreed to it. 'I think it was partly to prove a point to you,' she admitted. 'After we met at the airport... It felt like you thought I was nothing more than my parents' name and my own infamous internet appearance. I wanted to prove I was something more, I guess.'

'Good! Because you are. And I'm so damn glad you're starting to see it.' He took a long sip of his pint, then frowned. 'If that was only part of the reason, what was the rest?'

He was sitting too close to her to let her think straight. Violet wished she'd picked one of the other tables, one with two chairs on opposing sides, rather than this booth table with one long semi-circular seat. Here, he could keep sliding round until their legs were nearly touching and she couldn't concentrate on anything else...

A question. He'd asked her a question.

'I guess...I didn't want to let Rose down. Or my parents. And...'

'Yeah?' Another inch closer, and she could feel the length of his thigh against hers, warm and comforting. His arm was almost around her shoulders, resting on the back of the booth behind her, cocooning her, keeping her close and safe. Letting her know she could tell him her secrets.

'I wanted to do...more, I guess. I know you think I've just been hanging around at home, arranging the odd bouquet or something. And maybe that's what I wanted people to think, because then they wouldn't expect too much. I don't know.' She took a breath. This wasn't like her past, this was her life, and she wasn't ashamed of it—actually, she was pretty proud of it.

'I do a lot in our community, besides just the flowers, you know. I help out with pensioners' lunches at the church, I run a counselling group and...Mum and I, we set up a helpline. It's national, and it doesn't have our name on it anywhere. But we take calls from kids and teenagers who just need someone to talk to, or need help escaping from dangerous situations. I do a shift on the phones most days, and I take a lot of calls from teenage girls in their first relationships. Girls who've got in too far too fast and don't know how to get out again. I help them.'

She stopped, aware that Tom's hand was on her shoulder now and he was staring down at her, his eyes full of intensity and feeling she couldn't quite decipher.

'So, anyway. Not just sitting around arranging flowers,' she said. 'But I wanted to do more, and the concert... well, it wasn't about me, so it seemed like a safe way to try and do it.'

Tom shook his head. 'Every time I think I've got you sussed out, you go and surprise the hell out of me again and prove you're more than I could have even imagined.'

Violet stared up at him. 'Yeah?'

'Yeah.' Their gazes locked, and she knew before he dipped his head that he was going to kiss her again. And she wanted it so much...but something made her pull back.

'Wait,' she said, and hoped she wouldn't regret it for the rest of her life.

The woman was trying to kill him. That was all there was to it.

Swallowing hard, Tom backed up. Not too far—not far enough to let her forget that gorgeous chemistry that sizzled between them. Just enough for her to know that he wouldn't push anything until she was ready.

'What's the matter?' he asked, trying to find some rationality. But all he could think about was kissing her again, even when she'd made it very clear she didn't want that.

God, he was an idiot. What was he doing? Hell, what was he thinking? She was a subject. Not even that, the daughter of his subject. A secondary interest, worth about twenty pages in the book.

Not someone he should be falling for.

'I don't know.' Violet stared down at her hands, and Tom wished he could read her mind. 'I just...I'm not sure this is a good idea.'

Tom was. At least his body was damn certain it was the best idea he'd had in years.

'Why not?' he asked, disappointment clenching his chest even as he tried to fight it off. She was wary, he knew that. He just needed to win her over. Talk her round. It was all just words—and he was good at words. It was kind of his job, right?

'Because you're a reporter. Because I don't really do relationships. Because you're working for Dad. A million reasons.'

'None of which sound like you don't feel the same things I do when we're together.' She had to feel it too, right? No way that kind of connection only worked one way. It wasn't possible.

Violet sighed. 'Look, I'm not saying I'm not…that there isn't… Okay, fine. Yes, I'm attracted to you, even when I don't want to be. But that doesn't mean we need to…do anything about it. You're staying with my family, working with my parents… We can't risk screwing all that up.'

'It would be worth it.' He was damn sure of that. Even if she was only making the same arguments that had been buzzing round his head for days.

'Come on, Tom.' Violet's lips twisted up in a half smile. 'This is your big break. Don't tell me you'd be willing to risk that just for a quick tawdry fling with the Sex Tape Twin.'

'Don't say that,' Tom snapped. How could she still say that, after everything she'd just told him? 'That's not who you are. Not any more. And never to me.'

'I was, though. That was the first thing you knew about me. And the first thing I knew about you was that you'd watched that damn video.'

'It was work. I didn't…' God, there was no excuse here that would work, was there? 'You weren't…you to me then. You weren't Violet.'

Violet's smile was sad. 'But that's the point, isn't it? I'm not me to anyone. I'm just that stupid, naïve girl in a sexy video. I'm never just Violet.'

'You are to me now,' Tom promised.

'I hope so.' She looked up at him at last, blue eyes wide. 'But in lots of ways you're still just The Reporter to me. I don't…it's weird to think that I've opened up to you more than anyone since Will, but I still barely know anything about you.'

Well, that he could fix, surely? 'What do you want to know?'

'Everything,' Violet replied. 'But not tonight, I don't think. I need a little time to…process everything. I mean, I did something huge today, facing down Jake Collins. I couldn't have done that before, not even a month ago—I just froze up in front of people like that, knowing they were laughing at me inside. I'm changing, and I like it, and I think…I think a lot of it has to do with you being here. But it's all happening so fast, and I still have so much left to do for the concert, and…'

'You need time. I get that.' Disappointment warred with relief inside Tom. She wanted to know everything—and that meant she wasn't the only one who needed time. He needed to think about this too. To figure out how much he could tell her, how far he could let her in before she reached the stuff that would just make her kick him out completely. 'This wouldn't…this isn't a fling, Violet, not for me. And I don't think it is for you either. So we can take our time.' Even if the restraint it required was physically painful.

He managed a small smile for her, and shifted just a little further back. 'We'll talk soon, yeah? I need to go figure out all my cutest childhood tales and stories of selfless behaviour to win you over with.'

Violet paused with one hand on her handbag and threw him a serious look. 'Those aren't the ones I want to hear, Tom. I want the truth, same as you. It's the only way I can learn to trust you.' She leant over and pressed a kiss to the side of his mouth before grabbing her room key from the table and heading for the lobby.

The truth. Tom stared after her as she disappeared into the elevator, her golden hair flowing behind her.

The truth was the one thing he definitely *couldn't* tell her.

Draining the rest of his drink, Tom grabbed his own room key and prepared to head up. He had a lot of thinking —and writing—to do.

CHAPTER FOURTEEN

VIOLET HAD A horrible feeling that Tom was avoiding her.

They hadn't talked much on the way home from Brighton, mostly because Tom had been passed out in the passenger seat after muttering something about the mini bar, a spring sticking in his back, a broken window and a dripping shower keeping him awake. Violet hadn't slept much better, but since her room had been perfectly comfortable the only excuse she had was her own thoughts.

She did think, as she got back onto the motorway, that if he'd been that uncomfortable he could have always come and slept in her room...

Except she'd made it very clear that was off the cards, at least until she got to know him a little better. She'd been in a relationship before where the guy knew all her innermost thoughts and dreams and it turned out she didn't know him at all, and look how that ended. But while she knew that was a perfectly sensible decision in principle, that hadn't made it any easier to dismiss the thoughts of what might have happened if she'd just let him kiss her again.

In the days since then, he'd been nowhere to be seen. He hadn't even joined them for dinner last night. 'Working hard', her dad had said with a wink. And Violet might have believed it if it wasn't now *Friday* and she'd seen neither hide nor hair of him all week.

Oh, he'd been around, she knew that much. Locked away in the studio with her dad conducting more of the interviews he had, in fairness, travelled thousands of miles to do. She'd even overheard him talking with her mother once or twice—more interviews, she supposed—before she'd stopped listening at doors and got back to what she was supposed to be doing.

At least getting on with the planning for the Benefit Concert had mostly distracted her. With only a week left to go, she was reaching the hectic last few pages of Rose's carefully made lists. Jake Collins had even sent in the signed rider, so she didn't have to follow through on her publicity threats.

Things were good, and dealing with Jake had given her added confidence to get on with her job. She was on top of everything, had spoken with almost everyone involved, or at least their representatives, personally—without a single mention of the words 'sex' and 'tape' in the same sentence. She was making progress.

But, she had to admit, she missed Tom.

'Miss him how, exactly?' Daisy asked when she came over to try on potential wedding outfits the day before Henry Littlewood's wedding. 'I mean, he's right here.'

Violet sighed, and tried not to think that Rose would have understood. Even her twin would probably have struggled with this one, especially since Violet wasn't sure even *she* understood it.

'I guess I'd just got used to having him around.' She grabbed another dress from the pile of maternity evening-gwear Daisy had brought with her. 'How about this one?'

Daisy shook her head. 'Lily Taylor wore that one to a gala last month. It's already been photographed, and I don't want to be in any of those "which mum-to-be wore it best?" comparison pieces.'

So why did you bring it? Violet wanted to ask, but didn't. Pregnancy had made Daisy a little touchy.

'And he's still around.' Daisy shifted on the bed, her hand cupped around her growing baby bump. 'He's just a bit busy interviewing Dad and Mum, I suppose. And me.'

'He's interviewed you?' Violet stopped looking through outfits and stared at her sister.

Daisy blinked back blankly. 'Well, yes. He's interviewing all of us, isn't he?'

'Of course. Yeah.' She'd just imagined that he might start with her.

Daisy shifted again to tug on Violet's hand and make her sit on the bed. 'Okay, seriously. What's going on with the two of you? He's coming as your date tomorrow, Mum said the two of you disappeared to Brighton, of all places, last weekend, and now you tell me you haven't seen him all week. I know you'd probably rather tell Rose, but she's not here. So, fess up—what's going on?'

Violet bit her lip. In some ways, it was probably for the best that Rose wasn't there. She'd have sussed out there was something going on by the time Violet and Tom went for that first lunch. As much as she loved her twin, maybe it was better that she didn't have her über-protective identical sister around right now.

And Daisy...Daisy had always been a good listener, when they'd given her something to listen to.

'To be honest, I have no idea.' Violet fell back to lie on the bed, feeling lighter just for saying it. 'He indicated that he has...feelings, I guess. For me.' By kissing her and making her whole world spin.

'And you said?'

'That it was a bad idea.' Which, now, a week later, felt like a fairly epic mistake in its own right.

'Why?' Daisy asked, eyebrows raised in astonishment.

'He's gorgeous, seems nice, Dad adores him, which is always a good sign, and you're obviously a little bit besotted. So what's the problem? He's...oh. He's a reporter.'

Rose would have got there half an hour ago, but in some ways it was more useful to hear the reasons why Violet *should* say yes. Or maybe that was just wishful thinking.

'Actually, for a reporter, he's kind of...un-slimelike.' The admission didn't come easy.

'You really do like him, don't you?'

Violet sighed. Did she? She thought back over the last couple of weeks. Even after their awful first meeting, when really what she'd most wanted to do was strangle him, there'd still been a weird connection when she'd taken his hand. And he truly had been a help with the Benefit Concert. The way he'd spoken to Olivia's manager... He'd stood up for her, been offended on her behalf. And then he'd taken her out for lunch to cheer her up—and interrogate her, of course. Then he'd come all the way to Brighton and stood back and watched her deal with things herself, and knowing he thought she could had given her the confidence she needed to do it.

He understood about not trusting people. And she hoped he'd understood when she'd told him that she needed to know him better to trust *him*. Hoped he realised that just thinking she might eventually be able to trust him was a huge step for her.

Hoped he wasn't actually avoiding her.

'I do,' she admitted. 'I do like him. I just...he's asking all these questions about my life and my family. By the end of this book, he'll be an authority on all things Screaming Lemons and Huntingdon-Cross. I just want to know him as well. Does that make sense?'

'Of course it does!' Daisy stroked a hand down Violet's arm. 'Oh, Vi, I hope he opens up to you. And if he does...

if he gives you what you've asked for…you'll give him a chance, right? I know it's risky—relationships always are— but we all want to see you happy, and if Tom can make you that way…you have to let him try. Okay?'

Violet nodded. Eight years was too long to hide away, anyway. She'd dealt with pop stars, managers, suppliers and even the press covering the concert over the past week. She could deal with one date with a reporter who made her skin tingle. Right?

Saturday morning came almost too fast for Tom. He'd had a plan, a way to convince Violet that he was worth a chance. She wanted to know all about him? Fine. He'd tell her, up to a point. Nobody really needed to know every-thing about another person, right? She just needed to feel as if she understood where he came from, and that much he could give her.

Except, he realised quickly, he was always better with the written word than the spoken one. So he'd decided to find the time to write it all down, starting in a freezing, leaking hotel room in Brighton and continuing in between interviews and typing up his notes and a rush job on a short article for an editor who'd called and offered him a last minute slot.

Somehow, it wasn't until Saturday morning that he re-alised that what he'd written was his own obituary.

Tom stared at the words printed in front of him. Per-haps not the most auspicious start to a relationship, but it did give her all the pertinent information. At least all the information he felt able to share. And it was a start, right? A sign that he could give her what she wanted.

And besides, it was too late to change it now.

A quick shower and Tom dressed in his best suit, ran some gunky stuff through his hair to try and make it be-

have, and hoped he'd be good enough for the Littlewoods.
And Violet.

Rick was already in the kitchen pouring the coffee when
Tom made it downstairs, and Daisy's husband, Seb, sat
at the counter sipping his own mug as he read the paper.

'Ah, our third compatriot,' Rick said, grabbing another
mug and filling it to the brim with hot, strong black coffee. Tom took a sip the moment Violet's father handed it
over. Somehow, in the last three weeks, he'd actually con-
verted to *liking* his coffee black. 'This, gentlemen, is the
part where we wait.'

Tom checked his watch. 'Aren't we supposed to be leaving soon?'

'Theoretically? Yes. But in reality?' Rick shook his
head.

'We told them we needed to leave an hour before we
actually do,' Seb explained. 'That way, we might actually
get out of here on time.'

Taking a seat, Tom tried to imagine Violet taking hours
to get ready. For someone who mostly lived in neat jeans
and blouses, with her hair clipped back, it seemed unlikely.
But, then again, once Sherry got involved...yeah, he could
see things taking a while.

Violet, as a bridesmaid, should, by rights, have stayed
at the hotel the night before with the rest of the wedding
party. But, as she'd pointed out to everyone at dinner earlier in the week, she was only a bridesmaid on the bride's
sufferance, so she wouldn't inflict her presence too early.
'There are, like, ten others anyway. No one is going to
miss me.' So, instead. she'd arranged to have her hair and
make-up done to match everyone else's at the house and
would travel down early with the rest of them.

If she ever finished getting ready.

Two cups of coffee later, Violet appeared, dressed in a

pale blue bridesmaid's dress that left her shoulders bare. Her hair had been pinned back from her face and fell in curls at the back, and her wide dark-lashed eyes looked bluer than ever.

'They are coming, honest. Daisy's just changed her mind about which dress to wear. Again.' Violet swished across the room, her skirt floating around her legs, to fetch herself a coffee. Her shoes were silver, Tom realised. And sparkly.

And he was totally staring.

Blinking, he tore his gaze away, just in time to see Rick hide his smirk behind a coffee cup. Fantastic.

'I'll, uh, go see if the cars are here, shall I?' Tom said, heading out to the front of the house before anyone had time to reply. Maybe the fresh air would help clear his head.

Since they weren't expected for another thirty minutes, of course there were no cars. Stepping to one side of the front door, Tom leant against the brick wall.

'Hey.' He opened his eyes and found Violet standing beside him, cup of coffee in hand. 'You okay?'

'I'm fine,' Tom lied. 'No, actually, I'm not. I have something to give to you, and I'm not sure if I should, if it'll help or if it will scare you off for life...'

Violet raised her eyebrows. 'Well, now you have to give it to me. Because the things I'm imagining just *have* to be worse than whatever the reality is.'

Reaching inside his suit pocket, he pulled out the carefully folded sheet of paper.

'Okay, so you said you wanted to know about me. About my life. And so I thought I'd write it down—that's what I've been doing this week, when I wasn't interviewing your family. So...here it is.' He held out the piece of paper and waited for her to take it, half wishing that she wouldn't.

But she did, her wary eyes huge as they met his. Then she unfolded it, looked down and her eyebrows drew down as her brow furrowed.

'This is… Is this your obituary?'

'Kind of.' Tom hunted for a way to explain. 'When I used to work on a local newspaper, one of the things I was in charge of was keeping the obituaries up to date for local celebrities. So that if anything happened, we were ready to run. I have a few on hand for musicians I've written about or interviewed a lot, too, ready for when the time comes. So when I sat down to write about my life…it just kind of came out that way.'

Violet stared at him. 'You really are a journalist all the way to your core, aren't you?'

'Apparently so.' He just wished that wasn't the one thing she didn't want him to be.

'Is the car here yet, darling?' Sherry's voice floated down the stairs and out of the front door. 'We don't want to be late.'

Violet folded the paper again and slipped it into the tiny silver bag she carried. 'I'll read this later,' she promised. 'And then…maybe we can, uh, talk again?'

'I'd like that a lot,' Tom replied. Of course, first they had to get through the Littlewood wedding. Suddenly, he'd never been so unexcited at the prospect of spending a day with the rich and famous.

CHAPTER FIFTEEN

'So, what do we think?' Daisy asked as they finished up their puddings later that evening. 'Better or worse than my wedding?'

'Our wedding,' Seb put in, around a mouthful of chocolate and pistachio torte. Daisy waved a hand dismissively at him.

'Not a patch on yours, Daze,' Violet assured her sister. 'Was it, Tom? Wait, you weren't there, were you?' Maybe that third glass of champagne had been a bad idea. Bubbles always did go straight to her head.

But there'd been so many people, so many knowing glances. And even with Tom on her arm, she'd needed something else between her and all of them.

'I was not, unfortunately.' Tom smiled across the table at Daisy. 'But, delightful as today has been, I can't imagine it being a patch on a wedding organised by Sherry Huntingdon.'

'A safe bet,' Seb murmured.

Leaning back in her chair, Violet tried to spot the waiters coming round with coffee. Maybe that would help her focus on the special day going on around her.

Because all she'd been able to think about so far was the piece of paper folded up in her clutch bag.

She'd tried to concentrate on smiling as she and the

other bridesmaids walked in front of the beautiful bride down the aisle, and on Henry looking handsomely nervous at the front of the church. And she'd tried to listen to the vicar talking about the importance of love and forgiveness and understanding in a marriage. But really her mind had been buzzing with the knowledge that in her lap she held the history of Tom Buckley. His life and times. His secrets.

And she really, really wanted to know them.

But she wanted the time to savour them, too. To absorb and understand them. And she couldn't exactly sit there and read it at the dining table surrounded by her sister and brother-in-law, and three of Henry's cousins and their wives.

The cousins, fortunately, had wandered off towards the free bar before Daisy had started comparing weddings. But that didn't mean she could just get reading. Did it?

Violet glanced up. Daisy, Seb and Tom were deep in conversation and she didn't seem to be required. Mum and Dad were sitting three tables over, chatting with some old friends. It was entirely possible that no one would notice if she disappeared for ten minutes.

'I'm just going to…' She waved a hand vaguely in the direction of the bathrooms as she stood, but no one seemed bothered.

Pausing in the doorway to the main ballroom, where the wedding breakfast had been served, Violet checked to ensure no one was watching her, then headed in the opposite direction from the bathrooms—towards the gardens.

It was easy enough to find a secluded bench, hidden away behind the walls of the rose garden. If anyone stumbled across her, she could just say she needed a little air. After all, the weather was warm and the five hundred guests had made the ballroom a little stifling. No reason for anybody to suspect anything.

Especially not that she was hiding away to read the obituary of a man still very much alive.

She unfolded the piece of paper, wondering if the fact he'd written it told her more about him than even the words contained could. Only a journalist would think of doing such a thing, which was a permanent worry. But, on the other hand, he'd wanted her to have all the facts, the truth, laid out in a way they were only ever told after death.

This was who he was, how he thought he'd be remembered, everything he felt was important to say about his life. All in two pages—which Violet figured was probably a good page longer than hers would have been. Or a page and a half longer if you omitted the sex tape thing in the interests of good taste.

Yeah. No one was ever going to omit that.

With a deep breath, Violet focused on the words. Even with the dispassionate tone an obituary demanded, she could still hear Tom talking to her with every line.

She lived Tom's childhood in New York, his early career, his estrangement from his mother and his pain at her death, his tours with bands and his relationship history, all in his own words. And by the time she reached the end she almost, almost felt as if he was sitting there beside her.

'So, do you have questions?'

Violet jerked her head up at the sound of Tom's voice, blushing when she found him leaning against the garden wall watching her, one eyebrow raised.

'I probably will have, later.' After all, the plain facts weren't the same as actually *knowing* a person, were they? But after the last few weeks, it was really only the facts that she'd been missing. Swallowing hard, Violet got to her feet. 'But there's something else I want to do first.'

He didn't move as she stepped towards him, and she

understood that this was all on her now. This was her decision. And he would wait and let her make it.

She just hoped it wasn't a mistake.

She stopped, close enough that she could almost feel his breath on her face, but still not touching. Violet looked up into his eyes and saw the control there. He was holding back. So she wouldn't.

Bringing one hand up to rest against his chest, she felt the thump of his heart through his shirt and knew she wanted to be close to that beat for as long as he'd let her. Slowly, she rose up onto her tiptoes, enjoying the fact that he was tall enough that she needed to. And then, without breaking eye contact for a moment, Violet kissed him.

It only took a moment before he responded, and Violet let herself relax into the kiss as his arms came up to hold her close. The celebrity wedding melted away, and all she knew was the feel of his body against hers and the taste of him on her lips. This. This was what she needed. Why had she denied herself this for so long?

And how could it be that kissing Tom somehow tasted like trust?

Eventually, though, she had to pull away. Tom's arms kept her pressed against him, even as she dropped down to her normal height, looking up into his moss-green eyes.

'You liked my obituary, then?' he murmured.

Violet shook her head. 'Not one bit. I'd like it to never be written, please. But…I liked knowing you.'

'Is this where I give you some kind of line about getting to know me even better?' Tom asked, one eyebrow raised.

Violet's laugh bubbled up inside her, as if kissing Tom had released all the joy she'd kept buried deep down. 'I think it probably is, yes.'

'In that case, how long do you think we need to stay at this hootenanny?'

'There's five hundred people here,' Violet pointed out. 'What are the chances of them missing just two?'

'Good point.' And with a warm smile spreading across his face, Tom grabbed Violet's hand and they ran for the waiting car.

'Are you asleep?'

It was many hours later, and Violet's voice was barely more than a whisper. He felt it against his bare skin more than heard it.

'Not quite.' He shifted, pulling her closer against his side. Now he finally had her where he'd dreamt of her being, he wasn't willing to put up with even a centimetre between them. 'You okay?'

'Mmm, fine. More than fine. Kind of awesome, actually.' She smiled sleepily up at him, and he felt a puff of pride at the relaxation and satisfaction he saw in her face. She rubbed her cheek against his chest like a contented kitten.

'Told you this was a good idea,' he murmured into her hair.

Violet laughed, low and warm. 'You did. And you were right.'

Too damn right. This was more than a good idea. This was more than he'd dreamt it could be. He'd known from the first that he was attracted to Violet, but had never really expected to do anything about it. Never imagined he'd want to, not this badly.

But then he'd got to know her. Understand her. Even let her in a bit to understand him. And now look at them.

And she thought it was a good idea, at last.

'I'm glad you think so.'

'Plus, with the…last-minute nature of everything, I'm pretty sure you wouldn't have even had time to set up a video camera.'

It was a joke, he knew, but there was still something brittle behind the words. Something not quite healed. It made him want to wrap her up and keep her safe—not an emotion he was used to feeling about the women he dated. And in this case…he had a feeling that Violet had been kept safe for too long already. She'd had enough of being protected—and she was ready to take care of herself for a change.

Tom sank down a little lower in the bed, turning on his side until they were face to face. 'You know I wouldn't do that, don't you? You have to know that.' She might not need him to protect her, but she did need to trust him. To know he would never, never hurt her.

He wasn't that man any more.

'I do. I do.' Violet inched closer and placed another kiss on his lips. 'I'm just still…adjusting to the idea.'

'I can understand that.' Wrapping his arm around her waist, he pulled her against him. 'I just hope you can learn to trust me.'

'I think I already do.' The hope in Violet's eyes meant he just had to kiss her again.

But when they separated, the hope had faded away and left a question there. 'What is it?' he asked.

'I just wondered…in your obituary, you talked about your mum, how you fell out. And I know you said you hadn't made up when she died. But you never said what you argued about. I guess I just don't understand…what could have been that important that you didn't try to reconcile with her?'

Despite the warmth of the bed and Violet's body, a shiver ran through him and his muscles froze.

'Pride,' he whispered. 'What else? Stupid, pointless pride.'

Violet pressed a kiss against his collarbone. 'Tell me.'

Except he couldn't, could he? Because that one fact, that one omission from his obituary, was the one thing she'd never forgive. Still, he had to tell her something, and the trust in her eyes made him want it to be as close to the truth as he could manage.

'When I was just starting out as a reporter, I worked for a…less reputable paper. The sort that my mom felt was beneath me. It was run by a guy who believed that the ends—a good story—justified any means. And he expected his staff to do whatever they needed to, in order to get the copy.' And slowly, the longer he'd stayed there, the more desensitised he'd become to those methods.

'Mom said I was wasting my talents, that selling my soul for a job wasn't worth it.' He swallowed at the memory of his mother's face, full of righteous fury. 'She told me she'd brought me up better than that, that she didn't want to know a son who could sink to such depths.'

Tom risked a glance at Violet, where she lay silent, her cheek resting against his shoulder. Her eyes were damp and he fought back against the instinct to tell her how much he didn't deserve her pity or her tears.

'What happened next?' she murmured, her hand caressing his arm, a comforting, caring touch.

'I told her she didn't understand journalism, that she'd never get it. That this was what I had to do to build my career. She kicked me out of the house and told me to come back when I'd found my honour again.' He squeezed his eyes shut. 'It didn't take me too long to figure out she was right. But my pride made me stay away too long. I didn't know she was sick, and by the time I found out…it was too late.'

He'd quit the paper long before then, of course, the moment that terrible story broke and he realised what he'd done. But when he'd lost his mother's respect, he'd lost any respect he had for himself too. How could he go back until he'd regained that? And it turned out respect took far longer to earn than to lose.

Violet wrapped her arms tightly around his middle, shifting until she was almost lying on top of him, protecting him from the world. 'I'm so sorry.'

'It was a long time ago.' As if that made a difference to the pain.

'Still. I wish I could make it better.'

Tom curled his body around hers until they were touching skin at as many points as possible. 'Trust me, you are. Just being with you…watching you move past your own history, it helps.'

'Is that all that helps?' Violet raised her head slightly to look at him, and he felt himself warming at the heat in her blue eyes.

'I can think of one or two other things,' he said, and kissed her again.

CHAPTER SIXTEEN

VIOLET STRETCHED OUT against the sheets, listening to Tom's steady breathing beside her. The sun was almost fully up outside; it had to be around six. She'd heard her parents, Daisy and Seb returning hours ago, listened to their giggles and their good-nights. She'd texted Daisy from the car to say that she and Tom were heading home early—she figured she didn't really need to elaborate. Daisy might not be her twin, but she was still her sister. She knew her well enough for this.

What would they all think? Would they be pleased that she was moving on at last, or scared for her because of whom she'd chosen to move on with? Would they understand? And how would it affect the job that Tom was there to do?

'You're thinking too loudly,' Tom murmured, shifting beside her. 'Go back to sleep.'

'I will,' Violet lied. Running her hand down his arm, she listened until Tom's breathing evened out again. He probably wouldn't even remember his strange comment when he woke up.

But he'd remember the rest of the night, she was sure. That, at least, was impossible to forget. She might not be the most experienced of women, but the chemistry between them, the connection she felt when they were skin against skin…Violet had never felt anything like that before.

She stifled a laugh as she remembered Tom's first words to her—about how the frustrated look on her face reminded him of that hideous tape. Maybe Rose had been right when she'd recounted the incident to her. Maybe she really was finally able to laugh about the whole thing.

That had to mean she was moving on. And it was past time.

She glanced across at Tom, one arm thrown above his head as he slept, his dark hair rumpled and his bare chest so tempting. She could just curl back up beside him right now, rest her head on that chest and drift back to sleep until he woke up again for a repeat performance of last night.

The plan had many, many merits.

With one last look and a quiet sigh, Violet slipped out from between the sheets, slowly enough not to wake him. She needed to think, and that was practically impossible while in bed with Tom. The man was just too distracting—even asleep.

Grabbing a pair of leggings and a long T-shirt from a drawer, and, giving silent thanks that they'd made it back to her room, not Tom's, the night before, Violet dressed silently, then crept out of the room. She'd use the bathroom down the hall to freshen up, rather than her own en suite bathroom, then grab some coffee and head to Rose's study. No one was likely to interrupt her there, at least not for a while. After the late night at the wedding, everyone was likely to sleep in, and Tom…well, he was probably a little worn out too.

She couldn't help the smile that spread across her face as she thought about it. One thing she had no doubt about—last night had *definitely* been a good idea.

Now she just had to figure out what happened next.

The study was blissfully cool, quiet and private. Resting her cup of coffee on the corner of the desk, Violet curled up in her desk chair and stared out of the window. There was probably work for the Benefit that she should be doing, but she knew she'd be good for nothing if she didn't sort out last night in her head first.

He'd talked about his mother, and about the dark side of reporting—as if she didn't know it well enough already. But he'd got out, and the guilt he carried from his mother not knowing that before she'd died...Violet knew that was strong enough to keep him honest for ever. Tom would never be the sort of reporter Nick was. He'd told her the truth about everything.

This could have been history repeating itself all over again—but it wasn't. Because Tom wasn't Nick. And, for the first time in a long time, she honestly found herself hopeful and trusting in her future.

The phone on her desk rang, and Violet frowned at it. Who on earth would be calling so early on a Sunday?

'Violet Huntingdon-Cross,' she said, answering it.

'Miss Cross. It's Jake Collins here.' Ah, of course. Only the most offensive manager on her list of acts—who else? Probably looking for a way to get back at her for the rider thing. 'We're in Dublin airport right now, about to fly back across to your own fair green isle for the Benefit Concert.'

Well, that explained the early morning wake-up call. But not why he was actually calling. And wasn't Ireland the fair green isle, anyway? At least he was sounding civil. Almost friendly, in fact. It was enough to make her suspicious.

'Mr Collins,' she said as brightly as she could, 'how can I help you today?'

'It's rather more a case of how we can help you, I think. I appreciate that the news isn't official just yet, but you know how the industry is. There were enough people at that party last night that it really wasn't a surprise.'

What party? The Littlewood wedding? But the only thing that had happened there… Violet bit back a groan. She'd place money on some camera somewhere catching a shot of her and Tom in the garden. But did anyone really care about that? And what on earth did it have to do with Jake Collins, anyway?

'I'm sorry… I don't understand.' And she wasn't sure she wanted him to explain it, either.

'Of course, of course. I totally get that you need to await the official announcement. And, of course, there will need to be the appropriate period of mourning, especially for your family. But no one would want to see the Benefit Concert cancelled, I'm sure. So all I wanted to say was… if your father feels it inappropriate for the Lemons to perform, Olivia would, of course, be more than happy to help out by taking over the headline slot.'

Mourning? Why would they…and what would make them think of cancelling the concert?

'Mr Collins, really—'

'Oh, I know, too soon. Too soon. But it's out there now. I'll call again at a better time and we can talk. So sorry for your loss. Please, pass my condolences on to your parents.'

The line went dead, and Violet stared at it in her hand for a long moment before a truly dreadful thought hit her.

Rose and Will.

Violet's heart beat treble time in her chest. She had no idea where they were, what the time was there and she didn't care. Grabbing her mobile with shaking hands, she pressed the speed dial and prayed for Rose to pick up.

'Vi?' Rose's sleepy voice came over the line and Violet's breath burst out of her in relief.

'Oh, thank God. I just had the strangest phone call and

I thought…never mind. You're okay. Everything's okay. Go back to sleep.'

"Kay. Call you later.'

Violet hung up. Whatever Jake Collins's deal was, he was obviously mistaken. Everything was fine. Violet's heart rate started to return to normal and she reached for her coffee cup.

She only managed one sip before the police banged on the door.

'What's going on?' Tom asked as he stumbled into the kitchen, wishing he'd taken the time to go back to his own room and find something other than yesterday's suit to wear. But when he'd woken alone in Violet's bed, heard voices downstairs then spotted the police cars on the driveway…he hadn't really been thinking about his own sartorial elegance.

Violet looked across from the coffee maker, her expression tense. There were lines around her eyes he didn't remember from the night before and they looked puffy and red, as if she was trying really hard not to cry.

Sherry wasn't even trying. How she managed to still look beautiful with tears streaming down her face, Tom had no idea. Rick had one arm around her, his other hand covering his face. Seb held Daisy in the corner, her face hidden against his chest.

And next to the kitchen table stood two police officers and a man in a suit—utterly incongruous in the Huntingdon-Cross kitchen.

'I'm sorry, sir,' the suit said, not sounding at all apologetic. 'I'm Detective Inspector Trivet. And you are?'

'Tom Buckley. I'm here interviewing the family.' Except he'd never felt more like an outsider than at this moment.

'You're press.' The detective's mouth hardened. 'I'm

sorry, but the family has requested no reporters be allowed in at this time.'

Tom's heart sank, a dead weight in his chest. Of course not. Whatever was happening, this was for family only. 'Right. I'll just—'

'No!' Violet said, too loud in the subdued kitchen. 'Tom's a…family friend. Right, Dad?'

Rick looked up just long enough to nod. His craggy face looked ten years older, Tom realised.

'In that case, I'll tell you just what I've told the others,' Trivet said. 'I'm afraid that in the early hours of this morning one of Mr Cross's cars was discovered along the riverbank, halfway between here and London. The man behind the wheel was Jez Whittle.'

The Screaming Lemons' lead guitarist. But, more importantly this morning, Rick's best friend.

'Is he…?' Tom hardly dared ask. The answer was already written on the face of everyone else in the room.

'It appears that he died in the early hours of this morning.'

'From the car crash?' Tom asked, but Violet shook her head.

'Mr Whittle died from a fatal overdose of heroin.' Trivet's expression was solemn as he spoke. 'People at the party he'd attended in London confirmed that he had seemed unstable before he left and had talked about needing "something more" to take the edge off.'

'He'd been clean for years!' Rick's head shot up, his distress clear on his face. 'I mean, twenty years. You don't just fall off the wagon after two decades. Not without talking to someone first. Without talking to *me*.'

Oh, God, he shouldn't be here. This wasn't meant for Tom to witness. He shouldn't be watching Violet go to her parents and wrap her arms around them both, tears on her cheeks. Because if he was here…he had to write about this moment. Had to tell this story.

And how could he, now?

'What happens next?' Seb asked, his voice low and even. He was family now, even if he'd only married in. He could take charge and ask questions and take care of people. While Tom had to just fade into the background and pretend he wasn't intruding on this incredibly private grief.

Except he wanted to. He wanted to take Violet in his arms the way Seb had held Daisy, wanted to make this easier for her, any way he could.

'There'll be an official inquest, of course,' the detective said. 'And we'll need to ask Mr Cross a few questions about the car and such. But mostly, I imagine, you can expect an influx of paparazzi, and soon. I can leave a couple of uniforms here to watch the door, if you want. Might dissuade most of them from trying anything extreme.'

Like climbing in through windows, harassing the family every time they even looked outside. Oh, God, this was going to be hell for Violet.

Seb nodded. 'Thank you. And if that's all…' The Earl had the aristocracy's way with dismissal hints, Tom realised, and almost smiled.

'For now.' Detective Inspector Trivet motioned towards the door with his head and the policemen all filed out, leaving the family alone. With Tom.

'I should…' Leave, he wanted to say. But how could he when Violet's head jerked up, her blue eyes huge and wide in her pale face and her gaze pleading. 'Make more coffee,' he finished. 'Or food. If anyone wants something to… Or something else. Anything you need.'

'Thank you,' Violet whispered. But no one else was listening.

'I don't *understand* it.' Rick crashed his fist down onto

the table, rattling the coffee cups. 'Why didn't he talk to me? Of all the people…he knew! He knew I could help.'

'I set up a drug rehab and addiction counselling centre years ago.' Rick's words from one of many interviews floated through Tom's mind. *'I always felt it was important to pay back, for all the narrow escapes friends have had. I wanted to help.'*

And was this why? Had Rick been thinking about Jez when he'd started that project? That it would have made his friend's life easier—or even that it would be there, ready for him, if he ever needed it again?

Stories of Jez's addictions had appeared in the papers regularly, back in the day. But the band had always closed ranks around him, Tom remembered from his research. And in those days they hadn't had the internet or camera phones to contend with. By the time they'd been invented, Jez had sobered up and flown right.

Until last night.

'He was probably on his way here, Rick.' Sherry sounded exhausted, even though they'd all only been up for an hour or so, Tom guessed. 'He always, always came here when he was in trouble, you know that. He came to us and we fixed it.'

'Except this time he left it too late.' Rick's melancholy tone tore another sob from Daisy, and Violet looked paler than ever. Her hands were shaking, Tom realised. He wanted to go to her. Wanted to know what to say, how to help.

But then the phone rang and Tom realised there was, at least, one thing he could do.

'That'll be the papers,' Sherry said softly.

'Vultures.' Rick glanced up. 'No offence, Tom.'

'None taken,' Tom assured him.

'Do we answer it?' Daisy asked. 'Or just leave it.'

'They won't stop calling,' Seb said.

Tom took a breath. It wasn't his place. He wasn't part of the family.

But he would do this for Violet.

'I'll deal with them,' he said. 'All of them. You just... look after each other, and don't worry about the press, or the photographers, any of it. I'll take care of it all.'

He wasn't quite sure if Violet's expression was grateful or concerned, but it didn't matter. If she didn't trust him completely after this, she never would.

CHAPTER SEVENTEEN

NOTHING WAS EVER going to be the same again.

It wasn't the first time Violet had experienced that sort of revelation in her life, but this time it felt impossible to see how her family would ever find their way back to being whole again. The grief they were all experiencing permeated the house, a silence that crept through the hallways and clung to the curtains.

That silence had sent her running for Rose's study, the place she'd spent the most time over the last few weeks. The place she'd hoped would help her take control of her life again, to grow up and start living instead of just hiding.

But hiding was all she wanted to do now.

Uncle Jez. She'd known him since before she was born, had grown up with him always there for birthdays and parties and jam sessions and just when he was craving ice cream. He had free run of the house—especially the kitchen if he felt like making pancakes. He'd treated Dad's collection of cars as his own, had famously said he could never marry because Rick had stolen the only woman worth settling down for, then gone on and married—and divorced—four times. He was wild and free and enormous fun and she would miss him, always, in a corner of her heart that would never heal.

But most of her grief was for her parents. For their loss.

And for the horrible, unexpected proof that everything they'd told her, her whole life, was wrong.

Everything wouldn't be okay if they just stuck together. As long as they had each other, terrible things could still happen. There were some things in this world that family just couldn't fix.

And the worst thing was that she'd known that, really, of course she had. But she'd never actually believed it until this morning.

'Hey.' Tom stuck his head around the door at the same time as he rapped his knuckles lightly across the wood. 'Do you need anything?'

He hadn't asked if she was okay, which she appreciated. In fact, he'd been great at avoiding the stupid, unnecessary comments and questions and just getting on with what needed to be done. He'd gone out and faced the pack of press hyenas outside the house and asked that they respect the family's privacy and grief at this terrible time—not that any of them imagined that they would. Still, it had made it clear that no one intended to make a fool of themselves in front of them, or give them a new sound bite or photo to focus on.

Violet had watched him on the telly, too scared to even risk appearing at a window hiding behind a curtain to see it live. He'd looked in control, but also as if he cared.

As if he was part of the family.

Violet took a breath. 'To be honest, I could do with a hug.'

'That, I can do.' Tom smiled and shut the door behind him. Stepping forward, he opened up his arms and she practically jumped into them. How had it only been a matter of hours since she'd been curled up naked in his arms? And how could so much have changed since then?

'Rose is on her way back,' she murmured after a long

moment of just being held. 'At least she hopes so. She and
Will were heading to the airport to see if they could get an
earlier flight home when I spoke to them last. Although,
since I still have no idea where they are, God only knows
how long it will take them. I said I'd go pick them up if
they let me know when their flight gets in.'

'I'll come with you,' Tom said. 'Just let me know when.'

'I'd like that.' Violet wondered if he could sense the
relief in her voice. She could have sent a car, but it was
important to her that Rose saw family when she arrived.
But that didn't mean she wouldn't appreciate some backup
when the inevitable comments and photos and looks started
at the airport.

Strange to think that this time they'd be because of
Uncle Jez rather than her own mistakes.

'How's your dad doing?' Tom asked and Violet pulled
back from his arms with a sigh. Back to the real world.

'He's…devastated, basically. Mum's with him, though,
so that will help. Daisy and Seb are going to stay on for
the next week, too. Seb's popped home to get their stuff,
and Daisy has gone for a lie down.'

'And you? How are you doing?' That question at last.
She supposed even Tom couldn't hold off asking it for ever.

'I'm…angry. At Uncle Jez, at those vultures outside our
door—no offence—at the world.' But Violet had learned
that just being angry didn't get you anywhere. You had to
do something with it or it was just wasted.

She'd spent the last eight years being pointlessly angry,
and look where it had got her.

'I realised I'm angry because it's so meaningless,' she
said, looking straight into Tom's eyes. 'So I decided to
make it mean something.'

Tom blinked. 'Mean something. How, exactly?'

Taking a deep breath, Violet held up the new poster

mock-up she'd spent the morning working on. 'I know the concert's only five days away, and I know this would mean a ridiculous amount of work to pull it off—especially since we don't even know if Dad and the rest of the boys will even want to get on stage. But what do you think? Will you help me?' Violet glanced down at her newly appropriated poster, now proclaiming the Benefit Concert to be wholly in support of addiction support centres across the country. It would be a lot to do. But it would definitely mean something. It would be worth it.

A smile spread across Tom's face, and she knew she had him.

'Just tell me what you need me to do,' he said.

Violet had spent two days working like a woman possessed. Tom watched her in awe, taking every task she gave him and completing it as efficiently as possible, mostly because he wanted to get back to watching her work. If he'd ever thought of her as a spoilt celebrity kid who only wanted the spotlight without having to do anything beyond getting naked to earn it—and, okay, he had—she was proving him wrong by the second.

She amazed him. All day long she made the calls he knew would have terrified her a few weeks ago, speaking to not just people in the business but the media too. She fended off questions about her family and her dad's reaction to Jez's death like a pro, as though they didn't touch her at all. Tom knew they did—knew that when she clung to him in their bed at night she was thinking of all those people out there, desperate to know every detail of her life and use it against her.

He did his best to distract her at those moments.

And she amazed him there, too. When she wasn't being professional Violet, organising the Benefit almost from the ground up again, or family Violet, taking care of her distraught parents and pregnant sister, or even community Violet, fending off well-meaning locals who came with flowers or food. When she could just be his Violet, alone in the dark, letting him see the heart of her. As if Jez's death had torn down the last of her barriers and given him a clear path in to the real Violet.

They'd never really had The Talk—the one about their future and what they both expected out of this relationship, if it even was a relationship. But somehow, Tom felt, they didn't need to. They'd instinctively moved past that, to an understanding that this was what it was—and it was what they both needed right now. They mattered to each other, and the world was easier with each other in it. That was all Tom cared about.

'Okay, so what's left?' Violet asked, tapping her pen against her notepad as she frowned down at her list.

Tom refrained from pointing out that she was the one with the checklist in front of her. Instead, he moved behind her, rubbing her shoulders firmly as he looked down at the lines after lines of her handwriting, all with tiny check boxes beside them.

'Well, most of the stuff that needed printing—the new signs and programmes and stuff—that's all taken care of,' he said, assessing the ticks in the check boxes. 'And we've spoken to every act and sponsor and media partner between us, so they all know the score.'

'And they're all on board,' Violet added, a hint of amazement in her voice. As if she couldn't believe that *she'd* actually talked them all into it.

'With your incredible persuasive sell? Of course they are.' Tom dug his fingers into a particularly tight knot in her back. 'The riders for all the acts are sorted—even Olivia's. And all the technical stuff is more or less unchanged.

The new wristbands and such are en route, ready to hand out to the vendors when they arrive, to sell alongside everything else. What else is there?'

Violet's shoulders stiffened, beyond the power of his fingers to relax them. 'The headline act.'

'Apart from that.' Tom let out a long breath and moved his hands to just rest against Violet's skin, a reminder that he was there, that he wanted to help. 'Have you spoken to your dad yet?'

'Not about this,' Violet said. 'About the funeral arrangements, about the good old days, about the clinic, about what he'd have done to help if Jez had just come to him... But not a word on if The Screaming Lemons are planning to perform at the Benefit Concert.'

'He hasn't spoken to any of the rest of the band either,' Tom confirmed. 'Jonny actually asked *me* yesterday if I knew what was going on.'

'I need to ask him.' Violet put down her pen, obviously not willing to add this action to the list. 'If he wants to play...we need to get in another guitarist. They've worked with some great session musicians over the years...'

'Actually,' Tom said, the word out before he'd even completed the thought, let alone decided if it was a good idea, 'I might know someone. Someone I think your dad would approve of.'

Violet turned in her seat, twisting under his hands until she was almost in his arms. 'Really? Who?'

Tom shook his head. He didn't want to get her hopes up if it didn't work out. 'Look, you talk to your dad first. If he says he wants to go on...I'll make some calls.'

'Okay.' She gave him the sad half smile he'd grown too used to seeing over the past few days. 'Thank you, Tom. For everything you've done this week. I know this wasn't exactly what you came to Huntingdon Hall for.'

'Neither was this.' He dipped his head to press a kiss against her lips. 'And I wouldn't give us up for the world.'

A faint pink blush spread across her cheeks. Was that a step too far? Too close to the 'talking about things' line they weren't crossing? Because if there was one thing Tom had realised over the last couple of days, it was that he *wanted* to talk about things between them. He wanted to put a name on their relationship.

He wanted to tell her he had fallen in love with her.

But now wasn't the time. After the Benefit, once things had calmed down, and once Rose was back and her family was a little more stable again. They had time. He just had to pick the right one.

Love, it turned out, was worth waiting for.

'I mean it, Tom.' Violet's expression turned serious. 'You came here for a tell-all book, the exclusive stories that would make your name. And here you are, in the middle of the biggest story to hit the Lemons in thirty years, and you're spending all your time telling other reporters "no comment". I know it can't be easy for you—you're a born journalist; we both know that. But you haven't chased this story, haven't exposed Dad's grief. And I really, really appreciate that.'

Tom's smile felt fake and forced. A born journalist. Was that what he'd always be to her? And, worse, was it true? 'Of course I wouldn't. I'm here for you right now—and not as a reporter. When your dad is ready to resume our interviews, fine. But for now…let's just focus on the Benefit, yeah?'

Violet nodded. 'Are you still coming with me to the airport to fetch Rose and Will this afternoon?' The honeymooning pair had ended up having to take three separate flights over thirty-six hours to get home just one day earlier than planned, but Rose had insisted on doing it anyway.

'I'll be there,' Tom promised. 'I'll meet you at the front door at two, yeah?'

'Okay.' Violet leant up and pressed a kiss to his mouth. 'And, in the meantime, I need to go talk to Dad.'

'You do.' Neither of them were admitting it, but if the Lemons didn't play at the concert, the Benefit would lose a lot of impact. Yes, people might understand Rick's reluctance to get back on stage so soon after Jez's death, might even respect it. But without Rick Cross on stage, the Huntingdon Hall Benefit would just be another concert. And Violet, Tom knew, wanted this year's Benefit to be much, much more than that. She wanted to use it to change attitudes, to promote the availability of aid—for addicts and their friends and family.

She wanted to make a difference, and Tom honestly believed she might.

Plus, if there was anyone who could talk Rick Cross into anything, it had to be Violet.

'Wish me luck,' Violet said.

'You don't need it,' Tom told her, but he kissed her again for luck anyway. Just in case.

CHAPTER EIGHTEEN

VIOLET JANGLED THE car keys in her hand, barely resisting the urge to tap her foot. Where was he? It was quarter past two and still no sign of Tom. She really had to leave to fetch Rose and Will—unless she wanted them grumpy and fed up after a thirty-six hour flight with no one there to meet them.

'Any sign?' Sherry appeared through the kitchen door.

Violet shook her head. 'You haven't seen him either?'

'Afraid not. I checked the study again, and his room.'

'Did you ask Dad?' Violet asked, then regretted it when Sherry's face turned a little grey. Rick hadn't been in the best mood after Violet's conversation with him that afternoon.

'He's shut himself away in the studio,' Sherry said. 'I thought it best to leave him for now.'

'Yeah, I can understand that.' Guilt knotted in her gut. She shouldn't have pushed him, certainly not so soon. It was just that she was so desperate to make this year's Benefit Concert more of a success than ever. For Uncle Jez.

'Violet…' Her mother paused, and Violet felt the knot in her stomach twist tighter.

'I know what you're going to say, Mum. Don't worry. I'm not going to pester him again.'

But Sherry shook her head. 'It's not that. Sweetheart…

we're so proud of how you've stepped up these past few weeks. Taking over the Benefit, dealing with everything— even Tom being here.' She gave Violet a sly smile. 'Although I suspect that one wasn't quite the hardship you imagined, right?'

'Mum, I—'

'Darling, I think it's marvellous. He's a great guy, and it was past time for you to find something worth coming out of hiding for. No, all I wanted to say was…I'm so proud of what you're doing, turning this Benefit into a fitting memorial for your Uncle Jez, and a way to help others who might not know where to turn. It's important work, and I know how much it took for you to do it.'

Violet's eyes burned. 'Thanks, Mum.'

'So, so proud, darling.' Sherry wrapped her arms around her daughter and squeezed her lightly in a hug. 'And I do think the Lemons should play. I know your father isn't quite there yet, but I think he will be, once some of the fog clears. So…I'll talk to the boys, get them all on board. So we're ready when your dad bursts out of that studio ready to take to the stage, yes?'

'That would be great. Thanks, Mum.' Violet hugged her back, thinking, not for the first time, that the whole family would have been doomed years ago if Sherry hadn't been there to take them in hand.

'Now, you get off and fetch that twin of yours and her husband. We need all the family here right now.' She made a shooing motion with her hands. 'Go on. I'll tell Tom you couldn't wait for him when he shows up. He's probably on a call or something.'

Sherry was probably right, Violet decided as she pulled out of the garage and prepared to drive past the reporters still camped out on their doorstep. Tom wouldn't have left her to do this alone unless something important had come up. And since he'd taken on the job of distracting and dealing with the media and their many, many questions about Uncle Jez and the family, the chances were he was probably yelling 'no comment' down the phone at someone he'd previously considered a friend and colleague right now.

'Violet! Violet!' The calls started the moment her car pulled around to the front of the house and headed for the driveway out to the main road. She checked her windows were completely shut, but it didn't seem to do much for keeping the shouts out.

'How's your dad?' someone called.

'Any news on the car? How did Jez get hold of it?' yelled a less concerned reporter.

'Are Rose and Will coming home?'

'Is it true that Daisy went into premature labour and is now on bed rest?'

Violet had to smile at that one. Daisy was only five months pregnant and, if she was in bed, Violet was pretty sure she was 'seeking solace' in the arms of her rather attractive husband. Really, did they not think if something had happened to the baby they'd have seen the ambulances and medical experts lined up by the dozen? Sherry Huntingdon was taking absolutely no chances with her first grandchild.

The questions followed her as she sped down the driveway and faded away as she hit the open road. It was strange to think that the last time she'd driven this way had been when she'd headed to the airport to collect Tom. So much had changed since then, she barely recognised the frustrated, lonely woman who'd let loose on him in the coffee shop.

In the end, it turned out that Rose and Will's last leg flight had been delayed. Sighing as she checked the arrivals board for updates, Violet spotted a familiar-looking coffee shop and decided that was as good a place as any to try and avoid attention. Picking up a paper on her way, she grabbed a coffee, settled herself into a corner where she could still see the screens with flight information and prepared to wait.

She heard a few murmurs as people spotted her, probably exacerbated by the fact that the front page of the newspaper had a splashy sidebar about Jez's autopsy, but no one approached her directly, which Violet appreciated. In fact, it was possibly the most peace and quiet she'd had in days.

She should have known it wouldn't last.

Violet was halfway through reading an editorial piece about the price of fame, idly making her own comments in the margins with a pencil, when her phone rang. She didn't recognise the number, but that wasn't exactly unusual these days. She had all the main contacts for the Benefit Concert programmed in, but every time someone rang from a different office line or their home phone instead of their mobile, it threw her off.

'Violet Huntingdon-Cross,' she answered, trying to sound both welcoming—in case it was someone from the Benefit—and dismissive—in case it was another reporter who'd got hold of her number—at the same time.

'Hello, sweetpea.' The voice on the other end made her muscles freeze up, her whole body tense. For eight years she'd avoided that voice, and the man it belonged to. Eight years she'd spent trying to pretend he didn't exist—which was almost true. The man she'd thought she loved didn't exist at all. Only this man, who could betray her in a moment for a good story.

'Nick.' She should hang up, switch her phone off and pretend this never happened. Go back to hiding away from him and everything he represented.

Except she wasn't that Violet any more, was she?

'What do you want?' she asked, her tone clipped. She was so far past him now. One little conversation wouldn't kill her.

'The same thing everything wants from you right now,' Nick said. 'An official comment on the recent untimely death of your father's lead guitarist.'

Violet laughed, loud enough to draw attention from the people sitting at the next table. 'Why on earth would you imagine I'd give you that?' Or anything else he wanted, for that matter.

'Maybe for old times' sake?' Nick said. 'But I suppose I should have known better.'

'Too right you should.'

'I mean, you've got another journo on the line these days, haven't you? Stringing you along, just waiting for the story of a lifetime. I bet old Tom couldn't believe his luck.'

'You know Tom?' It wasn't really a question; Nick had always known everyone. Tom might be from the other side of the pond, but that wouldn't mean much. They ran in the same circles. But Nick was wrong if he thought Tom was anything like him.

'Doesn't everybody?' Nick said lightly. 'But I suppose the real question is how well *you* know Tom. I mean, have you ever read through his stories? Not the recent ones, but the early stories. The story that gave him his first big break, for example.'

'I don't know what you're talking about, and I don't want to.' Violet swallowed down the fear that rose up her throat as she remembered Tom talking about the first paper he'd worked for. The one that had caused such a rift between him and his mother. He'd never talked about the stories he wrote for that paper…a fact she'd wilfully ignored in the face of their romance. 'Tom's not like you. And what the hell does it matter to you anyway?'

'Maybe I just couldn't bear to see you taken in so completely all over again.' There was a pause, then Nick laughed. 'Okay, take this call as your reminder. When you figure out what he's really like and you realise that we're all the same, us journos, perhaps you might think *better the devil you know*, yeah? You've got to talk some time. Might as well talk to me as the next man.'

'It will never be you,' Violet bit out. How could he even think that? And what did he think he knew about Tom that would make *Nick* seem like the better option? She couldn't even think about it. 'Goodbye, Nick.'

She ended the call, her heart still racing. He was probably just winding her up. Taking a chance on having an in on the story of the century, or whatever. His editor had probably put him up to it. He couldn't have ever imagined she'd actually talk to him, right?

Which meant he was probably making it up about Tom, too. What the hell did Nick know, anyway? All Tom's stories were music based—even his early ones for that cursed paper were probably album reviews. What could possibly be contentious in that? Maybe he gave the Lemons two stars once or something, but that wasn't enough to drive a wedge between them. The past was the past; it didn't matter now.

Except…Nick had said they were all the same. And Violet knew some of the stories Nick had written. Had starred in a few.

Tom wouldn't write anything like that. Would he?

Violet glanced up at the arrivals screen. Still no word. So she had time to kill. It didn't mean anything.

At least that was what she told herself as she pulled her tablet out of her bag and began a search on Tom's name.

It took less time than she'd imagined. She wasn't exactly an internet geek, but even she could find basic information on a person—and the articles they'd written. And it wasn't exactly hard to figure out which one Nick had been referring to.

There, in amongst all the album reviews, band interviews and concert coverage, dated ten years earlier, was the story that had started Tom Buckley's career. And it made Violet's stomach turn just to read it.

Teenage starlet in nude photo scandal.

The photos had clearly been taken up close and in person, rather than by telephoto lens. Whoever had taken them had got close. Very close. And had been invited there.

Violet remembered the story breaking, remembered how these very photos had been splashed across the news, the papers and the internet within a matter of hours. And the text, the background info...he'd gone out looking for this, Violet could tell. Maybe he'd had a tip-off, maybe he'd played a hunch—whatever. Tom had deliberately and wilfully pursued and exposed this story. And maybe even seduced the actress to do it.

Kristy Callahan had been barely eighteen at the time, Violet remembered. She'd been famous for starring in a wholesome family sitcom. And Tom's story had destroyed her career.

Violet didn't want to know this. But now that she did... she couldn't pretend the story didn't exist. That she didn't know what Tom had done. He hadn't fallen out with his mother over the paper he worked for—it was because of this story. It had to be. He'd been lying to her after all, just at the moment she'd thought she had the truth. That she could trust him.

She glanced up at the screen; Rose and Will's plane had landed at last. She needed to find her sister and her best friend.

And then she needed to go home and find Tom.

CHAPTER NINETEEN

GOD, WHAT A DAY. Tom had been surprised when Rick had called him into his studio, and stunned when he'd insisted on doing an interview right now.

But the material he'd got was golden.

'I think, whenever you lose someone close to you, you always wonder if there was something more you could have done. Some small thing that would have kept them with you.' Rick shook his head, staring down at his hands. 'With Jez…knowing that I really *could* have done more—that I could have saved him if he'd let me, if he'd just called. That's going to be hard to live with. As is the guilt. Wondering if I should have seen the signs sooner, should have taken more precautions.'

Tom swallowed before asking his next question, reminding himself that today Rick was a subject, not a friend, not the father of the woman he was in love with. That he was here to do a job—one Rick had hired him for. That meant not shying away from the hard questions.

'Do you think…were there signs? Ones that you missed?'

Rick sighed. 'Probably. But, then again, maybe not. When an addiction takes hold…sometimes it can be a slow build towards cracking again, but more often it can just be one moment, one instant that flips you from recovering to addict again. There's such a thin line…and sometimes Jez liked to walk it. To put himself in the way of temptation.' He shook his head again. 'I don't know. If he wanted to hide it from me, he knew how. And with everything that's been going on here the last few months…maybe I wasn't paying the attention that I should have been.'

Guilt was etched in Rick's craggy face, whatever his words. Tom knew that guilt. That was the sort that never went away, the type you could never make up for once that moment had passed, the opportunity had been missed.

Rick Cross would blame himself for his best friend's death for the rest of his life, whether there was anything he could have done to prevent it or not. Facts didn't matter here, only love.

'Dad?' The door to the studio creaked open and Violet appeared through it. 'Rose and Will are here. And…have you seen…?' She trailed off as she caught sight of him. Tom gave her an apologetic smile, hoping she wasn't too mad about him missing the airport run. He'd planned to talk to her about it, but Rick had been very insistent that the interview was happening now or not at all.

'They're here?' Rick wiped his cheeks with the back of his hands and jumped to his feet. 'Sorry, Tom. We'll do this later, yeah?'

But Violet wasn't looking at her dad. She was still staring at Tom. And he had a horrible feeling that this might just have been his last interview with Rick Cross.

'I'm sorry I couldn't come to the airport with you,' Tom said as Rick shut the door behind him. 'Was it okay?'

'What were you talking to Dad about just then?' Violet's tone was clipped and her gaze sharp. 'Never mind; I'd rather hear it anyway.' She held out a hand for his phone and, with a sense of foreboding, Tom handed it over.

'He asked me to come in here,' he said as she fiddled

with the settings. 'He wanted to talk about some things with me now, while they were still fresh. He said you'd asked him about going on stage for the concert and he wasn't sure. He still needed to work some things out. He thought doing the interview might help.'

He sounded as if he was making excuses, Tom knew, when he had nothing to excuse. He'd been doing his job—and trying to help Rick at the same time. And Violet, for that matter, if it helped him get back on stage for the Benefit.

She had absolutely no reason to be mad at him, and yet he was pretty damn sure she was.

Violet pressed play and Rick's voice filled the room, cracked and broken and distraught.

'I think, whenever you lose someone close to you, you always wonder if there was something more you could have done. Some small thing that would have kept them with you. With Jez...knowing that I really could have done more—that I could have saved him, if he'd let me, if he'd just called. That's going to be hard to live with. As is the guilt. Wondering if I should have seen the signs sooner, should have taken more precautions.'

Violet jabbed a finger at the phone and the voice stopped.

'This is why you came, isn't it?' she said, her voice too even, too calm. 'I think I forgot that, with...everything that happened between us. But you were only ever here to do a job, weren't you? To find out all the dirty little secrets in the closets of my family and friends and put them on display for the world to see. Uncle Jez said—' She broke off, and Tom could see her hands trembling as she held his phone. He wanted to go to her so much it burned. 'He told my dad to find a better closet to hide those skeletons in. But in the end, he was the biggest story you could have hoped for, wasn't he? You must have been so frustrated to miss all the drama of Daisy's wedding, and then Rose's too. But at least there was still one sister here for you to get close to and seduce. And then Uncle Jez overdosed in Dad's car and you realised you had the story of the century right here. An interview with a grief-stricken Rick Cross. All you had to do was make sure none of the other journalists got to him first.' She gulped back a sob, and the sound broke his heart. 'And to think I thought you were doing *us* a favour, turning them all away.'

'Violet, no. You're wrong.' She had to be wrong. None of this had been planned—least of all the part where he fell for her. 'I told you. I'm not that kind of journalist.' He just had to reason with her. She was upset, and that was understandable, but she'd come round once she calmed down and saw the truth. That was all. He just had to be patient and not lose his temper and everything would be fine. 'Your dad asked me to come here; you know that. And he asked for the interview today.' He stepped closer, reaching out for her, but she flinched away. 'And I know you've had bad experiences before so I understand why you might be a bit sensitive—'

'A bit *sensitive?*'

Tom winced. 'Bad choice of words. I mean, I can see why you might worry about these things. But you don't need to. I'm not like your ex. I'm one of the good guys.'

'Yeah?' Violet's expression tightened. 'And is that what you told Kristy Callahan?'

The bottom dropped out of Tom's lungs, leaving him fighting to suck in the air he needed to respond. Just the sound of her name sent the guilt crashing in waves over his shoulders and, in that moment, he knew just how Rick felt. Worse, because Rick hadn't actually done anything wrong. Whereas he had known exactly what he was doing and had done it anyway.

God, Violet was right. He was every bit as bad as her ex; he just hid it better.

'How did you…? Never mind.' It didn't matter now, anyway. She knew, and that was enough. 'I can explain. Will you listen to me?'

Violet barked a laugh, harsh and uncompromising. 'Listen to you? I don't even need to, Tom. I know exactly what you're going to say. That she knew what she was doing. She was a celebrity; she knew the score, and the risks. That it was different then—that she meant nothing to you. That *I'm* different…we're different. If you're really desperate, you'll probably trot out the love line. How being with me has changed you, that now you love me you could never do something like that again.'

The vitriol and bitterness in her words was sharp enough to cut, and the worst part was that she was right. He'd tell her anything to win her back right now. And she'd never believe it was because he truly did love her.

She'd never believe anything he ever said again.

But he still had to try.

'It was a mistake. I was just starting out and the paper I worked for… I didn't take those photos; you have to believe that much. I wouldn't do that.'

'No, you'd just syndicate them in papers and news outlets around the world.' Her mouth tightened again. 'This was the real reason you fell out with your mother, isn't it? This was what she couldn't forgive.'

'Yes. It was. But…it wasn't like you think.' He had to find some way to make her understand. She might never trust him again, and his chances of getting her to fall in love with him were non-existent now. He'd thought he had time, and now he was scrambling just to make her believe he wasn't the biggest scumbag on the planet.

Which, given some of his past actions, was a lot harder than he'd like.

'Really, Tom? You're going to try and tell me what it was like?' She gave him a mocking half smile. 'Trust me, I know. I lived it, after all.'

No. He wouldn't let her think that he was just like her ex. He'd made a mistake, sure, but he hadn't planned it. Hadn't deliberately set out to destroy that girl. And she had to know that.

'It's not the same. Violet, you have to listen to me—'

'No! I don't! Not any more. I listened to you, right from that first night. And I should have known better. I *knew* what you were, and I *knew* how this would end. I should never have let you in, never let you close.' She shook her head sadly. 'You said it the night we met. I was never anything more than the Sex Tape Twin to you. Someone you could use to get what you wanted because I didn't matter at all. I'm just a punchline, right? Just a grainy video on the internet for late night comedians to use to get a cheap laugh, even all these years later.'

How could she think that? After everything they'd shared, after the way they'd been together?

'You know the worst part?' Violet asked. 'I actually trusted you. All that talk about never trusting anyone outside my family and I just let you in. Because you were nice to me.' She laughed, low and bitter. 'How desperate must I have been? God, you must have thought you had it made.'

Anger rolled through his body, working its way up through his chest and finding its way out of his mouth before he could even think to censor his words.

'You talk about trust? If you trusted me one iota you'd listen to me. You'd let me explain. You'd trust me enough not to jump to the worst conclusion at the first sign of trouble.' Violet stepped back at the force of his words, and he wanted to feel bad about that but he couldn't find it in himself. 'How did you even find out about that story? Did you go hunting for a reason to put between us? Or did someone tip you off?' The faint splash of pink that coloured her cheeks told him that he'd hit the mark. 'Who was it? Rose? Or another reporter?' The obvious truth slammed into him and he almost laughed at the ridiculousness of it. 'It was him, wasn't it? After everything he did to you, you still trust his word over mine.'

'I trust facts!' Violet shot back. 'How I found out doesn't matter—except that it wasn't from you. If you want my trust, you have to give me the truth.'

'How could I tell you this?' Tom asked. 'Violet, you've been hiding away here so long, so scared of what people might think or say, you don't even know what trust looks like any more. You wouldn't even talk to me about whether we were in a relationship! I was falling madly in love with you and I couldn't even say the words in case I spooked you. In case you jumped to exactly the conclusions you ran to today.'

'The *right* conclusions,' Violet countered, conveniently ignoring all his other points.

'No.' The anger faded, as fast as it had come, and all Tom was left with was that cold, hard certainty. 'You're wrong about me. I made a mistake ten years ago. But since I've come here the only mistake I've made was believing that you could move past *your* mistakes, your history, and find a future with me.'

Violet stared at him, her eyes wide, and for just a moment he thought she might actually listen to his side of the story. Then she held out his phone and her thumb grazed the play button again.

'Do you think...were there signs? Ones that you missed?'

His own voice, pressing Rick for more answers, a deeper admission of guilt.

Violet's face turned stony at the sound.

Rick's heavy sigh echoed around the studio.

'Probably. But then again, maybe not. When an addiction takes hold...sometimes it can be a slow build towards cracking again, but more often it can just be one moment, one instant that flips you from recovery to addict again. There's such a thin line...and sometimes Jez liked to walk it. To put himself in the way of temptation.'

She pressed 'stop' again and dropped the phone to the table as if it were poisoned.

'I'm not ignoring the signs,' she said, each word like a bullet. 'And I'm not staying anywhere near temptation. I want you to leave. Today.'

'Your father—' He couldn't go. Never mind the story of a lifetime; if he left her now Tom knew Violet would never let him back in, no matter how fast he talked.

'Will understand when I explain exactly what you've done.' Her eyes were cold, her arms folded across her chest like a shield. 'You're just a reporter. I'm family. Trust me on this. I know which one he's going to choose.'

So did Tom. And he knew when he was beaten.

He gave a slight nod and reached for his phone. 'I'll pack now and be gone within the hour.'

He'd gambled everything on this being more than a story. Time to admit he'd lost.

'Goodbye, Violet.'

CHAPTER TWENTY

VIOLET STOOD SHAKING in the middle of the studio for long minutes after Tom left. She needed to move, needed to talk to Rose, needed to explain to her father what she'd done. But how could she when she felt as if her heart, along with some other essential internal organs, had been ripped out?

She'd known, from the moment she saw that story with his name on it, exactly how the day would go. Had known she'd be standing here alone again at the end of it. Seeing Tom abuse her father's trust and exploit his grief for a story had only made it easier.

She'd made the right decision. She'd got out before Tom could tear her life apart again.

So why did she feel so broken all the same?

'Violet, honey?' When had her dad come in? How had she missed that? 'Where's Tom? Your mum said she just saw him walking out the front with a suitcase.'

'I told him to leave.' The words came out as barely more than a whisper. Would Dad be mad? He'd invited Tom here, after all. He was his guest—his employee, really. It hadn't been her place to send him away.

But what else could she do?

His expression cautious, Rick put his arm around her and led her over to the sofa, away from the chairs he and Tom had been sitting in when she'd entered the room. How long ago was that now, anyway? Time seemed strange. Confused.

'What happened, honey?' he asked, sitting beside her. 'Tell your old dad.'

Violet frowned, trying to find the right words to explain. In the end, what came out was, 'Did you really ask him to interview you about Jez today?'

'Why, yeah. I did.' Rick's eyebrows lifted with surprise. 'Is that what all this is about? Vi, honey, it was my choice. When you asked me earlier about going on stage this weekend…I wasn't sure what I wanted to do. I figured talking it out some might help. And Tom, well, he's a good guy, right? And since all this will probably end up in the book eventually anyway, I wanted to get it down—how raw it feels right now. In case it helps anyone else going through the same thing.'

In case it helped someone else. Sometimes Violet wondered if her parents thought too much about that and not enough about themselves. But that was who they were and she loved them for it, all the same.

'Are you sure it was a good idea?' she asked. 'I mean, everyone wants that interview, and you don't know what Tom is going to do with it now he's—' She broke off with a sob before she could reach the word *gone*.

Rick tugged her closer and she buried her face in his shoulder. 'Do you want me to get your mum? Or your sisters?'

Violet shook her head against his top. 'No. I just…I just need a few minutes.' A few minutes to let the misery out. To let go of all the hope she'd clung to over the last week or so. The chance that her future might be different to her past.

Uncle Jez had probably had that hope too, and look where it had got him.

That thought set off another wave of tears, and Violet didn't try to fight them. She might be all grown up these days, but sometimes a girl still needed her daddy's shoulder to cry on.

Eventually, though, the sobs faded and her tears dried and she knew her dad was going to want some answers.

'You sent him away,' Rick said. Not a question, not even a judgement. Just an opening, to show he was listening if she wanted to explain.

'I found something out about him,' Violet replied, unsure how much she really wanted him to know. Except this was her dad. He'd been there through everything. He'd understand, right? He'd want his little girl safe and happy. 'I know you thought he was a trustworthy journalist, I know that's why you picked him to write your book. But Dad, he wrote a story once. A story that destroyed a girl's life—just like Nick destroyed mine.'

Rick stilled, his arms securely tucked around her. 'You're sure?'

'Very. He admitted it.' Well, sort of. 'He claimed it wasn't the same but then he would, wouldn't he?'

Rick sighed, deep and heartfelt. 'Then I understand why you did what you did. But Violet, I need you to remember something very important, okay?' He pulled back to stare into her eyes, and Violet gave a small nod. 'Your life wasn't destroyed. Remember that.'

Shame filled Violet's chest. Here she was complaining when Uncle Jez's life was gone for ever. And she'd give anything for him to be caught up in a sex scandal right now, even if it meant the papers dragging up her own sordid story all over again.

'I know. Compared to Uncle Jez—'

'That's not what I mean,' Rick said with a sharp shake of the head. 'Think about it, Violet. You still have your home, your family. They took your confidence, and I'll never forgive them for that. But you're still you. You're still my daughter. And you are still loved.'

Warmth filled her, from the heart outwards. 'I know. And I'm so lucky to have you all. But it felt like…they made me someone I wasn't. So they took away who I really am.'

'But they can't.' Rick tapped her on the forehead with one finger. 'She's still in there. And it looked to me like Tom was helping you remember who she is.'

'I thought so too.' Until she'd found out the truth.

There was a pause, and when Violet looked up she saw her dad had on his thoughtful face. The one that always made her mother nervous.

'How did you find out about it? The story he wrote, I mean?'

Violet grimaced. 'Nick called. Told me I should look into his earlier stories.'

'Nick?' Rick's eyebrows launched upwards. '*The* Nick? And you *listened* to him?'

'I hung up on him,' Violet said. 'But…I was curious.'

'As ever.' Rick sighed. 'Did you talk to Tom about it before you threw him out?'

'A bit. I think he wanted to say more,' she admitted.

'Maybe you should listen.' Rick threw up his hands in pre-emptive defence. 'I'm not standing up for the guy—you get to make your own choices about him, and if you tell me he's not someone we should trust then I'll can the whole book idea altogether. He can publish what he has in interviews, but there's not even enough for a novella there. But Vi, if he matters to you—and I think he does—then you have to hear him out. Don't let someone else's version of who he is make your mind up for you.'

Violet nodded, and Rick bent over to kiss her on the

top of the head before moving towards the door. 'Listen to your old dad, yeah? He's been around awhile and sometimes, just sometimes, he knows what he's talking about.'

'I will,' Violet promised. But she couldn't help but be afraid this might not be one of those times.

'Hey, did you see this?'

Violet looked up from the file in front of her to see Rose in the doorway to the study, holding up a newspaper.

'It's less than twenty-four hours until the Benefit, Rose,' Violet said. 'I don't have time to read the paper.'

'You need to read this one.' Rose slipped into the room, revealing Daisy behind her. Daisy took the visitor's chair, rubbing her baby bump, while Rose perched on the edge of the desk, holding out the paper.

Violet sighed. Apparently she wasn't getting out of this without reading something. 'What is it?' she asked, reluctantly reaching out for the paper.

'Tom's first article from his interviews with Dad,' Daisy said, and Violet froze, her fingers brushing the edge of the newsprint.

'You really do need to read it,' Rose added.

God, but she didn't want to. One way or another, this would settle it. If he'd written the sort of story she expected him to, then there'd be no point listening to his side of the story about anything. It really would be over.

And if he hadn't…if by any chance he'd written the sort of story she'd want to read…what would she do then? Risk giving him a second chance?

She wasn't sure she could.

Swallowing, Violet took the newspaper from her sister's hand and skimmed over the section she'd folded it over to. Then, letting out a breath, she read it over again, slower this time.

'It's good, isn't it,' Daisy said after a moment. 'I mean, the guy can really write.'

'Sensitive, too,' Rose added. 'He really got Dad. I've never read an interview with him that made me feel like I was actually there talking with him before.'

'Vi, are you sure...?' Daisy trailed off as Violet shot a glare at her.

She really didn't want to talk about this. On the one hand, she should have known better than to get involved with a reporter in the first place. And if he really, truly did turn out to be a different breed, the lesser spotted good guy journalist...what did it matter now anyway? He was gone. She'd sent him away, and for good reason.

'Did you hear who he got to stand in for Uncle Jez tonight, by the way?' Rose asked. 'God only knows how. I tried to get the band to play second billing to the Lemons when we first put together the programme, but their schedule was crammed. Tom must have really pulled some strings.'

'I'm organising the concert, Rose. Of course I heard,' Violet snapped, then sighed. 'Sorry. I know. He's been great. Right from the start.'

'And yet...' Daisy prompted.

Violet dropped the paper to the desk. If there was anyone she could talk to, anyone who could tell her what she should do next, surely it would be her sisters. Especially since *they* at least seemed to have love all sussed out.

'Have Will or Seb ever done anything, like, in their past? Something you're not sure you could ever understand? Or forgive?'

Rose laughed. 'Vi, honey, Will left four women at the altar, remember? You're his best friend; you know he's not perfect. And was I damn afraid he might do the same thing to me? Of course I was.'

'But you married him anyway,' Violet said.

Rose shrugged. 'It's like Mum and Dad always say. When you know, you know. Will is the one for me. Once I accepted that…everything got a hell of a lot easier.'

Violet turned to Daisy. 'What about you?'

'I thought my marriage could only ever be a show, a business deal,' Daisy reminded her. 'But Rose is right— when you know, you know. So, the question is—do you know?'

Did she? Violet wasn't even sure. 'All I know is that it hurts, not having him here,' she admitted.

Rose and Daisy exchanged a look. Violet wasn't used to being on the outside of those looks. She didn't like it.

'Hurts like a dull ache, like something's missing but you can still feel it?' Rose asked. 'Like a phantom limb?'

'Or hurts like a sharp, blinding pain. The sort that consumes you until you can't think about anything else?' Daisy added.

'Both,' Violet admitted. 'And all the time.'

Rose and Daisy grinned across at each other.

'Honey, you totally know,' Rose said as she hopped off the desk.

'Where are you going?' Violet asked, standing when Daisy stood to follow.

Daisy flashed a smile back over her shoulder. 'To look at maternity bridesmaid dresses, of course. In lavender.'

Violet sank back down into her chair. She wished she could be so confident. Maybe she would have been, before Nick and everything that followed.

She took a deep breath. Maybe she would just have to be again; maybe she could find that lost confidence—if it meant winning Tom back.

He shouldn't be here. Tom was almost one hundred per cent certain he shouldn't be here. But Rick had called and said he was playing after all, and did Tom have any suggestions for a one-off stand-in guitarist for the night…and Tom couldn't not help. Not when he knew what a difference it could make to the night he and Violet had worked so hard to put together.

Even if she didn't want him there.

'Thanks again for doing this,' he said to Owain as a wide-eyed volunteer let them through the artists' gate.

'Are you kidding? Playing with the Lemons? It's an honour, man.' Owain's smile was wide, genuine—and world-famous. Tom had met the guitarist when his band was just starting out, and he'd rapidly become one of those friends he could call on for a night out whenever they were in the same city. These days, Owain's band played sold-out arena tours and, while the frontman might be the most famous member, any true music lover knew it was Owain's guitar playing that made their songs so memorable.

It didn't hurt that he had legions of female fans either, Tom thought. That had to be a bonus for tonight.

'I guess this is where I leave you,' he said as Owain headed through to the bands area. Normally, Tom would have been in there too, mingling, chatting, lining up interviews and soaking in the atmosphere. Tonight, he couldn't take the chance of bumping into Violet.

She had to be around here somewhere, he thought, as he waved goodbye to Owain. Probably racing around, double-checking everything, keeping everything under control in a way he couldn't have imagined her doing when they'd first met.

Strange to remember how he'd thought she was a spoilt rich kid, incapable of doing anything except trade on her parents' names and her own notoriety. He was happy to admit he'd been totally wrong about her.

He just wished she'd believe she was wrong about him, too.

'Tom! You made it.' Rick Cross clapped a hand on his shoulder and Tom tried not to jump.

'Hey. Things going well?' Tom asked, since he couldn't exactly ask, *How's Violet? Where is she? Will she ever forgive me?*

'Best Benefit Concert ever,' Rick announced, then lowered his voice. 'Don't tell Rose I said that, though, yeah?'

'Wouldn't dream of it.'

'Speaking of my girls, have you seen any of them yet?' Rick asked, his tone far too nonchalant. 'Say, Violet, for instance?'

'Ah, no. I thought it was probably best if I stayed out of the way a bit tonight,' Tom said. 'I really just came to bring Owain as a favour to a mate.'

'I see.' Rick subjected him to a long assessing look. 'And here I was thinking that you were here to set things right between the two of you. Never figured you for someone who'd quit at the first hurdle.'

'I'm not…I never said I'd quit.' Tom *wasn't* a quitter. But he also knew when he wasn't wanted. 'Maybe I'm just giving Violet a little space before I make my move.'

'Or maybe you're too scared she'll never trust you.'

How did the old man do that? See right to the heart of his every worry? Tom could understand it working with his daughters, but he'd only known the man a month.

Rick flashed him a quick grin and gripped his shoulder again. 'Don't worry, son. I'm not a mind-reader. But I've been where you are. Sherry and I always say "when you know, you know" and it's true. But we got married in a hurry, and knowing it's the real thing doesn't always make it any easier when times are hard. It just means you know it's worth fighting through.'

'And fighting for,' Tom murmured, almost to himself.

'Always that,' Rick agreed. 'Go on. Go find her. I think she's backstage.'

He shouldn't. This was her big night. She'd worked damn hard for it, and he didn't want to get in her way now. But on the other hand…how could he let this awful feeling in his chest that had started the moment he'd left Huntingdon Hall grow any bigger?

'Backstage, you say.' Tom squared his shoulders, wishing this didn't feel so much like heading into battle. 'Then I guess that's where I'm going.'

CHAPTER TWENTY-ONE

THE ATMOSPHERE BACKSTAGE was incredible. How had she never experienced this before? Normally at the Benefit it would be Rose rushing about behind the scenes, while Violet, Daisy and their mum would watch from a carefully sectioned off area of the crowd.

But now Violet knew—backstage was the place to be.

The act on stage finished their last song with a resounding chord that echoed off the trees surrounding the concert area, and the audience exploded into wild applause. Violet grinned and clapped along as the band traipsed off, high-fiving each other as they came.

'Great job, guys,' she told them, and got wide smiles in return. This was what all the work had been for. To put together a spectacular night that would help raise money and awareness for a cause that really counted.

It almost didn't matter that the person she wanted to share it with wasn't there.

Almost.

'Violet?'

Her breath caught in her throat at the sound of Tom's voice behind her. Of course he was here. How could a music journo miss a night like tonight?

She turned slowly, barely registering the next act as they took to the stage, even as the singer, Sammy, called back to her, something about a shout-out. There was cheering and music and noise all around her, and all she could see or hear was Tom, standing there, solemn-faced, watching her, waiting for her to speak.

And suddenly she had to figure out what she wanted to say.

She'd thought she would have more time. That she could tackle this at her own leisurely pace. But, instead, here he was and she needed to fix things. Somehow.

This could be her last chance.

'Tom.' His name was a start, right? A very small one, but still.

He stepped closer, just one pace. 'Things seem to be going great tonight.'

'They really are.' She bit her lip. 'I wasn't sure if you'd come.'

'Neither was I. But Owain asked me to come with him.'

'That's the only reason?' She almost didn't want to ask. Just in case.

'No.' How could one word send such a flood of relief through her system?

'I'm glad you came,' Violet admitted. 'I wanted to…I never gave you a chance to explain, last time. And I think…I'll listen now. If you still want to talk.'

'I do,' Tom said, but the hesitation in his voice made Violet nervous.

'But?'

Tom shook his head. 'You have a lot going on here today. It can wait.'

'I'm not sure it can.' Violet frowned. There was something more here. Something she wasn't getting. 'What is it?'

Tom leant back against the side of the stage with a sigh, and Violet had to step closer to even hear him over the noise of the band starting up. 'I can explain everything, and I think I can probably do it well enough to make you forgive me. This time.'

'Well, good?'

'But the thing is, Violet, that's only good for this time. What happens the next time I do something you don't agree with, or the next time something reminds you that I'm a hated journalist. You kick me out without listening again?'

'So…you're saying it's not worth trying?' Her stomach dropped lower and lower as every second passed without Tom's answer.

'I'm saying it's something I want you to think about. I want to know that you can trust me because I'm *me*. Not because I can tell you that my editor got a tip from an anonymous source and those photos in a brown envelope, and gave me the story to write as a test. To prove I could. To earn my stripes. And I thought it was just a practice run, that it wouldn't go to print. I don't want you to trust me just because I swear to you I asked him not to print it, and he laughed at me and I realised Mom was right all along.' He sighed, running a hand through his hair. 'I can explain as much as you want, Vi, and I will, probably often if we decide to make a go of things. But I need to know you trust me enough to not *need* the explanation to keep loving me. Does that make sense?'

It did. It was just an awfully big ask.

She opened her mouth to respond, to promise him whatever he wanted if he'd just *stay* long enough for them to sort things out. But then she heard her name blaring out of the speakers on stage, via Sammy, the lead singer's microphone.

'And a huge shout-out to Violet Huntingdon Cross for putting together such an epic party! Come on out here, Violet!'

'You should go,' Tom said, stepping back from her. 'I don't think she's used to being kept waiting.'

'But we need to—'

'I'll find you later,' Tom said. 'We'll talk then.'

But later would be too late; Violet knew it in her bones. Which meant it would have to be this way, instead. 'Go find Mum and Daisy and Rose. They're out front.'

Tom nodded, and was gone before Violet even stepped out onto the stage.

The lights flashed and burned her eyes and the cheers made her head pound, but nothing could dim her determination. She knew what she needed to do now. She just needed the courage to go through with it.

'Thanks, Sammy,' she said, stepping up to the microphone. She couldn't make out anything beyond the blurs of light in the crowd; she just had to trust that Tom was out there, listening. 'And thank you all for coming tonight.' She paused while the crowd cheered, and tried to ignore the way her knees were shaking. 'The Huntingdon Hall Benefit Concert is always a highlight of the year, but this is the first time I've been able to be so involved in it. You might have noticed that I've been keeping a bit of a low profile over the past few years. But that's...' she stumbled over her words for a moment and bit the inside of her cheek hard, determined to keep it together '...that's going to change.'

There were murmurs running through the crowd now, questions and speculations and probably a few off-colour jokes, too. Violet ignored all of them, looked up into the lights and said what she needed to say.

'I wanted tonight to be a memorial for my Uncle Jez, for his life, and a way of raising both money and awareness for people who find themselves in the same position and need our help.' She took a breath, drawing in courage.

'Whenever we suffer a loss—from a loss of a job, or our reputation, all the way up to a beloved family member—we have to grieve. We have to heal and we have to move on. And sometimes that can be the hardest part—letting go of the past and opening ourselves up to the possibilities of the future. It's taken me a while, but I'm finally able to do that. I am moving on. And you're going to be seeing more of me because of it. I'm going to be out there, raising awareness everywhere I can. I want to let people know that if they need help, it is out there for them. And I want to make sure they get it—because if I can spare one other family a loss like we've suffered this week, it will be worth every minute.'

The roar of the crowd's applause rumbled in her ears and the heat in her cheeks started to fade. She'd done it. She'd taken that step forward and moved on—she just hoped that Tom had seen it.

Because now she needed to find him for the next part.

Handing the microphone back to Sammy, she rushed off stage as the band started up their next song. Weaving her way through the business backstage, smiling vaguely at every clap on the back or supportive comment, she headed for where she hoped Tom would be—with her family.

The pride in his chest felt too big for his body, as if it might burst out of him at any moment. Never mind talking to the press on the phone or holding meetings with managers. Violet had put herself back out there—completely. She'd stood up in front of the crowd, the press and everyone watching on TV and declared herself part of the world again. A woman with a mission.

She wasn't ashamed any more, and it was beautiful.

'Did you *see* that?' Rose bounced up next to him, pure delight shining from her face.

'She was magnificent!' Daisy agreed.

'She most certainly was,' Sherry said, smiling with pride.

'Where is she?' Rose asked. 'I need to hug her.'

'Not until I do,' Tom murmured, and the three women turned to look at him.

Which was, of course, when Violet bounded in.

'Vi! You were brilliant!' Rose and Daisy reached for their sister, and Violet grinned—but her gaze was fixed on Tom's face. He could feel it, even as he stared back.

'Sorry, guys, but I need to talk to Tom,' Violet said.

They both ignored the knowing looks her family exchanged as they headed out of the private area, past the edge of the crowd and around through some of the smaller stalls set up on the outskirts of the concert. Tom vaguely recognised some of the women from the village manning one of the charity support stalls. As they passed them, Violet waved, then reached out to hold Tom's hand. Another sign she was done worrying about what others thought? He hoped so.

Of course, right now he was more interested in finding out exactly what *she* thought about their potential future together.

Eventually, they reached the security barriers out of the concert site, and Violet slipped them through with her pass. 'Where are we going?' Tom asked.

Violet shrugged. 'It doesn't really matter. I just…some things are still private, right?' She flashed him a quick smile and tugged him further along, until they were surrounded by trees at the edge of the wood. 'This will do.'

Tom wanted to ask what, exactly, it would do for. But Violet seemed nervous enough. For once, he'd have to curb his natural impulse to ask questions, lots of them, and let her talk in her own time.

Sometimes, he'd learnt, you got the best interviews that way.

Violet sucked in a deep breath, then let it out again. Tom stamped down on the impatience rising inside him. He had to let her take her time.

'Okay, so…I learnt something while you were gone. Or realised something, I guess. That…maybe people have never been able to move past my past, so to speak, because I've never done anything else. I need to replace those memories—those stories and those jokes—with new and better ones.'

'And that's what you were doing up there on the stage,' Tom guessed.

Violet nodded. 'Starting to, anyway. And it means moving on. Not just from that stupid sex tape, but from the last eight years of hiding, too. Of not trusting anyone and always expecting the worst.'

'Well…good.' Because that sounded positive. But he still needed to hear her say the words.

Violet looked up and met his gaze, her eyes wide and blue and totally open for the first time since he'd met her. 'My mum and dad, they always say that when you know, you know. And I think they're right.' The side of her mouth twisted up into a half smile. 'And I *did* know, deep down. It was just hard to see, behind all that doubt and fear and mistrust.'

'And now?' Tom asked, his heart thumping too hard, too loud in his chest.

'And being without you…it swept all that away. It hurt so much to be apart from you that none of the rest of it mattered any more. All that mattered was telling you that I love you. And I trust you. I do.'

'Really?' God, why couldn't he just take her words at face value?

Violet took his hand between hers. 'Enough to trust you with the rest of my life. If you'll have me.'

Tom blinked. 'You want to get married?'

Violet smiled, slow and warm. 'Why not? It seems to be all the rage this year. Besides, when you know, you know.' She reached up and kissed him once on the lips. 'And I know that whatever happens, whatever you've done or whatever you will do, I trust you to do it for us, not just for a quick story. I'm not the same person I was when that sex tape was made, and I know you're not the same person who let his editor use that story. And I'm not interested in who we were. Only who we can be together.'

And that was all he needed to know. Wrapping his arms tight around her waist, he pulled Violet close, kissing her long and deep until the sounds of the concert, the lights, even the breeze through the trees ceased to register. All that mattered was him and Violet, and their future together.

Finally, he pulled back, just enough to rest his forehead against hers. 'You did the same for me, you know,' he whispered fiercely. 'I spent so many years carrying around the guilt from that story, from my mom never knowing that I realised she was right, even if it was a little late. Meeting you…it made me face that guilt, and all my preconceptions about who you were. If you hadn't shown me that it was possible to move beyond our own pasts…I never could have come back here today. I never could have told you I love you too.'

Violet kissed him again, swift and sharp and full of feeling. But Tom wasn't done talking.

'I should get down on one knee, I know, but I don't want to move that far away from you,' he said, and Violet laughed. 'Violet Huntingdon-Cross. Will you do me the honour of becoming my wife?'

'Only if you'll do me the honour of being my husband,' Violet said, and kissed him again.

'Then it's settled. Your mum gets to plan another wedding.' He squeezed her tighter. 'What do you think? Next summer? Big celebrity bash?'

Violet laughed. 'Haven't you heard? The Huntingdon-Cross sisters don't wait that long for their happy ever afters.'

'True.' Tom smiled. 'Next month, then?'

'Sounds perfect,' Violet said. 'I'm ready to start our new lives. Together.'

EPILOGUE

THE SUMMER SUN shone down on Huntingdon Hall as crowds gathered for the fourth, and final, Huntingdon-Cross wedding celebration of the year. Violet peeked through the curtains of her bedroom, careful not to be seen, and watched the cars pulling up on the long driveway.

Somewhere out there, probably pacing with his soon-to-be brothers-in-law at his side, was her fiancé. She wondered what Tom was making of being the centre of attention for once, instead of just writing about other people's fame.

'Are you ready?' At the sound of her twin's voice, Violet let the curtain fall back into place and turned to smile at Rose.

'More ready than I thought I could ever be,' Violet said.

Stepping forward, the lavender silk of her bridesmaid's dress rustling around her, Rose hugged her sister, a feeling so warm and familiar that Violet felt love in every squeeze.

'Mum is downstairs, waiting to give final approval on the three of us before she heads out to the ceremony area,' Daisy said, her seven-months-pregnant bump appearing a moment before the rest of her came through the door. 'And Dad's just putting the finishing touches to his speech. Again.'

'"Final approval"?' Violet asked with a smile. 'Is she

worried Daisy might get jam on her dress, like she did when she was bridesmaid at Uncle Jez's second wedding?' The pang of pain at the thought of Jez was still there, but already it felt more like a loving memory than a searing loss. The hole he'd left would always be there, but they'd learn to live with it, Violet knew, to move on and make his death meaningful, at least.

'I was five!' Daisy pointed out indignantly.

'Just think, soon it will be your little bump trailing down the aisle in jam-smeared taffeta, leaving rose petals in her wake,' Rose said.

'Well, as long as it's not me, for once,' Violet said, checking her reflection one last time before they headed downstairs. 'I'm done being a bridesmaid, I think.'

'And today you're the bride.' Daisy's words came out a little watery, and Rose handed her a tissue for the inevitable tears.

'Don't start yet,' Rose said. 'We've got the whole ceremony to get through!'

'Not to mention Dad's speech,' Violet added. She wasn't sure if she was dreading or looking forward to hearing which tales of her life Rick Cross thought appropriate to share with the assembled company.

'Can't help it,' Daisy sniffed. 'Hormones.'

'Yeah, yeah,' Rose replied. 'A convenient excuse. They don't seem to be slowing you down any, though, do they? Seb was telling me all about your plans for Hawkesley Castle and his new TV series at dinner last night. It would be nauseating how much that man dotes on you if it wasn't so well deserved.'

Daisy elbowed Rose in the ribs. 'Don't tell me you didn't shed a tear or two when you were making those gorgeous rings for Violet and Tom.'

'Maybe just one,' Rose admitted. 'And they are very pretty, aren't they?'

'They're perfect,' Violet said. 'Just like everything else about today. Now, come on, let's go present ourselves for inspection.'

Violet followed her sisters out of the room, pausing to shut the door behind her. Strange to think she was leaving this place as herself, but would be returning as a married woman. Almost as impossible to believe as the thought of her getting married at all.

But here she was, with her sisters at her side, preparing to say *I do* to the last man she'd ever imagined marrying. And she couldn't be happier.

Sherry Huntingdon-Cross clapped her hands together with delight at the sight of them. 'Oh, don't you all look perfect,' she gushed before wedding planner mode took over again. 'Right, I'm going to head down and take my seat—that's the sign for the ushers to get everyone else seated. Rose, Daisy, you follow just behind me. Then Rick—where is your father, anyway?'

'Here, honey.' Rick Cross came rushing out of his studio, shoving pieces of paper into his pocket. 'Just a couple of last-minute edits. Don't worry,' he added with a wink at Violet. 'I kept the story about that time you fell in the pond at that hotel roof garden when we were on tour in Europe.'

'Oh, good,' Violet said unconvincingly.

'Right,' Sherry said again, commanding everyone's attention. 'I'm leaving. Daisy, Rose, prepare to follow.'

The wedding procession had been timed to perfection. As her father took her arm and led her out of the front door of her childhood home behind her sisters, Violet took a deep breath and followed her family down to the shady clearing, just behind the trees, where they'd set up the chairs and ceremony area. It wasn't a huge wedding—

despite Sherry's attempts—but neither was it the tiny one Violet would have insisted on even a few months ago.

She wasn't scared to share her new happiness, to let others see her moving on with her life in exciting new directions. She wasn't hiding any more.

At the front of the aisle, Tom turned, as if sensing her presence, and Violet couldn't hold back her smile at the sight of him in his perfect suit, waiting for her to join him.

'You ready for this, honey?' Rick asked as the string quartet struck up the canon.

'How could I not be?' Violet whispered back. 'After all, when you know, you know.'

* * * * *

THE BRIDESMAID'S GIFTS

GINA WILKINS

For Kerry.

Author of more than one hundred titles for Mills & Boon, native Arkansan **Gina Wilkins** was introduced early to romance novels by her avid-reader mother. Gina loves sharing her own stories with readers who enjoy books celebrating families and romance. She is inspired daily by her husband of over thirty years, their two daughters and their son, their librarian son-in-law who fit perfectly into this fiction-loving family, and an adorable grandson who already loves books.

Chapter One

"So you're the psychic."

Aislinn Flaherty had to make a massive effort to hold on to her pleasant expression in response to the drawled comment. She was doing this for her best friend, she reminded herself. Nic was so happy about her engagement, so pleased to be entertaining her future brother-in-law for the first time. Aislinn was going to do everything in her power to get along with him, even though she already suspected that it wasn't going to be easy.

"Someone has obviously been pulling your leg," she said lightly. "I've never even pretended to be a psychic."

"Hmm." Ethan Brannon was visibly unconvinced. Whatever he had been told—and Aislinn intended to grill Nic about that when they were alone—he apparently believed that she did, indeed, make claims to some sort of extrasensory abilities.

She had met Ethan only ten minutes earlier when she'd arrived at Nic Sawyer's house for this small dinner party. After introducing them, Nic and her fiancé—Ethan's brother, Joel—had moved into the kitchen to finish the dinner preparations, leaving Aislinn and Ethan to chat in the living room. This was Ethan's idea of a conversation starter, apparently.

In an attempt to dispel some of the awkwardness, she moved across the room to an antique buffet in one corner of the room. Nic had set the buffet up as a bar, and had encouraged Aislinn and Ethan to help themselves to a before-dinner drink while they waited. "Can I get you anything?"

"Yeah, sure. Whatever you're having."

She poured a glass of white wine for herself, a Chivas for him. Carrying both across the room, she handed him his glass. He frowned, looking suspiciously from the drink to her. "Parlor tricks?"

Sipping her wine, she lifted an eyebrow, then lowered the glass. "I beg your pardon?"

"I asked for whatever you were having, and you brought me my usual preference. I suppose Nic told you what I like?"

"Nic and I haven't talked about what you like or don't like to drink," she said, her brusque tone meant to hide a sudden wave of discomfort. "You just don't look like the white-wine type to me."

Still looking at her, he lifted the glass to his mouth. Despite the inexplicable antagonism she had felt from him from the start, she couldn't help noticing that his was a particularly nice mouth. He looked very much like a more sharply planed version of his younger brother. Both had crisp brown hair with a slight tendency to wave, clear hazel eyes and strong chins. Both were just under six feet and solidly built. Yet there was a...well, a hardness about Ethan that seemed to be missing in his more easygoing younger brother.

Ethan was three years the elder. A self-employed small-business consultant, he lived in Alabama in a house that Nic had told her was rural and rather isolated. This was his first visit to Arkansas, though his brother had lived here for almost two years. Having met Ethan eight months ago, Nic seemed to like her future brother-in-law, but she had admitted that he wasn't the easiest man to get to know.

"Joel says Ethan was born grouchy," she had confided with a laugh. "But he's actually quite nice."

Aislinn was reserving judgment on that.

"It was generous of you to offer to help Joel and his partner make their clinic run more efficiently," she said with a determined smile. "They're both wonderful pediatricians, but Joel claims they're both a little challenged in the business-management area."

Ethan shrugged. "I advised Joel to take some undergraduate business courses, but all he wanted to take were science classes. He spent so much time preparing for medical school that he forgot to prepare for the business of being a doctor."

"And that's what you do—teach small-business owners how to make their operations more profitable."

He nodded as he took another sip of his drink.

"Joel told me you're very good at your job. He said you've helped a lot of people stay in business who would have had to declare bankruptcy if they hadn't hired you. He said some of them have actually become wealthy."

He shrugged.

Aislinn swallowed a sigh. She had spent the day decorating a four-tier wedding cake with a couple of hundred tiny sugar roses entwined with frosting ivy vines. As tedious as that had been after a few hours, it was still less work than trying to draw conversation out of Ethan.

What a relief when Joel came back into the room to announce that dinner was ready. Both Aislinn and Ethan jumped to their feet with almost humorous eagerness to follow their host into the dining room.

Nic was just lighting the candles in the center of her mother's big mahogany table. She had been living in her widowed mother's house for more than two years, since Susan Sawyer had moved to Paris to live with her son, Paul, a U.S. Embassy employee. Nic had met Joel when he'd bought the house next door. Friendship had blossomed into much more, and now Nic and Joel were planning their wedding, which would take place in only a few days.

Taking her seat at the beautifully set table, Aislinn studied the happiness gleaming in her friend's dark-blue eyes. Though Nic had been dating someone else when she met Joel, Aislinn had never expected Nic's relationship with Brad to last. Yet she'd had a feeling from the first time she had seen Nic and Joel together that the two were meant for each other. She hadn't said anything to Nic at the time, but she had done her part to nudge them together—with obvious success.

They talked about wedding plans as they began to eat, Nic sharing a few anecdotes about how difficult it had been to choose the colors and flowers and music and menus for her upcoming wedding. "I had no idea there was so much involved," she added with a groan. "I thought all I needed was a dress and a minister, but people kept adding things to my list."

"What people?" Ethan asked.

"My mother, mostly. She'll be here tomorrow, but in the meantime she's been making long-distance wedding plans and she calls to update me three or four times a day. Sometimes she forgets the time difference and she calls in the middle of the night to suggest a brilliant idea she just had. And then there were my friends at work, who all had suggestions they thought I should be thrilled about. And my friend Carole, who volunteered to coordinate everything during the ceremony and immediately turned into a wedding-planner tyrant."

Ethan shrugged. "You should have told them all to butt out. If you wanted just a dress and a minister, that's all you should have."

Nic wrinkled her nose in a good-natured smile. "It isn't that I mind so much. Everyone knows I'm hopeless when it comes to these girlie things, so they were only trying to help. There were just so many decisions and details. It was mind-boggling at times, but I think it will all work out. I kept it as simple as possible."

"Seems like a lot of trouble. You're just as married

if you elope to a justice of the peace as you are after one of these fancy ceremonies."

This time it was Joel who responded to his brother's cynical observation. "That's true, but most people like to celebrate the occasion with friends and family. Nic's mother would have been terribly disappointed if we didn't make a bit of fuss—and, for that matter, so would ours. You know she's looking forward to it."

Aislinn was especially glad for her friend's sake that Joel's mother had endorsed the wedding. Elaine Brannon had made little secret of her reservations about the match when she had first met Nic eight months earlier.

She'd made it clear that it wasn't because she had anything against Nic personally. She had been concerned because Nic was so very different from her son's first wife, a supermodel-beautiful, socially conscious family counselor who had died in a tragic car accident less than a year after she and Joel were married. Elaine had wondered if her pediatrician son could be content with an impulsive, sometimes reckless small-town police officer who couldn't care less about being on the social A-list.

Once Joel had convinced his mother that he couldn't imagine being content without Nic in his future, Elaine had given her full approval to the match. All she had wanted, she assured them, was for Joel to find the happiness he deserved in life. If that was with Nic, then she was a welcome addition to the Brannon family.

Ethan mumbled something that seemed to imply that the mother-pleasing argument was no more likely to influence him than ordinary peer pressure.

"So you're saying when you get married, you just want a no-frills elopement?" Nic asked him with a grin.

He set down his fork and reached for his drink. "Marriage isn't on the agenda in my case. I've told you before that I can't imagine finding anyone who'd put up with me for long—or vice versa."

Aislinn's immediate reaction to that assertion was a vague feeling that he was wrong. Ethan would find someone, she sensed. And it would be a lifelong union.

She couldn't have explained how she knew that fact—and she did accept it as fact, since during her entire twenty-eight years she could count on one hand the number of times she had been wrong when her predictions had been accompanied by a particular feeling. It was not ESP, she had always insisted to anyone who questioned her. She just had better-developed intuition than most people.

Maybe she just paid more attention to her feelings, maybe she was just better at interpreting them—or maybe she was just a really good guesser. But she wasn't "different."

When they had all finished their chicken parmigiana, Nic rose to serve dessert. Reaching for plates, Aislinn offered to help.

"So?" Nic said when they were alone in the kitchen, loading plates into the dishwasher. "What do you think of Ethan?"

Aislinn shrugged. "He's okay, I guess. A little aloof."

"I agree that he's reserved. But underneath, there's a nice guy. He's been very accepting of me, even when his mother was still trying to convince Joel that I was all wrong for him. And he's obviously fond of Joel, very supportive and protective—which, of course, I find sort of endearing."

"He seems to be suspicious of me—as if he thinks I'm trying to run some sort of a con on his family."

Reaching into a cabinet, Nic shrugged. "He's just naturally cautious around new people, I think. He acted a little suspicious of me at first, too. Not rude or confrontational or anything. Just wary. Reserving judgment until he knew what my motives were. Maybe he's been burned a few times."

"A few." It was more a confirmation than a guess. She didn't have the details, but she knew he'd been hurt.

Maybe Nic was right. Maybe that was the reason Ethan tended to be cautious. She would try to be patient during the getting-acquainted process. For Nic's sake. And if it turned out that she and Ethan still didn't like each other after the wedding, it was no big deal. He'd go back to Alabama and they would rarely see each other again.

A funny feeling went through her with that thought. Oddly enough, she had no clue of what it meant that time, if anything. It was just a…well, almost like a mental shiver. Probably nothing at all, she assured herself.

She noticed that Nic was scooping whipped cream onto the first of four bowls of what appeared to be chocolate lava cake. "Leave the whipped cream off one of the desserts," she advised absently.

Nic didn't even blink at the suggestion. She simply loaded three whipped-cream-topped desserts and one without topping onto a tray. "Will you bring the coffee carafe?" she asked over her shoulder as she headed for the dining room.

The Brannon brothers were involved in a discussion of billing practices when Nic and Aislinn rejoined them. Aislinn poured coffee while Nic set the dessert tray on the table. "Is there anyone who doesn't like whipped cream?"

"That would be Ethan," Joel said with a grin. "He hates whipped cream."

Nic smiled at Aislinn before handing Ethan the untopped dessert. "Then I'm glad we left one plain."

Ethan gave Aislinn a hard look, but he didn't say anything as he dipped into his dessert. Concentrating on her own, she hoped the awkward evening would end soon.

Ethan was more than ready for this dinner party to be over. He didn't much care for dinner parties anyway, being the barbecue-and-beer type himself. He wasn't really into wedding planning, though he understood why Joel and Nic were preoccupied with that sort of thing now. And then there was the psychic....

Not that anyone had ever actually called her that. Joel and Nic had actually gone out of their way to avoid the label, claiming that Aislinn didn't like it. She simply had "feelings," they had assured him. She'd been gifted with a heightened intuition that made it wise to pay attention when she made predictions.

As proof, Joel had pointed to an accident Nic had been involved in while spending a few days in Alabama for Joel's high school reunion. It had been eight months ago, the weekend when Ethan had first met Nic. Aislinn had called Nic's cell phone several times during those few days with vague warnings of impending disaster.

As far as Ethan was concerned, it was simply an unfortunate coincidence that Nic had, indeed, been injured that weekend in an incident that had narrowly missed being tragic. There was no way Aislinn could have known a balcony would collapse beneath Nic's feet, sending her plunging twenty feet to the ground below.

If Aislinn *had* been psychic, she'd have been a lot more specific than saying something "bad" was going to happen, right? Even if so-called precognition existed, what good was it if she hadn't been able to stop her friend from being hurt? So far, all she'd done this evening was guess that he liked Chivas and hated whipped cream. Big deal.

Her alleged extrasensory abilities weren't the only thing about Aislinn Flaherty that made him uncomfortable, he had to concede. Joel had told him that she was very pretty, but that had been a major understatement. Aislinn was gorgeous.

He didn't know why she felt the need to pretend to have supernatural abilities. Surely it wasn't an attention-seeking ploy, since a woman who looked like that could attract all the notice she wanted. She certainly didn't dress for attention; she wore a modest beige knit top and brown pants that were rather plain in themselves but didn't at all detract from her own natural beauty.

As far as he knew, she hadn't asked for any money for her "services" from Nic or Joel—which didn't mean she wasn't conning other people. Perhaps it simply amused her to see how gullible others could be. Or maybe she sort of believed it herself, which was even more pathetic.

Reaching for his coffee, he hoped he would be able to make an escape as soon as dinner was over. He'd been sociable for about as long as he could manage.

"Good morning, beautiful."

The woman who called herself Cassandra looked up from her knitting with a smile and an instinctive little preen. She simply couldn't help reacting that way to young Dr. Thomas, with his warm green eyes and roguish smile. Even though she was old enough to be his mother, there was still enough of the flirt in her to respond to a good-looking man. And besides, this one was special.

"Hello, handsome."

Walking with a rolling gait that was deceptively lazy, he crossed the room and propped one hip on the windowsill near her chair. She liked to sit here in the afternoons, where she could look out at the beautifully manicured grounds and watch the birds nesting in the trees outside her second-story room. She had always loved spring, with its whispered promises of fresh starts and new lives. Even if those promises inevitably died in the cold darkness of winter.

"I've been told you had a difficult night."

Her smile faded in response to his gentle words. She looked down at her knitting, hiding her expression from him as she nodded. "Nightmares."

"They're getting worse again?"

"Not all the time. Just occasionally."

"Do you want to tell me about them?"

Her needles clicked in the silence that followed the invitation. After a moment she said simply, "I don't remember."

"Cassandra."

She could tell by his tone that he was disappointed she had chosen to lie to him. While she was sorry about that, she didn't want to talk about the dreams. About the faces that haunted her days as well as her nights. The memories that were simply too painful to dwell upon, much less to share.

"You have a date tonight," she said instead. "She's pretty, but she isn't the one. You're wasting your time."

Though she could tell he wanted to focus on her nightmares, he indulged her with a slightly strained smile. "You've been listening to the nurses gossip again, haven't you? I swear, you can hardly sneeze in this place without everyone knowing about it."

She merely smiled and continued to work her needles.

"That's what I get, I suppose, for going out with someone on staff here," he added conversationally. "Hard to keep it a secret. Not that I'm trying. But enough about me. Are you sure you wouldn't like to talk to me about your dreams? It just might help, you know."

She lifted her eyes then, studying him sadly. He was so young. So confident that he had all the answers. About her. About his other patients. About himself. Poor, sweet sap.

"It wouldn't help me," she told him quietly. "But thank you for caring, Dr. Thomas. You have a kind heart."

He didn't seem to know how to respond except to

stand and murmur, "Thank you. I'll prescribe a new sleep aid for you to try tonight. Maybe it will help you rest more peacefully."

"Whatever you think best, Doctor."

"I'll see you in a few days, okay? If you need anything at all, you be sure and let someone know. I or one of the other doctors will take good care of you."

"I know." She waited until he had reached her door before saying, "Try to have a nice time this evening, Doctor. Despite everything."

He chuckled quizzically. "You're something else, Cassandra."

"You have no idea," she murmured after he'd let himself out. And then she turned her attention back to the garment taking shape in her lap.

Chapter Two

Four days after the dinner party at Nic's house, Aislinn stood at the front of a small church, a bouquet of spring flowers clutched in her hands. As the traditional wedding ceremony began, she glanced toward the best man. A strange sensation coursed down her spine when she saw that he was studying her in return.

She looked quickly away, trying to focus on the minister as he spoke about the joys and responsibilities of marriage. But the uplifting message couldn't hold her attention. Her gaze turned again to Ethan, handsome and remote in his stark black tuxedo.

He wasn't looking at her now, but she sensed that he was still aware of her. Probably wondering why she kept looking at him.

She couldn't have explained. She was simply having a hard time looking away, for some reason.

"Do you take this man…?" the minister intoned, and Aislinn forced her attention back to the ceremony. Her part was coming up.

"I do." Nic's voice was strong and steady as she gazed into her groom's eyes. Eyes, Aislinn noted, that looked exactly like those of the best man—a thought that almost made her look his way again. She restrained herself with an effort, focusing almost fiercely on the bride and groom.

"I do." This time it was Joel who spoke, proudly and confidently. Joel was almost amusingly impatient to begin his new life with Nic and he made no attempt to hide his feelings.

It was time for the exchanging of the rings. As maid of honor, Aislinn had been responsible for holding the groom's gold band. She took Nic's bouquet, passing the ring to her at the same time. For just a moment they smiled at each other, their long years of friendship forming a bond that let them say a great deal to each other without words.

And then Nic turned to her new husband, and Aislinn was aware of the faintest pang of regret, almost as if an era were ending. She and Nic would always be close, she knew—but it would be different now. Nic and Joel would share a long, happy life together, one that would eventually include a child. A boy who would look exactly like Joel.

Though she had known for a few weeks now, Aislinn hadn't shared that tidbit with her friend. After all, it was only a feeling. A guess, really. And even though Aislinn's "feelings" had an impressive record of accuracy, there were times when it seemed best to keep them to herself.

She glanced once again toward Ethan, who was watching Joel and Nic now. Strange how she'd had so few insights about him since she had met him. As well as she usually read people, she'd gotten very little from Ethan—primarily that he seemed suspicious of her and had from the start. She still wondered what he had been told about her.

Ethan took great pride in being a realist and a skeptic. He didn't believe in mind readers, mediums, poltergeists, UFOs, vampires, Santa Claus or love at first sight. If he couldn't see it, feel it, touch it or prove it, he had no use for it.

And yet—every time he looked into Aislinn's exotically shaped near-black eyes, he felt something shift inside him. He couldn't explain it any better than that, but something definitely happened. And he had been on edge ever since he'd met her.

Lust, he told himself. Nothing more complicated than that. And who could blame him? On a scale of one to ten, this woman was a twelve. A perfect heart-shaped face framed by long, glossy black hair. Eyes as dark as still water on a cloudless night. A full, soft mouth that could make a man want to believe anything she might tell him.

As for the rest of her, well, he had to remind himself that he was in a church just to keep his eyes from lingering too long on curves that made his mouth go dry and his palms itch.

Realizing the fanciful direction his thoughts had taken, he had to force himself not to scowl. He didn't need to be standing up here glowering during the ceremony or people might get the idea he had a problem with the bride rather than the maid of honor.

It was too bad, really. Under normal circumstances, he might have been happy to spend some time with a beautiful woman like Aislinn while he was visiting the area.

It seemed appropriate that her bridesmaid dress was a bold, bright red. The color of danger.

"…I now pronounce you husband and wife."

The solemn words brought Ethan's attention back to the ceremony. He managed a slight smile as Joel enthusiastically kissed his bride to the accompaniment of sentimental sighs from the guests gathered to witness the occasion.

He was as pleased for his brother as everyone else was. Despite his initial concerns about police officer Nic Sawyer's suitability for Joel, he had quickly been convinced that they were a very good match. Though she couldn't have been more different from Heather, Nic was exactly what Joel needed now, six years after the tragedy that had changed the direction of his life. She made Joel happy again, which was all that really mattered as far as Ethan was concerned.

Beaming like two high-intensity bulbs, Nic and Joel turned to face their audience as they were introduced for the first time as Dr. and Mrs. Brannon. Holding her bouquet again in her right hand, Nic slipped her left hand beneath Joel's arm for their walk down the aisle. Following the instructions he had been given, Ethan moved to stand behind the couple, presenting his arm to Aislinn.

She hesitated only a moment before sliding her hand beneath his arm. The pause was so slight that he doubted anyone else had noticed, but he knew he hadn't imagined it.

Despite his skepticism of anything resembling premonition, he had the oddest feeling as he escorted Aislinn down the aisle in the wake of his brother and new sister-in-law. Had to be hunger, he told himself. Lunch had been a long time ago.

Aislinn had practiced walking out on Ethan's arm during the rehearsal the evening before. She had been surprised then to feel such well-defined muscles beneath the conservative but casual business-consultant clothing—and she was struck again now by how strong and solid his arm felt beneath her lightly resting fingertips.

Funny how nervous she'd been about touching him each time, she thought as she smiled at familiar faces she passed going down the aisle. Whatever inspired her hunches, she had never been overly influenced by physical contact. Yet she had been so wary of touching Ethan, almost as if she'd been worried that doing so would trigger some previously unknown ability within herself. How silly.

Or maybe the reason for her hesitation had been a lot more basic than that. Maybe it had more to do with the fact that she found Ethan Brannon just a bit too attractive for her own peace of mind. Dropping his arm the moment they stepped out of the sanctuary and into the vestibule, she reminded herself that he didn't seem to like her very much. She wasn't particularly fond of him, either, with his cutting remarks and obvious suspicions.

"Oh, my gosh." Nic looked a bit dazed as she turned to Aislinn. "I think I just got married."

Aislinn laughed, as did everyone else within hearing. "You did, sweetie."

"Too late to back out now," Joel said cheerfully.

His bride grinned up at him. "That goes both ways."

Aislinn noted that Joel didn't look at all perturbed by Nic's reminder.

The reception was held in the ballroom of a local country club. It wasn't an overly large room but big enough for the intimate crowd Nic and Joel had invited to celebrate their marriage with them. A local country band, made up of four talented teenagers who were already getting statewide attention for their singing and songwriting talent, provided the music.

Unpretentious but delicious food was served buffet-style, with coffee, fruit punch and sparkling grape juice for beverages. The lack of champagne or other alcoholic choices had nothing to do with the wedding budget but everything to do with Nic's relentless campaigning against drinking and driving. Through her career she had seen entirely too many tragic accidents involving alcohol and she had no intention of contributing to the statistics by serving drinks to people who had driven to her reception.

It wasn't as if public transportation was plentiful in the smallish central-Arkansas town. Whole months often passed without Aislinn seeing one cab. When the locals wanted to go somewhere, they drove. This was part of the reason traffic was such an issue as the thriving area grew more rapidly than the aging street system.

She cast a quick, assessing glance at the table that held the wedding cake, making sure it was still in pristine condition for photographs and the ceremonial cutting by the bride and groom. Though Nic had requested an understated cake to go with the simple theme of the wedding, Aislinn had spent hours crafting the perfect wedding cake for her best friend. She had taken her inspiration from Nic's heirloom wedding gown, first worn in the mid-1940s by Nic's grandmother, then by Nic's mother, Susan, in the early seventies.

The gown was satin, covered with lace painstakingly dotted with seed pearls. It had been hand sewn by Nic's great-grandmother, making it a priceless family treasure, immaculately preserved. Only a minimum of tailoring had been required for Nic, and Aislinn had no doubt that the gown would survive for another generation or two, perhaps to be worn by Nic's future daughter-in-law, or maybe a granddaughter.

Aislinn had so few heirlooms from her own family that she could only imagine how much the gown meant to Nic and her mother. So the dress had seemed to be the logical theme for the wedding cake. Borrowing Nic's matching veil for a few days and using photographs of the dress as inspiration, Aislinn had designed a white-on-white cake that looked as though it was covered in the same lace as the dress.

It had involved hours of eye-crossingly intricate string work and hundreds of tiny, hand-set edible "pearls." She had created gentle folds in the fondant "fabric" and had cascaded a spray of white-frosting roses entwined with green-tinted frosting ivy down one side, as if a bouquet had been carelessly laid upon the satin-and-lace cake. She'd forgone the overused bride-and-groom topper, using white gum-paste roses instead.

She had been pleased with Nic's reaction upon seeing the finished cake for the first time. Nic had acted as though she had never seen anything more beautiful in her life, even becoming uncharacteristically misty as she had examined every angle of the cake.

"It's gorgeous, Aislinn," she had said huskily. "The best you've ever done. I feel as though you should enter it in a competition or something, not just give it to me for my reception."

Laughing, Aislinn had shaken her head. "There's nothing I would rather do with it," she had assured her friend. "As far as I'm concerned, this is the most special cake I've ever created because it's for you."

The guests at the reception seemed to be properly appreciative of the effort. They gathered around the cake, oohing and aahing, asking Aislinn repeatedly if all the details were actually edible. Laughing, she assured them that, as intricate as the decorations were, the cake was meant to be eaten.

"So you made that?"

She turned to find Ethan standing behind her, a glass of punch in his hand, his gaze focused on the cake. "Yes, I made that."

If he noted her wryly mocking repetition, he ignored it. "It looks nice."

Feeling a little petty now, she replied more genuinely, "Thank you. It was the most important cake I've ever done."

"You and Nic are pretty tight, huh?"

"We've been friends for a long time. Since elementary school."

"And when did you start the psychic thing?"

She counted mentally to ten, then gave a fake smile and a slight wave aimed toward a pillar on the other side of the room. "If you'll excuse me, Ethan, I see someone I should say hello to. Perhaps you should offer your mother another glass of punch. She looks a little wilted."

Before he could answer, she was already moving away, congratulating herself on her restraint. There was absolutely no way she would do anything to put a damper on Nic's wedding reception, but Ethan Brannon could try the patience of a saint.

She didn't know what it was about her that made him feel compelled to bait her, but he never seemed to miss an opportunity. Fortunately she could think of no reason for spending any more time with him once this evening was over.

"Ethan."

Having been unaware that his brother was anywhere nearby, Ethan grimaced a little before turning around to face Joel with an expression of feigned innocence. "Hey, bro. Nice party."

"Yes, it is. So stop trying to mess it up, okay?"

"I'm not doing anything," Ethan muttered into his punch glass.

"You were picking on Aislinn again."

Faintly amused by his brother's wording, Ethan shrugged. "I was just talking to her. You know, making small talk. Isn't that what one's supposed to do at these things? I told her I liked the cake."

"There was more to it than that. I didn't hear what you said, but I could tell she didn't like it."

"So are you into mind reading now?"

"Leave her alone, Ethan. She's not a fraud and she's not a crackpot. She's Nic's best friend, almost a sister to her—which makes her, like, an honorary sister-in-law to me now. So be nice to her," Joel ordered sternly.

Ethan sighed. "I'll try. It's just that whole psychic thing. I'm not buying in to it."

"Nobody's asking you to. Certainly Aislinn's not asking you to. She hates when anyone calls her a psychic or talks about her...well, *gifts,* for lack of a better word. Just treat her like you do anyone else. No, scratch that. Be polite to her."

Because it was Joel's wedding day and Ethan was feeling uncharacteristically magnanimous, he said, "I'll work on it."

Joel clapped him on the shoulder. "I appreciate it."

Still looking radiant in her white satin and lace, Nic broke away from the final group of well-wishers who had lingered with her at the end of the reception line Joel had just escaped. "What are you two plotting over here?"

Ethan lightly chucked her chin with the knuckles of his free hand. "I was just commiserating with my kid brother. Now that he's married a cop, he's going to have to toe the line."

"You've got that straight." Nic's sudden tough-girl expression was especially funny considering the delicate lace draping her. "I've got handcuffs."

Looking intrigued, Joel slid his arm around her slender waist. "Maybe we should discuss those...later."

Ethan groaned and looked down at his empty punch glass. "I think I need some more of this fruity stuff. Since there isn't anything stronger."

"Nic. Joel." Nic's mother, Susan Sawyer, hurried toward them, a look of determination on her face, which so strongly resembled her daughter's. "The photographer wants to take a few more pictures of you while the guests are in line at the buffet tables."

Though Nic rolled her eyes a bit, she took Joel's arm and turned obediently with him. "Yes, Mother."

Joel looked back over his shoulder at his brother. "Try to look like you're enjoying yourself, will you? I know you don't like parties—but you could pretend you do."

"To paraphrase a cheesy movie I caught on cable recently—this *is* my party face."

Joel moved on with a resigned shake of his head, leaving Ethan to reflect that when it came to parties, he had always been pretty much hopeless. He didn't do small talk, he wasn't much of a dancer, he was uncomfortable in crowds and he was lousy at pretending to be having a good time when he wasn't.

He stood unobtrusively at one side of the room while

the other guests gathered around Nic and Joel or sat at the comfortably arranged small tables to enjoy the finger-foods buffet provided by the caterer. Ethan wasn't hungry, so he remained where he was, watching.

His gaze turned toward the cake table in its place of honor. The cake was so fancy that it was almost a shame to destroy it, he thought, wondering how many hours Aislinn had spent on those incredibly detailed decorations. Hers was an odd business. All that time and effort spent on something so transient. A plain cake tasted just as good as one covered in fake lace and flowers.

Still, as a small-business consultant, he appreciated the fact that she had found a market for her skills and was apparently making a living at it. He wondered idly if she was charging enough for her time, taking full deductions on her supplies and other expenses. If she had a solid business plan to keep her on track to grow and expand her cottage industry.

"You're thinking about work, aren't you?" His mother, petite, blond Elaine Brannon, slipped a hand beneath his arm as she spoke indulgently. "You always get that exact look in your eyes when you're trying to figure out how to make money for someone else. Are you already planning how to restructure your brother's business office?"

"Something like that. How are you holding up, Mom?"

She gave him a look and spoke firmly. "I'm fine. The wedding was lovely, wasn't it? Very simple and sweet."

"It was nice. Nic was right to resist overdoing things. I hate those splashy, overblown, pretentious affairs."

"You're referring to your cousin Jessica's wedding last year?"

He grimaced. "Bingo. The circus with the twelve bridesmaids and four flower girls and two dogs in tuxedos and the white doves and oversize ice sculptures and clowns and horse-drawn carriages and full orchestra and endless speeches by inebriated guests."

"There weren't any clowns," Elaine murmured, though she couldn't refute any of the rest of his drawled description. "I was sorry I coerced you into going to that one. I knew Marlene and Jessica would go overboard, but I didn't think they would get that carried away."

"Yeah, well, the worst part was that Marlene and Ted are going to be paying for that production long after the marriage is over."

"I'm afraid you're right." Elaine shook her head in disapproval. "Jessica and Bobby have already separated twice, and last I heard, things aren't looking any better for them. Still, Marlene could have made an effort to come to Joel's wedding after we all made the trip to Iowa for Jessica's."

As much as he knew his mother enjoyed family gossip—the reason he'd brought up the juicy topic in the first place—Ethan was bored with discussing his father's sister and her ostentatious lifestyle. "You and Susan seem to have been getting along very well," he remarked, glancing across the room to where Nic's mother stood chatting with the minister.

"She's an interesting woman," Elaine agreed. "She has some fascinating stories about living in Europe with her son. He has to return tomorrow because of job demands, but she's staying here another week to visit with her friends before rejoining Paul in Paris. She even offered to provide accommodations and guide service if your father and I would like to visit there. Wasn't that nice?"

"Good luck getting Dad to Paris," Ethan murmured. "He would be convinced his practice would collapse and termites would eat the house to the ground while he was gone."

Elaine sighed gustily. "He has to retire sometime, right? He can't keep practicing orthodontia for the rest of our lives."

"You know he would drive you crazy if he quit the practice. But maybe he'll agree to take you to Paris later this summer since Susan made such a nice offer. I'll even promise to check the house every day for termites."

Smiling at the gentle mockery of her husband's one odd obsession, Elaine said, "Between the two of us, maybe we can talk him into it. I would love to see Paris."

Ethan made a mental note to persuade his father to book the trip as soon as possible. And then, because his mother faced a rather significant medical appointment next week, he tried to assure himself that there would be no reason for her not to enjoy that long-overdue vacation.

"You're sure you don't want me to come back to Danston with you? Because I can come back and reorganize Joel's operations later…."

She shook her head sternly. "You will stay here, just as you've planned. It's the ideal time for you to look over Joel's office procedures and to keep an eye on things while he and Nic are away. I never should have told you about my appointment. If you hadn't happened to be there when the nurse called, I would have waited to tell you when I tell Joel—after I have all the results back."

"Yeah, well, Joel's going to be ticked off that you didn't tell him sooner, just as I would have been."

She leveled a finger at him in the same gesture she had always used when delivering a maternal order. "Don't you dare say a word to him, Ethan Albert Brannon. I won't have his honeymoon spoiled by worrying about something that will probably turn out to be nothing at all."

He sighed and responded as he always did to that particular tone. "Yes, ma'am."

"They're getting ready to start the dancing." Elaine glanced toward the corner where the band was starting to play again. "Interesting choice of musicians. They look young enough to be high school students."

"They are. I think a couple of them are Joel's patients."

"Really? How odd. But pretty much what I've come to expect from Nic."

"Admit it, you like her."

"More all the time," she confessed with a smile. "She really is a dear, isn't she? And she loves Joel so much."

"Obviously mutual."

"Oh, yes. He's crazy about her." Looking pensive now, Elaine gazed across the room to where Joel and Nic were moving to the center of the dance floor. "I can't help thinking back to Joel and Heather's big, formal wedding. It was so different from this intimate little affair. Beautiful in its own way but different. And as happy as Joel was with Heather, this seems so much more fitting for the man he is now."

Ethan didn't want to talk about his late sister-in-law tonight, six years after her death. "This *is* who

Joel is now," he agreed simply, then changed the subject. "Do you want something to eat? I'll get a plate for you."

"No, thank you. I'd better go join your father. He's starting to give me signals that he's ready to be rescued from Nic's uncle's fishing stories. By the way, you really should ask the maid of honor to dance. I know you don't care for dancing, but it is sort of tradition, you know."

He frowned as he glanced instinctively across the room to where Aislinn sat at a table eating with Nic's mother and brother. "Considering my dancing skills— or lack thereof—she would probably just as soon I didn't ask her."

"Nonsense, Ethan. You're perfectly capable of moving in time to the music. And why wouldn't you want to dance with her? She's very pretty. There's something a little…I don't know…different about her, but I suppose that's to be expected from Nicole's best friend, isn't it?"

Elaine seemed to have no idea just how "different" Aislinn was rumored to be—and not just in Nic's refreshingly unpredictable way, Ethan mused after his mother went off to rescue his dad. No surprise, of course. He wouldn't have known himself had it not been for that incident back in the fall, when Aislinn had called to warn of Nic's impending accident.

It wasn't as if anyone around here ever openly talked about it—not that he'd heard, at least. They simply acted a bit wary around Aislinn, as though they weren't quite sure what to say to her.

Oddly enough, he was sometimes treated the same way back in Danston. As though he didn't quite fit in with everyone else. Though, as far as he knew, no one had ever accused him of having any supernatural abilities.

The bride and groom finished their dance, and everyone else was encouraged to take the floor. With a slight shrug, Ethan moved toward Aislinn. What the heck. It wasn't as if there was anything else to do. And dancing with a beautiful woman—even one who pretended to be a psychic—was more entertaining than just standing there being bored.

Chapter Three

Aislinn was taken completely off guard when Ethan asked her to dance, which perhaps explained why she couldn't come up with a quick and polite excuse to decline. Not that there was any real reason why she shouldn't have accepted, of course, she reminded herself as they moved toward the small dance floor. It was sort of expected for the best man and the maid of honor to share a dance.

She was aware of that same odd hesitation when he turned to take her into his arms, almost a wariness of letting him touch her. She still couldn't understand why she felt that way around him. She'd touched nearly everyone else in this room, shaking hands in the reception line, exchanging brief social hugs with the people she had known most of her life. There had been no unusual flashes of insight, no unprecedented reactions to the physical contact. There was just something about Ethan....

"Why did you look so surprised when I asked you to dance?" he asked as soon as they music began.

Keeping as much distance between them as politely possible, she shrugged lightly before answering, "I just didn't think you would."

Mentally she dared him to make some smart-aleck remark about how he would have expected her to predict the invitation, but to her relief, he let it pass. Maybe he'd gotten tired of making digs about her so-called abilities. At least she hoped that was the case.

"I guess you and I haven't gotten off to a very good start," he said abruptly. "And I suppose that's my fault. I'm not very good at the social thing—meeting people, making small talk. Saying the right things."

"You choose not to be good at it because it isn't important to you," she murmured in return. "You're perfectly capable of making polite conversation when you make the effort."

She was almost surprised when he agreed with her rather than challenge her again. "You're probably right. I just don't choose to make the effort very often."

"I'm not exactly a party animal either," she admitted after a moment. "I prefer small gatherings to large crowds. And I sometimes have trouble knowing what to say to people I don't know very well. So I'll take part of the blame for any awkwardness between us."

"Very generous of you."

His tone sounded more humorous than mocking, so she smiled. "Yes, I thought so."

He seemed to search for something else innocuous to say. "They'll be cutting the cake soon, I guess. Will it bother you to watch them chop it up?"

"No." She was amused by his wording. "Why would it?"

"Well, you must have spent a lot of hours on the decorations."

"That's my job. I charge well for my time—though I made this one as a gift to Nic and Joel."

"Nice of you. Do you run your business out of your house or do you have a bakery with helpers?"

"I recently leased a small shop because I'd outgrown my kitchen at home. I have two part-time employees for baking and deliveries, but I do most of the work myself. I prefer it that way for now."

"As good as you are at it, you could probably build up a pretty decent business. Hire a few more people to do the mixing and baking while you concentrate on the arty part. Maybe teach a couple to decorate in your style for everyday orders, saving yourself for the really complicated stuff. You could advertise in Little Rock and online, get your name out there...."

Laughing a little, she tilted her head to look up at him, seeing a gleam in his eyes that had nothing to do with her and everything to do with her business. "Hey, just because you're here to organize Joel's office, don't make the mistake of thinking I want the same thing. I'm perfectly happy with my little operation and I'm making enough to take care of my needs for now."

"For now, maybe," he agreed, "but what about the future? You should be thinking about—"

"Ethan, this is a wedding reception, not a business conference."

His mouth quirked in a slight smile. "I'm painfully aware of that."

The weak joke passed by her as she found herself staring at his mouth. If just that hint of a smile had softened his expression so much, she couldn't imagine how much a full-blown grin would change him. Though she had a strong feeling few people saw him that happy and relaxed, she wished she could see him smile like that, just once. Only to satisfy her curiosity, of course.

He glanced toward the band. "They're pretty good, considering how young they are."

"Yes. They're going to hit it big," she agreed absently, still thinking about Ethan's smile.

He was quiet for a moment, then asked, "Was that just a guess?"

Feeling the muscles of her stomach tighten, she nodded coolly. "Of course. They're very talented. Why wouldn't they be successful?"

Aislinn knew very well that they were listening to a young band who would eventually be stars in their genre. A guess? Maybe, though without the doubt that usually accompanied a shot in the dark. *Intuition* was a more comfortable word for her—one she found easier to accept. Whatever lay behind her occasional predictions, she had enough experience with them to know that she was rarely wrong.

None of which she had any intention of discussing—

especially with Ethan, who had made his doubts about her very clear.

She was rather relieved when the song came to an end. She stepped away from him with a bright smile. "I guess I'd better get back to mingling."

He nodded, his own expression unreadable as he studied her face. "I'll walk you back to your table."

Because she didn't want to rebuff him when he was making an effort to be sociable, she nodded and fell into step beside him. On the way back to the corner where she had been sitting with Susan and Paul, they passed a table at which Ethan's parents sat chatting with the minister and his wife.

Elaine Brannon smiled approvingly at Ethan as they walked by, and Aislinn suspected that Elaine had pretty much ordered her older son to participate in the party. Had his mother been the reason he had asked her to dance?

Glancing at Ethan, she noted the expression in his eyes when he looked at his mother and she caught her breath. There was something she suddenly wanted to tell him, but she hesitated, knowing how he would react.

Maybe she should just keep her mouth shut. After all, these feelings of hers came with no guarantees. She and Ethan had just had a pleasant dance, ending on a fairly friendly note, for them. Why make waves now?

She sighed, aware that she was wasting time arguing with herself. After seeing the worry in Ethan's eyes and knowing it was eating at him, she had to at least attempt to set his mind at ease.

"You don't have to worry about your mother, Ethan,"

she murmured, turning to him just before they reached her table. "She'll be fine."

His brows dipped into a frown. "What are you talking about?"

"The tests will be clear," she continued quickly, before she changed her mind. "The mass is benign—nothing to be concerned about. So try not to worry too much about it."

"How did you—?"

"It's just a feeling I have, okay?" Anxious to get away from him now, she turned toward the table. "Thank you for the dance, Ethan. I'll see you."

He caught her arm. "Aislinn…"

Maybe it was because she hadn't braced herself this time. Hadn't been prepared for the touch. But she felt the jolt of reaction run through her, all the way from the contact between his hand and the skin of her arm to someplace hidden very deeply inside her. A place she had never wanted to examine very closely herself.

Something changed in his expression, irritation replaced instantly by reluctant concern. His hand tightened around her arm. "Aislinn? Damn it, you've gone white as a sheet. What's going on?"

"I—uh—"

"Aislinn?" Nic appeared suddenly at her other side, looking quickly from Aislinn to Ethan. "Is anything wrong?"

"I—" Abruptly brought back to the present, she looked around, relieved to see that no one else seemed to be looking at them. Not at the moment, anyway. "I think I need some fresh air. If you'll excuse me…"

"I'll go with you."

Aislinn forced a smile for her friend and spoke brusquely. "You'll do no such thing. This is your wedding reception. Go find your groom and dance again. I just need a couple of minutes alone. You know how I am when a lot of people are around."

Because she did know, Nic backed off. "All right. Let me know if you need anything."

"I will."

Without looking at Ethan again, Aislinn made her escape, wishing she could go straight home but knowing she had to stay a while longer yet. For Nic.

Ethan woke early Sunday morning with that sense of disorientation that usually accompanied waking in a strange bed. It took him only a moment to remind himself that he was in his brother's guest room, the only occupant of the house since Joel and Nic had left after the reception for a weeklong Caribbean honeymoon—the longest either of them could take away from their demanding careers. Ethan would stay here until they returned, at which time—assuming everything at Joel's office was running smoothly—he would head back to Alabama.

Joel had invited his parents to stay at the house, too, but they had chosen to stay in a nearby hotel instead, planning an early departure this morning. Their father was eager to get back to his routines. It was going to take a lot of persuasion for Elaine to get him away for that European vacation she longed for, Ethan thought with a shake of his head. Lou Brannon was the very epitome of a contented homebody. Something Ethan understood a bit too well.

Glancing at the clock on the nightstand, he saw that it was just after seven. Yet he'd bet his parents were already on the road. His dad liked to get an early start.

So here he was, the only member of his family in a town where he hardly knew anyone. During the five days he had been here, he'd spent several hours at Joel's clinic, meeting the partner and staff, looking over the operations with an eye toward streamlining bookkeeping and maximizing profits. Joel and Bob were literally putting their business into his hands.

He and their newly hired office manager, Marilyn Henderson, would meet with several software salespeople during the next week, as well as have long discussions about existing office practices. They would pore over the books and filing systems, deciding what to change and what to leave alone—though there would be very little of the latter.

Joel and Bob were great guys and excellent doctors, but neither of them had paid much attention to the business part of the practice they had opened just under two years earlier. They could definitely use some help in that area, and Ethan already had a plan in mind. Fortunately Marilyn seemed to be in agreement about the way a pleasant yet efficient medical office should be managed.

Since he was alone in the house, he pulled on a pair of jeans and zipped them but left the snap undone. Barefoot and shirtless, he wandered into the kitchen, yawning and wondering what Joel had left for breakfast. He found orange juice in the refrigerator and poured himself a glass, then popped a bagel into the toaster. Only then did he admit that from the moment he'd opened his eyes he had been trying without success to forget about Aislinn Flaherty.

He had every intention of avoiding her for the remainder of his stay in Cabot. Shouldn't be too hard. He doubted that she would visit the pediatric practice. And he wouldn't be ordering any cakes.

He'd given up trying to decide if she was crooked or crazy, but her comment about his mother's upcoming medical tests had made a cold chill go down his spine. He'd known for a fact that no one knew about those tests except his parents and himself. Just to confirm, he'd casually asked his mother afterward if she had mentioned the situation to anyone else. Anyone at all.

She had reminded him that she wanted to keep the tests absolutely secret until after she learned the results. She had been especially adamant that Joel was not to be told until after his honeymoon.

So how had Aislinn known?

He knew that so-called psychic con artists performed what were known as cold readings—throwing out vague comments and then watching carefully for the most minute changes in expression and subtle body language from their gullible marks. But as far as he'd been able to tell, Aislinn hadn't prefaced her remarks about his mother's health with anything he would have considered fishing for clues. And she hadn't spent much time talking alone to either of his parents, so he kept coming back to the same question....

How had she known?

Not that he had changed his mind about her alleged abilities. Guess or guile, she hadn't just pulled that prediction out of the ether. And while he fervently hoped she was right about the tests resulting in good news, he would consider it no more than a happy coincidence if it turned out to be true.

Just as well he wouldn't be seeing her again any-time soon, he told himself as he finished his breakfast. He was just too uncomfortable around her, for quite a few reasons.

Someone rang the front doorbell, startling him as he set his dishes in the dishwasher. He pushed a hand through his tousled hair and moved toward the front door. He couldn't imagine who would be at Joel's door on a Sunday morning when everyone knew Joel was out of town. Maybe his parents hadn't gotten that early start after all.

Having no psychic abilities of his own, he was sur-prised to find Aislinn on the other side of the door. She wore a gray T-shirt, jeans and sneakers, her dark hair pulled into a loose ponytail, no evidence of makeup on her striking face. She looked as though she had crawled out of bed, thrown on the first clothes she'd found and driven straight over. "What are you doing here?"

She didn't appear to take offense at the blunt greet-ing. "I need to talk to you."

"What about?"

She sighed. "May I come inside?"

For only a moment, he hesitated, tempted to close the door in her face. He finally stepped aside, not because he didn't want to be rude but because he didn't want to think of himself as a coward.

"Okay," he said, facing her from several feet away, his arms crossed over his bare chest. "What is it? Another 'prediction'?"

She looked around the room, her expression distracted, and then she turned and moved toward the hallway. Frowning, Ethan dropped his arms and followed her. "Where are you going?"

Without answering, she turned left, into Joel's bedroom rather than into the guest room on the right where Ethan had been staying.

"Aislinn, what the hell are you—"

"There's a photograph," she said vaguely. "I need to—oh, here it is."

The small, framed photo sat on top of a bookcase in one corner. The paperback mysteries Joel liked to read to relax at bedtime filled the bookcase almost to overflowing. On the wall above hung a framed watercolor painting of a peaceful lake cove surrounded by trees and boulders. Joel was the artist; until Nic had told him a few months earlier, Ethan hadn't even known Joel liked painting with watercolors.

"You sure know your way around Joel's house," he muttered as Aislinn picked up the photograph.

"I've never been inside this house before," she replied absently. "We've always gathered at Nic's instead."

So how had she…? Shaking his head impatiently, he told himself that he had no way of judging if she was even telling the truth. "Okay, what's going on?"

She drew a deep breath and looked at him. He noted abruptly that she still looked as oddly pale as she had when they'd parted last night. Perhaps that was why it was no surprise when she warned, "You aren't going to like this."

He was pretty sure that would prove to be an understatement.

Aislinn had been too focused on finding the photograph to pay much more than passing attention to Ethan when he'd let her in. She'd managed maybe two hours of sleep last night before she had finally given in to the overwhelming urge to drive to Joel's house. She'd waited as long as she could, doubting that Ethan would appreciate being awakened before dawn so she could find a photograph that was haunting her. Not that he'd been overjoyed to see her as it was.

Only now did she really look at him. He, too, seemed to have only recently crawled out of bed. His hair was mussed, he hadn't shaved and he wasn't wearing a shirt or shoes. His jeans weren't snapped. A stark contrast to the tidy and tuxedoed groomsman she had seen the evening before, she thought.

She wondered if it was weird that she thought he looked even better like this than he had at the wedding. More natural. This was the real Ethan—and despite his forbidding expression, he was a very attractive man.

Pulling her gaze away from the well-defined muscles of his lean chest and abdomen, she moistened her dry lips, her fingers tightening around the small silver frame clutched in her hands. She wasn't exactly sure how to begin, since she already knew he wasn't going to believe a word she said.

"Well?" he prompted impatiently.

Might as well stop stalling. She turned the photo toward him. "You recognize this picture, of course."

He glanced at it, then shrugged. "It's my family, obviously. Some thirty years ago."

"Your father. Your mother. You." She pointed to each figure as she named them. Ethan was perhaps six in the photograph, maybe seven. She indicated the younger boy next to him. "And this is Joel."

Ethan nodded, a muscle clenching in his jaw as they both turned their attention to the baby sitting in Elaine's lap.

"Who is this?"

For just a moment she thought he wasn't going to answer. And then he muttered, "That's Kyle. I assume you already know he died when he was almost two."

"Can you tell me what happened?"

He crossed his arms over his chest, making the muscles bulge just a little. If he was trying to look intimidating, he succeeded. Of course, he also looked sexy as all get-out, but she couldn't think about that right now.

"Why do you want to know?"

"Please, Ethan. Just humor me for a few minutes. I know this must be difficult for you."

"It happened a long time ago," he said with a slight shrug. "I hardly remember him."

It took no special ability at all for her to know that he was lying. She looked at him without responding.

After a moment he shook his head and spoke curtly. "He drowned. It happened during the aftermath of a tropical storm. There had been a lot of flooding, a lot of local destruction, and even though the weather was still bad, Mom had gone out with one of her charity groups to try to help some of the people who had suffered the most damage to their homes. Dad was at his office, making sure everything there was okay. They left Joel with the nanny who took care of us while Mom was busy with her volunteer work, which was pretty often back then."

"And there was an accident?"

He nodded. "Joel and I were spending the week with our maternal grandparents in Tennessee, as we did every summer while they were living. Mom thought Kyle was still too small to be gone for that long. Anyway, for some reason, the nanny took him out during that heavy rain. No one knows why they left the house. They were in her car, a cheapie little compact."

He cleared his throat, then continued, "Apparently she hydroplaned, went off the road and was swept into a flooding river. The car was found a few days later, overturned in very deep water, but it was empty. Several other people drowned during that same tropical storm and resulting flood. There was another man whose body wasn't recovered for several months, but neither the nanny's body nor my brother's was ever found."

There was no identifiable emotion in his tone, though his eyes looked darker than usual. He obviously believed every word of the sad story he had just told her. The story that had been told to him.

She moistened her lips again. "It isn't true," she whispered.

He frowned more deeply at her. "What isn't true?"

"Any of it. I mean, I know that's what you think happened. What you all believe. But…"

Ethan's arms dropped to his sides, the fists clenched. He took a step toward her, making her instinctively move backward. "If you're going to try to feed me a load of crap about how you've been talking to my dead brother…"

"No!" She shook her head forcefully. "It's not like that, Ethan. I'm not a medium. And even if I were, it wouldn't apply in this case."

"And just what is that supposed to mean?"

She drew a deep breath, then blurted out the words before she could lose her nerve. "Kyle isn't dead."

Chapter Four

A gentle breeze ruffled Cassandra's snow-white hair, one straight lock tickling her right cheek. She reached up to tuck it back, savoring the scent of the flowers that bloomed in the gardens around her.

As she often did, she thought of how fortunate she was to be at this pleasant, exclusive, private facility. It was expensive, but her late husband had made sure she would be well cared for after his passing. Just as she had known he would when she'd married him.

She sat alone in her little corner of the garden. She didn't mingle much with the other residents here, most of them being quite a bit older. Besides, she wasn't interested in socializing. She actually enjoyed her solitude, for the most part.

She didn't come outside very often, but she had

allowed herself to be persuaded this afternoon, thinking that the fresh, warm air might clear her mind. She didn't like the new medications. They left her feeling groggy. Lethargic. And she still had the nightmares. Not as often, maybe, but just as vivid and disturbing when they came.

She would have to ask Dr. Thomas to make another adjustment.

Her knitting needles clicked with a slower-than-usual rhythm as she tried to immerse herself in the soothing sounds of the birds singing in the trees above her head, the water splashing gently in the nearby fountain. Lovely, peaceful sounds that almost—but not quite—drowned out the echoes of her dreams.

"Here you are."

She couldn't have said how much time had passed between her thoughts of him and his appearance. A few minutes. An hour, perhaps. Time had a trick of slipping away from her. "Hello, Dr. Thomas."

He sat on a concrete garden bench, crossing one leg over the other. The casual pose stretched the fabric of the khaki slacks he almost always wore with a solid-color shirt and brightly patterned tie beneath the required white coat that made him look so handsome and professional. She liked the way he dressed. Not too stuffy but neatly enough to show regard for his patients here.

There had been a trend away from ties and white coats a couple of years ago, but the residents hadn't liked seeing their physicians in blue jeans and polo shirts and other members of the staff in T-shirts and flip-flops. Now that the doctors were back in their white coats and the rest of the staff wore tidy uniforms, everything seemed to run much more smoothly. More civilly. She firmly believed that the general decline in polite society could be measured by the pervasive loss of respect for proper attire.

And weren't there people in her past who would find that attitude hilarious, coming from her?

"What are you thinking about so seriously?"

She made herself smile as she replied candidly, "Neckties and panty hose."

To give him credit, he didn't seem at all taken aback by the non sequitur, asking merely, "Are you for 'em or agin 'em?"

She chuckled, thinking of how much she liked this nice young man. "I'm for 'em."

He tugged lightly at the blue-and-green-patterned tie he wore with a blue shirt that contrasted nicely with his light tan. "I was afraid you might say that."

Laughing again, she shook her head. "Don't try to con me. You like looking nice or you wouldn't give so much thought to matching your shirts and ties. Unlike some of the doctors who show up in mismatched patterns and colors that make one's head hurt to look at them."

"Now, Cassandra, don't make fun of Dr. Marvin. Everyone knows he's color-blind."

"Then he should always let his wife dress him in the mornings, bless his heart."

Grinning, the doctor nodded. "You're probably right. So how are you?"

She told him about the effects of the new sleep aid, finishing with a request for a change.

Dr. Thomas nodded gravely. "We'll make another adjustment. I still think it would be good for you to talk about your dreams with someone, though. If not with me, at least with your counselor. We don't discuss specifics about our clients, as you're aware, but I get the feeling you aren't being much more forthcoming with her than you are with me."

"I tell you both everything you need to know," she assured him, catching a dropped stitch.

"I would like to think you trust me, Cassandra."

The sincerity in his voice was genuine, not like some of the doctors who only pretended to be truly concerned about the residents here. Dr. Thomas cared so much that she was tempted at times to advise him to put a bit more distance between himself and his patients. As appealing as his empathetic nature made him, it also made him more susceptible to burnout and disillusion. As fond as she was of him, she would hate to see him fall prey to either of those conditions.

"I trust you as much as I trust anyone."

He sighed lightly. "I suppose I have to be satisfied with that."

Nodding, she let her hands rest. "How was your date last week?"

"We were talking about you, not me."

She lifted her needles again.

After a moment, he conceded. "We attended a symphony performance. We had a flat tire on the way to the concert hall, but I was able to change it without messing up my clothes or making us late to the concert. On the whole, it was a pleasant evening."

"But a little dull," she interpreted, reading easily

between the lines. "You probably won't ask her out again. I told you she wasn't right for you."

He shook his head in obvious exasperation. "Maybe you can introduce me to Ms. Right," he muttered.

"I can't introduce you, but I can tell you that you'll know when you find her. And you will find her."

"A seer, are you?" he teased.

She didn't smile in return.

"You're crazy."

Aislinn flinched in response to Ethan's blunt words. "I'm not crazy."

"Then you must think *I* am. Because there is no way I'm buying whatever it is you're trying to sell."

"I'm not trying to sell anything, Ethan. I just…know."

"You don't know anything." He took the photograph out of her hands and set it a bit too forcefully back into place on Joel's bookcase. "I think you'd better leave now."

She sighed wearily. "I knew you would react this way."

"Did you? Well, hell, maybe you *are* psychic."

He stalked to the doorway, pausing there with one hand motioning for her to precede him. It wasn't a request.

Though she moved past him out of the bedroom, she wasn't ready to completely give up. "If you would just let me tell you what I—"

"I'm really not interested." He kept walking, straight toward the front door, making her have to hurry to keep up with him. "I know Nic thinks the world of you, and Joel seems to like you, too, so I'm giving you the benefit of the doubt. Maybe you really believe the things you say. Maybe you've guessed correctly so many times that you've convinced yourself you really do have some sort of gift. But this time you've taken it too far."

"Don't you think I know how bizarre this sounds?" she retorted. "Can't you understand how hard it was for me to come here, knowing how you would respond?"

"Then why did you come?"

She sighed and pushed her hands into her pockets. "I had to," she muttered. "I couldn't sleep last night and I knew I wouldn't be able to rest until I talked to you about the...about the feeling I had about your brother."

"And just when did you get this ... feeling?"

The slight note of mockery behind the word wasn't lost to her, but she answered evenly, "Last night. At the reception. When you touched me, I—I knew there was something I had to tell you. I wasn't sure what it was until later, during the night, when I got...I don't know...some sort of a mental image of this photograph. When I looked at it, when I held it, I knew what I had to tell you."

Ethan's expression didn't change during her halting, stumbling explanation. She swung out her hands in frustration. "I know it sounds crazy! I spent most of the night wondering if I really have lost my mind. I don't have visions, Ethan. I don't get flashes when people touch me. Like you said, I make guesses—and they usually come true. But this is different. This isn't something that has ever happened to me before."

"Really?" He made no effort to hide his disbelief. "How about last year, when you kept calling Nic in Alabama to warn her that something bad was going to happen to her?"

"I told you—that was a feeling. Just a vague sense

of uneasiness that made me worry something might go wrong. The sort of premonition ordinary people get all the time."

Ordinary being the operative word. It was all she had ever aspired to be.

Ordinary.

Normal.

He shook his head. "Coming into my brother's house, going into his bedroom, telling me Kyle didn't drown thirty years ago—that's not the sort of thing ordinary people do, Aislinn."

She swallowed. "I know."

Letting his breath escape in a long, slow exhale, Ethan pushed a hand through his hair, leaving it even more mussed than it had been before. "I'm not sure what I should say here. I'm not very good at this sort of thing. Maybe you should get some help. You know, see someone. If you need me to call anyone—a friend, maybe, a family member—just tell me the number."

Oh, great. Now he was trying to be nice even as he suggested that she should be taken away in a straitjacket.

"You know what, Ethan? You're right. I shouldn't have come here," she snapped, moving toward the door. "I should have known how you would react. I *did* know, but I thought I could persuade you to listen. I was wrong about that, but I wasn't wrong about Kyle. He didn't die in that flood. He's very much alive."

He didn't respond, but she hadn't really expected him to. She grabbed the doorknob and jerked open the door. She'd stepped only halfway through when she turned to throw one last reckless comment over her shoulder.

"You want a real, live prediction from a real, live freak? Fine. Your parents are on their way home. They'll arrive just fine, but they'll be delayed by several hours because they're going to have a blowout in a little town just inside the Alabama border. The left rear tire, and it's going to take them a while to have it repaired. So figure out how I 'guessed' that, why don't you? *I* certainly don't know."

She slammed the door behind her with enough force to rattle the diamond-shaped glass pane in the center. And still it didn't seem hard enough to express the full extent of her anguished frustration.

Ethan was trying his best to concentrate on his work when the telephone rang later that afternoon. Glancing at his watch, he decided it was exactly the time his parents should be arriving safely at their home, probably without any untimely delays at all. "Hello?"

"Hey, bro, it's Joel."

So he'd guessed wrong. "What are you doing calling on your honeymoon? You don't have enough to keep you entertained there?"

Joel chuckled. "Trust me, I've got plenty to do here. I just forgot to do something yesterday and I wanted to ask you to take care of it for me."

"Sure. What is it?"

"There's a stamped envelope on my desk, made out to the American Cancer Society. It's a memorial for one of my patients that I meant to mail before I left—but, well, I got kind of distracted yesterday. I just remembered it and I hate to let it wait until I get back. So would you mind sticking it in the mailbox for me later?"

"No problem. It'll go out first thing tomorrow."

"I appreciate it. So how's everything else? Any problems there in the house?"

"Joel, you've been gone less than twenty-four hours. The place isn't going to fall apart just because you aren't here."

His younger brother chuckled ruefully. "I'm turning into Dad, aren't I?"

"I'm not going to lie to you, kid. You're sounding a lot like him. Now go concentrate on your beautiful bride and quit worrying about things here."

"Nic wants to say hello." He handed the phone over before Ethan had a chance to send his regards through Joel.

"Hi, Ethan."

He answered in patient resignation. "Hi, Nic. Did you forget to mail something, too?"

"No, I think I took care of everything," she replied, missing the joke. "Have you seen my family today?"

"I saw them earlier. Your brother came over to tell me goodbye as he left for the airport. He asked me to keep an eye on your mom's house while I'm here."

"Oh, good. I was going to ask you the same thing."

"I'll tell you the same thing I told them. If your mother needs anything while I'm here next door, all she has to do is ask. She would probably tell you the same thing she said to me—she'll be just fine. She said she expects to be so busy catching up with all her old friends before she rejoins Paul that she won't be home much, anyway. I believe she's at a party of some sort now."

"That doesn't surprise me. So what about you, Ethan? How are you entertaining yourself there?"

"I've been working. Trying to go over Joel's books before I meet with Marilyn and the software people tomorrow."

"That doesn't sound like much fun. You shouldn't work the whole time you're there. I know you don't know many people, but maybe you could call Aislinn? She'd probably be happy to show you around...or something."

Ethan pulled the telephone receiver away from his ear to stare at it incredulously. Was Nic actually trying to fix him up with her spooky friend? He knew they hadn't spent all that much time together yet, but he'd have thought his new sister-in-law would still know him better than that!

"I'm going to be pretty busy while I'm here," he said after a moment. "Joel's billing procedures are a mess."

He had no intention of telling either Nic or Joel about Aislinn's weird visit that morning and certainly not the reason why she'd claimed to have come. He only wished he'd thought to forbid her then to call and bother Joel and Nic on their honeymoon with that wild tale. Surely even she wouldn't go to that length for attention—would she?

It took him a moment to realize that Nic was speaking again, and that she sounded a bit disappointed. "Oh. Well, if you're not interested... But she really is very nice. Like you, she's just a little hard to get to know."

"Oh, I don't think Aislinn's at all like me," he muttered.

"What was that? I didn't hear you."

"Nothing. Look, Nic, you and Joel should be out snorkeling or horseback riding or sailing or something. Don't worry about anything here, okay? Just enjoy your honeymoon."

"Okay, but—"

Joel apparently took the phone from Nic's hand. "We'll talk to you later, Ethan. You know how to reach us here if anything comes up."

"Yeah, I know. Have fun."

He hung up with a frown, hoping nothing would happen to spoil his brother's honeymoon.

Though Aislinn wasn't officially open for business on Sundays, she spent Sunday afternoon in the shop she had recently rented in a strip mall on the outskirts of town. She had a lot to do during the next few days. While it was nice to be doing well in her business, there were times when it all seemed to be moving too quickly. She'd had half a dozen serious inquiries just at the wedding reception.

She was piping a delicate string of yellow frosting when someone hammered on the shop door early that evening, ignoring the Closed sign. Her hand jerked, ruining the effect of the decoration she'd been trying to complete. Swearing beneath her breath, she determined that the damage was repairable before she set her tools aside and went to answer the door.

She passed by the display counter and the table and four comfortable chairs where she sat with clients as they discussed details of their orders. Photo albums of her work were neatly displayed on a small bookshelf, and framed enlargements of some of her best cakes decorated the walls. A few green plants were scattered through the room, but nothing else that would detract from the photos. More out of habit than anything, she glanced around to make sure nothing was out of place.

Though she hadn't been expecting him exactly, it didn't take much effort to figure out who she would find on the other side of the glass door with its drawn shade. "There's no need to knock it down," she said as she released the locks and opened the door.

Ethan dropped the fist he'd been using to knock on the thick glass stenciled with the words *Cakes by Aislinn.* "How did you do it?" he demanded, pushing past her without waiting for an invitation. Once inside, he turned to glare at her. "How did you know?"

She closed the door, knowing it would serve no purpose to ask him to leave, the way he had kicked her out of Joel's house earlier. "I take it you've heard from your parents?"

"They called me when they got home," he agreed gruffly. "They were running a few hours later than they expected. They had a blowout."

"Left rear tire?"

He nodded without taking his eyes away from her face. "How did you know, Aislinn?"

"What? You don't want to accuse me of somehow sabotaging their tires?"

He shook his head impatiently. "I know you couldn't have done that. But I still don't know how you predicted the tire was going to blow."

Her head was starting to hurt. She rubbed irritably at her left temple as she turned toward the kitchen.

"I need some tea," she said, figuring he deserved the same abrupt treatment he'd given her. "We can talk in the kitchen while the water comes to a boil. But, I warn you, I'm not in the mood for any more of your accusations. You can listen and you can ask questions, but start calling me a liar or a con artist again, and I'm throwing you out on your ear."

It was just as well he didn't ask how she intended to do that, since he outweighed her by some fifty pounds. Still, as grumpy and unfriendly as Ethan had been to her, she wasn't afraid of him. When she wanted him to go, he would leave.

She had leased this shop because of the large, utilitarian kitchen. Big enough to hold a sizable work island, with two ovens, a six-burner gas range and an industrial-size freezer and refrigerator, it was the place where she spent the most time, even more than she did at her home these days. A small, rectangular metal table sat against one wall, with four simple metal chairs so she and her employees could take occasional breaks.

Ethan glanced at the towering cake on the work island. "Another wedding cake?" he asked, picking up a long, serrated knife she used for torting—slicing layers into thinner layers.

"It's for a golden anniversary celebration tomorrow night," she answered, reaching for the teakettle.

He walked slowly around the island, studying the very traditional cake Aislinn's client had chosen. A lemon cake filled with raspberry jam, it was covered in golden-yellow fondant, draped in icing shells and strings and topped with two entwined translucent golden rings made of sugar. Lovely but quite simple, actually, in keeping with the unpretentious personalities of the celebrants. "It's nice."

It was the same adjective he'd used for the much

more elaborate cake she'd made for Joel and Nic's wedding, she remembered. An all-purpose cake compliment, apparently. "Thank you."

She opened a stainless-steel cabinet to take out a mug. "Would you like tea?"

"You tell me."

Closing the cabinet a bit too firmly, she snapped, "I have no idea."

"Sorry," he muttered after a moment. "No, I don't want any tea just now, thanks."

He took a seat at the table, and a short while later she joined him, a steaming mug of chamomile tea in her hand. She set the beverage in front of her as she sank into a chair on the opposite side of the table from him. It wasn't that she wanted the tea so badly; she had simply needed something to do to occupy her hands while she talked to him.

"Okay," she said. "I'm ready to talk."

He rested his forearms on the table and looked intently at her face, as if to watch for any sign that she wasn't being entirely honest with him. "How did you know about the blowout?"

"I don't know."

He cursed beneath his breath, slamming one hand down on the stainless-steel tabletop. "You said you were ready to talk."

"And I *am* talking," she replied defensively. "You asked me a question. I answered honestly. I don't know how I knew. I just did."

"Did it come to you in a vision?"

"I don't have visions."

"A little voice in your head, maybe?"

"I don't hear voices."

"So…?"

"I just knew," she repeated, unable to think of any other way to explain it. "I have these feelings some- times. And sometimes they come true. I've always believed that everyone has them. Maybe I just pay more attention to them."

"I don't have them."

"Surely you've had odd premonitions. The feeling that something's going to happen. Or the phone rang and you somehow knew who was on the other end. Or maybe you were thinking about someone and then co- incidentally ran into them."

"Well, yeah, but—"

"That's all it is with me. Feelings. Intuition. Whatever you want to call it."

"I think you're the one playing with semantics. In- tuition doesn't explain the things you've said to me during the past couple of days. No one gets a vague feeling that a near stranger's left rear tire will blow out just over the Alabama state line. That's a little more specific than a good guess."

Her fingers tightened spasmodically around the mug. "I know," she said, her tone sounding rather miserable even to her. "I—it's not usually quite that detailed."

"You said the same thing about your 'feeling' about Kyle still being alive."

A slight tremor went through her, causing hot tea to splash on her fingers. She quickly released the full mug, reaching for a paper napkin to dry her fingers.

"Are you all right?"

"I'm fine," she said without looking at him. "I just spilled a little tea."

Though she was still looking down at her fingers, she knew he hadn't turned his gaze away from her face. "I want to know what made you come to Joel's house this morning," he said, getting to the real reason for this visit. "What did you hope to accomplish with that crazy story about my little brother?"

Chapter Five

This was so much more difficult than Aislinn had anticipated. Even with Nic, she rarely talked about her insights. She simply stated what she thought Nic needed to know, and Nic took the warnings to heart with a matter-of-factness that Aislinn had always appreciated. No comments or questions about how Aislinn had known, just an acceptance that somehow she did. And that she was usually right.

It was one of the reasons Aislinn was so fond of Nic. Nic had never treated her as an oddity, unlike so many other people they knew.

"I try to avoid the *C* word," she muttered, glaring into her mug again. "I'm not crazy."

"Whatever. So how long have you had these feelings?"

The slight hesitation before the word let her know

that he was as uncomfortable talking about this as she was. "A long time. Most of my life."

"And how many people know about them?"

"Only a few," she answered with a shrug. "Though even most of them don't know quite how often it happens."

"You downplay your abilities."

It wasn't a question, but she nodded. "Yes. As it is, there are those who make too big an issue of it."

She thought of her friend Pamela, who sometimes bragged about her friend the psychic, even though Aislinn had asked her repeatedly not to say that. Pamela had a good heart and was a loyal friend, bringing Aislinn a lot of customers for her cake-decorating business. She didn't mean any harm by her comments; she actually considered it a compliment, since she was fascinated by anything that appeared in the least paranormal.

Aislinn, on the other hand, assiduously avoided any hint of such a thing. She was as normal as anyone else, she had spent her entire life insisting.

"So most of your friends just think you're pretty good at guessing things that are about to happen and take it for granted that they should listen to you."

"Something like that."

"But what they really think is that you're at least somewhat psychic and you just don't like to admit it."

"I—" She stopped, then sighed. "Maybe," she conceded reluctantly, suspecting that was exactly what others secretly thought. Even Nic, probably.

"I don't believe in psychics."

So why did he keep insisting on calling her that?

Shaking her head in exasperation, she said, "I don't care. I'm not sure I believe in them myself."

"What was the point of coming to Joel's house this morning?" he asked again.

She took a sip of her cooling tea, mostly to give herself a moment to put her thoughts in order. "I probably shouldn't have done that," she conceded, setting the cup down carefully in front of her. "I'd had a bad night and I thought if I could just look at the photograph, maybe convince myself I was making too much of it..."

"You'd seen the photo before?" he asked when her voice trailed away.

She shook her head. "No. I told you, I'd never actually been in Joel's house before."

"Then how did you know where you would find it?"

"Maybe I should start from the beginning."

"That's probably a good place to start."

He was still being sarcastic, but rather absently now, without the aggressiveness of earlier. Almost like a habit he had developed very quickly around her.

Giving him only a mildly chiding look in response, she began, "It happened at the reception last night. You touched my arm—"

"I remember. You went pale. I asked you about it."

She nodded, feeling again the jolt that had gone through her with that contact. She hadn't known what it was then, only that she'd felt almost as though she'd been body-slammed. It was later, during the long, nearly sleepless night, that she had begun to see that portrait in her mind.

Every time she'd tried to close her eyes, she'd envisioned the photograph sitting in Joel's bedroom—and had recognized that bedroom even though she had never stepped foot in it. She'd never experienced anything like that before, but she had been compelled to drive to Joel's house that morning, knowing she wouldn't be able to stop obsessing until she did. It was almost as if her movements had been controlled by some force outside herself, drawing her to Joel's house and then into his bedroom, to the photograph she had seen in her mind.

Only when she had held the frame in her hands had she understood exactly what she needed to tell Ethan. She had looked at the face of the baby boy in the photo—and she had seen the man he had become. Not *would have* become. *Had.*

"I'm sorry, Aislinn, I just can't buy it," Ethan said, shaking his head when she finished. "There's no way Kyle survived that flood. The police found the nanny's car upside down, twelve feet deep in water."

"But no bodies."

"Well, no. It was thirty years ago, after all. Toddler seats weren't as secure as they are now. The seat apparently broke loose."

"And the nanny's seat belt?"

"Undone. Either she wasn't wearing it or she managed to get herself free and was swept away in the deluge. One of the car doors was open."

"Or she was able to get out with the child and neither one of them drowned."

"That's what you think happened?"

She twisted her mug in front of her. "That's what I know happened."

"You just know."

She nodded. "I just know."

"And you expect me to believe you."

She felt her mouth twist in a wry smile. "No."

"Then what do you want from me?"

"Nothing," she replied simply. "I just needed to tell you. What you do with the information, if anything, is up to you."

He brooded about that for a moment, then asked, "So what else do you know?"

"What do you mean?"

"Do you know where this man is? The one you say is my brother?"

"No."

"What about the nanny? Is she still alive? Can you tell me how to find her?"

"I don't know."

"Then what the hell do you expect me to do?" he asked irritably.

She spread her hands. "I'm sorry, Ethan. I keep trying to explain that nothing quite like this has ever happened to me before. I don't know what it means or what to do with it—and I'm almost sorry I said anything to you about it. Maybe I should have just kept my mouth shut."

"No," he said after a moment. "I'm the one you should have told. The only one, by the way. I don't want my parents or my brother to hear about this until I look into it."

"You're going to look into it?"

"I'm not saying I believe you," he responded quickly. "I don't. But I'll try to check it out, if you'll promise you won't say anything to Nic or Joel."

She didn't like the implication that he was offering to indulge her in exchange for her silence. It wasn't as if she had anything to gain either way. "You do what you want," she said stiffly. "I won't mention any of this to anyone else."

He nodded. "Good."

"So how are you going to begin? Looking into it, I mean."

"Beats the heck out of me. I don't suppose you can do some sort of woo-woo thing and give me a starting point?"

She didn't even bother to get annoyed that time. "Sorry. I'm all out of woo-woo at the moment."

"Guess I'm on my own then."

"Guess so."

But he continued to sit there, looking at her across the table.

Growing self-conscious after a few moments, she asked, "Are you sure I can't get you anything?"

He glanced at the work island, then drawled, "I wouldn't turn down a piece of cake."

Something about the way he said it made her laugh. "I'm afraid that one's spoken for. But as it happens," she said, rising, "I have something that might appeal to you."

"Do you now?"

She faltered for just a moment in her steps, then made herself keep moving toward the refrigerator. No way he'd meant that the way it had sounded, she told herself. Had it been anyone else, she'd have thought he was flirting. But this was Ethan, who thought of her as a crackpot who couldn't quite be trusted. She would be the last woman he would consider flirting with.

She pulled out a cake plate and set it on the counter. She had tried a new cake recipe, making a small, round chocolate cake torted into four layers with caramel filling, then frosted with white-chocolate-flavored butter cream. She had topped the cake with a few yellow-frosting daisies and piped a simple yellow shell border around the edges.

"Do you like chocolate?"

"I consider it one of the essential food groups," he replied. "Especially if you've got a glass of milk to go with it."

She set the cake on the table and opened the refrigerator again. "Of course."

Ethan was studying the cake when she returned to the table with a full glass of milk. "Looks too nice to cut just for me. Did you have plans for this one?"

"Not really. I make small cakes sometimes to try out new recipes. I keep them on hand for walk-in business, people who need a cake for a special occasion but forgot to place an advance order. I get several requests for those each day."

"I guess you get tired of cake for yourself."

"No. I love cake." She served him a generous slice, cutting a smaller piece for herself.

"You must not eat it all that often."

The rather clinical once-over he gave her in tandem with the observation made her shake her head. Did the man have absolutely no tact or did he just rarely bother to make an effort?

"I try to keep balance in my life," she said mildly. "When I eat cake, I exercise a bit more to make up for it."

"Wow. This is good."

The compliment pleased her since it seemed completely sincere. "Thank you. I'll have to consider adding this recipe to my menu."

He nodded, washing down another bite with a sip of his milk. "How long have you been running your own cake-decorating business?"

"Just a couple of years. I started out in high school decorating birthday cakes for a supermarket, and it expanded from there as I became interested in more intricate designs."

"You didn't go to college?"

"No." She had no intention of going into her family history with him just then. "What about you? You have a degree in business, I assume?"

"Double major. Business and economics."

"And how long have you been self-employed?"

"Five years. I quit my job with an accounting firm on my thirty-first birthday to open my own business."

"You like being your own boss."

"Right. Just like you do."

She nodded to concede his point.

Apparently out of small talk, he finished his cake, drained his milk, then stood. "Thanks for the cake. I'll let you get back to work now."

"Wait a sec." She crossed to the counter where she'd left the chocolate cake, took out a small delivery box and carefully set the cake inside it. Closing the lid, she turned and held it out to him. "Here. Something for you to snack on while you're staying at Joel's."

He hesitated only a moment, studying the box with

her logo printed neatly across the top. And then he accepted the gift with a slight smile. "Thank you."

"You're welcome."

Carrying the box, he preceded her through the shop to the front door. He paused with one foot outside on the sidewalk. "I assume you'll let me know if you get any more, uh, feelings about my family."

"I would have thought you'd want me to keep any future feelings to myself."

He frowned. "Just come to me if there's anything you feel you need to pass along."

She didn't respond.

After a moment, Ethan turned away. "Goodbye, Aislinn."

Closing the door behind him, she thought about the finality with which he had spoken. Ethan wasn't expecting to see her again. And while she almost never had premonitions involving herself, she knew somehow that he was wrong.

"Are the books that badly messed up?"

Ethan blinked and looked away from the computer screen. "I, um…what?"

A curvy brunette in pale blue scrubs leaned against the countertop beside him. "The way you're glaring at that computer, I figure what you're seeing must be really bad."

Clearing the screen, Ethan leaned back in the chair, grimacing when stiff muscles protested. Apparently he'd been sitting there longer than he'd realized. Unfortunately he hadn't accomplished much, since he'd been having a hard time concentrating on the numbers. "It's not so bad. Just a little disorganized."

"Yes, well, Carla Colby set up the books when Joel and Bob went into practice together. Carla used to be the bookkeeper for old Dr. Green before he retired, and Joel and Bob figured she must know what she was doing, but her methods were a little outdated. She retired a few months ago. I think Marilyn's going to be a great office manager once you get all the systems up to date."

"Yes, she's very efficient." He looked around the empty office. "Where is Marilyn, anyway?"

"She went home. It's five o'clock, Ethan. We're closing up for the day."

He glanced at his watch in surprise. Now that he thought about it, he sort of remembered Marilyn saying something a few minutes earlier. Must have been goodnight. He hoped he had at least grunted a response—and that she had assumed he was preoccupied by work.

"Guess I let time slip away from me."

Nurse Lizzie Murdoch laughed quietly. "I know when a man is obsessed with his work. I see that look all the time around here with Joel and Bob. But you've got to take a break sometime, you know?"

"Yeah. As a matter of fact…" He pushed himself out of his chair, knowing he would accomplish nothing more by sitting there any longer. "I might as well head out myself."

"Do you have plans for dinner?"

He shook his head. "Joel stocked his kitchen for me. I'm sure I'll find something edible."

"There are some pretty decent restaurants around here, you know. Do you like catfish?"

"Yeah, I—"

"I know—why don't you and I go grab something to eat? I don't have any plans this evening, either, and it's always nicer to eat with someone, isn't it?"

Actually, he was just as content dining alone most of the time. And Lizzie was being about as subtle as a semi with her "spur-of-the-moment" invitation. He supposed she was attractive enough and she seemed like pleasant company. But he wasn't really interested in getting involved with one of Joel's employees during the short time he planned to be in town.

"Just a friendly dinner," she said quickly, as if sensing the direction his thoughts had taken. "Seems only hospitable, since you're a visitor to our town and your brother is away on his honeymoon."

Ethan shrugged. Her tone had reassured him that she wasn't going to expect much from their dinner, and he supposed there was no need to be antisocial. "Okay. Catfish sounds good. You think anyone else wants to join us?"

The expression in her eyes let him know she'd gotten the message. But something about her smile hinted that she hadn't completely written him off. "I'll ask around," she said, "though just about everyone else is gone for the day."

As it happened, he and Lizzie were the only ones free for dinner. They agreed to meet at the restaurant at six-thirty, giving them both a chance to freshen up first. Lizzie had swapped the scrubs for a low-scooped T-shirt and a short denim skirt with high, wedge-heeled sandals when she rejoined him. Even though he couldn't help noticing how nicely she filled out the rather skimpy garments, Ethan kept his behavior politely distant as they were seated at a booth and served fried catfish, hush puppies, coleslaw and green tomato chowchow.

Lizzie kept the conversation moving with talk about the wedding. "It was really nice, wasn't it? Simple. Like Nic. Not that I mean Nic is simple, of course. I meant, you know—"

"Unpretentious."

"Yeah. That's it. So, anyway, everyone thought you and Joel looked so handsome up there in your tuxes," Lizzie continued flirtatiously. "Y'all really look a lot alike, you know?"

"So I've heard." Ethan stuffed a hush puppy in his mouth.

"And Nic looked so pretty in her heirloom gown. All feminine and delicate, which certainly was a change from seeing her in her police uniform all the time around town. And then Aislinn, of course, well, she's just gorgeous no matter what she's wearing."

Ethan took a deep swallow of iced tea to avoiding having to respond.

"The cake was fantastic. Aislinn's had cakes featured in cake-decorating magazines, you know. She did one for my niece's sweet-sixteen party. It looked like a filigreed jewelry box with the lid partially open and a string of pearls spilling out of it. It had ribbons and flowers and glittery jewels—and every bit of it was edible. Made out of frosting and sugar and stuff, you know? Cost my sister a freaking fortune, but everyone said it was worth it. Aislinn took a picture of the cake and put it on her Web site."

"So do you know Aislinn very well?" Ethan asked casually, dragging a strip of fish through tartar sauce.

"I wouldn't say *well*," Lizzie replied with a shrug. "I don't think anyone knows her well—except Nic, of course. The two of them have been tight since grade school. They were a few years behind me in school," she admitted with a rueful wrinkle of her nose.

"What do you mean about no one knowing Aislinn well?"

"She's just very private. Reserved. A result of her childhood, I guess. I mean, she's nice enough. Her business is pretty successful—lots of word-of-mouth referrals. And you don't hear anybody say anything bad about her. Well, not very often, anyway. There are people who think she's a little spooky. Something about the way she looks at you sometimes, you know? Like she knows something you don't. But personally I think maybe she's just a little shy and occasionally her shyness comes across as sort of distant."

While he would have liked to follow up on that throwaway comment about Aislinn's childhood, he refused to gossip about Aislinn behind her back. He'd found out what he wanted to know already.

There didn't seem to be any general talk about Aislinn being psychic. Just "a little spooky." She'd apparently been telling the truth when she said that only her closest friends knew about her extraordinary intuition.

Which didn't mean he completely believed in it

himself, of course. Even if she had been uncannily accurate so far.

And speaking of spooky…

Something made him look up and across the room, toward the cash register. His eyes met Aislinn's just as she turned, holding a white take-out bag.

She blinked a few times in surprise, then nodded a greeting before turning and walking out the door.

"Ethan?" Her back to the registers, Lizzie hadn't realized that the woman they'd just been talking about had been in the restaurant. "Still with me? You look a million miles away."

He pulled his attention back to the table. "Sorry. I guess I got distracted."

"You really are a workaholic, aren't you?" She shook her head in resignation, and Ethan got the impression that she had just written him off as a potential for anything more than a temporary coworker.

Though he would just as soon keep it that way, he made an effort to be a bit more companionable during the remainder of the meal. Yet he found it harder than he would have expected to put thoughts of Aislinn out of his mind.

Ethan went straight back to Joel's house from the clinic Tuesday afternoon. Lizzie didn't bother to ask him to dinner again, probably knowing he would have declined if she had.

The phone rang only a few minutes after he walked in. He picked it up, thinking his brother might be checking in again. Instead it was his mother's voice he heard on the other end of the line.

"You can stop worrying," she told him, her tone much lighter than it had been the last time they'd spoken. "The tests came back clear. It's just a little benign cyst. The doctor said I'll be just fine."

Ethan felt relief flood through him. "That's great news, Mom. Must be a load off your mind. Not to mention Dad's."

"Oh, yes, we're both quite relieved."

They talked a few minutes longer about everything her doctor had said that afternoon. And then Elaine said that she had to go. Lou was taking her out to dinner to celebrate, she added.

"Have a good time. Love you, Mom."

"I love you, too, sweetie. See you soon."

Hanging up the phone, Ethan spotted the telephone book lying on the counter nearby. On an impulse, he picked it up. Turned to the *F*s. There was only one Flaherty listed, with the initials A.J.

Even as he dialed the number, he wondered why he was doing it. Wondered what he would say if she answered.

"Hello, Ethan," she said calmly.

Caller ID, he realized abruptly. That invention let everyone sound a little psychic.

Rather than comment about her greeting, he said, "A. J. Flaherty. Aislinn…Jean? Joanne?"

"Joy," she replied.

"I see." A little more frivolous than he had expected. It made him curious again about the veiled comment Lizzie had made about Aislinn's childhood. "I heard from my mother today. The doctor's report came back exactly as you predicted it would."

"I'm glad. I know you were worried about her."

"Yes, I was. I still don't understand how you knew."

She remained silent. Maybe she felt as if there was just nothing left to say in response to his continued skepticism.

"I saw you yesterday," he said. "At the restaurant."

"Yes, I saw you, too."

"You know Lizzie?"

"In passing. She grew up around here, too."

"She works for my brother, you know. We were both free for dinner, so we ate together."

"Okay."

He didn't know why he'd felt the need to explain. She certainly didn't seem all that interested. "So anyway…I just wanted to tell you about my mom."

"I'm glad you called."

"Yeah." An awkward silence stretched through the line, and then Ethan cleared his throat. "So have you had any new visions?"

"I told you—I don't have visions."

"Any new 'feelings,' then?"

"No."

"Nothing more about my supposedly missing brother?"

"Kyle is alive, Ethan." Her tone seemed to say that she knew she was wasting her breath trying to convince him.

Because he couldn't tell her otherwise, he said nothing.

"Thanks again for calling me about your mom's tests," she said after a moment. "If there's anything else you need while you're in town, feel free to call."

He felt as though there was something else he wanted to say to her, but his mind remained frustratingly blank. "Uh. Yeah."

Very smooth, Brannon.

"Goodbye, Ethan." Aislinn disconnected before he could make a further fool of himself.

He supposed he should be grateful for that.

Chapter Six

"Good morning, Cassandra." The nurse entered the room with a broad, fake smile, her voice artificially cheery. She carried a paper cup that held several pills.

Already in her chair by the window, her knitting in her lap, Cassandra made an effort to speak warmly, though this was one of her least favorite of the facility's staff. "Good morning. How are you today?"

"Me? Oh, I'm fine. It's you we're worried about. Did you sleep better last night?"

"A little," she lied, taking the cup and the glass of water Nurse Chirpy handed her. She had pretty much given up hope that her problems could be solved with a colorful little capsule.

As much as nice, young Dr. Thomas wanted to help her, there was little he could do to heal the wounds of her past. But, just to make everyone happy—and because there was always the outside chance she could be wrong about their benefit—she dutifully swallowed the pills he had prescribed for her.

Sometimes Aislinn dreamed about cakes. Some of her best designs had come from her dreams, causing her to keep a pad beside her bed so she could make rough sketches before the elaborate dream designs escaped her. She might have worried about that being a little weird, but having heard that writers and designers described similar experiences, she figured maybe it was relatively normal for creative types to dream up ideas.

She woke Wednesday morning groggy. Not particularly well rested. She could vaguely remember tossing and turning during the night and she thought maybe she had sketched something on her pad, though she couldn't remember exactly what. Probably a cake. Considering that she'd been mostly asleep when she'd drawn it, she doubted that the idea would be worth pursuing.

It was quite a shock to see a man's face staring out at her from the notepad. Drawn with some detail, the face was strong, handsome, appealing. He looked a little like Ethan. A little like Joel. But not exactly like either of them.

Although Aislinn had always thought Joel was nice-looking and she was a bit too attracted to Ethan for her own peace of mind, she had to admit that the man she had drawn was more striking than either of them. And there was no doubt in her mind that this man was their brother, Kyle.

Shaken, she sat on the edge of the bed, staring at the

drawing. She didn't remember sketching the face. But, even more disturbing, she had never shown any talent for drawing portraits. Were she to try, she wouldn't be able to do it again now, wide-awake.

She picked up the phone. "Ethan?" she said a few moments later, hearing the unsteadiness of her own voice. "There's something I think I need to show you."

Twenty minutes later he was at her door. From the look on his face, she must have sounded more disturbed than she had even realized when she'd called him.

"What's going on?" he asked the moment she opened the door. "Are you okay?"

Now that she'd had time to think about it, she rather regretted calling him. Had she been more awake, less perturbed by seeing the drawing, she would have talked herself out of making that call. Ever since she'd hung up the phone, she had been berating herself. She had pulled on jeans and a T-shirt, brushing her hair into a ponytail and forgoing makeup, trying to brace herself for Ethan's disbelief and renewed suspicions about her.

She hadn't expected him to look so worried about her.

"I'm fine." She motioned him into her living room, which was decorated in soft creams and taupe. Soothing colors.

Aislinn's home was her retreat from a hectic world that could be overwhelming to her at times. When she was here, she sought peace and refuge. She rarely even turned on the television. She met with clients only at her shop these days. Only a few close friends spent much time in this sanctuary.

She hadn't expected to invite Ethan here.

"I'm sorry I disturbed you so early," she said, self-consciousness causing her to babble a little. "I had a small shock when I woke up and I called you without stopping to think about it. You told me to call you if I had any other insights about your brother."

His eyebrows dipped downward into a frown as he turned to face her. "You've learned something new? You've had another…what do you call them? A flash?"

"No, I don't call them flashes. I just have feelings." She'd said the words so often they were starting to sound clichéd even to her. She shook her head impatiently. "I made coffee after I called you. Would you like some?"

He looked as though he intended to refuse and then he stopped himself. His expression wry, he nodded slowly. "Yeah. I haven't had any coffee yet this morning. Something tells me I'm going to need it."

"Have you had anything to eat?"

"No. I jumped in the shower to wake myself up and then headed straight over here. You gave good directions, by the way. I had no trouble at all finding your house."

She glanced at his damp hair and pictured him taking a quick shower and throwing on the polo shirt and khakis he wore. Deciding she'd better put all thoughts of that out of her mind if she wanted to be relatively coherent, she motioned toward the kitchen. "At least let me feed you while I talk."

He hesitated, then nodded again. "I could eat."

Like the rest of her house, her kitchen was done in peaceful, earthy colors. A commercial-type refrigerator/freezer, double ovens and abundant counter space remained from when she had operated her business out of her home. She had bought the house specifically for the spacious kitchen, the largest room in her otherwise smallish home.

"Nice," Ethan said, glancing around as he took a seat at the small oak table. "Did you grow up in this house?"

"No, I bought it a few years ago." The down payment had come from an insurance payoff after her grandfather's death. Because that was a long, complicated story, she didn't elaborate. "Do you like oatmeal?"

"Don't know. I haven't had oatmeal since I was a kid."

"Really? I have it quite often. It's what I had planned for my own breakfast this morning. It will only take me a few minutes to make some, if you want to try a bowl."

"Yeah, that's fine." There was a note of impatience in his voice, as if food was the last thing he wanted to talk about just then. "I still don't know why you called me over this morning," he reminded her as she started assembling the ingredients for their breakfast.

She stilled her hands for a moment, then went back to work. "I think I've been stalling a little. I know how you'll react."

"You think you know," he corrected her. "Why don't you tell me and find out for sure?"

She was glad to have something else to do while she talked, so that she didn't have to look at him while she told him about her restless night. About waking to find the drawing on her nightstand.

"It's there," she added. "In that sketch pad."

He picked up the pad she had set on one corner of the work island and turned pages. The first few sheets were filled with cake designs, roughly drawn with little detail, difficult to decipher for anyone except her. He stopped on the sketch of the man's face. "Is this what you're talking about?"

She glanced over her shoulder, then looked away again. "Yes. I don't remember drawing it. I didn't even know I could draw like that. I've never been able to sketch a recognizable face. But when I woke up— there it was."

"Do you know who it is?"

"Yes." She could tell by his tone that he'd already guessed her answer. "It's Kyle. The way he looks now, I mean."

Ethan looked at the sketch for a long time in silence, then set the pad aside. "You understand that I'm having trouble believing this."

"I knew you would."

"So you just sat up at some point during the night, drew this face in your sleep, and decided this morning that it must be my brother."

"It sounds strange when you put it like that."

"You think?"

She winced in response to his tone, but didn't pause in her breakfast preparations. "As I said, I probably shouldn't have called you. It rattled me a little to see the drawing this morning, and I acted without taking enough time to talk myself out of it. But since you're here, I feel like I should tell you everything."

"Definitely tell me everything."

She carried two bowls of steaming oatmeal to the table, then returned to the counter for a pitcher of milk and small bowls of brown sugar and raisins. Spreading a napkin in her lap, she sat across from Ethan and picked up her spoon.

"As I said," she began, sprinkling brown sugar and raisins into her bowl, "I knew who I had drawn as soon as I saw the sketch pad this morning. But that wasn't all I knew. Which is why I felt that I should call you."

Having heaped a generous spoonful of brown sugar onto his oatmeal, Ethan paused in the process of adding raisins. "What are you talking about?"

"I got a couple of names. Do you know someone named Mark?"

"I've probably met a few Marks in my life, but no one comes immediately to mind."

"What about Carmen?"

Watching him closely, she saw a muscle twitch in his jaw. "What about Carmen?" he asked.

"Who is she?"

"As if you don't already know."

"I don't know," she refuted. "The name popped into my head this morning, and I knew it was important, but I don't know who she is."

"Carmen was the name of Kyle's nanny. The one who disappeared the same day he did."

Aislinn's expression didn't change. Either she had already known the answer to her question—despite her assertion otherwise—or she wasn't particularly surprised by his response.

Deciding to play along until he could figure out what she was up to now, he asked, "The name just came to you this morning?"

She nodded, dipping a spoon into her bowl. "Mark and Carmen. Both names just kept repeating in my mind. You must think that sounds strange—and, trust me, it feels that way to me, too. I know I keep saying this, but this is all so different for me. So unlike anything I've sensed before."

Yes, she kept saying it. And he still didn't know what to make of it. "I suppose it wouldn't have been that hard for you to find out the name of Kyle's nanny. Old newspaper reports of the storm and its victims, maybe even something Joel let slip one time."

"Joel never talks about your brother's accident. Neither Nic nor I knew anything about it until we'd known him for almost a year—when she went to Alabama with him for the reunion. He has never mentioned the nanny at all."

While she obviously resented his implication that she had looked up the information she claimed had simply come to her in her sleep, she managed to keep her irritation in check. Only her slightly clipped tone let him know how she felt about his comment.

"I didn't say you did look it up. I merely pointed out that you could have," he said mildly. "Is that all you have? The two names?"

She started to say something, then fell quiet, nodding as she ate another spoonful of her oatmeal.

He swallowed a bite of his own, savoring the creamy, brown-sugar-sweetened taste. It was good. Much better than he remembered from childhood. Either his tastes had changed or Aislinn cooked oatmeal better than his mother had. Didn't mean he could believe anything she told him, of course. "What were you going to say just now? Before you changed your mind."

"I—nothing."

He set down his spoon. "Aislinn, I may not be psychic, but I can tell you're holding something back."

She sighed and pushed her half-empty bowl away. "It's all mixed up in my head," she admitted. "I don't like sounding like a flake when I've never thought of myself that way. Before now, everything I've felt or guessed seemed so...I don't know, normal. Maybe a little more intuitive than most people but nothing too far out of the ordinary. To be honest, I worked pretty hard at maintaining that illusion. Keeping some of my feelings unsaid, even with Nic, drawing little attention to myself, putting all my energy into my cake-design business. And then you came to town."

"And what exactly changed when I came to town?"

She motioned toward the sketch pad, still open to the drawing of the man she said was Kyle. "That, for one. I really can't draw like that. If you asked me to draw a face now, I wouldn't be able to. Not with that kind of detail. And I've got to tell you, it creeps me out to think of myself sitting up in the night drawing in my sleep like some sort of zombie."

Her wording might have been amusing had he not identified a bit too closely with the distaste in her voice. He suspected he would have felt much the same way had he been presented with evidence that his actions had been controlled by some outside force. He was way too much of a control freak to be comfortable with that image.

"And then there were the names," she continued, her

hands clenched into fists on the tabletop. "Mark. Carmen. Carmen. Mark. Just hearing them over and over in my mind, like when you get a snippet of music in your head and it just won't go away. That's what those names became to me. Annoying and repetitious."

"I can ask my mother if she remembers anyone named Mark. Maybe Carmen had a boyfriend. Or a brother."

"Maybe." But neither of those explanations seemed to completely satisfy her. After a moment, she shrugged. "It would be a start, anyway."

"You can't give me any other leads?"

She shot him a quick glance, as if trying to determine whether he was making fun of her, and then she replied, "Just one other possibility."

"Which would be?"

"The state of Georgia has some connection to your family."

"Georgia," he repeated.

She nodded.

"I've never been to Georgia. As far as I know, my family has no connection to the state. We lived in North Carolina before we moved to Alabama."

"I don't know what the connection is. Just that your search will eventually lead there. Whether it will end there, I don't know."

Having nothing else to say about that at the moment, Ethan finished the last of his oatmeal, then set his spoon in the empty bowl and reached for his coffee. "That was good. Thank you."

Clasping her hands in front of her, she nodded. "You're welcome."

He drained his coffee cup and set it next to the bowl, giving himself a moment to choose his words. And then he looked somberly at her across the table.

"I still don't know exactly how to get started, but I'll look into all of this," he said. He had told her that before but had yet to make the first inquiry. Probably because doing so would have felt almost tantamount to saying he believed she somehow knew things that other people did not, and he hadn't been ready to do that.

She surprised him then by smiling, though faintly. "You still think I'm a nut. And maybe you're right. But I wish you *would* look into it."

Actually, the more he got to know her, the less he thought of her as a nut. Which didn't mean he accepted everything she said, of course, but he was beginning to acknowledge privately that there were things about Aislinn that weren't easily explained.

She rinsed out their bowls and stacked them in the dishwasher. He stood and picked up the sketch pad, examining the drawing again. Kyle had been little more than a baby when he was lost in that storm, and Ethan's memories of him were hazy, to say the least. But he had looked at enough photos of his little brother to believe that this could be the man he would have become. This drawing resembled quite a bit photos of their father at that age, actually.

"Do you mind if I take this?"

Glancing over her shoulder, she shook her head. "You're welcome to it."

"Thanks." He tore the page neatly from the pad, folded it and slipped it into his shirt pocket. "I'll let you know if I find any evidence at all that either Carmen or Kyle survived that flood."

"Thank you."

She walked him to the front door. He looked around a bit more on the way through the house this time. Her home was tidy, as he had expected, but he was a bit surprised by the lack of color. Shades of brown and cream. Relaxing, he supposed, but it lacked a certain…spark. Passion.

Come to think of it, she tended to dress much the same way, he thought, glancing at her jeans and navy T-shirt. Somewhat colorless. Subdued. With the exception of the flame-red dress Nic had chosen for Aislinn's bridesmaid dress, he couldn't remember ever seeing her wearing bright or bold colors. Another sign of her determination to fit in? Not to call attention to herself, outside of the spectacular cakes that took so much of her time and effort?

They reached for the doorknob at the same time, his hand landing on top of hers. He should have removed his immediately, but instead he lingered, intrigued by the feel of her. She glanced up at him, their eyes meeting. Holding.

She really did have amazing eyes. So dark and deep he could almost fall into them. And her lips. Full. Curvy. Just slightly parted in an invitation he doubted was intentional. Her flawless skin was fair in contrast with her dark hair and eyes, a slight wash of color warming her cheeks as he studied her. He could easily imagine how soft it would feel against his palm.

From the first moment he had seen her, he had been aware of her beauty. He had pushed the attraction to the back of his mind as he had tried to deal with his wariness of everything else about her.

She didn't go pale in response to his touch this time. Instead, her cheeks turned pinker. He wondered what visions, if any, were going through her head this time. He certainly had a few of his own—not that there was anything at all otherworldly about them.

Because those images were becoming just a bit too vivid, he removed his hand slowly, letting her open the door for him. She turned the knob, then stepped back to allow him to pass through the open doorway.

His intention was to walk to his car without looking back. Her voice stopped him before he stepped off the front porch. "Ethan?"

He glanced over his shoulder. "Yes?"

"Be careful at the stoplight."

"What stoplight?"

"Every stoplight," she answered and closed the door.

Shaking his head, he climbed into his car. Seemed like every time he managed to forget the more troubling things about her, she found a way to remind him. Be careful at stoplights? What sort of psychic advice was that? Wasn't that sort of a "duh" admonition?

And yet he found himself hesitating when the light turned green, long enough for the guy in the pickup truck behind him to blow his horn impatiently. Shaking his head at his own gullibility, he started to accelerate—then slammed on the brakes when a teenager in a wannabe sports car squealed through the intersection, not even slowing for the red light.

Had Ethan not waited, the kid would have broadsided him. As it was, he came within an inch of being rear-ended by the pickup, which had moved forward when he did.

Drawing a deep breath to steady his pulse, he proceeded on with caution. There were definitely things about Aislinn that were getting harder all the time to explain, he thought grimly.

Chapter Seven

Even as he dialed his parents' phone number Wednesday evening, Ethan wondered what he was doing. Was he really starting an investigation into his brother's death? All because Aislinn had a feeling Kyle was still alive?

Remembering the incident with the traffic light, he glanced at the drawing that lay beside him. So maybe it was worth asking a few questions. "Mom? Hi, it's me."

"Ethan. Hi, sweetie, how are things there?"

"Okay. We installed some new software on Joel's computers today. Should simplify his bookkeeping quite a bit."

"Oh, that's nice. Are you almost finished with his new business plan?"

"Yeah. I think he'll see a jump in profits within the next few months."

"You didn't increase his prices, did you, Ethan? Because you know, he takes care of a lot of children whose families don't have a great deal of money."

"I'm not advising him to gouge his patients, Mom. Nor their insurance companies. I've simply found places where he and his partner and staff could cut overhead and minimize waste."

"Oh. That's good then."

He smiled faintly. "Yeah. That's good."

Shifting into a more comfortable position in his brother's easy chair, he cleared his throat. "Mom, do you mind if I ask you a couple of questions about Kyle's accident?"

After a slight pause, she replied, "No, of course not. But what made you think of that tonight?"

He had no intention of mentioning Aislinn, of course. Instead he said, "I guess it's just been on my mind for the past few days. It's been thirty years next month, hasn't it?"

"Yes." She obviously hadn't needed the reminder of the sad anniversary. "What do you want to ask, sweetie?"

He'd made a few notes. He glanced at them, though he didn't want to sound too prepared to his mother. "The nanny—Carmen Nichols, right?"

"Yes. You should have some memories of her. She was with us from the time Kyle was only six months old. That's when I went back to my volunteering and charity work after his birth."

Ethan knew his mother still struggled with guilt that she hadn't been home with Kyle that day. Though she had never worked out of the home full-time after having children, she had been extremely active in local schools and charities, spending part of almost every day volunteering and organizing fund-raisers and other events. It had been almost a year after Kyle's death before she had been able to start volunteering again, and then only during the hours when he and Joel had been safely in school.

As much as he hated bringing those bad memories back to her, he pressed on carefully. "She was nice. Sort of quiet, from what I recall. I remember that she was particularly close to Kyle."

"She adored him. Of course, she was with him more than she was with you and Joel. You were both old enough to be more self-sufficient when she joined us and you were involved in activities of your own before long—preschool and playdates, teeny-league sports activities, that sort of thing."

"How old was Carmen, anyway? I thought of her as being pretty old, but to a little kid, anyone over sixteen is old."

"She was just shy of thirty. She was only a couple of years younger than I was, actually."

"Older than the average nanny."

"A bit. But I'm afraid she wasn't trained to do much else. She told me that she dropped out of high school during her junior year to get married to a young man in the Army. A few years later, he was killed in a rather sordid incident overseas—a bar fight or something—leaving poor Carmen with little means of support. She was estranged from her family, who hadn't approved of the choices she had made, and she was pretty much on her own."

"How did you meet her? Did she apply for the job?"

"Not exactly. I hadn't quite decided whether to hire a nanny, but one of my friends suggested that I should meet Carmen. Carmen was working part-time for a day care center where my friend sometimes left her children, and my friend Angela was very impressed with her. She recommended her to me, and your father and I met with her and decided to give it a try. She was wonderful with Kyle, and you and Joel liked her, so it all worked out nicely. We never regretted hiring her. Even after…"

Her voice faded, but Ethan was able to fill in the rest of the sentence. "So she just became a part of the family? Didn't have an outside life of her own? No boyfriends?"

"No. She had a couple of friends around town but no one particularly close to her. I used to try to talk her into going out more, getting a life outside of our house, but she was too shy. She said she was happy with the way things were and she made it clear that she didn't want me to interfere, so I stopped trying. I always assumed she was still grieving over her husband and that she would decide in her own time when she was ready to move on."

"She didn't live with us, did she?"

"No, she had a little apartment not far away. Ethan, these are very odd questions. It isn't that I mind answering them, but what has made you so curious about Carmen?"

"Just working out some old memories in my mind," he prevaricated. "Do you mind answering a couple more questions, even if they sound a little strange to you?"

"All right. If it will help you."

"It will." At least he hoped so. "Do you know Carmen's maiden name? And where she grew up?"

"Her maiden name was Smith, I think. And I believe she once told me that she came from Florida. I'm not sure how she ended up in North Carolina, where we lived."

"Does the name Mark mean anything to you?"

"Mark?" She thought a moment, and then he could almost hear her shrug as she replied, "Not particularly. There's a Mark who works in the post office I use. I know because it's printed on his uniform shirt. And Mark Campbell, who goes to the same church your father and I attend. You know him, Ethan. He sells insurance."

"Yeah, I know him." But he doubted that the balding, avuncular insurance salesman had anything to do with Aislinn's premonition. His family hadn't even moved to Alabama until several years after Kyle's disappearance.

There had been a time when he would have thought of it as Kyle's death, he realized abruptly. Was he really letting Aislinn affect his thinking this much? Maybe he was if he was willing to put his mother through what had to be a difficult inquisition. And it was about to get harder for her.

"Why do you ask about the name Mark?"

He shook his head even though she couldn't see him. "Just a name I thought I remembered."

It was the first outright lie he had given her about this, and he didn't like the way it tasted on his tongue. He moved on quickly. "I seem to remember being told that no one knew exactly where Carmen was taking Kyle that afternoon. Is that correct?"

After a moment of silence Elaine replied, "Yes, that's

right. As far as anyone knew, there was no reason for her to have left the house with him that day. She rarely took him out, except to the park, occasionally, and the weather was much too bad for that on that day. He didn't have any doctor's appointments, and as far as we could determine, she had no appointments, either. If there had been an emergency of some sort, we'd have expected her to try to reach someone, but we couldn't find any evidence that she'd tried to call anyone."

"Strange."

"Yes. After obsessing about it for a long time, I decided she must have needed something from the store or some other sort of errand, though she drove much farther than she should have had to. There were plenty of stores and shops closer to our house than where her car was found."

"There were no witnesses to the accident?"

"No one who was willing to stay around to talk about it, anyway."

"What does that mean?"

"Don't you remember us talking about it? Well, maybe you wouldn't. Your father and I tried not to discuss the accident much when you and Joel were young. Anyway, there was an anonymous report. A woman called in the details of where Carmen's car had gone off the road, but she didn't give her name. By the time the police arrived, no one was there, though they found evidence that a car had gone into the river."

"How did they know it was Carmen's car even before they found it?"

"The woman gave a license plate number. She said

she caught a glimpse of it just as the car went over. The police seemed to think she might have somehow caused the accident. Maybe skidded or crossed the center line into Carmen's path, and didn't want to admit it. She panicked, apparently."

"Yet she had the presence of mind to note the license plate number?"

"Some people just notice things like that, I guess." She sounded a little weary now, as if this conversation was taking a toll on her. "Anyway, the police found the car a couple of days later, some distance downriver. Very deep. As you know, they never found Carmen or Kyle. It was months later before they recovered the poor old man who was swept into the river in another part of the state the day earlier, when he got out of his flooded car in chest-deep water. Everyone said it was the worst flooding of the past fifty years.

"That's what made it even harder to imagine why Carmen would have risked taking Kyle out that day," she added. "Everyone knew how bad the flooding problem was. The earlier drownings had been all over the news. It just didn't make sense. It still doesn't after all these years. I've just finally had to accept that we'll never know the answers."

Something he should be telling himself, rather than following the suggestions of a pseudopsychic, Ethan reminded himself grimly. "That's all I wanted to ask, Mom," he said somewhat abruptly. "Thanks for being so patient, okay? I hope it wasn't too distressing for you."

"Of course not, Ethan. I'm always available if you need to talk, you know that."

Feeling decidedly guilty now, he said, "Thanks, Mom. But you've answered all my questions. I'll let you go now. I'm sure you have things to do."

"Actually, I do have a book club meeting this evening. But if you'd rather talk…"

"No. Go to your meeting. And tell Dad hi for me, okay? I'll see you both next week."

"All right. Good night, Ethan."

Feeling like a jerk, he hung up the phone. He wished he could say that conversation had managed to convince him that everything Aislinn had said was a load of bunk. Unfortunately it had only served to remind him that there were still a great many unanswered questions about the events of that long-ago afternoon.

While he wasn't prepared to admit that Aislinn had provided any of those explanations, he knew his mind wouldn't be at ease until he'd made an attempt to pursue a few more answers on his own.

"You haven't been cooperating with the staff, Cassandra. That isn't like you."

She shook her head, speaking patiently. "It isn't the way you make it sound, Dr. Thomas. I'm not exactly refusing to cooperate. I've simply chosen not to take the sleep medications anymore. They don't help, and I don't like the way they make me feel the next day."

"Then let's try another prescription. There are several we haven't tried yet. As you know, everyone reacts differently to medication, and there's a good chance the next one won't cause the aftereffects you don't like. You need your rest. It's obvious that your health is being affected."

She didn't bother to argue with him on that point. She had been feeling weary. Lethargic. Too weak at times to lift her knitting needles. She never complained, but apparently the staff had been watching her a bit more closely than she had realized—and reporting their observations to her doctor. "I'll be fine."

He frowned, and she could see genuine concern in his pretty green eyes. "I worry about you, Cassandra."

"Do you?" She smiled at him. "That's very sweet, Dr. Thomas."

"It's also my job."

Reaching out, she patted his arm in a maternal gesture. "But it's more than that to you. You worry too much about us. Remember what I warned you about burnout."

"We aren't talking about me," he reminded her, though he couldn't seem to help smiling back at her. "We were discussing you. You aren't sleeping. You're refusing your medications. And you haven't been talking with your counselor. According to her, you're always pleasant and polite but not at all forthcoming about anything that might be bothering you."

"I prefer to keep my problems to myself. Do you have any plans for the weekend, Dr. Thomas?"

Sighing impatiently, he shook a finger at her. "You're trying to change the subject again. Why won't you talk with your counselor? Don't you like her?"

"She's nice enough. A little too perky. I prefer people with a little pepper to them. Like you."

He chuckled. "Flirting with me won't make me forget what we're talking about."

She laughed softly. "Maybe not now. But there was

a time when I could have smiled at you and made you forget your name."

"I have no doubt of that."

"My late husband said I mesmerized him the first time he met me. Little did he know I planned it exactly that way."

"Set your cap for him, did you?"

She nodded, remembering her certainty that marrying Lawrence would be vital to her future. Turned out she had been right. Had he not left her so well provided for, who knew where she would be now? "He never knew what hit him."

The young doctor laughed again, though Cassandra hadn't actually been joking. And then he sobered. "You and your husband had no children?"

She shook her head. "I was almost fifty when we married. He was seventy-five and had outlived a wife and a son. I made him very happy for the last few years of his life."

"And did he make you happy?"

She suspected that her smile looked rather sad to him, though she tried to keep her emotions hidden. "He was very kind to me."

After a moment the doctor spoke again. "Forgive me if you think I'm prying, but I've noticed you never have visitors. You have no family?"

"None that I would have any interest in seeing. Or vice versa."

That seemed to surprise him. "I can't imagine anyone not wanting to spend time with you."

"Yes, well, you haven't known me very long. I

haven't always been the charming and gracious lady you see now."

He looked at her as though he wasn't quite sure if she was teasing him. She had spoken the truth, of course.

"Still," he said, and something about the way he watched her told her that he was choosing his words very deliberately, "it's a shame you never had children. You wouldn't be so lonely now."

Did he think that was what was bothering her? Loneliness?

Perhaps he was right in a way, she conceded. But she had no intention of telling him everything. "Not everyone is meant to be a mother, Dr. Thomas," she said gently, even as the memory of a baby's cries echoed hauntingly through her mind.

"Maybe not," he said, standing, as if sensing that he'd gotten all he was going to get out of her this time. He paused for a moment beside her chair, setting a gentle hand on her shoulder. "I'd like to try another sleep aid for you, Cassandra. If this one doesn't help you, then perhaps we should pursue some different avenues. Are you willing to work with me?"

Because the poor man looked so genuinely distressed, so anxious to help, she nodded.

"I'll try the new sleep aid," she said. "Maybe this one will work."

He seemed relieved that she had agreed to let him try again to help her. He wanted so badly to be of assistance to her.

His kind nature was going to be severely tested someday, his tender heart broken. That wasn't a guess.

It was a certainty. But because she wasn't ready to talk to him about such things, she kept her thoughts to herself.

She waved him out with a smile that faded the moment the door closed behind him.

Ethan left the clinic early Thursday afternoon, but rather than heading back to Joel's house, he drove to Aislinn's shop. She would probably be busy, but he had an urge to stop by anyway. He didn't pause to ask himself why.

She *was* busy, as it turned out. She was meeting with a giggling young woman and her mother, who were trying to decide on a wedding cake design. Sitting at the reception area table with her clients, Aislinn glanced up when Ethan walked in, excused herself and walked over to greet him, leaving the women to leaf slowly through the photo albums of cakes she had previously designed.

"Hi."

He nodded. "Sorry, I didn't mean to interrupt your meeting."

"No problem. I have fresh coffee in the kitchen if you'd like to have a cup while I finish up here."

"Sounds good. Thanks."

"There's cake, too," she added with a smile. "Cupcakes, actually. In the fridge. Help yourself."

"I'll do that."

Leaving her to her customers, he walked back into the kitchen. She had been busy that day, he noted immediately. There were not one but two cakes on the work island.

The largest was obviously a wedding cake, though a bit different than the usual tiers-on-pillars design. This one was stacked in four graduated layers covered in a shiny, almost pearlescent frosting tinted a pale lavender. Amazingly realistic flowers in graduated shades of purple were arranged on the top layer and cascaded down both sides, intertwined with glossy green leaves that he could almost have believed were real had he not looked more closely. Rather than a bride and groom, a delicate white cage sat in the very center of the top, holding two white doves and decorated with thin, purple satin ribbon.

The second cake was more whimsical. A groom's cake, maybe? It looked amazingly like a fisherman's creel with a fly-fishing reel lying on top. Fascinated, he studied the woven effect of the piped frosting, making it look exactly like a natural rattan basket. The top was brown and actually had a wood-grain pattern to it, and the hinges and clasp could well have been made of metal, though he knew they were edible. The reel was made of a small, round layer, decorated so realistically he could almost hear the line zing through it.

Amazing. He couldn't help but wonder if Aislinn was wasting her talents here. It wasn't as if she had family holding her in this area. Not that he could tell, anyway. With the exception of a few close friends and her thriving business, she seemed to live a very solitary life. He'd gotten the impression that she loved her rather colorless home but rarely shared it with anyone else.

Because that seemed all too familiar to him, he winced. He was often called a loner. He, too, kept his somewhat isolated home as a retreat from the demands of the outside world. Nic had once remarked that he and Aislinn were alike in some ways, and he had immediately denied that they had anything at all in common. He didn't want to start rethinking that denial just now.

He poured himself a cup of coffee and opened the refrigerator. The cupcakes were stacked on a plate, arranged almost like a cake themselves. Cheerfully decorated with yellow frosting and pink flowers, they were sort of sissy but looked too good to resist. He plucked one from the top of the stack and carried it and his coffee to the table to wait for Aislinn.

From where he sat, he could easily overhear the conference going on in the other room. He made no effort not to eavesdrop. This was business, after all. His specialty.

He could hear papers rustling as Aislinn began to talk. Probably taking notes. "So your colors are pumpkin and chocolate, is that right? Interesting choices, and very nice for a late fall wedding."

The bride spoke warmly. "Thank you. My fiancé keeps saying I've picked brown and orange and he thinks those are weird colors for a wedding, but I told him pumpkin and chocolate aren't just brown and orange."

"No, of course not," Aislinn agreed.

Bull, Ethan thought. He agreed with the absent fiancé. Call the colors what you wanted, they were still brown and orange. And they did seem like sort of weird colors for a wedding.

Aislinn spoke again. "Have you seen a cake you like in the photo albums? Or do you have ideas for a design you would like me to create for you?"

"Since our wedding will take place in October and the colors are fall colors, I thought maybe something that fit the season, you know? Like maybe leaves and gourds and pumpkins and stuff."

For the first time, the mother of the bride spoke up. "Really, Lacey? Wouldn't you rather have flowers and scallops and more delicate-looking things on your wedding cake?"

"No, Mom. I told you—I want my wedding to be different. I don't want the same stuff everyone else has."

For the next twenty minutes they debated traditional versus creative wedding rituals while Aislinn contributed an occasional calming suggestion. At times, the discussion between mother and daughter grew rather heated, and Ethan suspected that there had been other such arguments during various stages of the wedding planning. But Aislinn seemed to be an old pro at keeping such conflicts under control, and by the time the duo left a short while later, they seemed to be satisfied with the results of the meeting.

Despite how calm she had sounded, Aislinn looked a bit stressed when she joined Ethan in the kitchen. She headed straight for the coffeepot.

"The wedding isn't until October and they're already ordering the cake?" Ethan asked, watching her.

"I prefer six months' notice," she replied with a shrug. "They're actually running a little behind. But I think I can work them in, since the cake she wants doesn't sound overly complicated."

"You're booked six months ahead?"

"Yes. I can usually work in a few birthday and special-occasion cakes, but when it comes to the very complicated and labor-intensive cakes, I need lots of notice."

"Do you charge by the hour?"

"By the serving," she corrected. "The price per serving depends on the time involved and the cost of the supplies required."

"Makes sense."

She carried her coffee to the table and slid into the chair opposite him. "Did you have a cupcake?"

"Actually, I had two of them. They were good. What was that filling? Sort of lemony?"

"A lemon-orange flavor. A new recipe I'm trying."

"I'd add it to the menu."

"Thanks. I'll take your advice into consideration."

"I usually get paid for my advice."

"And I usually get paid for my cupcakes."

He chuckled. "We'll call it even."

They smiled at each other across the table, and he was rather surprised by how friendly and relaxed they were being with each other. Usually there was an undercurrent of tension, if not open antagonism, between them—and he was well aware that it was mostly his fault. He didn't know exactly what had changed in his attitude toward her—heck, he didn't even know why he was with her now, but it felt kind of nice.

Maybe that was what spurred him to tell her, "I talked to my mother yesterday."

She looked at him over the rim of her coffee cup, waiting for him to continue.

"I asked her some questions about Kyle's accident."

"That must have been a difficult conversation for both of you."

Major understatement. "Yeah. It was."

"Did you tell her about me?"

"No. I just implied that the subject was on my mind because the thirtieth anniversary of Kyle's death is coming up soon."

Aislinn didn't bother to remind him that she didn't believe Kyle was dead. Instead, she asked, "Did you learn anything new from your mother?"

He repeated the conversation as best he could remember, and she sat quietly listening and drinking her coffee.

"The authorities looked for Kyle and Carmen for weeks before giving up," he added. "They said they could have been carried miles away from the place they went in, considering how fast and how high the river was that week."

She remained silent.

Looking at her narrowly, he asked, "I don't suppose you can give me any other details about what happened that afternoon?"

Frowning a little, she seemed to look inward, as if searching her mind for the answer to his question. But then she shook her head. "All I know is that they didn't die that day."

"That day?"

"Kyle is still living. I don't know whether Carmen is alive."

He stood and poured himself another cup of coffee. "This gift of yours," he said, annoyed at his own awkwardness, "have you ever used it to—you know—like, help Nic or something?"

"I don't—"

"I guess I'm trying to ask if you've ever worked with the police to find missing persons. Anything like that."

She frowned. "Of course not. I couldn't do anything like that."

"Don't you ever get feelings about the cases Nic works?"

"Sometimes, but I rarely say anything to her about it. I wouldn't want to mislead her in any way. I make guesses, Ethan, and they aren't always right."

"So how often are you wrong?"

"I don't keep records."

This time he was the one who remained silent, looking at her steadily across the table.

She sighed. "When I get a certain type of strong feeling, I'm almost always right. But I rarely have clear enough details to help the police or anything like that. For example, I had a premonition that Nic was going to be injured in an accident last year in Alabama—but I didn't have a clue how or when it was going to happen. I couldn't prevent her from being hurt. So what good was it, really?"

He twisted his coffee cup between his hands, thinking of how frustrating that would have been. To know her friend would be hurt yet not be able to prevent it.

"It's the same with you," she added. "I know your brother is alive, but I can't tell you where he is. Where he has been for the past thirty years. What happened on that long-ago afternoon. So you tell me—just how useful is this so-called gift of mine?"

Ethan didn't know quite how to respond to her plaintive question. Yet he was struck by the sincerity of her expression. The visible distress in her eyes. If she was faking, she was perhaps the best actor he had ever encountered.

"You kept me from being broadsided at a traffic light," he offered, compelled for some reason to try to encourage her.

"Did I?"

He nodded. "You didn't provide specifics, but I kept your advice in mind. Maybe that's what makes it useful. You give warnings, but it's up to the people you tell to figure out how take advantage of them."

"Does that mean you're starting to believe I'm not just making up the things I tell you?"

Had he just been cleverly manipulated? He frowned, searching her expression again for any subtle sign of satisfaction. Seeing nothing, he shrugged, saying noncommittally, "Let's just say I'm keeping an open mind."

"That's something, anyway," she said.

"Best I can do." He stood, carrying his coffee cup to the sink. "Are you about done here for the day? If so, you want to go have dinner somewhere?"

"Dinner?" She seemed as surprised by the invitation as he was that he had impulsively issued it. "Now?"

"Whenever you're ready." After all, he reasoned, he was tired of eating alone. And at least Aislinn was good company who wouldn't read anything more than he intended into the outing. Heck, she would probably know how the evening would end before he did.

She studied him a moment from her chair, as if trying to determine his motive for asking—and then she nodded and stood. "All right. I can clear up here in about ten minutes, if you don't mind waiting."

"Not at all."

He wandered into the reception area to leaf through

albums of her work while she prepared to leave. He noted there wasn't one wedding cake with pumpkins on it. Yet he had no doubt that if Aislinn designed one, it would look good. When it came to her business, he had complete faith in her abilities.

Chapter Eight

She wouldn't exactly say she was winning Ethan over, but at least he didn't seem openly antagonistic anymore. She supposed that was a step forward.

Not that she was trying to win him over, exactly, Aislinn assured herself as she sliced into a steak at the restaurant where she and Ethan had decided to dine. He would be leaving town in a few days, after all. She just didn't like the thought of him leaving while still thinking of her as a con artist or a crazy person.

Maybe he was finally starting to see that she was just an average woman with above-average intuition.

Even with his self-proclaimed ineptitude at small talk, Ethan managed to carry on a civil conversation with her as they ate. They didn't talk about anything of particular importance. Mostly business stuff—his and her own. If there was one thing that got Ethan excited, she thought with a secret smile, it was business.

"Aislinn." Pamela Maclure stopped by the table, looking delighted to see her. Her round, reddish-toned face beamed with the smile she turned from Aislinn to Ethan. "It's great to see you. And you're Joel Brannon's brother, aren't you? I saw you at the wedding."

"Ethan Brannon," he confirmed with a nod, rising to greet her.

Looking pleased with the small courtesy, she extended her hand. "I'm Pamela Maclure. An old friend of Aislinn's."

"Nice to meet you."

"You, too. Please, sit down. I only stopped by to say hello."

Ethan returned to his seat and picked up his fork again.

Pamela turned back to Aislinn. "Look, call me tomorrow, okay? I need to talk to you about something."

Aislinn groaned, knowing exactly what Pamela wanted to talk to her about. "Not another one, Pam. I'm really not interested, okay?"

Pamela frowned and glanced quickly at Ethan. "No, really, this might really work out. Unless you're, um—"

"No," she said firmly, shaking her head. She and Ethan were definitely not an item, which was what Pamela had implicitly asked. "Still not interested."

Happily married Pamela had been trying for months to fix her up with a string of men, none of whom had been in the least compatible with her. It didn't help that Pamela billed Aislinn as her friend the psychic, which intrigued some men for all the wrong reasons. She would rather spend an evening with Ethan, who openly expressed his skepticism of such abilities, than with a guy who hoped to profit from them, as had the man who'd offered to split the take with her if she would help him place bets on winning football teams.

Pamela sighed. "This is what I get for being friends with someone who knows what I'm planning," she muttered, only half-teasingly. "I can't get anything past you."

Aislinn gave her a warning look.

Sighing again, more gustily this time, Pamela took a step backward. "Call me anyway," she said. "Just to talk."

"I will," Aislinn promised. And she would, because despite everything, she was fond of Pamela.

Smiling at Ethan again, Pamela excused herself and went to rejoin her husband, who had just finished paying at the cash register.

"What was that about?" Ethan asked quizzically.

She lifted a shoulder. "Long story."

He didn't push. "You say you've known her a long time?"

"Yes. Since high school. She's a good friend."

"Does she know about your...well, you know?"

Resisting the impulse to roll her eyes, Aislinn said shortly, "She knows."

"Have you ever had a feeling that helped her out?"

"A few times."

"And she believed you. Took your advice to heart."

She nodded. "Of course."

"Can you give me an example?"

She lifted her eyebrows at him.

"Hey, you're expecting me to go to a lot of trouble to

pursue one of your hunches. It wouldn't hurt to give me some verification that I wouldn't be wasting my time."

"You're asking for references?"

His mouth twitched. "Just anecdotal evidence."

"Fine." She propped her elbows on the table and loosely clasped her hands. "I told her where to find her husband."

"Had she lost him?"

"Not like that. I told her where to go to meet him initially. I had a feeling she should go to a certain store at a certain time, and she did—and as she was driving through the parking lot, looking for an open space, someone backed into her car."

Ethan lifted an eyebrow. "And that was a good thing?"

"Yes. Bill, her husband, was driving the car that hit hers. He apologized, they exchanged insurance information— and phone numbers—and a year later they were married."

"And you knew she was going to meet him that way."

"Oh, no. I just knew she should be at that place at that time. I wasn't sure why, but I felt like it was important."

"And now she's trying to repay the favor."

"I beg your pardon?"

He smiled briefly. "It was obvious that she's trying to set you up. With someone you're not interested in meeting, apparently."

Aislinn sighed, wondering if she was the only one at this table with better-than-average intuition. "I don't know who she's picked out for me this time, but you're right. She's undoubtedly got another prospect in mind."

"Another prospect?"

"She's been trying to match me up for more than a year. She's made it her personal mission."

"Actually, she reminds me of someone. My dad has this office manager—Heidi Rosenbaum. Nice woman, but she can't bear to see a single adult. She's always trying to match people up. I ran into her at the grocery store last month and she started telling me about some woman she wanted me to meet. A schoolteacher."

"And you told her you weren't interested."

"I told her I was fully capable of finding my own dates if I wanted."

"Why do I get the feeling you weren't particularly polite about it?" she asked, amused by the image.

"Let's just say subtlety doesn't work well with Heidi."

"Did you hurt her feelings?"

"Not possible. She just patted my arm and told me I knew where to find her if I got too lonely."

She studied his face. She doubted that he had much trouble finding companionship when he wanted it. But she suspected that for the most part he was content with his own company.

"You don't get lonely very often."

"Right."

"But you get sad sometimes."

He frowned. "I don't know what you're talking about."

He knew. But he didn't want to talk about it. And she wouldn't press just now, while they were getting along so well.

Ethan changed the subject rather abruptly. "How are you with a computer?"

"In what respect?"

"I thought I'd go online on Joel's computer this evening, maybe do a little research about Carmen

Nichols. Needless to say, I don't have a lot of experience with that sort of investigation. I just wondered if you have any advice to offer."

"I haven't had any experience at finding long-lost people, either," she replied. "But I spend a lot of time online looking for inspiration for new cake designs, learning new methods, that sort of thing."

"Maybe between the two of us, we could find some information—if you're not too busy and you're interested in looking into it with me, of course."

"You're asking me to come to Joel's this evening and help you do computer research?" she asked for clarification.

He nodded. "Unless you have other plans."

He had taken her by surprise again—just as he had when he'd shown up at her shop and when he'd asked her to dinner. Why was Ethan suddenly looking for ways to spend time with her?

"I don't have other plans, actually," she admitted. "But I don't know how much help I would be to you."

He shrugged. "It was just a thought."

Maybe he was just trying to make amends, of sorts, for the way he had treated her from the time they'd met. Maybe he figured that since she was his new sister-in-law's best friend, it was better to stay on friendly footing. Or maybe, despite his denials, he was just getting a little lonely after all, here in this town where he knew so few people.

"All right," she said, hoping she wasn't making a mistake. "Maybe together we can find some information that would lead you to your brother."

While he looked far from convinced that their search would change his mind about what had happened to Kyle all those years ago, he seemed satisfied that she had agreed to assist him.

Aislinn followed Ethan to Joel's house after dinner. She stopped by to say hello to Nic's mother next door before joining Ethan. Susan seemed to be enjoying her visit home, but she admitted to Aislinn that she was looking forward to returning to Europe to be with her son. She would spend another couple of weeks here after Nic and Joel returned, visiting with them, and then she would return to Paris until her next visit home at Thanksgiving.

Susan didn't seem to find it odd that Aislinn was visiting Ethan that evening. She seemed to believe that Aislinn was simply being sociable, keeping her friend's brother company for a few hours. Aislinn was content to leave it at that. Taking her leave of Susan after a brief, pleasant exchange, she walked back to Joel's house to help Ethan search for his long-lost brother.

Curled into a chair next to Ethan's, Aislinn arched her back and was rather surprised when several muscles protested. She glanced at her watch. Had they really been sitting here for almost two hours, staring at Joel's computer monitor?

Ethan sat in another chair at the keyboard, a legal pad with several pages of scribbled notes at his elbow. He looked around when Aislinn moved. "Getting tired?"

"Just a little stiff." She stood, stretching out the kinks. "Do you mind if I have a glass of water?"

"Of course not. There's a filtered pitcher in the refrigerator. Help yourself."

"Thank you. Can I get you a glass?"

"Yeah, that sounds good. Thanks."

She was returning with a glass in each hand when the telephone rang. "That's Joel," she said without checking caller ID. "I assume you're not going to tell him yet what we're doing."

"You assume correctly." He answered the phone, chatting for a few minutes with his brother while Aislinn sipped her water.

She was beginning to think he wasn't going to mention her at all when she heard him ask if Nic was nearby. "Aislinn's here, keeping me company for a while," he added. "They'd probably like to say hello to each other."

Taking the receiver from him with a smile, Aislinn said, "Hi, Nic. How's the honeymoon?"

"Paradise," Nic answered fervently. "It's so beautiful here, you wouldn't believe it. It's going to be tough coming back home and going back to work. And speaking of home, how's everything there?"

"Same as always. I saw your mom earlier. She's having a great time catching up with her old friends."

"I talked to her yesterday. It did seem like she was enjoying her visit. I could tell she's looking forward to rejoining Paul, though. She really loves it over there." Changing the subject, Nic continued, "So, you're spending the evening with Ethan."

"Yes, we've been having a nice visit."

"Have you?" Nic sounded surprised—and a bit suspicious, as if she wondered what exactly was going on between Aislinn and Ethan.

Aislinn didn't blame her for being curious. After all, neither she nor Ethan were overly sociable types. And they hadn't exactly gotten off to the best start.

"Has Ethan been giving you advice about your business? Joel said there's nothing he loves to do more than talk to small-business owners about ways they can restructure."

"Yes, he's given me a few tips about my business." He had advised her to add the chocolate-caramel cake and the lemon-orange cupcakes to her menu, which she supposed made her answer an honest one.

Looking around from the computer, Ethan gave her a quizzical look. She wrinkled her nose at him and returned her attention to the phone call.

"I'd better go," Nic said. "Joel and I are going for a late-night walk on the beach."

"Sounds very romantic."

"I guess it would be if one of us didn't insist on starting a footrace every time."

Aislinn laughed. "Gee, I wonder which one of you that would be."

They hung up shortly afterward.

"I appreciate you not telling them what you and I are really working on this evening," Ethan said without looking around again.

She returned to her seat beside him. "I promised you I wouldn't."

"Do you always know who's calling before you pick up the phone?"

"It was a pretty safe guess that would be Joel."

"True, but you didn't answer my question."

She sighed. "I usually know, especially on my home phone."

"How often? On your home phone."

"Maybe nine out of ten calls."

"That's a little more than random chance."

"Maybe."

To her relief, he let it go. "I don't think we're going to find anything else tonight, do you?"

"No." She was sure they wouldn't, actually. She'd known for the past half hour that there was nothing left to find online, but she'd kept quiet, letting Ethan check every possibility he could think of.

Pushing away from the desk, he turned his chair to face hers, the legal pad in his hand. "So we've read every old news report we can find of the storm and the accident. We've learned that a couple of people expressed concern at the time that the bodies were never found, but that eventually everyone seemed to accept that the severity of the flood made the search too difficult. Prevailing theories seemed to be that Carmen and Kyle were trapped at the bottom of the river somewhere beneath debris and would never be found."

Aislinn nodded. "That's what most people believed."

"I remember that my dad went out every day for a long time, driving down the river, taking his fishing boat out whenever he could. After the first night, he didn't believe Kyle was still alive, but he hoped to finally find him so they could give him a decent burial."

Her heart twisting at the grief the family must have

experienced, Aislinn murmured, "There was nothing for him to find."

"From what I recall, my mother was amazingly strong during the whole ordeal. Later I heard her tell people that she got through it by concentrating on Joel and me. She said she didn't have the luxury of going to pieces because we depended on her so much."

"I could tell your mother is a resilient woman. She's been through a lot."

"She has."

"Was she close to your sister-in-law? Joel's first wife?"

It was probably because she was watching him so closely that she saw the emotions swirl in his eyes. Most people wouldn't have seen them, she guessed. Ethan was very good at hiding his feelings.

"Yes, she and Heather were very close."

"I'm glad she's been able to welcome Nic to your family as warmly as she has. I know it was difficult for her at first."

"Mom never wanted Joel to be alone forever. And it had been six years since Heather died. Nic was just a little different than Mom had expected. Once she got to know her, she couldn't help but like her."

She'd picked up some undercurrents in that exchange that she wanted to mull over later. For now, she directed the topic back to their search. "So now that we've found out all we can online, what are you going to do to find more information about Carmen?"

"I don't know," he admitted. "I'm no private investigator."

"Have you considered hiring one?"

"And tell him what? That a woman who denies being a psychic has a feeling my long-lost brother is still alive and possibly living somewhere in Georgia?"

"It does sound a little far-fetched when you put it that way."

"Yeah. A little."

"But I'm sure private investigators have heard stranger stories."

"Probably. But I'm not sure I'm willing to pay some guy an outrageous hourly fee to look into this."

Especially since he was still a long way from being convinced there was anything to look into, Aislinn finished silently.

"Maybe you should look up some of Carmen's surviving family members. Maybe some of her friends."

"And ask them what? If they've heard from her?"

She shook her head. "They wouldn't have. But maybe they had noticed odd behavior from her in the days or weeks leading up to the accident. Maybe they heard her talk about places she wanted to visit or things she wished she could do. Anything that might lead you into a new direction."

"Sounds like a lot of trouble," he grumbled.

"It will be," she agreed. "But it's worth a try, isn't it?"

"Is it?" His expression had turned distant and brooding again, to her regret. It had been kind of nice working side by side with him, having him seem open to her input, willing to accept the possibility that there could be some validity to the things she had told him. But something had changed, and it seemed to have happened when she'd mentioned his late sister-in-law.

Clasping her hands in front of her, she leaned slightly forward in her chair, their knees almost touching as they faced each other. "If there's a chance—even a very slim chance—that I'm right about Kyle still being alive, wouldn't you want to find him?"

Ethan was silent for so long that she began to wonder if he was going to respond. And then he lifted one shoulder. "I guess so. I mean, I haven't ever really considered the possibility that he survived that flood. What you're talking about—kidnapping—was never something my family even considered after he disappeared. Yeah, sure, they wondered why Carmen took him out that day in weather like that. They wondered why no bodies were ever found, but considering the circumstances, that wasn't out of the realm of possibilities."

He pushed his chair back and stood, walking across the room to stare out a window. She doubted that he saw anything out in the neatly manicured back lawn. Even though he wasn't looking at her, his attention was focused entirely on her as he said, "Now, thirty years later, you tell me there's a chance Kyle could have survived. That he somehow grew up without us, matured into a stranger with a different history than ours, probably no memory of any of us."

She had already thought of those things—how painful it would be for the family to accept the years they had lost with Kyle, how wrenching it would be for Elaine and Lou, especially. Moving to stand beside him, she spoke quietly. "It's going to be difficult, for all of you."

He turned, glaring at her in a way that might have intimidated some people. "I'm beginning to wonder if we're both crazy. You for the things you say and me for listening to them."

Though she could understand why he would feel that way, she couldn't help flinching in response to his adjective. "Neither one of us is crazy," she said more forcefully than she had intended.

"Then why am I listening to you?"

She gazed up at him. "Because you're keeping an open mind—just in case I'm right."

"I'm not sure that's it."

"Then why *are* you listening to me?"

He surprised her by reaching up to cup her face between his hands. "Maybe it has something to do with your eyes."

"What—" She had to stop to clear her throat. "What about my eyes?"

Looking somberly down at her, he murmured, "They're mesmerizing. Maybe you're really a hypnotist rather than a psychic."

She tried to smile. "Very funny."

His head lowered toward hers. "I don't think I was joking."

His lips were on hers before she had a chance to say anything else.

Chapter Nine

There were no predictions or special insights in Aislinn's mind when Ethan kissed her. Actually, there was nothing at all. He had rendered her completely incapable of forming a coherent thought.

She hadn't kissed many men in her solitary, self-protective life. But she didn't need much of a base of comparison to know that Ethan was pretty much a pro at this. Amazing, actually.

She couldn't imagine why he was kissing her. And it utterly astonished her to realize that she was kissing him back.

She gaped up at him when he lifted his head. Then, concerned that she probably looked like an idiot, she closed her mouth and jerked away from him.

Ethan spun on one heel and moved back to stare out

the window again. He stood straight and stiff, tension vibrating from every inch of him. Was he regretting kissing her? Wondering what on earth had possessed him? She didn't have a clue what he was thinking.

"I suppose you were expecting that," he said after a moment.

"What are you talking about?" Peevishly, she pushed a lock of hair out of her face. "I had no idea."

"You mean you didn't predict it?"

"No," she answered shortly.

"Interesting."

She stared at his back with mounting irritation. "You're *testing* me? Trying to see if I can predict your actions?"

Without looking around, he shrugged.

"What more do you want me to do to convince you that you can trust me?"

"You could always try some more parlor tricks."

Planting her fists on her hips, she drawled, "Want me to read your mind?"

That made him turn toward her. "You can't."

"You're right. I can't. I have no idea what's going on in that head of yours just now."

She thought she saw a brief flash of relief in his eyes, but that couldn't be right, since he didn't believe she had any special abilities anyway. "You want to convince me? Help me find my brother."

"Isn't that what I've been doing tonight?"

"Hardly. We looked up a couple of old reports of the accident. Easy enough to do. For all I know, you'd already done so."

"I told you I hadn't. But that goes back to whether you can trust anything I say, doesn't it?"

He nodded to concede her point. "Help me find some proof that Kyle survived that flood, and I'll be a lot more likely to believe you."

"I wouldn't know how to begin."

"I have a few ideas."

"Such as?"

"You're the one who suggested I contact Carmen's surviving family and friends. Go with me to talk to them."

"Go with you? I thought you would just talk to them by phone."

He shook his head. "This is too complicated to handle by phone. I need to see their expressions if there's any chance that one of them knows anything about that day that hasn't already been revealed."

"Maybe. But why on earth would you want me there with you?"

"You're the one who claims to just know things. Maybe you'd know if anyone tries to hide something from us."

"So I'd be your human lie detector."

"Something like that."

She shook her head. "I really don't think this is a good idea. For one thing, I'm very busy right now."

"I can wait until you aren't busy. It isn't like there's any hurry."

But there was, she thought, chewing on her lower lip. Somehow she knew that he needed to start his search soon or he would never find the answers. "I really see no need for you to take me along."

"Because you know there's very little chance that there's anything for me to find?"

He was trying to trap her, she thought with a glare. To somehow make her admit she wasn't really convinced Kyle was still alive. "You know what I believe."

"So are you willing to back up your words with action?"

"You really are testing me," she said slowly. "Why?"

He seemed to mull over the question for a moment before replying. "It seems like something I need to do."

It was like him not to try to offer rationalizations. But she could figure out part of his reasoning. He was still concerned about her closeness to Nic—which made her a part of Joel's life, as well. He had an older-brother protectiveness toward Joel. Toward his whole family, for that matter.

He was undoubtedly worried that despite her promises to him, she would say something to Joel or his parents about her belief that Kyle was still alive. It wasn't necessary for him to explain how distressing that would be for them without proof of her claim. It would be hard enough for them when it turned out to be true.

And it wasn't only his family he was worried about, she sensed. There was a tiny part of him that was starting to believe her, and that disturbed him as much as anything.

She knew he had been burned in the past. She knew he had put his faith in at least one person who had turned out to be untrustworthy. Because of those betrayals, combined with the hard losses his family had known, he had become guarded. Wary. Unwilling to open himself to further disillusionment.

It would be hard for anyone to believe the earthshaking news she had shared with him, she mused. For Ethan, it was almost impossible, based on nothing more than her instincts.

He would never know, of course, how difficult it was for her to accept it herself. He didn't know how hard she had tried to talk herself out of confiding in Ethan, telling herself that he would probably throw her out on her ear, and that even if he gave her the benefit of the doubt, it would be cruel to raise his hopes with so little evidence. And yet she had known that she was right. Believed it with every fiber of her being. And she had been compelled to tell him, feeling that he had a right to know his brother was alive.

He didn't believe her. He didn't trust her. And yet, rather than keeping her at a distance and refusing to listen to her, he had been spending time with her. Trying to figure her out. And even though he saw it as more of an invitation than a dare, in effect, he was giving her a chance to prove herself to him. To help him find the brother she knew was still out there somewhere.

"Have you gone into a trance?"

His sarcastic question brought her attention back to the moment. "I can take off the week after next if you can," she said, and it was as much a challenge as the one he'd thrown at her. He wanted her to prove herself? Fine. She was demanding that he give her a real chance to do so.

For only a moment he looked startled that she'd accepted his dare. Had he been bluffing?

But then he nodded. "I can probably arrange that."

She swallowed, wondering if she'd made a mistake. But she hid her doubts behind a brusque tone. "Fine. We'll need to work out a plan. And a cover story, if you're still opposed to telling your family what we're doing."

"We can do that. You don't have any cakes ordered for that week?"

"Actually, I'd blocked that week out for a vacation," she said, wondering now if she had somehow sensed that she needed to leave some spare time in her calendar.

"And you're willing to spend your vacation helping me track down a ghost?"

"He's not a ghost," she said firmly. "He's as alive as you are."

"Looks like you've got one week to prove that."

"That will be enough."

His eyebrows rose. "Something else you just know?"

She shrugged. "I guess we'll find out, won't we?"

Turning on one heel, she snatched up her purse as she headed for the door, suddenly needing some distance from him. "I'm heading home. We'll talk later about the details of our search."

"Right." He followed her toward the door.

She opened it before he could reach her, stepping quickly out into the evening air. Her hand was still on the door when she turned to say, "By the way, Ethan—"

He stood just inside the house, watching her make her exit. "Yeah?"

"You didn't kiss me as a test. You kissed me because you wanted to."

He crossed his arms over his chest in what might be

interpreted as a defensive posture, though his drawl was meant to sound rather mocking. "Think so, do you?"

"I do." And that was the woman speaking, not the sort-of psychic. "But from now on? Wait for an invitation."

She closed the door with a snap, giving him no chance to respond.

"So, Cassandra, have you been sleeping better since Dr. Thomas changed your medications?"

"Much better." Whatever name she had used, whatever identity she had assumed, Cassandra had always been a highly skilled liar.

"That's wonderful." Melanie Hunt, the counselor who had been assigned to Cassandra, smiled her cheery smile and made a note in the file she held.

Cassandra had often wondered whimsically if Melanie had found a way to have that smile permanently affixed. Some sort of clever plastic surgery, perhaps. She was pretty sure she could tell the perpetually perky psychologist that she was planning to sneak out of the institution that evening and rob a bank, and Melanie would just smile and nod and make another note in the file. Maybe ask Dr. Thomas to prescribe some new meds.

But that was unkind. And she was trying to be a better person these days. She was sure Melanie meant well. Hers wasn't an easy job, and she was performing it to the best of her abilities. Which were just a tiny bit limited, that old, less charitable voice whispered.

"What shall we talk about today?" Melanie asked brightly.

Arranging the almost-finished sweater she was

knitting more comfortably on her lap, Cassandra started another row. "You're directing this session. Isn't that your call?"

"I'd like to talk about something important to you, Cassandra. Why don't we chat about your childhood?"

The needles stuttered a bit, but she spoke evenly. "It was fine. Quite nice, actually."

She really was a very accomplished liar.

"Would you like to tell me any amusing stories from your youth?"

"Not particularly."

Melanie managed to smile and sigh in exasperation all at the same time, proving she had some impressive talents of her own. "Oh, Cassandra, you are such a hoot."

A hoot. Well, she supposed it was better than some of the names she'd been called in her time.

Someone tapped on the open door. "Is this a bad time?"

Both Cassandra and Melanie smiled then. Cassandra noted that Melanie's smile had a newly flirtatious element to it. Melanie was wasting her time in that respect, she thought as the handsome young doctor strolled into the room. Dr. Thomas wasn't interested. He'd learned his lesson about dating coworkers.

"Dr. Hunt." He greeted her with professional courtesy, then turned to pat Cassandra's shoulder, his tone turning warmer. "How's my favorite patient?"

Even though she suspected he said that to everyone here, she couldn't help but respond, "I'm doing very well, thank you."

His eyes were more perceptive than Melanie's as he searched her face. This one was a little harder to deceive.

"I was just trying to persuade her to tell me a funny story from her childhood," Melanie chirped. "But she doesn't seem to be in the mood to reminisce."

Cassandra almost told her that she was never in the mood to reminisce. Living in the present had been her philosophy for the past twelve years, since she had married Lawrence and put her past behind her. But she kept those thoughts to herself.

She sensed that the doctor and the psychologist shared a look before Dr. Thomas said, "That sweater is a very intricate pattern, isn't it? You've made quite a bit of progress on it. It looks almost finished."

"Almost." It had taken her quite a while, actually, since she'd never become very fast at knitting and this was the most complicated pattern she had ever tried. But there had been no reason to hurry, after all.

"Are you making it for yourself?"

"Oh, no. It wouldn't fit me."

"Someone special?"

"Mmm."

The doctor laughed ruefully. "You don't give an inch, do you?"

"You know what they say. Give an inch, and they'll take a mile."

Shaking his head, he patted her shoulder again. "Then we'll wait until you're ready to share."

What he didn't add was, *If ever,* though it was implied. That was one thing about this private and very expensive facility. As long as she had the money to stay, she could pretty much cooperate with the staff or not, as she desired. And since she had plenty of money and cooperated just enough not to be a problem for the administration, she wasn't going anywhere.

The headphones covering Aislinn's ears discouraged conversation from the chatty-looking little lady sitting in the seat next to her. It wasn't that Aislinn was trying to be unsociable, exactly. She was simply too nervous to engage in conversation with an overly friendly stranger.

She didn't do well in close quarters, like this airplane cabin. So she sat here, crammed into a window seat, her hands clenched in her lap and soothing music playing in her ears, trying to focus on the melodies and the lyrics.

Unfortunately the music didn't drown out the insights she picked up from all the people crowded around her. The sweet-natured woman next to her wanted to talk about her grandchildren, whom she was on her way to visit. The man in front of her was a salesman wearily embarking on yet another business trip. Someone else was traveling with a woman who was not his wife—and hoping his wife would not find out.

She wasn't reading thoughts. She couldn't add many details to those flashes of information. There was nothing she could do for any of them, though she supposed she could inform the philanderer that his wife would learn about the girlfriend—and that it was going to cost him. Big.

Maybe it was possible that she would learn something she could change. An impending car accident or some other tragedy she could divert with a warning. But that would involve tracking down whomever she'd picked up on, and then convincing that person that she wasn't a nut and that her warnings should be taken seriously. And because she didn't want to be led away in a straitjacket or—equally daunting—believed and then expected to possess more wisdom and guidance, she had no intention of opening herself to more.

She cranked up the music just a little, as if doing so would drown out any extra thoughts in her head. Instead she found herself thinking about an all-new problem. The man who was supposed to be waiting for her when the plane touched down at the airport in North Carolina.

It had been more than a week since she'd last seen Ethan. He'd left Arkansas on Saturday, two days after they'd spent the evening with Joel's computer. They had seen each other only once after that night: he'd stopped by her shop to tell her he was leaving, and to inform her that he would call with details of their trip. Unless she'd changed her mind? She had coolly informed him that of course she hadn't changed her mind and she would look forward to his call.

She had spent the eight days since staying very busy at work and firmly not thinking about kissing Ethan.

She couldn't quite believe she was doing this, joining Ethan in another state on a search for the brother he didn't even believe was still alive. But he had pretty much dared her to prove she wasn't crazy, and she'd been unable to resist the challenge.

Maybe she needed to prove a few things to herself, as well.

Ethan was waiting at the baggage claim, as he had promised he would be. She spotted him almost immediately after turning the corner. Though he wasn't tall enough to tower over the milling crowds and was doing nothing to call attention to himself, her gaze went straight to him.

He leaned against a wall, arms crossed over his chest, his expression inscrutable. More than one passing woman checked him out, some rather lingeringly, but he didn't seem to notice any of them. He simply waited. For her.

Spotting her, he straightened away from the wall and moved toward her. He wore jeans. And wore them well. His shirt was a green polo that fit just tightly enough. He was a man who would look equally masculine and comfortable in a three-piece wool suit as he did in denim and soft knit.

She had hoped the week they'd spent apart had given her a chance to recover from her initial problematic attraction to him. It hadn't.

Telling herself this was simply a normal reaction to a good-looking man and that there was no reason she couldn't put it aside and concentrate on their mission, she stepped forward to greet him. "Hello, Ethan."

"Did you have a good flight?"

"Yes, it was fine," she replied blandly, seeing no need to embellish.

"I've rented a car. Let's get your bags and get out of here."

She nodded and turned toward the luggage carousel, hoping she looked as blasé about this whole thing as Ethan did.

Chapter Ten

Fifteen minutes later they were on the road in the small but comfortable vehicle Ethan had procured for them. "Did you have any problems clearing your schedule for the trip?" he asked.

"Not too many. My employees can take messages until I get back. How about you?"

"I had to reschedule a few things, but I handled it."

"One of the perks of being self-employed, right?"

"Yeah."

She shifted into a more comfortable position, rearranging the seat belt across her lap. Like Ethan, she had dressed casually for travel. She wore a tan wrapped top over a cream-colored tank, slightly darker brown twills and brown leather flats. She hadn't given a great deal of thought to her outfit, simply choosing pieces that were nonbinding and wrinkle-resistant.

"So what was your cover story to get away? I assume you didn't tell anyone you were joining me here?"

She shook her head, trying not to feel too guilty about the fibs she had left behind her. "I told everyone I'd been working too hard and needed a week to rest. Since that wasn't much of a lie, no one really thought too much about it. Except for Nic, of course."

"And what did you tell her?"

"I just told her I had some things I needed to do and I didn't want to talk about it yet."

"That satisfied her?"

Aislinn smiled a little. "Of course not. But we respect each other enough to give each other space when we need it. She knows I'll tell her what I want her to know when I'm ready."

When he merely nodded, she asked, "What about you? What did you tell everyone about being out of town this week?"

"I go off on business trips fairly often. No one thinks twice about it. They know they can reach me on my cell phone if they need me."

"Same here." Which reminded her that she hadn't turned her phone back on after getting off the plane. She dug into her canvas-and-leather bag and rectified that right then. Not that she expected any calls for a while.

"I thought we would grab a bite of lunch and then get started," Ethan said a few minutes later.

"Fine."

"You in the mood for anything in particular?"

"No. Anything's okay with me."

Taking her at her word, he turned into the parking lot of a tidy diner that advertised "country cooking" and appeared to be popular, judging by the number of vehicles in the smallish parking lot. "There should be something here we'll both like," he remarked.

"I'm sure you're right."

A smiling waitress in jeans, T-shirt and apron greeted them at the door and escorted them to what appeared to be the last available table. "What can I get you to drink?"

"Iced tea for me, please," Aislinn replied.

Ethan nodded to second the order, and the busy waitress bustled off to get their drinks, leaving them with menus to peruse until she returned. Aislinn took a moment to look around. It was a little early for the Sunday after-church lunch crowd, but the diner was still full. The other patrons seemed to be enjoying their meals, talking and laughing so that the room was filled with the clatter of tableware and the sounds of camaraderie.

No one seemed particularly interested in her and Ethan, and for once she was picking up nothing from anyone else that gave her any cause for concern. She could enjoy her lunch and feel as normal as anyone else here.

She looked back across the table to find Ethan studying her over the top of his menu. "What?"

"I was just wondering what was going through your mind when you looked around the room," he answered candidly.

She glanced down at the menu, trying to concentrate on the choices. "I doubt that you would understand," she murmured.

"Try me."

It was almost tempting, just to see how he would react. She was rather relieved when the waitress returned then with their drinks, giving her a chance to change her mind.

"Have y'all decided what you want?"

Aislinn looked quickly down at the menu again and chose the first thing that appealed to her. "I'll have the grilled chicken breast."

"Just bring me the special," Ethan said, handing over his menu.

Making note of their orders, the waitress nodded and hurried away again.

"Well?" Ethan prodded.

She spoke brightly. "I was just wondering what our agenda is for today. Do you have an idea of where we should start?"

He frowned, making it clear he knew she was holding back, but he let it pass. "I thought we'd examine the accident site first, maybe get a feel for the surrounding area."

She nodded. "That sounds like a good place to start."

She suspected that it wouldn't be easy for Ethan to go to that spot. It might be less difficult for him if he could truly believe, as she did, that Kyle hadn't died there—but maybe not. Either way, Ethan had lost his little brother that day. Even if they did find him again, those missing years could never be recovered.

Their food was delivered with impressive promptness, and they ate without much conversation. Aislinn's meal was very good, well cooked, nicely seasoned. The juicy chicken breast was accompanied by side orders of rice and steamed broccoli. Judging from the speed with which it disappeared, Ethan's lunch must have been good, too. The daily special turned out to be fried pork chops with red potatoes mashed with the skins, green beans and corn. Country cooking, just as the signs outside had advertised.

"You chose well," she said when they'd both eaten all they could. "That was delicious."

He shrugged. "You know what they say—if you want a decent meal, look for the place with the most pickup trucks in the parking lot."

She chuckled. "An interesting measure for culinary excellence."

A fleeting smile quirked his lips. "Probably not the best way to choose gourmet cuisine."

"True. But I'm not all that into gourmet cuisine, anyway. Though I do enjoy a place that serves interesting desserts," she added lightly.

"Even though you don't want to be a pastry chef in one of those snooty places."

She shrugged. "Doesn't mean I can't appreciate the efforts of the ones who do enjoy it."

"Can I get y'all some dessert?" their waitress asked, approaching the table again. "The coconut pie's good today. Got some chocolate cake, too."

Neither of them wanted dessert. "I'll take the check now," Ethan said.

Aislinn reached for her purse. "I'm paying my own way."

"I've got this." Obviously Ethan wasn't in the mood to argue about it just then.

Because she didn't want to cause a scene, Aislinn gave in, promising herself they would talk about the expenses of this trip later. While they were on a quest to find the truth about his brother, she had made the decision to accompany him. He hadn't offered to pay her, and she didn't want him to. Taking pay—even letting him buy her meals—felt too much like some of the "psychic" cons he'd been so leery of when he had first met her.

Aislinn was dressed in brown again. Ethan was beginning to seriously question her predilection for the rather drab color. Not that she could ever look drab, with that striking black hair and those dark chocolate eyes—but still. Remembering how good she had looked in the bold red of her bridesmaid dress, he wondered why she didn't choose bright colors more often.

"What's your favorite color?" he asked as he drove the windy mountain roads, breaking a silence between them that had stretched almost since they'd left the restaurant a half hour earlier.

The question seemed to startle her. He rather liked being able to take her by surprise occasionally.

"My favorite color? Why?"

"Just making small talk. You have a favorite color, don't you?"

"I—um…green. Emerald-green, a little brighter than your shirt."

"Really?" Seemed she could startle him a bit, too.

"Why does that surprise you?"

"I guess because I haven't seen any evidence of it. I've never seen you wear that color, didn't see it in your decorating, either, at your home or your shop."

She gave a self-conscious smile. "I don't have to wear it or decorate with it for it to be my favorite color. It just gives me pleasure to see it."

"Bet it would look good on you."

"It looks good on you. Green, I mean. What's *your* favorite color?" she asked quickly, as if to cover a slip of the tongue.

He didn't even have to stop to think about it. "It's red." As of fairly recently, actually.

"Do you wear red very often?"

Chuckling at the way she had turned the question back against him, he admitted, "Not since I quit going to football games back home. The Danston Cardinals," he explained. "Everyone wears red."

"Actually, I knew that. Nic told me. It's why she picked red for her wedding color—because she and Joel fell in love during his homecoming weekend."

"Yeah, that was quite an event. Heidi, the class officer who arranges all those events, kept them busy partying all weekend—until the balcony collapse that last morning, anyway. That put an end to the reunion. It was a miracle no one was more badly injured."

Nodding her agreement, Aislinn asked, "Does your class have reunions?"

"Yeah."

"And do you go?"

He gave her a look that effectively answered her question.

"Oh," she said, smiling wryly. "Of course you don't."

"No. I see the people I want to see when I want to see them. As for sitting around with a group of near strangers, reminiscing about stuff we did twenty years ago, well, that would bore me into a coma."

"Somehow that doesn't surprise me."

"Has your class had a reunion yet?" He wasn't sure exactly how old she was, but he assumed she had to be close to Nic's age.

"They had a ten-year reunion last summer."

"I suppose you went?"

"No, actually. I skipped out on it."

Something in her voice made him glance her way. She was looking out the side window, so that all he could see of her face was her profile. Yet that was enough to let him see that she didn't really want to talk about her school years.

"Neither one of us is interested in reliving the past, I guess," he remarked lightly.

"I suppose not."

"So why are we making this trip?"

That made her look at him. "This isn't about the past," she reminded him. "Not primarily, anyway. It's about the present—and the future."

"So what do you see in my future? Do you predict that I'll find my brother and we'll all live happily ever after?"

"You'll find your brother. But whether you live happily ever after is up to you."

Inexplicably amused by her slightly acerbic tone, he chuckled. "Maybe I like being grouchy and bitter."

"Trust me, you wouldn't be the first person I know to enjoy living that way."

It was obvious that she was referring to someone in particular. One of her parents, maybe? Both?

He realized that he knew absolutely nothing about her past except that she had grown up in Cabot and had been friends with Nic for most of her life. Lizzie had implied that Aislinn's childhood had been a difficult one, but he didn't know what that meant. How hard it had actually been.

Because this didn't seem to be the time to ask, he changed the subject. "Look at those directions I've written in that pad in the console, will you? I'm not sure where I'm supposed to turn once I get to Bellamy, the town where we lived. I looked up the directions on the Internet last night."

"Have you been back since you moved away?" she asked, opening the notepad.

"No. We moved three years after Kyle...disappeared and we never went back. I was nine. As far as I know, my parents pretty much lost contact with all their friends there, and we had no relatives there to visit."

If she had noticed his slight stammer about Kyle's fate, she didn't comment. "They wanted to start a new life in Alabama—away from people who knew them before they lost Kyle."

"Yeah, I guess. And it worked. We all made friends and felt at home there. Joel barely remembers living in North Carolina at all."

"But you do."

He shrugged. "I was older. But I wasn't opposed to

the move. Even that young, I knew somehow that it would be easier for Mom to live in a new house, away from all the reminders of Kyle."

He paused a moment and then something made him add, "I still remember the day we moved into our house in Danston. Mom told us to choose our rooms. Joel looked up at her and asked which room was going to be Kyle's. I can still see her face when she told him that Kyle wouldn't have a room in the new house but he would always have a place in our hearts."

And then, embarrassed that he had revealed so much and wondering what it was about Aislinn that brought out things like that from him, he spoke again before she could comment. "So where do I turn? It's a highway number, I think."

Probably sensing that he needed the change of topic, she began to read the directions to him.

Ethan guided the rented vehicle to the curb and put it into Park. "That's it. That's the house where we lived."

Aislinn studied the tidy redbrick, ranch-style house across the street. The trim and shutters were cream, as were the posts that supported the roof of the long front porch. A redwood fence surrounded the backyard, but the neatly manicured front lawn was open and inviting, with a couple of large shade trees and flowers in well-tended beds.

Whoever owned the place now took pride in their home and kept it looking nice. It appeared much the same way when the Brannons had lived here, Aislinn thought. There had been toys on the lawn and a swing set in the backyard. A happy home but a noisy one, with three boisterous little boys inside.

It had been very quiet in that house after Kyle's disappearance, she thought sadly. While the laughter had gradually returned, the tone had forever been altered. The family's broken hearts had mended but had never been made completely whole again. And no matter what happened in the future, those scars would never completely heal.

"Your Christmas tree was always in that window," she said, pointing. "And you had a dog. A small brown one."

"A dachshund," he confirmed. "We called him Teddy."

She could almost see him, a dark-haired little boy chasing after a small, brown dog. "You had a hiding place in the backyard."

"There was a big bush. The branches came all the way down to the ground, and I could hide inside them and watch people without them seeing me." He looked at her as he spoke, evidently trying to determine if she was only guessing or if it was more than that.

"You went there a lot after Kyle left. And you took something of his in there with you."

"A toy," he said, speaking more slowly now. "A stuffed cat. I thought if I concentrated really hard on the toy, Kyle would come home. He'd be okay, and my parents would stop crying."

"You kept that cat. Even when your parents packed away Kyle's things, you kept the toy and you didn't tell them. You took it with you when you moved—because you thought as long as you kept it, there was always a chance Kyle would come home to claim it. Do you still have it?"

"No."

She frowned. "Yes, you do. It's packed away. You haven't looked at it in a long time. But you have it."

"Okay, I do," he admitted a bit crossly. "How do you know these things, Aislinn?"

She was appalled to feel her eyes suddenly fill with hot tears. "I don't know," she whispered.

Visibly rattled, he asked quickly, "You aren't going to cry, are you?"

Forcing her eyes to dry, she shook her head. "No. Sorry."

She didn't know how to explain her uncharacteristic emotionalism. Part of it was because of the vague images that had filled her mind. The sad little boy grieving for his lost brother. The happy family whose lives had been so tragically and so permanently changed.

She was also genuinely unnerved by the clarity of the images she was receiving. She didn't see the need to tell him again that she didn't usually pick up so much information. That the past few weeks had been different for her—and more than a little frightening.

She had learned to live with what she considered heightened intuition. She had never asked for more. Never wanted more.

Clearing her throat, she spoke more brusquely. "So Carmen left here with your brother that afternoon. In the rain, knowing there was extensive flooding in the area."

Seeming relieved by the return to objective facts, Ethan nodded. "Yeah. She left the house at about two o'clock that afternoon. One of the neighbors saw her drive away and thought it was strange that she would go out in that weather."

"When did the anonymous call come in about the car going off the road?"

"An hour and a half later. Just after three-thirty."

"It took her that long to get there?"

"We'll find out. We're going to drive there from here."

"Were any of her things missing? Clothing, money, that sort of thing?"

"I don't know yet. If so, Mom didn't seem to know anything about it."

"From what we saw in the newspaper accounts, there didn't seem to be much of an investigation. It appeared to be taken as fact that the car went over and the bodies were washed away."

"There was no real reason to think otherwise. Carmen had been our nanny for eighteen months. She seemed perfectly content with her life. She had no money, nowhere to go. Why would she have faked her death?"

"Maybe you'll have the chance to ask her." But something about that statement didn't feel right. Maybe he would never find her. Or maybe Carmen had died since. Except for the picture of Kyle she had drawn in her sleep, she had no insight into what had become of Carmen or Kyle since they'd disappeared into that storm.

Ethan put the car into gear. "Let's find the spot where the car went over. Check your watch. We'll see how long it takes to get there from here."

* * *

"It was somewhere along this stretch of road. I'm not sure exactly where."

A metal guardrail provided a border between the two-lane highway and the steep drop-off to the river below. Ethan had already informed her that the river was popular for canoeing and kayaking in the shallows and white-water areas and for fishing in the deeper parts. It was deeper in this area, the ever-moving surface glittering in the late-afternoon sun, a few fishing boats tucked into small inlets or drifting with the current. She pictured it as it had been on that afternoon, swollen several feet above its current level, rushing violently downstream and carrying anything in its path along with it.

Glancing at her watch, she said, "We've driven twenty-five minutes from the house. There's no way it took her almost an hour and a half to get here."

Doing his own mental calculations, he nodded. "Even in the bad weather, it shouldn't have taken her that long. Either she drove a more circuitous path to get here, for some reason, or she made a stop along the way."

He pulled over to the narrow shoulder and stopped the car. "This guardrail wasn't here thirty years ago. Just the shoulder and then the drop-off. The newspaper report said there weren't any skid marks from braking—though the water on the road could have had something to do with that, if she hydroplaned."

Gazing at the river, Aislinn chewed her lower lip, trying to visualize the accident.

"Well?" he prompted after a moment. "Are you picking up anything?"

She turned to look at him. "'Picking up anything?'"

"You know. Getting any additional information by being here at the actual site. Like you did at the house."

She supposed she couldn't blame him for asking. She had sensed several details at the house that he hadn't told her. Turning toward the river again, she tried to focus. Open her mind.

"Well?" he asked again.

Sighing, she shook her head. "I don't know what I'm supposed to be doing. I just feel kind of foolish, like I'm—I don't know—playing psychic or something."

"What were you doing when that stuff came to you back at the house?"

"Nothing. I just looked at the house and I saw the Christmas tree and the puppy. And you, hiding in the backyard."

He looked beyond her to the river, then put the car into gear again. "Let's try something. Keep looking out the window."

"What?"

"Just let me know if you get anything," he said, pulling back onto the highway and proceeding slowly down the road.

She wasn't sure what he was talking about, but she cooperated by gazing out the passenger window, watching the river go by. The passing scenery was rather mesmerizing, and she could feel her thoughts drifting like the lazy current.

Until she suddenly went tense and said, "Here. Pull over."

They were perhaps a mile and a half farther than before. Glancing into the rearview mirror to make sure no one was coming up behind them, Ethan drove onto the shoulder again and pushed the gearshift into Park.

The road was a bit wider here, with shoulder on both sides and a clear view of the river. No trees to impede the view, or to have stopped a car had there not been a guardrail.

"It happened here," she said, staring at the water with a heavy feeling in her chest.

"What exactly happened?" He spoke very quietly, matter-of-factly, neither belief nor skepticism audible in his tone.

She frowned. "There was another car."

"Someone ran her off the road?"

"No."

"The witness was driving the other car? The woman who called in the accident?"

"I don't—no."

"Then what is it about the other car?"

Dragging her gaze from the river with an effort, she looked at him instead. He was watching her closely, his expression unreadable but his body tense behind the steering wheel.

She wished she could know what he was thinking. But because he seemed to be willing to listen to what she said, she told him what she had just realized. "Someone picked her up here. Her and Kyle."

"After the accident, you mean?"

She shook her head. "They never went into the river, Ethan. There was no accident. The car was deliberately pushed over the side, and she and Kyle left the scene in someone else's car. I think Carmen was the anonymous woman who called the police."

Chapter Eleven

"Cassandra. Cassandra, can you hear me?"

She opened her eyes blearily, wondering why the voice sounded so strange and hollow. Why it was so hard to clear her vision. To clear her mind.

"There you are. Can you see my face? Do you know who I am?"

Blinking a couple of times, she forced herself to focus. "Dr. Thomas. What are you—what's going on?"

He patted her hand, and she realized that his smile was strained, his face tight. "The staff couldn't wake you," he explained quietly. "You were out so deeply that they were getting ready to call for an ambulance by the time I arrived."

"No. No ambulance. I don't want to go to a hospital. I'm fine."

Slipping his stethoscope into his ears, he pressed the bell to her chest. "I'll be the judge of that."

She concentrated on keeping her breathing and heart rate steady. Calm. "I'm fine," she repeated evenly. "I guess I was just really tired. I haven't been sleeping well lately, you know."

"Cassandra, that was more than just sleeping. You were unconscious. But your heart sounds good," he conceded slowly, wrapping the stethoscope around his neck again. "Your blood pressure is normal."

"Perhaps it was a reaction to the new medication," she suggested.

"Maybe." But he didn't look convinced, and she was beginning to worry that he was still considering hospitalization.

"I really do feel fine," she said. "Why don't we give it a few hours and let me prove that there's no lasting effect? It isn't as if I won't have people to check in on me."

He nodded reluctantly. "If that's what you want."

"It's what I want. Please."

Sighing, he gave in. "All right. We'll see how it goes."

Relief flooded through her. "May I have a glass of water? I'm really quite thirsty."

"Of course." Glancing around at the nurse who'd hovered behind him, the doctor satisfied himself that water was being fetched before turning back to Cassandra. He sat on the side of the bed, the concern slowly fading from his face. "You gave us quite a scare."

She smiled briefly. "I'm sorry. It wasn't intentional."

"You've been feeling well lately? No shortness of breath? No dizziness?"

"Except for a few episodes of insomnia, I've been very well. No complaints at all."

Those too-perceptive eyes searched her face. "And when you do sleep, do you dream?"

An odd question. She mulled it over for a moment while she sipped the water the nurse had given her before leaving to take care of other duties. She wasn't sure how to respond. It wouldn't be with the truth. "Sometimes. Nothing particularly interesting. But no nightmares like before, if that's what you're asking."

A lie, of course. But if it kept her out of the hospital, she considered it justifiable.

Still in that casually conversational tone, he asked, "Do you dream of the past or the present?"

Not certain where he was going with this, she shrugged lightly against the pillows. "I don't remember, exactly. Just dreams."

"Many of the residents here dream of their childhood, you know. They tell me about reliving some of their happiest moments when they're asleep."

"Lucky them to have had such happy childhoods to relive."

"Does that mean your own wasn't so happy?"

She merely looked at him.

"Ah. Now you've gone quiet again."

"I can't say the same for you."

He chuckled. "Always have a comeback, don't you?"

"Oh, I try."

"I'd like to think we've become friends, you and I."

"I'm very fond of you, Dr. Thomas."

"Then why won't you talk to me? Tell me a little about yourself?"

"Why is it so important to you to hear about my past?"

"Because I think it's haunting you," he replied simply. "I think you've been carrying some very heavy baggage that's weighing you down now, causing you a great deal of pain. And it seems to be getting heavier, for some reason. I'd like to help you with that load if I can, Cassandra."

"You're a fine young man," she told him, touched by the sincerity in his voice. "You care very deeply about your patients. Too much, perhaps. But there comes a time when all of us must accept that we've done as much as we can. There's nothing you can do for me, Dr. Thomas, except to take care of my physical health, as you do the other residents here."

"I'm not sure I can accept that."

She shrugged again.

He shifted and reached for the chart that had rested beside him on the bed. "The medical history you've given us is far from complete, but from what I've read, you've had a difficult time of it even before you were stricken with MS."

"I've had my share of ailments." Some of which she had brought on herself, through dangerous and self-destructive behavior. That was before she had learned to accept—and forgive—herself.

"You told me you married your last husband when you were fifty. Were you ever married before?"

"Once. Briefly. What about you, Dr. Thomas? Ever come close to getting married yourself?"

She could see that he was on the verge of telling her that they were talking about her, not him—but then he seemed to think better of it. Perhaps it occurred to him that she would be more likely to share if he did. "I almost asked someone to marry me once."

"Really? Why didn't you?"

He chuckled. "Someone else beat me to it."

"Then you weren't meant to be with her."

"That's what I told myself at the time. Didn't stop me from kicking myself for waiting too late, though."

"You'll find someone else." She had no doubt of that.

"Maybe. I'm not in any hurry, though I wouldn't mind having a family someday." Turning that into a smooth segue, he asked, "You never had children with your first husband?"

She turned her head on the pillow, looking away from him, trying to hide the sharp pain that went through her in response to his question. It wasn't the type of pain that he could treat, so there was no need to burden him with it. "I'd like to get up now, Dr. Thomas. Would you mind sending someone in to help me on your way out?"

He sat without moving for a few moments longer, obviously aware that he had just been gently dismissed. And then he stood, looking grave. "I'll be back to check on you this evening. And I'll probably have you monitored periodically during the night, just to make sure you don't slip too deeply into unconsciousness again. In the meantime, if you need anything, anything at all, have someone contact me, will you?"

"Thank you, Dr. Thomas. I want you to know that I

deeply appreciate your concern. There haven't been many people who have cared for me as sweetly as you have."

He leaned over to touch her cheek, the gesture so tender that it almost brought tears to her jaded eyes. "Someday you'll feel like talking to me, Cassandra. And then maybe we'll find a way to take some of that weight off your shoulders. You must be awfully tired of carrying it by now."

"Go take care of Mrs. Kennedy," she said, her voice a bit hoarse as she blurted the first thing that came to her mind in an attempt to control her strained emotions. "She's not doing so well today. She needs you worse than I do."

He straightened. "Now how would you know that? You've only just started the day."

"I, um—she was feeling poorly yesterday. I don't expect she's any better today."

"I'll go check on her. Remember, call if you need me."

"I will. Thank you."

She watched the door close behind him and only then did she allow herself to swipe at her eyes. She would never reveal all the details of her past, of course. Dr. Thomas would never understand—and she couldn't bear to see the disillusionment in those gentle eyes if he ever learned the truth.

It was hard enough for her to remember the things she had done before she had taken the name Cassandra and created yet another new life for herself.

"Where do you want me to put your bags?"

Aislinn looked rather blankly around the nondescript

motel room, then waved a hand toward one of the two beds. "Just put them there."

It was one of the handful of complete sentences she had uttered in the past hour, since they'd left the spot by the river and had driven back into town. She'd had no comment about the motel he had selected, speaking up only to insist on paying for her own room. And now she stood in the center of her room, frowning at her bags as if she had never seen them before.

She was pale again, he noted, studying her face. The skin around her mouth was tight, as if she were holding her emotions in check by force. He thought again that she would have to be an extremely gifted actress to be faking her reactions to the visions she'd been having— or whatever he should call them.

He was a long way from believing that what she had told him was anything more than figments of an overactive imagination, but he conceded that she seemed to believe everything she said. Whatever she was going through while she struggled with these episodes, it looked real. And obviously difficult for her.

"Do you want to rest a while before dinner? We can start tomorrow looking for people who knew Carmen."

"I, um—whatever you want to do."

"Get some rest. I'll be next door if you need me."

She nodded but remained where she stood.

He moved toward the door, then paused before opening it. He felt funny leaving her here like this, so dazed and wan. "Aislinn."

"Yes?"

"Are you okay?"

"Yes, I'm fine," she said in that same monotone.

He sighed and moved back toward her. Taking her arm, he guided her to the bed and put both hands on her shoulders, pushing downward until she sat on the edge. "Lie down."

She blinked a couple of times, rousing a bit. "What?"

"Lie down," he repeated, punctuating the command with another little shove that tumbled her backward against the pillow. Lifting her feet, he removed her shoes, tossed them on the floor and then stepped backward. "Get some rest."

She started to say something and then she fell silent, curling one hand beneath her cheek as she turned on her side and closed her eyes. He thought she might be asleep by the time he reached the door.

He stood there for a few more moments, just looking at her. She was absolutely one of the most beautiful women he'd ever met. He wouldn't have been a normal, straight male had the thought of joining her there in that cozy bed not crossed his mind. But talk about complications…

Pushing a hand through his hair, he let himself out of the room, closing the door silently behind him.

Aislinn woke with a start, not quite certain where she was. She was wearing her clothes, though her feet were bare, and she lay on top of the covers. There was a light shining in her eyes.

Pushing her hair out of her face, she sat up, only to find herself facing the chair in which Ethan sat reading a newspaper. His long legs were stretched out in front of him, feet crossed at the ankles, and he looked quite comfortable there in her room. *Why* was he there in her room?

He looked up in response to her movement. Checking her face with a shrewd glance, he nodded in satisfaction. "You look better."

She had only a vague memory of checking in. Of being urged by Ethan to take a nap. It embarrassed her now to think about how out of it she had been.

"What are you doing in here?"

Setting the newspaper aside, he straightened in the chair. "You were sleeping so heavily I was a little concerned about you. You've been out for several hours."

It was unlike her to sleep so deeply that he had been able to enter her room without rousing her. It made her uncomfortable to think that he'd been there watching her sleep, even though she was touched that he'd done so out of concern.

"I don't know why I was so tired," she said, swinging her feet to the floor. "I hardly ever do that."

"Are you hungry?"

She pressed a hand to her stomach. "Actually, yes, I am. What time is it?"

"It's almost eight o'clock." He turned to the small, round table tucked into the corner and picked up a white paper bag. "I didn't know if you would want to go back out tonight, so I brought food."

"That sounds good. Give me a minute to freshen up."

He nodded. "I'll go get some cold drinks out of the vending machine. What do you want?"

"Anything diet."

"I'll be right back."

As she washed her hands a few minutes later, it occurred to her to wonder how he had gotten into her room while she was sleeping. The door automatically locked when closed. The only explanation was that he had taken her key with him.

At least he knocked when he came back from fetching drinks. Crossing the room to let him in, she had the uncomfortable suspicion that he had knocked, before, too, but that she'd been sleeping too deeply to hear him. No wonder he'd been concerned about her.

They sat on opposite sides of the little table, knees almost touching as Ethan pulled food out of the bag. As he unwrapped deli sandwiches, he explained that he'd chosen something that didn't have to be served warm. Turkey, cheese, lettuce and tomato on whole-wheat bread, along with two bags of baked potato chips. For dessert, he'd purchased two white-chocolate-and-maca-damia-nut cookies.

Aislinn picked up her sandwich. "This looks very good."

"I figured you wouldn't mind a light dinner since we had a heavier lunch."

"I don't mind at all." It was funny how ravenous she was all of a sudden. She ate the sandwich and all the chips, then started on the cookie, washing it all down with the diet soda Ethan had brought her.

She looked up to find him watching her. Self-conscious now, she wiped cookie crumbs from her fingers. "I was hungry."

"I noticed."

"It was good," she said, reaching for her soda can. "Thank you."

"You're welcome. So what happened to you this afternoon, Aislinn?"

She had been expecting the question. She wished she knew how to answer it. "I'm not sure, exactly."

"You keep saying this is all different for you. Does that include the way you zoned out after having those visions by the river?"

"They weren't—" She had started to speak automatically, but she stopped herself, knowing that this time she wouldn't have been telling the truth. They *had* been visions. There was no other way to refer to them. "No. Nothing like that has happened to me before."

"You really believe the things you saw are true?"

"You can confirm part of them," she reminded him. "Everything I saw at the house. As for what I learned at the river, yes, I believe it's true. Carmen Nichols faked her own death and kidnapped your brother. Someone helped her. I don't know who. I don't know where they went when they left there. But I know that's the way it happened."

"And you expect me to believe it, too. Just because you say so."

She sighed, thinking that they had been over this too many times already. "Believe what you want, Ethan. I'm only trying to help."

He leaned back in his chair, slinging one arm over the back, his expression thoughtful. "Has it occurred to you that you continually send me mixed signals? Even as you continue to deny that you are a psychic or a seer or whatever people might call it, you tell me you somehow know things you couldn't possibly know without some sort of extrasensory perception. You tell me you're simply a good guesser, but then you ask me to accept that you are absolutely certain that Carmen stole my brother."

Nervously gathering the debris from their casual meal, she nodded. "I can't blame you for being confused. I'm pretty bewildered myself by all of this."

He thought about that, then asked, "Why do you fight it so hard? Your ability, I mean."

She flinched. "Wouldn't you? Would you want to be seen as a freak? An oddity?"

"I've been considered an oddity for most of my life," he answered with a shrug. "People don't understand why I'm not interested in amassing a fortune for myself. Why I choose to live quietly, in solitude for the most part. Why I don't play the social games most people choose to play."

"But you came from a good family. You live the way you do out of choice, not because there's something 'strange' about you. People may call you odd or antisocial, but they don't call you 'spooky.'"

A muscle twitched in his jaw, letting her know that the label rang a bell with him. Either he'd already heard someone refer to her that way or he had thought it himself. Maybe both.

"You haven't said much about your family," he commented instead.

She hadn't said anything about her family, actually. And she wasn't sure she wanted to do so now.

And yet…she was aware that she and Ethan had been discussing the most intimate details of his own family's past, things that had to have been painful for him to share with her. She doubted that anyone else knew he still had Kyle's stuffed cat tucked away in his possessions, yet she had forced that admission out of him by confronting him with what she had seen. Despite his expressed doubts, he was here, looking into the things she had told him, on the off chance that she could actually be right.

The least she could do would be to tell him a little more about herself, since she was asking him to have so much faith in her word, she thought reluctantly.

"I don't talk about my family much because it's too painful," she confessed.

"Then forget I mentioned it," he said immediately. "We'll talk about something else."

She suspected that he wanted to change the subject as much for his benefit as for her own. Ethan wasn't comfortable with delving into emotions, as witnessed by his near panic when he'd seen the threat of tears in her eyes. That was probably a result of surviving too many emotional scenes in his past, when his family had lost their youngest child and, later, Joel's beloved first wife.

"It's okay," she assured him with a slight smile. "I don't mind so much telling you about it."

Still looking a bit doubtful, he nodded.

Aislinn drew a deep breath. "I should start with my grandmother, I suppose. She died before I was born," she said, keeping her tone even, impassive. "Everyone said she was a troubled woman who suffered from bouts of depression. She died of a heart attack just after her fortieth birthday."

"That must have been hard on her family."

She nodded. "My grandmother was an only child whose own parents both died relatively young. She and Granddad married when she was in her early twenties. From the few stories I heard about their marriage, it wasn't a particularly happy one. Granddad was a rather humorless man, hardworking, extremely religious, old-fashioned when it came to gender roles. He didn't know what to do with my grandmother during her 'spells,' so he pretty much let her suffer through them on her own."

"How many children did they have?"

"Just the one. My mother."

"Having a child didn't make your grandmother happier?"

"I'm afraid not. And my mother wasn't an easy child. She was unruly, stubborn, rebellious. Maybe it was her nature, maybe a result of the way they raised her—or a combination of all those things—but by the time she was twelve she was already sneaking out at night, running wild with kids who were a lot older than she was, regularly getting into trouble with the law. I was told that my grandfather tried everything he could think of to straighten her out, from preaching to punishment to counseling, which wasn't exactly common in the early sixties—but nothing worked."

Ethan took a sip of his soda without commenting, though Aislinn knew he was absorbing every word.

"My mother was fifteen when her mother died. A lot of people blamed it on her—including my grandfather,

I think. Maybe he never told her so, but she probably suspected it."

Wincing, Ethan muttered, "Rough on her."

"Yes. It must have been horrible for her. Anyway, after that, she went completely out of control. My grandfather washed his hands of her a year later."

"She was on her own at sixteen?"

She nodded.

"And then she had you."

He was obviously envisioning a teenage pregnancy. Logical assumption, but she shook her head. "Not for another sixteen years."

That made his eyebrows shoot up in surprise. "She was thirty-two when you were born?"

"Yes. She would be sixty now. About the same age as the nanny who took Kyle, I guess."

"What happened during those years before you were born?"

"She took off right after Granddad threw her out, and no one heard from her in all those years. And then she showed up with me. Granddad was seventy, still living in the same house where he'd raised my mother. He still owned and operated the hardware store he'd bought just before my mother was born. Granddad was stunned to see his daughter after all those years, but he welcomed her home and invited her to stay with him as long as she needed to. He once told me that he loved me from the moment he saw me. He said I looked like his mother, whereas my mother looked like his late wife."

"What was your mother's name?" he asked, as if suddenly realizing that she hadn't mentioned it before.

"She was christened Mary Alice Flaherty. When she was six, she insisted on answering to Maxie. At fourteen, she became Butterfly. Remember, this was during the early hippie years, a culture she embraced wholeheartedly."

"Butterfly Flaherty." He shook his head. "And people called her that?"

"Her friends did, I guess. Her father called her Mary Alice."

"So then she came back to town, carrying you," he prompted, totally into the story now.

"Right. She used the nickname Allie then. She was past thirty but still eccentric. The way she was described to me, her hair was waist-length and dyed bright red. She wore peasant clothes and sandals and she was driving a '69 VW van. I was six months old."

"Your father?"

"She never mentioned him," she said with the slight pang that always accompanied the awareness that she would never know her father. "She told my grandfather that it wasn't relevant. He rarely talked about my mother to me, but I once heard him mention to my aunt that my mother had implied there had been another child—a boy—that she had abandoned. That she still felt guilty about leaving behind. He told my aunt that he couldn't believe then that his daughter would have abandoned a child, but when she did basically the same with me, he figured it was probably true."

She cleared her throat, trying not to think about lonely childhood longings. "Granddad never knew I heard him say that, but I was pretty stunned by the revelation. It's possible I have a brother somewhere I've never met. I don't know for certain, but then, I've never been able to sense much of importance about anything that matters most to me."

"But your mother chose to keep you."

"She said she'd wanted to try to be a mother to me but she'd realized she couldn't handle it alone."

"So she stayed in town then? Raised you with her father's assistance?"

"No." She laced her fingers together on the tabletop, trying to keep the pain in her heart out of her voice. "Apparently they spent a very strained evening together, and then she left town again before dawn the next morning. Alone."

Chapter Twelve

She had caught him by surprise again. "She left you with your grandfather?"

"She didn't even tell him she was leaving," she added grimly. "He woke up the next morning to find her van gone and me crying in the playpen she'd put me to sleep in. She didn't even leave a note, but Granddad said he knew when he saw me that she wouldn't be back."

"What kind of mother would do something like that?"

"Mine."

The stark reply hung in the air for a moment before he asked, "So you were raised by your grandfather?"

"Believe it or not, yes. He had a younger sister, Maureen, who'd been widowed a few years earlier. She moved in with him to help raise me. She was in her early sixties, and her own son was long grown."

"Still, they were both fairly old to become responsible for a six-month-old baby."

"There were people who suggested that they should give me up for adoption, but they both refused. I think my grandfather felt guilty that he'd failed with my mother. As for Aunt Maureen, she was lonely and at loose ends since losing her husband and she told me later that I gave her new purpose in her life. Her son, my cousin Alex, was and still is a confirmed bachelor, so she didn't expect grandchildren. She and Granddad both saw me as a way to atone for past parenting mistakes, I guess."

"A big load for a small girl to carry."

She shrugged.

His eyes grave, he asked, "What was your childhood like?"

"Quiet. Orderly. I had everything I needed."

"Not everything."

Because she couldn't really argue with that, she let his comment slide. "I was a very good child," she informed him. "I never broke the rules, never talked back, never missed curfew."

"That doesn't surprise me," he murmured.

She drew another deep breath. Since she had told him so much already, she might as well tell him the rest. "When I was five, I told my grandfather that the house across the street was going to burn down. Two days later, it did."

"How did he react to that?"

"With fear. And anger. He ordered me to close my mind to thoughts like that. He said they were unnatural. Probably unholy. And that they could only lead me into misery and isolation."

Ethan rubbed his chin thoughtfully. "Your grandmother had the gift?"

"Probably."

"Your mother?"

She nodded. "Whenever I slipped during my childhood and said something I shouldn't have known, Granddad gave me the lecture again. He said my mother had always pretended to be 'special' and that it had only led her into trouble. He said he had tried to punish those thoughts out of her and it hadn't worked, so with me he wanted to use reason. Logic. He told me no one would like me if they thought I was weird. That people would be afraid of me. Or that they would try to use me to their own advantage. He told me that I should pray every night to be normal."

Ethan said something beneath his breath that might have been a curse.

"He meant well," she said wearily. "He'd seen his wife descend into depression and his daughter lose herself in drugs and rebellion. He didn't want the same things to happen to me."

"So you listened to him."

"Yes. I worked even harder to be the perfect child. But I wasn't very good at being 'normal,'" she added with just a touch of bitterness. "I didn't always know I was saying something that other people would find strange. So I quit talking much at all, which made me even more of an oddball among my age group. Nic was the first person I met who never seemed to find me strange. Who accepted my occasional insights with such matter-of-factness that it made me feel almost average."

"You continued to live with your great-aunt after your grandfather died?"

"Yes. She was in good health until I turned seventeen, when she suffered a mild stroke. I took care of her during my senior year of high school and for six months after my graduation. She suffered another stroke then. A fatal one."

"That's why you didn't go to college. You were taking care of your aunt."

"She took care of me all those years. It seemed only right."

Ethan was quiet for so long that Aislinn became self-conscious again. What was he thinking? She didn't want his pity; that wasn't the reason she'd told him the things she had. She certainly didn't want him to wonder about things like hereditary mental illnesses. He wouldn't be the first to mention that possibility.

After another few moments he said, "You've had an interesting life."

She was surprised into a weak smile. "Not so much. I told you, I've lived very quietly. I discovered my talent for cake decorating when I was in my teens and I parlayed it into a career. I learned to interact better with people through my business and I've made a few good friends. I'm quite content, but my life is hardly noteworthy. I suppose my mother was the one whose life could be considered interesting."

"Is she still living?"

"I don't know."

"You've never heard from her?"

"I got a birthday card from her on my tenth birthday. All it said was, 'I think about you every day.' Granddad and Aunt Maureen considered not giving it to me because they thought it might upset me, but eventually they decided to show it to me and warn me not to read too much into it."

"It must have meant something to you for her to tell you she hadn't forgotten you."

"I wasn't sure how I felt about it," she admitted. "In some ways, it was harder to know that she hadn't forgotten me but she still chose not to see me. I still wonder what became of her. Why she left me with her father, whom she never got along with herself."

"If it's true that she knew things, maybe she somehow understood that you would be better off there. That you would grow up safe and relatively happy there. You can't argue that you've turned out well. You have friends, a nice home, a successful business. You probably had a much better life than you'd have had with her, drifting around in an old VW van."

"You're right, of course." But there had been many times in her quiet, predictable, ordinary life when she had fantasized about being on the road with her wild, free-spirited, adventurous mother.

"Did she name you?"

"Yes. I was lucky, I guess, that she didn't name me Rainbow or Strawberry or Moonbeam, not that Granddad would have left it at that. Aislinn isn't exactly a common name in Arkansas, but at least it sounds like a name. Even my middle name is ordinary enough."

"Joy," he said, proving that he remembered. "Much better than *my* middle name."

Intrigued, she cocked her head. "What is yours?"

His mouth twisted. "Albert."

She didn't laugh. But it took an effort. "You don't really look like an Albert."

"It was my grandfather's name. My paternal grandfather. He lived in Michigan with his third wife. We used to go visit him when I was a kid. He had a fishing cabin on a lake that I thought was the greatest place in the world. I always said that when I grew up I was going to live in a house just like it."

"And do you?"

"Pretty close. I've got a house on a river. You can fish off the dock in my backyard. Sit outside in the evenings and watch deer walk along the riverbanks."

"It must be lovely."

"I like it."

She stood to throw away the trash from their dinner. "Well, now you know my entire life story," she said lightly. "Sorry you asked?"

He didn't smile. "No."

"Anything else you want to know?"

"How can you know what happened to Kyle and not know whether your own mother is still living? Or whether she had any other children?"

She sank onto the foot of the bed, resting her hands on either side of her. "As I said, I almost never get any feelings that affect myself. I don't know why I pick up some things and not others. It seems to be completely random and usually pretty vague. Today was literally the first time in my life I've been able to deliberately focus and pick up such clear details."

"Doing so seemed to take a lot out of you. You went out like a light when we got here."

"I felt completely drained," she admitted. "It was a little unnerving, actually."

"Tell me about it."

She cleared her throat. "Sorry if I worried you."

He inclined his head. "I don't know what to make of you," he said after another pause. "I still have trouble believing that you can somehow know all these things."

"That's understandable. I just hope you no longer think I'm some sort of con artist. Or crazy."

"I don't think you're a con artist."

After another moment she smiled ruefully. "I notice you didn't reassure me about the craziness part."

He pushed his chair back from the table and stood, looking down at her with an expression she couldn't quite decipher. "I told you once that I thought maybe we're both crazy. The more we get into this bizarre investigation, the more I wonder if I was right."

Rising, she gazed up at him. "You came here because, even though it's hard for you to believe, you had to know if there was a chance I'm right about Kyle."

"Yeah. I guess."

"What other reason would there be?"

He reached out to cup her cheek in one hand. "You can't think of any other reason I'd want to spend time with you?"

Warmth flooded through her, centering in the skin

beneath his palm. She blurted the first words that came into her mind. "You think I'm spooky."

"Hell, yeah."

Her sputtered laugh was smothered beneath his mouth when he lowered his head to hers.

Aislinn's slender body arrowed neatly into the water of the swimming pool, creating hardly a splash. Standing in the shadows of the motel building, Ethan watched her begin to swim laps, her strokes steady and strong. She seemed to be working off some sort of tension.

He knew the feeling.

She was the only one in the pool. Technically it was after hours, and the pool was closed, though no effort was made by management to stop late swimmers. She shouldn't be out alone at night like this. He supposed she felt relatively safe because of the motel rooms surrounding the pool, but it still wasn't a good idea. Crossing his arms over his chest, he leaned against the wall, silently standing guard.

Watching over her was hardly a hardship. He didn't think he'd ever seen anything more beautiful than Aislinn moving so sleekly through the glistening, softly lit pool water. She was modestly dressed in a one-piece black bathing suit—another example of her habit of dressing to fade into the background. He could have told her she was wasting her time. Aislinn could wear a sheet of burlap and still catch the eyes of every man within sight of her.

He understood now why she worked so hard to blend into the crowd. She had been abandoned by her mother and raised by aging relatives who'd done their best to drill the uniqueness out of her. *Different* was a pejorative to her. *Average* a compliment.

She did a practiced turn at the deep end of the pool and swam in the other direction. He'd heard her leave her room earlier, an hour after he'd surprised them both with a good-night kiss. He had been tempted to follow that kiss up with more…and then some…but a remaining shred of common sense had given him the strength to pull away, to tell her good-night and walk out of the room. She hadn't tried to detain him.

This wasn't a woman he wanted to get involved with. For one thing, Aislinn wasn't the no-strings-dalliance sort. She came with complications he had assiduously avoided during the past few years. Not to mention the complications that had to do with Aislinn herself.

He was giving her a few more days to show him any evidence that Kyle was still alive, and then he was putting both her and her psychic claims out of his mind, he promised himself. That was the best he could do—even if it was taking every ounce of self-control he possessed to keep himself from taking her slim, wet body into his arms and making them both forget about anything beyond tonight.

Wrapping herself in a large towel, Aislinn slid her feet into sandals and shook her dripping hair out of her face. The grounds of the little, out-of-the-way motel were quiet, pretty much deserted at this hour, but she wasn't concerned for her safety. Her room was only a few steps away.

She had needed the exercise of swimming. Maybe

she'd slept too long that afternoon or maybe she was still keyed up from her talk with Ethan. Or from something else with Ethan. But after he'd left her, she'd been filled with pent-up energy that no amount of pacing the small confines of her room could burn off. Looking out her window, she'd seen the pool and had impulsively changed into the bathing suit she had packed at the last minute.

The swim had helped. A little. Maybe she would be able to sleep now. If she could find a way to prevent the memory of Ethan's kiss from keeping her awake all night.

Fat chance.

She moved toward her room, resigned to a restless night. Her breath caught when someone moved out of the nearby shadows.

"You really shouldn't be out here by yourself at night," Ethan said, his expression grim when the light fell on his face. "Especially since you're no good at seeing your own future."

Trying to steady her racing heart, she cleared her throat. "You startled me. But I was ready to run and scream if I had to."

"If I'd been someone who wanted to hurt you, I wouldn't have given you a chance to run or scream," he pointed out.

He stood between her and her door. She took a step toward him. "Then it's a good thing you don't want to hurt me, isn't it?"

"Yeah." His voice was rougher now. "I guess it is."

The same restless energy that had driven her into the pool impelled her forward. He remained where he stood until she stopped, inches away from him. The cool water still dripped from her hair and slid down her body. She could almost fancy that it evaporated in the heat of Ethan's gaze.

Sliding a hand up his arm and around to the back of his neck, she lifted herself onto tiptoes and pressed her wet body against his dry one. Her lips only a breath from his, she asked, "How are you at telling the future, Ethan?"

"Not worth a damn," he muttered hoarsely.

"So I guess you weren't expecting me to do this," she murmured and pressed her mouth to his.

"No," he said when she gave him a chance to speak a few moments later. "I wasn't expecting that."

"Then this should come as a real surprise to you." She wrapped both arms around his neck and kissed him again.

With a low laugh deep in his chest, he pulled her closer, smothering her mouth beneath his.

"I wasn't going to do this." Ethan's voice was low, his expression rueful as he loomed over her.

Lying on her back on her bed, she reached up to him. "Neither was I."

He slid the straps of her bathing suit off her shoulders, lowering his lips to her still-damp skin. "Probably not a good idea."

Arching her neck to give him better access, she sighed. "No, probably not."

"There's still time to come to our senses."

She nuzzled her cheek against his soft brown hair. "You first."

He pushed her suit farther down and groaned. "Maybe it's too late after all."

Offering herself to him, she closed her eyes. "Definitely too late."

Drifting in a haze of satisfaction, Aislinn forced her eyelids open when the bed shifted. "Where are you going?"

Reaching for his clothes, Ethan replied, "I'm heading for my room. Get some sleep. We'll get an early start in the morning."

Lifting herself to one elbow, she pulled the sheet across her and watched him dress. "Second thoughts?"

"Second. Third. Fourth."

She couldn't be offended since she felt much the same way. "You don't have to worry about it, Ethan. I'm not going to cause any scenes when you ride off into the sunset."

He looked down at her. "Suddenly you know the future?"

Chuckling wryly, she murmured, "I think pretty much any woman could tell what you're thinking now."

Looking annoyed, he shrugged into his shirt. "That's bull."

"Maybe."

"So *you're* not having second thoughts?"

"Second. Third. Fourth."

Her dry repetition seemed to ease some of his tension. He paused by the side of the bed. "Sorry. I guess I've just had a lot to process today."

"I know. It's been a long day for both of us."

He leaned over to brush a surprisingly gentle kiss against her lips. "I'll see you in the morning."

"All right. Sleep well."

He paused again at the door, one hand on the knob. "Aislinn?"

"Yes?"

"No matter what happens, I'm not really sorry."

She smiled. "Neither am I. No matter what."

He let himself out the door, closing it firmly behind him.

Aislinn fell back against the pillows. Okay, maybe that had been a mistake. And she was well aware that she was the one who had initiated it, though Ethan had certainly been a willing participant. And maybe her heart was going to be bruised, if not broken, before this rather quixotic quest was over.

But whatever happened, she wasn't sorry. For once, she had done something bold, reckless, a little wild—and while she had no intention of radically changing the quiet, rather conservative life she had led to this point, it had felt good to step out of her rut for just this one night. Amazing, actually.

Maybe there was a tiny bit of her mother in her, after all.

Chapter Thirteen

"Little Ethan Brannon. I can't believe it."

Ethan forced a smile, though he was more tempted to grimace.

Eighty-year-old Odessa Hester folded her hands across her large stomach and beamed at him and Aislinn as they sat side by side on the afghan-draped and pillow-crowded sofa in her overfurnished living room. There was barely room for their knees between the sofa and the knickknack-covered coffee table. The big recliner that supported Odessa's substantial weight was wedged between another table and a three-light floor lamp.

The smallish room also held an entertainment center with a medium-size television set, two packed-full curio cabinets, a wing chair, a rocking chair and a large leather ottoman. Every flat surface was covered in bric-a-brac, most of it of the inexpensive, dollar-store variety, but there wasn't a speck of dust in sight.

He vaguely remembered this house. Every room was like this one, filled almost to bulging with furniture and decorations. When he was little, he'd found it fascinating, with so many things to see, so many nooks and crannies to explore. Odessa had happily invited him and his brothers to explore as much as they wanted. To make it more fun, she'd hidden candy and small toys before they'd arrived to keep them entertained while she and his mother visited. Funny how he'd forgotten that until today.

"How is your dear mother, Ethan?"

"She's fine, thank you, Mrs. Hester."

"Oh, honey, you might as well call me Odessa now. Everyone does. Are you sure I can't get either of you some pie? A soda?"

Both he and Aislinn politely declined. He could tell Aislinn was captivated by the large, friendly woman in the colorful clothing.

"So tell me why you're here, Ethan. Are you showing your girlfriend where you lived when you were a little boy?"

He didn't bother to correct her about Aislinn's identity, though the term made him vaguely uncomfortable. "Something like that," he said instead. "I haven't been back here since we moved away, you know."

His former next-door neighbor sighed lightly. "I know. I'd hoped your folks would come back to visit sometimes, but I guess it was just too painful for them, bless their hearts."

"They've made a good life for themselves in Alabama," he assured her. "Dad stays busy in his orthodontics office and Mom's involved in a half dozen charities, of course."

"She always did love to stay involved in the community."

"Still does."

"And your brother? How's Joel doing? I know he's a doctor, because your mother still sends me a Christmas card every year and tells me family news. He lives in Arkansas, doesn't he?"

"That's right. Did you know he got married again two weeks ago?"

"No, I didn't. Good for him. Do you like your new sister-in-law?"

"Very much," he said sincerely. "I think she and Joel will be happy."

"That's nice to hear. Your family's suffered enough loss. It's time for you all to be happy." She beamed at Aislinn, who squirmed a bit self-consciously on the couch. "How long have you known Ethan, hon?"

"Not very long," Aislinn replied. "I met him through Joel's new wife, Nic, who's been my best friend for years."

"Well, isn't that nice? Do I hear more wedding bells in store for the Brannon family? You aren't getting any younger, you know, Ethan. What are you? Thirty-three? Thirty-four now?"

Tempted to squirm himself, Ethan said lightly, "I'm thirty-six. I'll turn thirty-seven in a few weeks."

"Thirty-six," she repeated with a slow shake of her head. "Can you imagine that? I'll have to tell Vic when he gets home from visiting his brother out at the nursing home. He'll be sorry he missed you. He always thought the world of your dad, you know."

Ethan barely remembered Odessa's husband. He had a faint memory of a large, quiet man who always carried sticks of gum that he liked to hand out to the neighborhood kids. Odessa and Vic had never had children of their own, but they'd taken pleasure in being honorary aunt and uncle to dozens.

More than ready to change the subject, Ethan got to the point of their drop-in visit. "Odessa, do you remember Carmen Nichols?"

"The nanny who died with poor little Kyle? Of course I remember her. She used to have coffee with me sometimes while Kyle took his nap. Nice woman, if a little reserved."

"Reserved in what way?"

"Oh, you know. Didn't talk about herself much. Wouldn't really share details about her life. She'd talk about you kids and about movies and television programs she enjoyed, books she'd read, that sort of thing.... But getting her to talk about herself was like pulling teeth."

"So you don't really know anything about her."

"Well, you know I'm pretty good at drawing people out. I learned a few things."

Sitting up straighter, he asked, "Like what?"

"Mind if I ask why you want to know?"

"Aislinn and I are looking into the accident," he said candidly. "My family still has a lot of questions about exactly what happened that day, and I decided it's past time one of us tried to find some answers. Like why

Carmen took Kyle out that day and where she was going when she left the house with him."

"I don't blame you for wondering," Odessa said with a sigh. "I've asked myself those same questions many times during the past thirty years."

"You were the one who saw her leave the house that afternoon, weren't you?"

Odessa nodded. "I was looking out to see if the rain was letting up. I saw her putting Kyle in the toddler seat she kept in her car for him. Never was a very good seat," she added with a shake of her head. "But she didn't take him out very often, so your mama wasn't too worried about it, though I know she planned to buy a new one when she got the chance."

"Did Carmen see you watching her? Did she look upset or anxious?"

"I don't know if she saw me. I don't think so. I was too far away to see her expression, exactly. And she had a hood over her head to protect her from the rain. One of those yellow slicker-type raincoats. She was very fond of that coat. She wore it every time it even drizzled a little. Your daddy used to tease her about it, call it her banana coat."

"You said you drew a little out of her about her private life. Can you remember anything in particular?"

Odessa waved her pudgy hands in a vague gesture. "She told me she'd married young but that he'd died. She said she'd grown up in Mississippi but that she was an orphan."

Ethan frowned. "Mississippi? Not Florida?"

"No, I'm pretty sure it was Mississippi."

"She told my mother she was from Florida and that her family disowned her when she married."

"That's odd. It's not at all the story she told me."

"Did she have any special friends around here? Anyone she dated or just hung out with?"

Odessa nodded. "There was one woman about her age. They used to go to movies and stuff together. Sometimes the other girl would come over to your house while your mama was off volunteering, and she and Carmen would watch soap operas together in the afternoon."

"Do you remember her name? Do you know if she's still in this area?"

"Oh, yes, I still see her occasionally. She works over at the Kroger store on Maple Street. Her name is Natalie, but I can't recall her last name, if I ever knew it."

"That's fine. You've given us quite a bit as it is."

"I wish I could tell you more. I can understand why you'd be struggling with this. It has bothered me for thirty years that I didn't try to ask Carmen where she was going on such a stormy day."

"No one would have expected you to do so, Odessa. Just one more question, if I may. Does the name Mark mean anything to you in connection with Carmen?"

Aislinn looked at him thoughtfully while Odessa gave the question a moment's consideration. And then Odessa shook her head. "Not that I know of."

Ethan couldn't think of anything else to ask. Though he was impatient to move on, it took another twenty minutes for them to take their leave of Odessa. She wanted to reminisce a bit more about the years when his family had lived next door, and Ethan didn't want to be rude when she was being so nice and helpful.

"Thought we were never going to get out of there," he said when he and Aislinn were on their way.

"Mmm. She was nice."

She sounded distracted, distant. She'd been rather quiet all morning—and he supposed he couldn't blame her for that, considering the way he'd run out on her last night, but this was different. He was beginning to recognize this tone.

"What did you pick up in there?" he asked.

"Carmen wasn't from Mississippi. Not from Florida, either."

"So where was she from?"

"I'm not sure. But it was somewhere in the South," she suggested tentatively.

"Have you ever figured out what connection the state of Georgia has to all of this? Do you think that's where Kyle is now?"

"Maybe."

"You're full of maybes today."

"Sorry. It's the best I can do."

"It does seem suspicious that Carmen told my mother and Odessa different stories about her past," he conceded. That was hardly proof that she had snatched his brother, of course, he reminded himself.

He didn't have to express his lingering reservations. Aislinn merely nodded. "She had a lot to hide."

"Did you sense anything else while we were talking to Odessa?"

Her face was somber when she nodded. "Only that

it's a good thing you had a chance to visit with her today. You'll appreciate that memory soon."

Startled, he tightened his hands on the steering wheel. "You think she's ill?"

"Very ill."

"Should we go back and tell her? Maybe she should go to the doctor...."

"She knows, Ethan."

He reminded himself that Aislinn could be wrong. He still wasn't ready to accept everything she said as fact. But still, he was glad now that he'd spent that extra twenty minutes with Odessa.

"Of course I remember Carmen. She was the best friend I ever had."

Natalie Mitchell's pale blue eyes filled with tears as she spoke, and she dabbed at them with the back of one weathered hand. A hard-lived sixty, Natalie had once been a redhead, though her hair was mostly gray now. She had probably never been pretty, but the face they saw now was the victim of too much sun and too many frowns.

They'd found Natalie at her home, after being told by one of her coworkers that she wasn't working that day. The coworker had given them her last name, and Ethan had found her address in a local telephone book. More trusting than she should have been, she had let them into her rented duplex when they'd told her that they were there to ask about Carmen.

"Who did you say you are?"

"Ethan Brannon," he told her. "My brother was with Carmen the day she...died."

If Natalie noticed the slight hesitation, she didn't react. Aislinn, however, had noted it.

Natalie swiped at her eyes again. "You were the oldest," she murmured. "I remember you. I used to come over to your house to visit Carmen sometimes. Don't you remember?"

Sitting in one of two undersize armchairs in the shabby living room while Aislinn sat in the other and Natalie on the couch, Ethan shook his head. "No, I'm afraid not."

"Well, you were little. And, come to think of it, you were already in school. Joel was in kindergarten. I'd come over while the baby was asleep and me and Carmen would watch TV and sometimes play cards."

Aislinn studied the woman, picking up no trace of deception in her. Sadness, yes. Regrets, definitely. But there seemed to be no doubt that Natalie believed her friend had died when everyone else thought she did.

"I'm simply trying to understand exactly what happened that day," Ethan explained to her.

Natalie sighed heavily. "If you knew how many times I've asked myself that same question…"

"Can you tell me about Carmen? I don't remember her very well. I remember that she was quiet."

"She was a little quiet around people she didn't know very well," Natalie agreed. "But once you got to know her, she was a lot of fun. We used to laugh over those card games…." She sighed again as the words trailed off.

"Did she talk to you much about her past?"

"Neither one of us wanted to talk much about our pasts," Natalie muttered. "Mine hadn't been so great, and she told me hers wasn't, either."

"Did she say where she grew up? I've heard Florida—or maybe Mississippi."

Natalie frowned and slowly shook her head. "She just said she moved around a lot when she was growing up. She didn't claim any particular state that I recall."

"What about boyfriends? Did she date? Do you remember a guy named Mark?"

"I don't remember anyone named Mark. Carmen didn't date much. She didn't meet many men working at the day-care center where I met her. Nor sitting there with you kids. After work, she tended to go straight home and watch a lot of TV. I didn't date much, either," she added. "Not for lack of wanting to. I just rarely met anyone who was interested in going out with me."

Aislinn sensed that there was something more. "So she wasn't seeing anyone before she disappeared?"

Natalie hesitated, then said reluctantly, "Maybe someone in the weeks before. There were several nights when I asked her if she wanted to do something and she told me she had other plans. It hurt my feelings that she wouldn't tell me more. Up until then, I thought we told each other everything."

Someone had picked Carmen up on that highway that afternoon, Aislinn mused. Someone who had agreed ahead of time to meet her there and help her spirit away the child in her care. She didn't know who it had been, whether man or woman, but it hadn't been Natalie.

"You've been very generous with your time," Ethan said, standing, which signaled Aislinn to rise to her feet, as well. "Just one more question, if I may, and I'm afraid it's going to sound strange."

Rising, Natalie looked at him questioningly. "What is it?"

"Do you think there's any possibility that Carmen didn't die that day? That she chose to simply disappear instead, taking my brother with her?"

Aislinn was startled to hear him so bluntly sum up her theory of what had happened that day. This was the first time he had even suggested to anyone else that there was a possibility Carmen had survived.

Natalie had started shaking her head before Ethan even finished asking the question. "I don't know where you got that idea, but it's crazy," she said flatly. "Carmen was happy here. There was no reason at all for her to do anything like that."

Holding up a hand in a conciliatory gesture, Ethan spoke soothingly. "I didn't say it did happen that way. I was just asking. You can probably understand that I've always looked for reasons to hope that my brother would be returned to the family someday, and since the bodies were never found…"

Calming a little, Natalie nodded. "I can see why you wouldn't want to give up hope. I felt the same way for a long time after Carmen disappeared. I missed her so much, you see. She was the only real friend I had back then. And it bothered me to know she would never have a proper burial, never have a place where I could take flowers every so often and, you know, sort of talk to her.

"So every weekend for the next year I'd go out and drive along the river, as far down as I could imagine the flood carrying her. Sometimes I'd get out and walk the banks, looking for something, anything, that would give me a clue of what happened to her. I thought the authorities gave up too soon, you see. I wanted them to keep looking, even after they called off the search. And then one day I found proof that Carmen had been washed downstream, several miles from where the car went over the side."

Aislinn and Ethan exchanged a startled look.

"You found proof?" Ethan asked.

Natalie nodded. "Wait here."

She disappeared into the back of her home, then rejoined them carrying an old-looking, square cardboard box. She set the box on the table, lifted the lid and carefully drew out a tattered, stained strip of once-yellow weatherized fabric.

"This was a piece of the coat she was wearing that day," she murmured, stroking it gently with one hand. "I found it wedged under a rock along the riverbank. There was a lot of other debris from the flood in that area, too, at a place where the river is really wide and deep. I figured the stuff was deposited there as the water receded and that Carmen's body was probably trapped under more rubble somewhere underwater. I go there now every year on the anniversary of her death and throw flowers in the water. It makes me feel like she has a burial place after all."

Ethan was obviously shaken by the revelation, but his voice was steady when he asked, "How do you know this was a piece of her coat? It's just a scrap of cloth."

Natalie turned the fabric to reveal the other side. "Her initials are embroidered on it. See? C.N. She did this herself one day while I was visiting her. This was her coat, Ethan. I guess it was ripped off her in the flood, then shredded by debris. It's one of the few things I have left of her."

"Do you know what became of her belongings?" Aislinn asked, one of the first questions she had asked of the woman.

"There weren't that many. Since she didn't have family, the things she'd left at her apartment were sold to pay off her bills. She didn't have a life insurance policy, nor a will. Whatever was left over was donated to charity, I believe."

"Do you mind if I touch that fabric?"

Though she looked surprised, Natalie shrugged. "I suppose not."

Aislinn sensed Ethan watching her closely as she placed her hand on the torn cloth. A moment later she dropped her hand. "Thank you."

"You're welcome, I guess." Natalie folded the fabric back into the box. "Is there anything else you want to know?"

Shaking his head, Ethan put a hand on Aislinn's arm and nudged her toward the door. "That's all, thanks."

She saw them out with polite bemusement.

Sitting across a restaurant table from Ethan, Aislinn watched him pick at his plate of spaghetti without much evidence of either appetite or pleasure. His thoughts were obviously far away.

It was early for dinner, but he hadn't seemed to know what else to suggest when they'd left Natalie's place. He'd said he was hungry, but the way he acted now proved that hadn't been true. She knew he'd needed time to think about what they had learned today and something to occupy his hands while he did so.

Having ordered a chef's salad for herself, she poked her fork into a plump cherry tomato and asked, "What's our next step?"

He looked up from his plate, fully meeting her eyes for the first time since they'd left Natalie. "I don't know about you, but I think I'll head back to Danston in the morning. I have work that needs to be done there, and I'm pretty sure I'd be wasting my time staying here any longer."

"What about the search for your brother?"

He set down his fork, giving up all pretense of eating. "Isn't it obvious that we've reached a dead end? We've talked to everyone we can find who even remembers Carmen from thirty years ago. There isn't a shred of evidence that she didn't go over the side of that road. We don't know where she lived before she came here, don't even know for certain that Carmen Nichols was her real name. Though I can't imagine why she'd have lied about that."

"You're starting to doubt me again, aren't you?"

"I have always doubted you," he reminded her. "Not your motives, necessarily. You seem to believe the things you say. But as for their accuracy—"

"You think I'm making it all up."

"I didn't say that, either. Don't put words in my mouth. I'd be a fool to deny that you have some special gifts. An ability to sense some things that most people can't. I don't think you're crazy or unnatural or any of the things your grandfather obsessed about. Maybe it's like you've always said, just heightened intuition or a real talent for guessing things. But this time I think maybe you let yourself get carried away."

"Carried away," she repeated, pushing her salad bowl aside. "You're suggesting that I've concocted this whole tale about Carmen faking her death and disappearing with Kyle."

"Not intentionally," he assured her.

"That's supposed to appease me?"

"I'm not trying to appease you," he said crossly. "I'm just trying to be honest."

"And you honestly think I'm wrong about what happened to Carmen and Kyle."

He sighed and pushed a hand through his hair. "I have to repeat, there's no evidence at all that they're still alive. We have a witness who saw her get in her car with Kyle and who saw her wearing the yellow coat that Natalie found months later, far downriver from where the car went in. Though we never found her, there was a witness who called the police and reported the car going over. There were certainly some inconsistencies with the stories Carmen told about her background, but it's a big leap from a few fibs to kidnapping."

"Kyle is alive, Ethan," she said wearily, knowing she had already lost.

"Then tell me where he is."

"I wish I could."

"You touched Carmen's coat. Did you get anything from it about what really happened that day? Where she is now if not in the river?"

"No. I didn't get anything. I didn't expect to, really, but I thought it was worth a try."

"So there's nothing more we can do, is there? Unless you get some sort of vision that leads straight to Kyle, it looks like you and I have done all we can."

But he didn't expect that to happen, she thought sadly. Because he had closed his mind to the possibility that she might be right.

As they drove in silence back to the motel, she thought about his turnaround. She knew he had been on the verge of believing. That she had almost convinced him she could be trusted.

But then they had made the mistake of getting too close—and in his self-protective retreat, Ethan had looked for any excuse he could find to pull away. For some reason, that scrap of yellow cloth had provided all the proof he needed to put an end to this uncomfortable journey.

He walked her to her door but made no move to enter. "I'm going to make arrangements for a flight home in the morning. I assume you'll want to do the same."

She nodded, hearing defeat in her voice when she said, "Fine."

"I'm planning to spend the evening in my room, catching up on some computer work."

"Yes, I'll do the same."

"Let me know what time you need to be at the airport. We'll want to get an early start."

"I'll call you as soon as I have a time."

"Good." He hesitated a moment longer. "You probably shouldn't swim after the pool closes tonight. It really isn't safe for you to be out alone like that."

"I won't be swimming tonight."

He nodded and turned away. "Good night, Aislinn," he said without looking back at her.

"Goodbye, Ethan," she whispered as she closed herself into her room.

Aislinn's plane was scheduled to leave before Ethan's, and their gates were at opposite ends of the airport. "There's no need for you to stay here with me," she told him after he walked her to hers. "I have a book in my bag."

"Are you sure?"

"I'm sure. It's only going to be an hour, and I've been trying to find time to finish this book for weeks."

He looked almost relieved, which didn't do a lot for her ego. "I guess I'll leave you to your reading then."

"All right." She held out her hand. "Have a safe flight, Ethan."

He looked at her hand a moment before taking it. And then he spoke impulsively. "Look, I'm sorry, okay? I guess there was a part of me that really wanted to believe you."

She drew her hand from his. "And another part of you that never wanted to even try."

"You can't say I didn't give it a shot," he said, sounding defensive. "I came here with you, didn't I? I spent the whole day yesterday talking to strangers, pretty much making a fool of myself."

"I didn't force you to do that. It was always up to you whether you wanted to act on the information I gave you."

"And I acted. But you still seem to be disappointed that I'm ending the search. What else would you have me do, Aislinn?"

"I'm not sure. Maybe try to find employment records or tax records or something to trace Carmen's background, which might give us a clue where she went."

"That would be a major undertaking, even if we could find anything useful. I don't have that kind of time to spend on what would probably turn out to be a futile exercise. You don't, either. You have a business to run. Orders to fill."

"I'm aware of my responsibilities to my clients," she said coolly.

"So go back to them. I appreciate your effort to help my family, but in the long run, maybe it's better this way."

"Better?"

"I don't believe Kyle's out there, okay? But if he is, maybe he's perfectly happy. Maybe he's got a great life and we'd just be messing it up by tracking him down. Maybe he wouldn't want a new family. For that matter, my family's doing pretty well right now. Mom and Dad are healthy and content, Joel's a blissful newlywed, I'm satisfied with my life. Why risk upsetting everyone again?"

She was stunned by his seemingly careless words. "Are you saying that if I could give you definitive information on how to find Kyle, you would turn your back on him? Because it would be easier to pretend none of this ever happened?"

They stood in a relatively private spot in the busy terminal in a back corner of the waiting area. Still, Aislinn was aware of a few curious looks as passing strangers sensed the tension between them. She didn't care.

"You really think I don't know why you've been such a loner the past few years, Ethan?" she continued in a low voice. "Why you avoid people except in the line of business? Why you live in your isolated river cabin where no one but family ever visits you?"

"You don't know me at all," he growled. "No matter what you think you might sense about me."

"I know you've been hurt. Disappointed. Betrayed. You've lost people you loved, you've loved people you shouldn't have. And now you protect yourself. Too well, maybe."

He moved a step backward. "You're really reaching now."

"Am I? Because I think you're afraid, Ethan. I think you're afraid to start believing Kyle might still be out there. Because you think it would hurt too much if you found out later that you were wrong."

"I don't—"

But she didn't give him a chance to finish the denial. "It all comes down to me, doesn't it? Whether you can trust me. And trust is something you don't give anyone anymore.

"You're afraid," she said again. "Afraid that if you did start to trust me, you could end up disillusioned if it turns out that I really have been playing you for a fool. Afraid that I see too much when I look at you, more than you let most people see. Afraid of getting your heart broken again. That's why you don't trust me to get near it."

His brows were drawn downward into a fierce frown. "You don't know what you're talking about."

"I know you were in love with Heather. And that the night she married your brother, you told yourself you would never open your heart like that again. And you haven't. Whenever anyone gets too close, you run. Just like you're running now."

The words had left her before she could stop them. Maybe because she knew this was her one last chance to convince him that she understood his fears. And that he should believe what she told him.

But she had gone too far. His face white, Ethan took another step away from her. "Goodbye, Aislinn. Have a safe trip home," he said, his voice harsh.

Conceding defeat, she nodded. "I will. And so will you."

He ignored the dry prediction as he turned. And then he paused and glanced back over his shoulder. "Like I said, I don't believe it will ever become an option. But for the record, no, I wouldn't turn my back on my brother."

"And yet that's exactly what you're doing," she whispered.

He spun without another word and walked away. Effectively turning his back on both of them.

Chapter Fourteen

"I'm glad to hear you've been sleeping better, Cassandra."

"Yes, it's been much better. Thank you, Dr. Thomas."

He glanced at the sweater folded neatly on the end of her bed. "It looks like you've completed your project."

"Yes." Her hands felt empty without the knitting needles, but she knew she would never hold them again. "I finished yesterday."

"It's great. A beautiful color."

"Thank you."

"I suppose you'll be starting a new one soon."

"Mmm." Because she didn't want to talk about that now, she changed the subject. "You've been very good to me, Dr. Thomas. I'm going to miss you."

He went still, then asked cautiously, "Are you going somewhere?"

Smiling indulgently at him, she replied, "No. I'll be staying here. You're the one who's leaving, aren't you?"

"I, um, what do you mean?"

"Now, Dr. Thomas, don't be evasive. I know you're making a career change. And I don't want to spend our last few days together pretending ignorance."

He shook his head. "How could you possibly know I've accepted a partnership in a new clinic? I haven't told anyone here yet."

"I have my ways of knowing things," she replied with a faint smile.

He looked at her, sitting by the window in her wheelchair, and then at the closed door through which so few people ever entered. "Has anyone ever told you you're a little scary, Cassandra?"

"All the time," she assured him. "So when will you be leaving?"

Sighing in resignation, he replied, "At the end of the month. I had planned to make the announcement early next week."

"You can still do so. I haven't mentioned it to anyone else."

"I'll miss everyone here, you know."

"I know. But you're making the right move. Your life is going to change a great deal in the next year. It's going to be stressful for you at first, as change always is, but everything will work out fine. You're going to have a good life and you deserve it. You're a fine young man."

"And you know all of this...how?"

"Let's just say I have certain talents and leave it at that, shall we?"

He cleared his throat, obviously uncomfortable. But she was used to that. There was a great deal more she could tell him about the changes awaiting him, but she thought she'd better stop now. He would have to find his own way in his future, and she knew he would do so, though not without difficulty. But then, life wasn't meant to be entirely easy, was it?

"I think you have a lot of talents, Cassandra. I'm not sure predicting the future is one of them," he added with a faint smile, "but I'm not ruling it out, either. I've never met anyone quite like you. Would you mind if I come visit you sometimes after I leave?"

"I would be delighted to see you. Anytime," she assured him, though she suspected there was a sad edge to her smile.

"Is there anything else I can do for you before I go today?"

"As a matter of fact, there is. See that envelope on my nightstand?"

He picked up the envelope and glanced automatically at the front. "This one?"

"Yes. I'm afraid I don't have any stamps. Would you mind mailing that for me?"

She knew he was a little curious about why she'd asked him rather than a member of the staff, but he merely nodded. "I'd be happy to. Don't you want to put a return address on it first?"

"No, it's fine, thank you." She didn't add that the reason she had asked him to mail it was because she knew he would do so from a post office near his home, which was in a different city than the residential facility where she lived.

"Well, I'll see you tomorrow then. I'd better go now and check to see how Mrs. Campbell is settling in. She's the new resident two rooms down. Have you met her yet? She seems nice."

"No, I haven't met her." Mrs. Kennedy had occupied that room until recently, when she had died rather unexpectedly. It had happened the day the staff had encountered so much trouble waking Cassandra and had called Dr. Thomas as a result.

"Maybe you should join some of the activities this afternoon. You might just surprise yourself and make some friends."

He was still worried that she was lonely, she thought after he let himself out. He couldn't know that she was most content when she was alone these days. Which didn't mean the same applied to him. It would be good for him to have new people in his life. But she would miss him.

The plastic line on the gasoline-powered weed trimmer sliced through the grass that had grown high around the concrete pad of the cedar-shake-topped gazebo in Ethan's backyard. Cuttings flew through the air, sticking to his jeans and boots. Sweat dripped from his hair and from beneath his protective goggles. Trimming was his least favorite part of yard work, but it was the price he paid to keep his place looking good. Strictly for himself.

Moving on to trim around the stone barbecue, he

thought about the raspberry iced tea that waited in the refrigerator. The cold beverage was going to taste great after all this manual labor in the heat of the summer afternoon.

He pictured himself sprawled in one of the rockers on the deck, sipping tea and watching the river roll by. There was nothing he'd rather be doing. No company he'd rather have than his own.

At least that was what he had always believed.

He'd never been lonely here before. Never regretted his choice to live a rather solitary existence in his rural refuge. Never entertained the thought that he had done so out of fear rather than simple preference. Until Aislinn had made him start to question himself.

It wasn't fear, he assured himself now, angrily attacking a new patch of weeds. He was no coward. So maybe he'd suffered some losses in his life. Maybe his heart had been bruised a time or two. Maybe he had loved unwisely once or twice. Didn't mean those experiences had left him afraid. Just cautious. Maybe a little hardened.

On the rare occasions when the thought of settling down with someone had crossed his mind during the past few years, he'd always assured himself that he was fine on his own. He was too obstinate to be married, too set in his ways. Too jaded to fall in love again now. He'd long since stopped believing in fantasy or magic. Until Aislinn had told him things no one else could have known and made him start questioning everything he had believed before.

He had accused her once of hypnotizing him, he remembered, staring out at the river for a moment, the machine still chugging in his hands. He wondered now if she really had. How else could he explain the fact that she still haunted him two weeks after he had walked away from her? Two long, restless weeks since he'd told himself she came with too many complications and too many strings to make it worth pursuing anything with her?

What else could account for the way he kept seeing her, even here in his home where she'd never stepped foot? In his bed, where she had visited only in fevered dreams?

What else could make him still want to go to her now despite the acrimonious way they had parted? He had been furious with her when he'd stalked away from her, dismayed that she guessed things about him that he'd thought he'd hidden deeply away from everyone. Including himself.

And yet he'd spent the past week trying to talk himself out of contacting her again. He had even considered resuming the search for the brother he didn't believe was out there, just because it would provide another excuse to see Aislinn again.

He'd known he was in trouble when he had started trying to convince himself that being with Aislinn again would be a smart move. That spending more time with her would let him work her out of his system in a way. That his lingering fascination with her would surely fade away with familiarity.

It had been lust, plain and simple, he told himself. And that was something that faded rather quickly, in his experience. So maybe it felt different this time with Aislinn. But then, Aislinn was very different from the women he had known before.

Silencing the noisy trimmer, he pushed the goggles

to the top of his head and turned, grimly trying to think about anything but Aislinn. When he saw her standing on the pathway behind him, he thought at first that he was being haunted by another memory of her.

And then she spoke. "Hello, Ethan."

She looked as beautiful as ever, if a bit pale. Her dark, wavy hair was loose around her face and shoulders, her body very straight and rather tense in a cream-colored top and brown slacks. She gripped a crumpled envelope in her hands so tightly her knuckles were white around it.

Very conscious of his sweat and dishevelment, the dirt and grass stains on his torn T-shirt, jeans and old boots, he asked more gruffly than he'd intended, "What are you doing here?"

"I know I should have called," she said apologetically. "But I had to talk to you and I didn't want to do it over the phone."

He figured she must have thought it was important or she wouldn't have come all this way. Which meant it probably wasn't going to be a quick conversation.

"Let me clean up first," he said, not liking the feeling that he was at a disadvantage. "You can have a glass of tea or something while I shower. Then we'll talk."

She didn't attempt to argue with him.

By the time he had showered and changed into a clean shirt and jeans, he felt a bit more in control of his emotions. Aislinn might have caught him off guard, showing up without warning as she had, but he was ready now to deal with her. At least he hoped so, he thought as she looked up at him with an uncharacteristic vulnerability that tugged at his hardened heart.

She started to stand, but he waved her back onto the sofa where he'd left her with a glass of tea when he'd gone to shower. Like her, he had furnished his home for comfort, with deep, overstuffed furniture, functional tables and built-in shelving for books and entertainment equipment. A stone fireplace dominated the living room, and in the winter there was usually a warm fire crackling there. Glass doors at the back of the room provided a view of his deck, picnic pavilion, private boat dock and the river beyond.

He had put a great deal of himself into this house and its furnishings. He doubted that Aislinn had missed a thing during the short time she'd been alone in here.

"You want any more tea?" he asked, moving past her toward the sunny, eat-in kitchen with its industrial appliances.

"No, thank you."

He poured himself a glass, then carried it back into the living room and sat in a chair across from her. He didn't quite trust himself to sit on the couch beside her. "Okay," he said after taking a long swallow of his tea. "I'm ready."

She laced her fingers in her lap. "First, I want to apologize for the way we parted at the airport," she said. "I was out of line and I'm sorry."

He shrugged, not wanting to discuss the details of what she had said. "We were both mad and frustrated by the dead ends we'd hit," he said. "Forget it. That wasn't the only reason you came, was it?"

She shook her head.

"Have you come up with more details about Kyle?" he asked, wondering what he would do if she had. He should tell her he wasn't interested in any more wild-goose chasing. If he was smart, he would keep his distance from her from now on, hoping his unwelcome fascination with her would fade in time. But he would still listen to what she had come to say.

She smoothed the white envelope she had been holding since she'd arrived, but she didn't open it just then. "Since I got home, I've been working very hard, trying to put your family issues out of my mind," she admitted. "You didn't want me to tell anyone else about what I believed happened to Kyle, and I had no way to prove any of it. Like you said, we had hit a dead end. And I was still upset over the way we separated, so it just seemed easier not to think about it."

He knew that feeling. He wondered if she had been any more successful than he at blocking the memories. Something told him she hadn't. "So you haven't learned anything new?"

"Not—not on my own."

"What does that mean?"

She held out the envelope then. "This was in my mail two days ago. I don't know who sent it."

Looking into her troubled eyes, he took the envelope from her and opened it, taking out a single sheet of paper. Unfolding it, he frowned when he saw the drawing. He recognized the face. It was the same one Aislinn had supposedly drawn in her sleep. Though the pose was different, the style was almost identical. He would have sworn they had been drawn by the same hand.

He still wasn't sure they hadn't, he thought, looking up at her slowly.

"I didn't draw this one," she insisted, obviously reading his thoughts in his expression. "It came in the mail. No return address. Postmarked Atlanta, Georgia."

He looked at it again. The face that she had told him was his brother. He'd looked at the drawing she'd given him a dozen times since he'd returned home, and there were very few differences between the two.

This wasn't what he had expected at all. He'd thought maybe she would tell him some more details about the accident or more vague clues about where Carmen had supposedly taken Kyle. But this, if he were to believe her, made everything even more strange and unsettling than anything she had told him yet.

"Look at the back," she urged, her voice strangely flat, uninflected.

He turned the sheet over. There was a name written in small block print. *Dr. Mark Thomas.* And an address below it, located in Georgia.

"Mark," he said, the significance of the name hitting him then.

Aislinn nodded.

"And you don't know who sent you this."

"I—no."

He sighed impatiently.

"I don't," she said defensively. "But when I held it, I thought I should know, for some reason. That's the best I can do to explain it."

He set the drawing aside and stood, moving to look out the window. He felt strangely as if his entire future hinged on however he handled the next few minutes—and he wasn't sure if he was ready for this at all.

As she'd said, he didn't give his trust easily. And what she was asking him to believe now required a leap of faith greater than any he had ever taken before.

Still sitting on the couch, Aislinn studied Ethan's back, giving him time to process what she had told him. She knew how difficult this must be for him. It had been one of the hardest things she'd ever done to come here at all.

She remembered the impact of seeing that drawing that had arrived in her mail. It had hit her with such a physical force that she'd staggered, almost falling into a chair. She still couldn't look at it without a chill running down her spine.

It had been the truth when she'd told Ethan she didn't know who sent it to her. But every time she touched it, she got a...feeling. A nagging whisper at the back of her mind that she should know. That she wasn't letting herself know.

After another moment, she stood and moved closer to Ethan, stopping a few steps away. "Ethan?"

"You must realize how this sounds."

"Trust me, I know. I was aware of how hard it would be for you to believe me when I came. I tried to talk myself out of coming, since you'd made it clear you wanted to stop searching. But I knew I had to tell you about this."

He turned then to look at her. "It would be easy for me to believe that you're trying to put something over on me. That you're playing with my mind. That you drew both those pictures and that you've made up this whole bizarre tale, for some reason."

"I can see why it would be reasonable for you to think that," she agreed evenly. "All I can tell you is that you would be wrong. Everything I've said to you happened exactly the way I told you it did. I drew the first picture I showed you. Someone else drew this one. Someone who then mailed it to me, along with the name and address on the back."

"And you think that name is the one my brother is using now."

She nodded. "I know it is. Dr. Mark Thomas is your brother, Kyle."

He moved a step closer to her and cupped her face between his hands, looking deeply into her eyes. "Tell me one more time."

Though her pulse raced in response to his touch, her voice was steady when she said, "I'm telling you the truth, Ethan. And despite how improbable this all sounds, I'm asking you to trust me."

His gaze traveled from her eyes to her mouth and then back again. She held her breath while he made up his mind, taking so long that she was beginning to get a little light-headed by the time he finally dropped his hands and stepped away.

"All right," he said brusquely. "I'll throw some things in a bag."

She breathed deeply, then let it out on a slow, unsteady exhale. "We're going to Georgia?"

"We're going to Georgia."

* * *

For some reason, Aislinn had thought the address on the back of the drawing might be an office. Maybe because of the title before the name. Instead she and Ethan found themselves in a residential neighborhood of nice, tasteful brick homes. A young-professionals neighborhood, she thought, filled with couples on the rise in their careers.

It hadn't occurred to her that Kyle could be married now or have children. He would be thirty-two, certainly old enough—and yet she had the feeling that he was still single, despite the family-style house.

Sitting behind the wheel of the rental car, Ethan studied the windows of the house. It was early evening, not dark yet, so it was hard to tell if the lights were on inside. But Aislinn sensed that Kyle—or Mark, as he was known now—was home. Blissfully unaware that his life was about to change drastically.

"This is nuts," Ethan grumbled beneath his breath, sounding a little nervous.

"Maybe," she agreed. "But we have to do this."

He turned in the seat to look at her. "You're asking me to take a huge step here. To risk making a complete fool of myself."

"I know."

His eyes grave, he murmured, "I wouldn't have done this for anyone but you."

She let the meaning of that sink in. Ethan was telling her that he trusted her. And that hadn't been an easy admission for him.

"Thank you," she said unsteadily.

"Okay." Dragging his gaze from hers, he reached for his door handle. "Let's do this."

They walked side by side to the front door of the Georgian-style house. There they paused and looked at each other again. After a moment, Ethan held out his left hand. Swallowing hard, Aislinn put her right hand in his palm, feeling his fingers close around hers. And then he pushed the doorbell.

The door opened a few moments later. Aislinn stared at the nice-looking man who stood just inside the house. There was a definite family resemblance, she noted, though Ethan and Joel looked more like each other. But she had no doubt he was their brother.

"May I help you?" he asked, looking from Ethan to her and back again.

"Dr. Mark Thomas?" Ethan asked.

"Yes."

"I'm Ethan Brannon. This is Aislinn Flaherty."

"Nice to meet you." The way his voice rose a little at the end turned it into a question.

Ethan glanced at Aislinn again, then, when she nodded slightly, looked back at the other man. "This is going to sound strange, I know, but I hope you'll give us a chance to explain. There's a, um…there's a chance that you and I could be brothers."

Mark Thomas looked hard at Ethan for a moment and then he took a step backward. "I think you'd better come inside."

Chapter Fifteen

At least he hadn't thrown them out, Aislinn thought a half hour later, after she and Ethan had told Dr. Mark Thomas everything that had led them to him. To be honest, they'd made such a mess of it that she was rather surprised he hadn't called the authorities.

"So let me get this straight," he repeated slowly, the first time he had spoken in a while. "You—" he looked at Aislinn "—are a little bit psychic. And you got the feeling that Ethan's brother was kidnapped thirty years ago."

Trying not to grimace at the way he made it sound, she nodded.

"And you—" Mark turned to Ethan "—aren't sure you believe in psychics, but because you believe in Aislinn, you were willing to come with her here."

Ethan glanced at Aislinn. "Something like that."

Mark pushed a hand through his hair in a gesture that reminded Aislinn very strongly of Ethan. He exhaled gustily. "I assume you know how crazy that sounds."

Ethan put a hand on Aislinn's knee. "We try not to use the *C* word," he murmured.

She and Ethan sat side by side on a couch, while Mark faced them from a mismatched chair nearby. It was the only furniture in the room. There wasn't even a table. She got the impression that he had only recently moved into this house and hadn't yet gotten around to buying furnishings.

Focusing on his face, she said quietly, "You wouldn't have heard us out if you hadn't had some reason to think we could be telling the truth."

He shook his head slowly. "I can hardly believe I'm even entertaining the possibility, but there are a few things that make me wonder...."

"Such as?" Ethan asked, leaning forward a little on the couch.

Mark looked back at him steadily. "I can see a resemblance," he admitted. "I'd be lying if I said I didn't."

"What else?"

He drew a slightly unsteady breath and nodded toward the drawing and the envelope in Aislinn's hands. "That."

"You know who drew this?" Aislinn asked.

"I'm not sure about that. But I know who mailed it."

"Who?" Ethan demanded tensely.

Mark spread his hands. "I did."

Cassandra sat in her chair by the window, letting the late-afternoon sunlight wash over her. Her hands were folded in her lap, resting on the soft package she held there.

A slight smile played on her lips. The peacefulness she felt inside her was new, something she'd never known in her footloose, rebellious life. It felt good to finally make amends for some of the mistakes she had made. To repay some of the kindnesses that had been shown to her during the past few years.

She had brought a family back together. Something she had never been able to accomplish with her own. That had been as much her fault as anyone else's, she admitted now.

But she was most satisfied with the knowledge that Aislinn now had someone to believe in her. To accept her in a way that Cassandra herself had never been fully accepted. Someone dependable enough and strong enough to stay beside her, so she would never feel abandoned again.

Maybe if Cassandra had found someone like that in her youth...

But, no. It was too late for regrets now. She'd lived her life on her own terms, and despite the people she had hurt along the way, she knew there was no other path she could have taken. She was who she was. Who she had chosen to be. Maybe someday Aislinn would understand why it had had to be that way.

Understand...and perhaps someday forgive.

"My mother's name was Carmen Thomas," Mark said into the stunned silence that followed his announcement. "She told me my father was a soldier who died overseas. She said she had no family of her own and had never been accepted by his family. I never tried to find any of my father's family because I didn't want anything to do with people who had treated my mother badly. She raised me on her own in a little town in southern Georgia. Sometimes she worked two jobs at a time to support me."

He swallowed, his throat working with the force of it. "She was very shy. Didn't socialize much. I was pretty much her whole world. She made sure I had everything I needed. Most of what I wanted, though there wasn't a lot of extra money for luxuries. She made sure I made good grades in school, had friends and extracurricular activities to keep me out of trouble. She always wanted me to become a doctor."

"And you did," Aislinn murmured.

He nodded. "I went to medical school on loans that I've only recently finished paying back."

Again it was Aislinn who spoke, while Ethan digested what Mark was saying. "She must have been proud of you."

"She didn't live to see it," Mark answered dully. "She died the summer after I graduated from college. A car accident."

The irony of that didn't escape any of them.

"I'm sorry," Aislinn told him. "You must have felt very much alone."

He nodded, seeming to appreciate that she understood. "Now you're telling me that she wasn't my mother at all. That she stole me from a loving family, faked her own death—and mine—and lived out the remainder of her life in hiding with me."

"That has to be a hard thing to hear."

"That's an understatement," he said on a long exhale. "I'm still not sure I believe it. Nothing about the shy, gentle woman who raised me would lead me to believe she was capable of doing something like that."

"I wouldn't believe a couple of strangers who showed up with a story like that, either," Ethan agreed. "My first thought would be that they were trying to pull some sort of scam on me. I'd demand proof. To be honest, I'm only now starting to believe you might really be Kyle. And before we go any further with this—before we tell anyone else—I think we should get that proof."

"DNA testing, you mean."

Ethan nodded. "I'll give blood. Cheek swabs. Whatever it requires."

"So will I," Mark said.

But Aislinn thought she detected a note of resignation in his voice, as if he had already predicted the results of that testing. And his heart was aching despite the brave face he was putting on for them.

"I still don't understand about this drawing," Ethan said with a frown. "You said you mailed it?"

Drawing his attention back to the present, Mark nodded. "I'm an internist with a specialty in gerontology," he explained. "The care facility where I've been practicing is filled with very wealthy people who expect regular, personalized care and can afford to pay for it. I've been paid well enough there to help me pay off my loans, though I'm planning to join a family-practice clinic in a few weeks."

He went on to tell them about a particularly intriguing patient there, a woman who never had visitors, whose past was a mystery to the entire staff but who had enough money to make their questions discreetly disappear.

"She...sees things," he added. "I don't know how, but she's told me things she couldn't possibly have known. I tried not to think about it much, but I've always wondered about her. Anyway, a few days ago she asked me to mail an envelope for her, and I agreed. I didn't know what was in it, but I recognize it as the one you're holding. I remembered that it was addressed to someone in Arkansas and that she declined to put a return address on it."

"What's her name?" Aislinn asked, holding her breath.

He hesitated. "I'm not supposed to discuss details like that. Privacy is one of the primary rules of the facility. Not to mention the law when it comes to doctor-patient confidentiality."

"I'd say the circumstances warrant some leeway," Ethan muttered.

"Her name is Cassandra Jamison," Mark revealed after another hesitation.

It didn't mean anything to either of them. But Aislinn had a feeling that it should. "How old is she?"

Mark stood abruptly. "I think you should ask her these things yourself. I'll take you to her and ask if she'll talk to you."

Aislinn knew that Mark had quite a few questions he wanted to ask her himself. His life as he had known it had just been turned upside down—and he wanted some answers.

* * *

Aislinn followed Mark and Ethan down the impeccably decorated hallways of the care facility, watching as various staff members nodded at Mark, showing little surprise at his unscheduled visit. She suspected that he had spent many hours with his patients here, that he was a dedicated doctor who took his work very seriously. It was just something she had sensed about him.

She couldn't help noticing how much he resembled Ethan. Their coloring. Their build. The way they walked. They would have their DNA tests, but as far as she was concerned, the answer was obvious.

Nerves gripped her as they neared the room in which the mysterious Cassandra lived. Something told her that this woman was as important to her as she was to Ethan and Mark.

A nurse flagged Mark down as he turned a corner. "Dr. Thomas," she said in surprise. "I was just about to call you. Have you already heard about Mrs. Jamison?"

Mark spun on one heel, while both Aislinn and Ethan went very still. The truth flooded Aislinn's mind even before the nurse explained in response to Mark's question. "She passed away a few hours ago. Dr. Marvin said it was her heart. She just…slipped away, sitting in her chair by the window."

It was at that moment that Aislinn realized who the woman who had called herself Cassandra had been.

She must have made a sound. Ethan wrapped an arm around her shoulders, while Mark talked quietly with the nurse, asking questions in medical terms Aislinn didn't completely understand. It didn't matter, she thought as she leaned into Ethan's strength. The end results were the same. Cassandra was gone.

Mark turned back to Aislinn and Ethan, his eyes as tormented as Aislinn's heart. "I don't…this was unexpected," he said, and she heard the self-blame in his voice. "She refused to go the hospital for tests, and I couldn't force her, of course, but I would have tried if I'd had any idea.…"

"This wasn't your fault," Aislinn said firmly, stepping away from Ethan to rest a hand on Mark's arm. "She didn't want you to do anything."

He squeezed the back of his neck with one hand, unable to accept her exoneration yet.

"Is there any way we can go into her room?" she asked him, knowing he would have to come to terms with this in his own way—just as she would.

He nodded. "I'll take you in. Let me get the key."

She didn't know what strings he had to pull to accomplish that, but he was back a short while later, the key in his hand.

The first thing they saw when they entered the room was the package on the dresser. It was wrapped in brown paper and had two words written in large letters on top. Staring at her own name, Aislinn put a hand to her throat.

Mark was the first to move, picking up the package and staring down at it. "I think I know what this is," he said, turning to hand it to Aislinn. "But maybe there are some answers inside, as well."

"Open it," Ethan urged when Aislinn hesitated.

Moistening her lips, she peeled the paper away to

reveal a beautiful emerald-green sweater, hand-knitted in a luxuriously soft yarn. Mark nodded as if in confirmation of his guess as to the contents.

She would ask him later how he had known, but her attention was drawn then to another white envelope. This one had been enclosed with the sweater. Her name was printed on the outside in the same handwriting that had been on the one that had held the drawing she'd received in the mail.

Ethan and Mark stood nearby while Aislinn sank into a chair to draw out the three handwritten pages that had been enclosed in the envelope. They both waited while she began to read. She took her time about it, the moments ticking silently into minutes, but neither of them tried to rush her. They knew she would fill them in when she finished.

Her hands were amazingly steady when she refolded the letter, though Ethan and Mark's images swam through tears when she looked up at them. Ethan moved immediately to her side, setting a hand on her shoulder. "Are you okay?"

She nodded. "I will be."

"Was she…?"

She nodded again. "She was my mother."

This time it was Mark who had to sit down, as if his knees had suddenly given out on him. He perched on the end of the bed while he absorbed this latest stunning revelation. "I don't understand any of this," he muttered.

"I know what you mean," his brother said, remaining close to Aislinn. "I've been feeling just the way you look for the past month."

Aislinn drew a deep breath. She kept her eyes on Mark as she began to speak, afraid that looking at Ethan just then would tip her over the edge of her self-control. "I'll tell you about my mother later, but let's just say she was a free spirit who changed her identity as often as some people swap cars. I never knew her. I was raised by my grandfather and my great-aunt."

He nodded to encourage her to continue.

"According to this letter, she did a big favor for a woman thirty years ago. She regretted it soon afterward, but she didn't know how to atone for her mistake, so she put it behind her, along with quite a few other bad choices she had made during the years. And then she met you, and when she realized who you were, she saw a chance to make things right."

"Your mother was the one who picked Carmen and Kyle up on the side of that road thirty years ago?" Ethan asked in dismay, leaping to the obvious conclusion.

Aislinn nodded. "She was pretty vague about it in the letter, but apparently Carmen convinced her that Kyle was her son and that they were running from an abusive spouse. I don't know how they met exactly, but they hadn't known each other very long, apparently. They planned the whole thing in a bar. My mother said she spent a lot of time in bars back then, using the alcohol people bought for her to dull her senses and mask her pain. Carmen must have bought her a lot of drinks."

"She believed that story about the abusive spouse?" Ethan asked.

"She chose to believe it." Aislinn was able to fill in some of the blanks on her own, from the messages she got while holding the pages. Messages that hadn't been put into writing. "It seemed like a great adventure to her, and she liked the idea of herself as a rescuing heroine. She helped Carmen push her car off the side of the road and she drove her away. They drove for three days, until Carmen asked her to leave her and the baby on their own. Apparently Carmen had squirreled away enough money to set up housekeeping in a small town and begin a new life.

"By that time, Mother knew something was wrong about the story she'd been told, but she was too absorbed with her own problems to stay around and try to find out. She said she told herself that Carmen was probably just taking you away from your father. A custody-battle thing. That was easier for her to justify than the truth."

"She knew she had helped to kidnap a child, but she did nothing about it?" Mark shook his head slowly. "That just doesn't fit at all with the image of the woman I thought I knew here."

"I told you—she was very good at reinventing herself. Maybe the woman you knew wouldn't have done anything like that. I think she tried to tell my grandfather what she'd done once, but they never communicated well. He misunderstood when she talked about a little boy she had abandoned. I guess she thought she was finally setting things right by sending me the drawing."

"But how?"

"Some things are better left unasked," Ethan advised glumly. "They defy explanation."

Aislinn couldn't smile. Clearing her throat, she said, "I'll let you read the letter for yourself, Mark, but she said to tell you she was sorry. She said the same to me, actually. She said she knows it will be difficult for all of us to come to terms with the past in regard to her, but she predicted we'll all find happiness as a result of her intercession. She sounded rather pleased with herself. Maybe she was picturing herself as the heroine again."

"Aislinn."

She shook her head in response to Ethan's murmur, blinking back a fresh film of tears when she added, "She named me as her heir. Apparently there's a will on file with the management here to make it all official. So you don't have to worry about breaking patient confidentially after all, Mark. I'm fully entitled to be here, to knowing all the facts about her."

"She knew she was going to die?" Mark asked, still frowning in bewilderment.

"Yes. She said she lived life on her own terms and she left the same way."

"Now that sounds like Cassandra," he murmured, his voice thick.

Her own unsteady, Aislinn said, "Maybe you can tell me about her sometime."

He nodded as Ethan pulled Aislinn up and into his arms. Burying her face in his shoulder, she allowed herself to shed a few tears for the mother she would never know.

Because Mark's spare bedrooms were unfurnished, Aislinn and Ethan checked into a hotel not far from his house, telling him they would see him the next day. He seemed relieved to be left to himself for the remainder of the night, and Aislinn didn't blame him. He needed time and privacy in which to adjust to everything that had been dumped on him that day.

He and Ethan had parted rather awkwardly, but both of them had seemed willing to spend time getting to know each other. Whatever relationship developed between them after that remained to be seen, but Aislinn thought they would become good friends, at least in time.

They didn't even bother getting two rooms this time. Carrying their bags inside, Ethan dumped them unceremoniously on the floor. "Are you hungry?" he asked her. "I could order room service."

She shook her head. "I couldn't eat. But order something for yourself, if you want."

"No. I'm not hungry, either." He took her hands in his, drawing her to sit beside him on the bed. "I'm so sorry, Aislinn."

She nodded. "This was the way she wanted it. She said in the letter that she wouldn't have been a good mother now, any more than she had been before. She didn't want me to look at her, knowing the things she had done, the person she had been. She didn't consider herself to be Mary Alice Flaherty anymore. She was Cassandra Jamison, wealthy widow and kindly older woman. She wanted that to be her final identity."

"What are the odds that we all came together like this? That Joel married your friend and that your mother was the one who helped Carmen all those years ago? Hell, it makes my head hurt to think about it."

She tried to smile, though it was a weak attempt.

"Mine, too. Especially since my mother left some images in there that I'm going to have to spend a while deciphering."

"What kind of images?" he asked warily.

"Just little details about her past. Flashes, I guess you would call them. Maybe she wanted me to know her a little after all."

Still holding her hand, Ethan said, "I think it's going to take all of us a while to get used to this."

"Yes. We'll have to tell your family, of course. How do you think they'll react?"

"The same way I have. With disbelief and then stunned acceptance. My parents will be shocked but overjoyed to have Kyle back, although I guess he'll be Mark to them now. It's the only name he remembers."

"Will they blame me, you think? For my mother's part in his disappearance?"

"Why would they blame you?" he asked roughly. "You had nothing to do with it. It happened before you were born. Besides, she might have helped take him away, but you helped bring him back. They won't forget that. I won't let them."

Biting her lip, she looked up at him through her lashes. "Does that mean—"

"You were right, you know. It's been a long time since I've really trusted anyone. I've been burned a few times and I let myself get bitter. Withdrawn. Then I met you, and you asked me to trust in things that didn't even make sense. Things that went against everything I'd ever believed before."

"I know," she whispered.

"And somehow I did," he went on wonderingly. "Whether it was magic or hypnotism or plain old love at first sight, it hit me the first night we met, and I went down hard. Which didn't mean I didn't go down fighting."

She smiled through tears at that. "You fought pretty hard."

"We've known each other for a month," he reminded her. "I didn't hold out all that long."

"I didn't think I would ever meet anyone who could accept me just for who I am," she said unsteadily. "And I thought you were completely wrong for me because you were so determined not to trust me from the very start. But I went down hard that first night, also—and, trust me, I fought it, too."

"So did we both lose?"

She chuckled faintly. "I'd like to think we both won."

He kissed her lingeringly. "I love you, Aislinn."

"I love you, too."

And then he straightened, frowning. "Um, about Heather—"

"It doesn't matter."

"Yeah, it does. I want to put this behind us. And keep it forever just between us, okay?"

"Of course." She already sort of knew what he was going to tell her, but maybe he needed to put it into words.

"Joel was really busy with his residency. Didn't have a lot of time to spend with his family—or with his fiancée, Heather. She and I ended up spending some time together during the summer before they were married, just hanging around, you know. Family-type stuff. They had been together a long time, since high school, and I knew her pretty well. She was pretty amazing—beautiful, brilliant, popular. I always thought Joel was a lucky guy and hoped I would meet someone like her, since my own relationships tended to end badly."

"What happened?" she encouraged when he paused, knowing he needed to get it off his chest.

"One thing led to another—and there were some kisses," he admitted reluctantly, self-recrimination heavy in his voice. "Though I never asked her to, she told me she had considered dumping Joel for me. And then she said she changed her mind because she wanted to be a doctor's wife. I wasn't ambitious enough to be a suitable match for her."

Aislinn must have made a sound, because he spoke quickly, shaking his head. "Heather was a good person. And she loved Joel, despite her understandable last-minute doubts. She was ambitious, sure, but so was he back then. She and I agreed that nothing had really happened between us, so there was no need for Joel to ever know anything about it. We put it behind us and we never let it affect our friendship."

"Not outwardly at least," Aislinn murmured.

He sighed. "Okay, so I thought I was in love with her. After all, she died just six months after they married, and I still hadn't really had time to get over her yet, which I would have done eventually."

"But she hurt you. In a way, she betrayed both you and Joel with her flirtation. And because you felt guilty and defeated, you told yourself you weren't going to let anyone hurt you like that again."

"Maybe," he admitted. "But I know now it wasn't

really love. Affection, maybe. Attraction, of course. But nothing I ever felt for her—or for anyone else—ever came close to being as powerful as what I feel for you now. For always."

"It won't be easy," she whispered, leaning into his arms. "I come with some pretty daunting complications."

"So I'm in love with a sort-of psychic. Might take some getting used to, but I've come a long way in that direction already. I'll just have to stay honest, since you would know in a heartbeat if I were trying to get away with anything."

She looked up at him with a smile. "I trust you, Ethan."

"And I trust you," he murmured, lifting her hand to his lips. "With all my heart."

It was all she had ever wanted, she thought as they sank onto the bed and into a kiss that warmed all the cold, formerly lonely places inside her. Love that came without reservations. Love that trusted. That was the greatest gift of them all.

* * * * *